Alindarka's Children

Alhierd Bacharevič

ALINDARKA'S CHILDREN

THINGS WILL BE BAD

translated by Jim Dingley and Petra Reid

A NEW DIRECTIONS
PAPERBOOK ORIGINAL

Copyright © 2014 by Alhierd Bacharevič
Translation copyright © 2020 by Jim Dingley & Petra Reid

Originally published as *Дзеці Аліндаркі* by Halijafy, Minsk
Published in arrangement with Scotland Street Press, Edinburgh

This book has been selected to receive financial assistance from English PEN's
"PEN Translates" programme, supported by Arts Council England.
English PEN exists to promote literature and our understanding of it, to uphold
writers' freedoms around the world, to campaign against the persecution and
imprisonment of writers for stating their views, and to promote
the friendly cooperation of writers and the free exchange of ideas.

WWW.ENGLISHPEN.ORG

Manufactured in the United States of America
First published as a New Directions Paperbook (NDP1534) in 2022

Library of Congress Cataloging-in-Publication Data
Names: Bakharèvich, Al'herd, author. | Dingley, Jim, translator. |
Reid, Petra, translator.
Title: Alindarka's children : (things will be bad) / Alhierd Bacharevič ;
translated by Jim Dingley & Petra Reid.
Other titles: Dzetsi Alindarki. English
Description: New York : New Directions Publishing Corporation, 2022. |
"A New Directions book"
Identifiers: LCCN 2022005800 | ISBN 9780811231961 (paperback) |
ISBN 9780811231978 (ebook)
Subjects: LCSH: Child internment camp inmates—Fiction. | Belarusians—Fiction. |
Belarusian language—Fiction. | Genocide—Fiction. | Escapes—Fiction. |
LCGFT: Thrillers (Fiction). | Novels.
Classification: LCC PG2835.2.B284 D9413 2022 |
DDC 891.7/9934—dc23/eng/20220204
LC record available at https://lccn.loc.gov/2022005800

2 4 6 8 10 9 7 5 3 1

New Directions Books are published for James Laughlin
by New Directions Publishing Corporation
80 Eighth Avenue, New York 10011

It isn't a question of how accurate our history is,
It's more a matter of who gets to tell it.

—Tsering Wangmo Dhompa

Nous nous tournons vers l'Écosse pour trouver toutes nos idées sur la civilisation.

—Voltaire

In parts of Belarus, language, religion and custom vary from village to village, and the only common cultural experience is of brutality at the hands of invaders. There, peasants who are confronted with "who are you?" will often reply: "We are tutejszy—we are 'from here' people." But the world will not allow them that answer for much longer.

—Neal Ascherson (1996)

Contents

Introduction

You live in a country where your language has long been under insidious attack. It is one of the two official languages of the country, but it is denigrated at every turn. The number of schools that use it for teaching has been reduced to almost zero. There is no university that uses it for teaching. If you use it in a store, you run the risk of at best not being understood, or at worst of being told that you should speak like a human being. The people of your country are not encouraged to develop a sense of national identity separate from that of the much larger, imperial eastern neighbour. They have been systematically stripped of any historical memory by other countries' claims. You live in Belarus.

You feel passionately about your language and the hidden history of the land on which you live. You are hemmed in by your country's adherence to its Soviet past, and harassed by obsessive Belarusian language zealots who drove your wife, a singer, to attempt suicide because she sang songs in Belarusian that were not on the "right" subjects. So it is that you find yourself having to bring up your little daughter on your own. You believe she is destined to preserve the Belarusian language for future generations. She needs to be isolated from her surroundings. She must be protected from nosy neighbours and the prying eyes of agents of the state. You must find a protector for her at the same time as finding consolation for yourself in vodka. And then you lose her ... twice.

These are the bare bones of the Hansel-and-Gretel story told by Alhierd Bacharevič. Born in 1975, he experienced firsthand the collapse of the Soviet Union and the emergence of an independent Republic of Belarus in 1991; it was then that Belarusian was declared the sole official language. Brought up as a Russian speaker, Bacharevič discovered the language for himself. He wrote songs for the punk rock group Provocation, of which he was lead singer, and iconoclastic poems for the writers' group Boom-Bam-Lit in Belarusian. The cultural freedom that independence brought with it gradually began to wither after the inauguration in 1994 of Alexander Lukashenko as President, an office he still holds over a quarter of a century later.

Russian was declared an official state language alongside Belarusian which had the intended result of pushing Belarusian, once again, to the fringes. However, despite the restrictions imposed on society by the Lukashenko government, the Belarusian cultural sphere has continued to show signs of flourishing. Bacharevič has by now completed several books of fiction and some deliberately contentious works of literary criticism, all in Belarusian.

Alindarka's Children, originally published in 2014, is the first of Bacharevič's novels to appear in a translation for anglophone readers. (A French translation was published in 2018.) The book is written in two distinct languages, Russian and Belarusian. In addition, many of the characters in the book speak the mixture of the two languages that is called "trasianka" (a shake-up). Any translator is faced at once with a serious problem: how to render the different languages? This translation seeks to match the original by contrasting English with Scots. The choice of Scots stems from the classification of both Belarusian and Scots as "vulnerable" in the UNESCO *Atlas of the World's Languages in Danger*.

The novel is full of Belarusian and Russian cultural references. They form an essential background "noise" to the linguistic clamour. The poet Petra Reid has created a linguistic and cultural noise that acts as the perfect foil to the original text. True, there aren't any statues of Lenin in Scotland or hotels in small provincial towns that charge extra for toilet paper (at least I don't think there are). Remember, though, some of the action in this fable takes place in the dense forests of Belarus. And anything can happen in a forest: you can wander round and round in circles, always in fear of what is lurking behind the next tree and never knowing where you will end up.

There is one aspect of the background that deserves special mention. The whole of what is now Belarus fell within the Jewish Pale of Settlement of the Russian Empire. The frontiers shifted several times between the world wars, but many of the small towns of the area retained a majority Jewish population. The Nazi occupation of 1941–1944 changed all that. Belarus is haunted by ghosts; the far-flung suburb of Šabany, Minsk, in which Bacharevič was brought up, is built close to the site of one of the Nazi death camps.

Before the story begins

Who is Alindarka? There is a poem running like a thread through the story. It was written by a man who can be regarded as the first poet in modern Belarusian literature: Frańcišak Bahuševič (Frantsishak Bahushevich) (1840–1900). The poem is entitled "Things Will Be Bad."

A baby boy is born to a family of impoverished, illiterate peasants living in the Northwestern Territory of the Russian Empire. He is born in March, a bad month in which to come into the world, when the food stored for the winter is almost exhausted. His parents take him to the local Roman Catholic priest to be baptized. The priest speaks Polish. To decide on a name for the boy, he asks the parents to pass him his book of saints' days, his *kalendar*. The parents do not understand the word, mishear it, and think that this is the name to be given to the boy. Hence Alindarka. So his life starts out badly, and does not improve. He is constantly in trouble with the authorities and ends up in prison.

JIM DINGLEY

A Note from the Scots Translator

There are several poems and songs incorporated with this translation, and the list of them in the "Scots Dimension" at the back of the book can be read as a fair reflection of my personal experience of "Scots."

"In finding a voice for these women, I've considered the question of Scotland's three native languages—Gaelic, Scots and English."
—Gerda Stevenson, *Quines* (2018)

Speaking only one of the above (English), albeit with a strong accent, and harbouring ambivalent feelings towards the other two, means that I confess from the off to the "Scots" herein being both variable and fabricated. It's made of things my granny used to say, alongside Scots law, Rab C. Nesbitt, Gavin Douglas, Stanley Baxter, Irvine Welsh ... the usual romantic variety of Scotticisms. Some of the words I have made up myself, and some seem as if I have: "Niaroo" for example, used to name houses, pubs, caravan parks etc. (read it backwards). The grammar, at times, is of my own invention, in the spirit of a language imagined. The poems and songs are exactly transcribed from a variety of sources.

So far, so MacDiarmid lite. The filter through which it all passes is my reflection on being the child of a parent who was absolutely committed to a cause, Scottish independence in this case. I was well versed in the ideology and language of a parent's cause from a very young age, like Alicia/Sia.

What future do Scots and Gaelic have in relation to English? Alan Riach suggests that "... there's one (Gaelic) word that helps bring together our interrelated understanding of land, people and culture: *dùthchas*." I think, I hope, the concept of *dùthchas* will only become more exciting, more sanity-preserving. Everywhere.

PETRA REID

1

Ma tittie wis eatit bi wulves

Ma tittie wis eatit bi wulves.

These words had Avi really worried. They had just come into his head from God knows where. It was just as if he had swallowed those words together with the bilberry leaf that had a little beetle stuck to it. There was a speck of light on the beetle's back. Avi was so upset, in fact, that he even stopped chewing, straightened up, opened his eyes and with a kind of solemn horror in his voice uttered:

"Ma tittie wis eatit bi wulves."

The voice seemed to belong not to Avi, but to someone completely different.

It was like there was someone standing behind Avi's back.

He opened his eyes wide and looked around. Fortunately, there seemed to be no special meaning in the smooth swaying of the pine trees. There was no hint of anything out of the ordinary in the way in which the sun mimicked the movement of the forest. Even so, in the midst of the bilberry bushes those words did indeed sound as though a green mouth had opened, lips had stirred and something had been said, words that should never under any circumstances be spoken. At least, not when Avi's sister was around. But right now there was no sign of her. Now and again she would suddenly emerge from the trees in the most unexpected places, as if from under the ground. To Avi, Alicia seemed to be digging subterranean passageways rather than gorging herself on berries.

tittie: sister (there is a phrase that denotes the close relationship between brother and sister: "tittie-billie")

Any minute now she's going to jump out from under his feet with moss flying in all directions; the bilberry bushes are still shaking and that terrible phrase is still hanging in the air—it's snagged on a spider's web and trembling, like there's still something that needs to be said, although Avi hasn't the faintest idea what the continuation could be. Alicia will hurl herself at him, blocking out the gentle sun with her body, making him fall right on to the bilberries. She'll begin to strangle him with her terrifying blue tentacle-like fingers. "They're aw blue—aff o me, get them aff o me!" "Non! Ah willna!" And there are Alicia's eyes pressed close up to his face with the red tinge like you get in photographs. He suddenly pictured to himself how Alicia's ballpen had leaked in her pocket, the ink flooding her shorts and running down her legs. She shoved her hand into her shorts, retrieved the pen and her fingers were all blue, a really tenacious kind of blue. She maun heave her claes oot, the hale load o thaim, thare's nae weys tae wash oot yon stain, thought Avi.

But it's not his fault, it's those sourish, mind-bending little berries that are to blame, those tiny wee spheres, those tablets that flood your head with all kinds of nonsense, that give you that tight feeling in your chest. Bilberries, bletherberries that befuddle the mind, babbleberries that give you a kick—a really hard kick. The beautiful green forest scales, the timber songs, play out like a kaleidoscope before his eyes. It's hard tae breathe, yer haunds skeedaddle awa. Canna seem tae shake the bletherberries.

The bilberries were indeed very much like the tablets that were given to them in the Camp. It was easy to tell the difference between those tablets by their colours. The dark blue ones were given out after breakfast. The girls said that they were for the memory. Avi had his own thoughts on that.

maun: must   *heave out*: dispose of   *claes*: clothes   *hale*: whole
thaim: them   *haunds*: hands

Lassies ayeweys ken that wee bit mair,
Aye but they dinnae get tae drain oor quair!

Ye shoudnae listen tae them! Yon blue, awmaist black tablets
mak ye feel bamboozle'd wi awthings ye hear an see. Aye right
eneuch, each nicht i the Camp ye'd mynd o the day jist past wi
bricht, nigglin nagglin particularity; it wis awfy hard tae sleep.
Each muivement, each soond's fixed i yer mynd: yon clatterin o
spoons i the canteen, yon wey the flag crawls up the flagpole tae
heiven, yon shairp crack whanever the baw's hit o'er the stane
Ping-Pong table that's aye gravestane cauld. (That's a trick that
Avi never did learn, and now it looks as though he never will.)
Unlikely tae be ony Ping-Pong action whaur thay're aff tae.

In the Camp there were also green tablets—"vitamins"—and
brown ones. These were the nippiest sweeties. For a long time
Alicia resisted mentioning the rumour that was circulating among
the girls about what these elongated capsules were for, but then
finally she did admit that no one actually knew. Apart frae fact
those brune tabules mak ye awfy keen oan buryin yirsel intae the
groond. Tolik—the laddie wha'd pished himsel t'ither day—he'd
done it. The troop leaders found him in the evening behind the
kitchen up to his neck in the ground; someone had put the caps of
two toothpaste tubes in his nostrils. It was decided not to tell the
Camp Director about the incident, but everyone continued to be
amazed for some time afterwards by Tolik's ability to dig himself
in, and to do so in such a neat way, right up to the chin. After all,
it would be difficult to find a creature more cack-handed, short-
sighted, generally repulsive and less fit to live than Tolik.

Avi screwed his face up as he recalled all this—there was this
really sour taste in his mouth—and looked around. There were
no fewer bilberries than there had been to begin with. Quite
the reverse, in fact—they seemed to grow back instantly on the

eneuch: enough   *ye'd mynd o*: you would remember

bushes that had already been stripped of their fruit. An endless patch of bilberry bushes, bushes that bear berries and can never be consumed. If it weren't for the midges, he probably wouldn't be able to remember where their car was.

Alicia and Avi probably resembled mosquitoes themselves. They stuffed these intoxicating little spheres into their mouths and kissed the juice off of the palms of their hands. They gobbled them up as if they had been stolen, as if they wanted to poison themselves with them. They shifted restlessly among the trees, coming closer together and then moving further apart, pressing their noses into the ground. It was a habit of theirs—always rushing around.

Ma tittie wis eatit bi wulves. In the Middle Ages, par exemple, naebuddy wud've been surprised wi biographical fact likes o yon, thought Avi to himself. Yon sortae thing happens, folk wid say. Weel, last winter ma aunty wis bit bi some big rat, folk wid say back in the day, an she got deid o the plague. Yon bubonic one, tae be precise. Whit aboot ma tittie, the wan wha got merrit tae yon humpybackit swineherd? An therr wis ma uncle; he went aff tae liberate the Tomb o' Oor Lord, and naebody's heard frae him foriver an iver agin. Mynd whit oor troop leader said tae us aw at line-up yestreen, that he was gonnae mak a real medieval hell fur us, cause Tolik hae'd pished his cot again. Whit the leader meant tae say wis that he'd tie them aw up likes o he'd done afore. As if yon sadist had ony clue as tae whit "medieval" meant. Whan folk had bairns back i the day, they reck'd tae be lucky if hauf thair off-spring made it tae saxteen years o age. Avi wasn't yet sixteen, but knew he would live to that age. He felt such power run through his whole body. Even if ye jist had a guid stretch, ye felt lik ye could hoist up the hale country an cairy it oan yir shouders. Nae matter whare tae. The troop leaders used tae say that it wis the Camp that gied us strength. And Avi believed them; nothing like that had ever occurred to him before. Sic a power: bilberries, pine trees, the sun, whitiver. Ye coud reach oot an touch awthings.

Funnily enough he didn't feel at all hungry. Only that morning they'd woken up in the Camp, surrounded by the same old, same old wooden walls of their barrack block, and even managed to have breakfast in the canteen—milk, porridge, bread and butter, and the cheese that Alicia didn't finish and gave to him. After breakfast they had to take their tablets. Today they didn't have to go to the medical examination room and so they had a little bit more free time.

Whenever there was no session involving the examination room, they always went after breakfast to their special, secret place beneath the fir trees; they would meet by the loos, behind the wooden shacks where they stood right next to the Camp fence; there was a heap of chairs there, an old piano in which wee-sleekit-cowerin-timorous-beastie-mice were living and hackneyed hand-printed posters full of mistakes. Some old window frames had been left standing upright in the grass. There was someone living in between the panes of glass; when the sun shone you could occasionally see weird reflections on the glass—reflections, perhaps, of people or shadows, and behind their backs, in the very depths of the glass, you could make out a gleaming, brightly lit corridor full of languid, fishlike movement. The wonderful three-dimensional quality of this glass world was striking; on one occasion, Alicia confessed that whenever she was there she wanted simply to step into the glass because she knew that she could. "Non, dinna dae that," Avi begged his sister, and she gave him a dour look, the kind of look a nun would give.

Over there by the fence the ground was strewn with light grey pine cones and motionless pine needles; they looked as if sugar had been scattered over them. Alicia and Avi used to walk up and down on them, listening to the pleasant rustling sound under their feet. Often they'd lie beneath the trees discoursing on this and that; the one thing they never discussed was the Camp. Just beyond the pine trees was the metal wire-mesh fence, and on the other side of the fence was the forest. The dappled light on the forest made it look just as enmeshed, as though it had walked into a trap.

This morning, all of a sudden, there was someone calling out to them from behind the fir trees. This had happened before. Alicia and Avi would saunter up to the fence quite unafraid—it was unlikely that anyone could contrive to get into the Camp through the wire. The Camp had a proper entrance: a gateway painted yellow. There was a wheel hanging over the gate with a lot of shiny metal spurs sticking out of it. Somehow, the two of them knew that these shiny spurs were there to protect them; the wheel was in some way connected with the mesh fence and the Camp perimeter which they had not yet had time to wander all around. That's why they felt no fear now when someone called to them by name.

True, Alicia did once say that going right up close to the fence was dangerous—what if people on the other side had long hooks to grab hold of a person and drag them out of the Camp into the forest? Just after they had first been brought here to the Camp, an old man had started talking to them across the fence. He offered them nuts to eat and even shoved some through the wire mesh. They said nothing but he kept blathering without stopping, and even crying at the same time. Back then they still didn't know the Lingo very well. Alicia went up to the fence, and Avi came tramping unwillingly after her. It was then that the man turned his back on them. One hand he used to push nuts through the mesh and the other he shoved into his pocket: he looked really odd standing there like that. The scene seemed to last for ages, and the nuts fell on to the pine needles. How many nuts did that guy have with him, thousands, millions? The words flew into the forest, turning into sighs and groans. "Yon nuts are pushionous," said Alicia when the man finally walked off. You could tell how insulted he was by the way his back disappeared behind the trees. "We durna eat thaim." And then they walked off.

durna: dare not

However, what they saw more often on the other side of the fence were local yokels from the villages nearby; they did all kinds of daft things to attract the children's attention. "Howzit gaun oan the ither side, heidcases?" they shouted, and their voices would grow hoarser and hoarser. "Bawheids, the load o yese. Ur theys cuirin' yese? Hud yer jags yet? Did they gie yer harnpans a right guid gardyloo?" Sometimes one of these yobbos would whip his cock out of his trews and wave it merrily at them, but it was only the boldest souls who did this; most of them simply bent over and mooned them with their suntanned arses. Alicia smiled without turning her eyes away. Avi, on the other hand, desperately wanted to throw something over the fence, and throw it so as to hit one of them and make blood flow. Avi loved it when blood flowed.

But what happened this morning was completely, utterly different.

This morning, there really was someone calling to them by name from the other side of the wire fence. By their real names.

They heard a hushed voice call out, "Alicia! Hey, Avi!"

They looked at one another. It was an insistent, commanding voice that was calling them, quiet yet very familiar. Avi took his sister by the hand, and they raced headlong into the fir trees towards the wire. However, they stopped several metres before they reached the fence. After all, familiar voices could have poles with hooks on the ends.

It was Faither. He was standing on the other side and calling them. His face lit up as they came nearer, just as though the forest had slowly parted its crown of treetops. A young woman with short yellow hair

Yellow hair, beyond compare,
Comes trinklin' doon her swanlike neck,
An' her twa eyes like stars in skies,
Would keep a sinking ship frae wreck

bawheids: fools, idiots   *harnpans:* brainpans, skulls

was standing next to Faither; she was observing the children with such unfeigned interest that Avi tried not to look in her direction.

"Come awa here, closer," whispered Faither, and they took a few more steps towards the wire. Faither pushed his fingers through the mesh. The scene was really rather repulsive: his fingers were wiggling around, but they were in the Camp, whereas Faither was There, on the outside.

"He's wantin us tae gang o'er there tae see him," said Avi.

"Ye canna come here awa," Alicia begged Faither, and kept looking cautiously around her. Faither had never seen her like this. "We maun be oan the Parade Groond the noo. Thare's a competeetion the day an we've practised!"

Surprisingly, Avi had forgotten all about that. There was the song that they had been learning. It had these cunning words scattered right through it that were bound to trip you up, however many times you tried to get them right.

As I was walking up the street,
A barefit maid I chanc'd tae meet;
But O the road was very hard
For that fair maiden's tender feet.

"Haud yer wheesht!" said Faither hastily, pressing his fingers around the wire. "We're gonnae dae aw things swiftly, wi silence, an yese huv tae harkit me. This here's Kenzy, she ..." He looked—rather pathetically, the children thought—at her.

"She's oor helpie. Nou jist hang oan ..."

This Kenzy woman—whoever she was—suddenly drew a huge pair of shears out of her rucksack. They were just like the shears that hung on the wall of the medical examination room with their blades gaping open. The Doctor never took them down, but for some reason Avi's eyes were always drawn to

gang: go   *the day*: today   *haud yer wheesht*: keep quiet

them whenever he was in the room. Kenzy handed the shears to Faither, and Faither let them fall to the ground; knelt down and then stood up; in his hands the shears sprang to life and started clicking away. He was in a tearing hurry. For as long as they could remember, he had always been in a hurry. Faither seized the shears with both hands and began to cut the wire.

It was harder than he thought. Faither was puffing and panting, wiping the sweat from his forehead. It was funny how his upper lip was dancing beneath his nose. From time to time he looked pleadingly first at Avi and then at Alicia, as if asking them for help, but they just stood there watching him suffer. Meanwhile Kenzy

Mally's meek, Mally's sweet,
Mally's modest and discreet;
Mally's rare, Mally's fair,
Mally's every way complete

was observing the children closely, now and again looking around nervously. Avi also had the feeling that someone would come running up because of the noise. One of the troop leaders. Avi tried not to think of how things would end. Blood would flow, perhaps.

"Whit ye doin doon therr?" Trying to drive the midges away made Kenzy finally lose her patience. "Whit ur ye *doin*? Dinnae tell me ye've forgot ..."

"Jist a wee minuit mair," Faither groaned. The shears bounced around, refusing to stay where he wanted them. "Jist a second. Thare yese go!"

Alicia looked at Avi. Avi looked at Alicia.

They sighed, took each other by the hand and started walking slowly towards Faither. The wire of the fence got snagged on Avi's T-shirt, but Kenzy carefully freed him; she pulled it out like it was a splinter.

"It's aw fur aw the best," said Faither. "Ah luve the baith o yese. Nou we'll n'er . . ."

And, still wielding the shears, he burst into tears. Kenzy had to snatch them out of his hands. "Less o yon panic i yer breastie," she said and grabbed the rucksack. "Therr's nae time! Leave it tae the morn!"

They set off running down the hill, first Kenzy, then Faither behind her, holding Avi by the hand, and Alicia in the rear. The forest was gradually thinning out, and from somewhere they could hear the sound of a tractor working in the fields. Jumping across streams and stumbling over tree stumps, they reached the bottom of the hill and emerged on to a road. There stood the car with its snout buried in the bushes. The sun had heated the car up; inside was a fat gadfly desperately beating itself against the windows in a struggle to get out. It took no notice when they opened the car doors. They sped off along the forest road with the fly hurtling around inside the car like a mad thing. The bumpy ride over ruts and broken branches could not shake off the stuffiness inside or the pine needles on the windscreen.

Avi and Alicia sat on the back seat, looking at the forest jumping up and down on the other side of the windows. At one moment, Avi thought he spotted the wire fence somewhere out there among the trees. The Camp was big—and now there was a little hole in it; nevertheless, one big enough to let a child out. It was a hole that could cause all kinds of things to happen inside the Camp.

Faither drove out on to a main road, and the bumping stopped. He smiled for the first time since he arrived at the fence. He glanced at the bairns in his rearview mirror, but neither Avi nor Alicia was smiling, and Faither's face once again became serious.

"'Nane will stop nor halt us . . .'[1] Are yese faimisht? Eh, Avi?" he asked. "Nae matter, we'll soon be someplace sauf, an thare . . ."

"Shame we didnae think oan yon afore," said Kenzy. She turned and stroked Avi's hair. Avi didn't like it. It was as if she wanted to make an impression on Faither—this woman with the yellow hair and her two eyes, like stars meant for skies that desperately wanted to escape the pretty face. Kenzy gave Alicia a packet of crisps; the children made no attempt to start eating. They simply sat there, Alicia with the packet in her hand, Avi all tensed up, staring out of the window. Villages and small towns flew past, then more villages. They all resembled old furniture that had been put out on the grass, waiting for strong pairs of arms which—after resting for a while—would drag them up the steps. There were people sitting here and there by the roadside; in front of them there were piles of apples and berries. "Ah'm faimisht," said Avi all of a sudden. Faither was on the point of slowing down so he could stop and buy some fruit from the sellers who were hanging around in their filthy panama hats in the full glare of the sun.

"Whit ye *daein*?" screamed Kenzy. "We cannae stop! An youse perr jist eat yer crisps! Therr yese go!" Their car took a breather, then gave a roar and raced on along the road.

All the same there was a feeling that they were travelling slower and slower ... Avi even felt that the sellers by the roadside managed to look him straight in the eye. Kenzy noticed this and said to Faither:

"Mebbe the bairns shoud hunker doon oan the flair o the motor—folk micht remember thaim. Hae a look at whit een thay've goat—like lasers!"

Faither said nothing. Avi looked at all these plums, pears, strawberries and raebucks that no one was buying; they all looked as though they were waiting—together with the people—for a vehicle to come along and take them to the local town to sell. If ah wis ahint yon steering wheel, thought Avi, ah'd tak yon basket. Yon wan wi raebuck berries. An ah'd set yon richt whaur

youse perr: the pair of you   *ee* (plural *een*): eye   *raebuck*: roebuck berry

Kenzy's sat. An then ah'd set yon basket oot the motor whaur it tellt me. Or mebbes naw. Ah'd cart it tae the forest an eat aw they raebucks. Efters ah'd put stanes in it an hurl yon in tae yon loch, n'er tae be discovered. He glanced at Alicia and thought that if anyone understands him, surely she does. No words needed.

"We shoudae brought them some gemms or playocks." This was the restless back of Kenzy's head talking. "Or fired up some cartoons oan yer laptop. Thay're bored oot their skulls, an thare's lang roads yet tae gang."

She was holding a large map on her lap and making it look as though she was busy studying it.

"Kenzy!" said Faither softly, "Ye huv tae comprehend these bairns arena likes o yon."

With one hand he fished a book out of the glove compartment; both Avi and Alicia eagerly reached out to take it—so eagerly in fact that they nearly tore it apart. It was a German road atlas of Europe dating back to 1939. They shifted closer to each other and began enthusiastically leafing through the pages.

"Ho, hae a deek o this! The Polski names've been scored oot!" Avi shouted. "Startin pynt—Breslau!" Alicia suggested. "Than it's aff tae Danzig!" Avi warned her in a stern voice. "Awricht," she replied.

And they began to trace the route on the map with their fingers, reading the place names aloud. This occupied them for about half an hour. Then Avi noticed that Alicia had fallen asleep on his shoulder. He looked out of the window and saw a wolf.

In all honesty it wasn't exactly a wolf. Their car was being overtaken by a huge jeep. In the jeep there was a dog sitting on the back seat behind two adults, looking intently at Avi as though trying to fix him in its memory. It was a thickset animal, dunnish red in colour, with muscles that you could see working furiously

gemm: game   *playock*: toy   *deek*: look

on either side of its tense neck. Around its neck was a collar that reflected the fast-moving sunlight on the road so harshly that Avi was near blinded by it. Its ears stood erect, its eyes shone with intelligence. There was a boy in a sleeveless T-shirt sitting next to the dog, making rude hand gestures at Avi. All this lasted no more than a moment. The jeep was steadily overtaking them on the broad highway that gradually rose towards the high transparent sky, pulling the fields on either side—yellow as Kenzy's hair and beyond compare—up with it. Avi made a brief eye movement as if winking at the dog, although he didn't entirely shut one eye, merely squinted. With lightning speed, the dog twitched and sunk its teeth into the boy's bare shoulder. The dog's gloating mouth opened as wide as it could. It was as if the boy had been turned inside out, right to the glands. Before Avi's eyes everything went red, like it does when you lie in the sun for too long with your belly up, and then he could see nothing at all—the jeep had overtaken them and sped forwards, but then the taut line of speed snapped, the jeep swerved and came to a stop by the roadside.

Meanwhile the travellers in the car continued to forge ahead. Faither didn't notice a thing. He just looked at Kenzy from time to time, and she responded by casting strange glances at him. Avi thought that what the pair of them sitting in front really wanted was for him to drop off as well; after all, they were both being shaken up and down. He felt like saying this to Alicia, but she was already asleep and he didn't want to wake her. The two adults were swaying slightly on the front seats, inebriated with speed and danger. If you're drunk, you shouldn't get behind the wheel. Avi was desperate to say all this, but he was well aware that he himself had already been dozing for a long time.

"Mind an turn aff the main drag," said Kenzy to Faither, and licked her lips.

drag: road

13

On Cessnock banks a lassie dwells;
Could I describe her shape and mien;
Our lasses a' she far excels,
An' she has twa sparkling rogueish een.

Then they did turn off on to a forest road, and at this point Alicia woke up. She took a look at the wet patch that had spread on Avi's T-shirt and then switched her gaze to the window, obviously not quite understanding where she was.

"Whaur's yon beastie? Yon pudgie wan!"

True, it hadn't been heard for a long time. "Deider'd," said Kenzy. "It's bylin in here."

Alicia knew what Avi was thinking: She's the wan wha pits us aff frae unsteekin the windaes. An Faither's obedient tae her.

The metalled road soon gave out, only to be replaced by the kind of rutted track that would really shake you up. It was easy to imagine that they were back where their journey had begun. However, the Camp was a long way away. It was impossible to say in what direction, although Avi realised that if he really wanted to find it, he could. Aw he'd tae dae wis lift his heid high as he coud, an aw wad be perceivt. He'd scoor the hale country, aw the villages, toons an ceeties, an sooner or later his ee wad light oan the spiky yett. Aye, thare's yon—the locus whaur they wis bein treated fur thingummyjig. Precisely whit it wis they were bein treated fur wis nane o thair business.

Oan Campside o the yett, somebody wouda savvied thair absence bi the nou. The competeetion wad be scrubbed, an yon scoot-hole i the wire fence uncovered bi thair troop leaders. Thay'd be walkin aboot the forest yellin; lobbin echas tae each ither lik baws, inspectin each timmer an ony trampit gress, wreckin spiders' wirm-wabs.

pits: puts   *unsteekin*: opening   *yett*: gate   *echas*: echoes   *baws*: balls
timmer: tree, timber

Leafy timmer green the simmer through, Sir.

Thay'd be pledgin no tae bind onybody, lang as Alicia an Avi shouted back tae let oan thair whauraboots. He shoudna hae slain yon big beastie. He shouda pit yon i a wee jam jar—yon beastie wad shuirly hae shown them the retour. But richt eneuch, Avi thought, ah've nae wee jam jars. Aw ah've goat's a T-shirt, ripped at the shouder, breekums an gutties. Alicia hae likewise. Awmaist identikit claes, exceptin fur Alicia's breekums' white an mine's blue. The real Mackay of blue.

Tak thaim aff … non, ah willna.

And nothing else. It was a baking hot summer.
Right then the car sputtered and died.
Everyone looked at Faither, and he—or so it seemed—was quite pleased with what had happened.
"Ah've nae idee," he said in response to Kenzy's quizzically raised eyebrows. "Ah tellt ye ah'd nae idee aboot motors."
"We've goat anither hunnert kilometre tae gang yet," said Kenzy.
"Naebody spied us turnin oan tae this track," said Faither, looking straight ahead. He put a hand on her knee. "Yon main drag wis totally deserted. Ah'd baith ma een peeled. Nae motors."
"But whit ur we …" Kenzy began. "Och well, it doesn't really matter."

Her voice is like the ev'ning thrush.

"Doesn't really matter." She said that in the Lingo. It was a phrase that both Avi and Alicia knew. They exchanged glances. The car stood still; you could almost see the heat that was rising

pledgin: promising   *breekums*: shorts   *gutties*: plimsolls

15

from it into the air. There was an occasional clicking sound coming from inside. Surprisingly, the car seemed to fit quite well into its surroundings. It blocked the narrow forest road: tree branches swayed right above its roof, pine cones looked through the windows at the people in it.

A little bird that sings on Cessnock banks unseen

settled on the bonnet and fluttered off as soon as the windscreen wipers shuddered, scattering the pine needles that had collected on them. Faither

While his mate sits nestling in the bush

opened the windows. The car still retained the smell of that strange, anxious morning—something that was so unfamiliar to Avi—but now it was joined by the scent of the sun-warmed forest. It crept in and filled the entire sedan. It was a different forest. A forest that was completely unlike the forest that he and Alicia had observed for months through the wire fence.

They got out of the car, groaning and stretching their aching bones. Alicia rubbed her backside.

"Och, let me hug the baith o yese!" said Faither, but both Avi and Alicia could see that he wasn't thinking about them at all.

An' she has twa sparkling rogueish een.

That's why they didn't stir, and Faither—without giving them a hug—pointed to the path that led into the depths of the forest: a narrow pathway beneath low-hanging branches that were like dipped flags.

"See, see aw they hunners and thoosans o blaeberries! Awa an gather aw yese're wantin!"

Avi and Alicia mistrustfully bent down right to the ground.

The berry bushes led them along the path and from there up the hill to a real bilberry kingdom. Bilberries, bletherberries, babbleberries. "Ah propone a Treaty o Tordesillas," said Avi hastily, filling his mouth with the first berries from this green, blue, black, golden, mysterious India. "An ah'm d'accord" retorted Alicia. "East o yon meridian's aw mine!" They both fell on their knees, their mouths open wide, and crawled each to their own side.

"Ma tittie wis eatit bi wulves," said Avi for the last time and opened his eyes. It was then that a terrible green force knocked him off his legs and he tumbled face down into the moss. Alicia pummelled him with her heels and tightened her fingers around his throat from behind. "Get aff o me!" he croaked.

"It's ye, ye're the wan that goat eatit, they've eatit ye an splotter'd aw the wee bits oot," said Alicia, breathing heavily. At last she relaxed her grip. "Ye're slaithered wi wulf slime an glit. Ye're hauf undigestit, aw chowed likes o goury. Yuck!"

"Ye're droukit yersel! Ye're aye droukit!" Avi muttered under his breath

She's no bow-hough'd, she's no hen-shin'd.

Havin such a strang tittie likes o her—whan she lays intae ye, it's like ye've bin mouildert alive. The Camp's tae blame, aw they vitamins an yon sweet air.

"See whit ye've scriev'd aw o'er me," he shouted, and the forest caught his words and carried them off somewhere, as if they had never been uttered. C'mon, forest, gies back ma voice! Voice, gies back the forest!

"Whit d'ye mean? Whaur?"

"Here!" And he pointed to his T-shirt. It really was covered with blue marks left by Alicia's fingers, nose and even lips; as

glit: slobber   *goury*: (lit.) the refuse of the intestines of salmon   *droukit*: sopping wet   *scrieve*: write

if she had indeed written something on the white cloth of the T-shirt with the hole in the shoulder that he wore. Some kind of long sentence in mysterious, unintelligible hieroglyphs.

"They're no aw that unintelligible," said Alicia, peering closely at the T-shirt. "See, ah writ 'b' here, an here coud be a Latin 's'—in Gothic-write. An here's a wee thing like script auld monks wid use . . ."

"We huv tae decipher yon," said Avi. "Ah think ah've goat the boak."

"Vomit," said Alicia and burst out laughing. "In the Lingo you say 'I will have a vomit.'"

"Naw, ye semply say 'I will vomit,'" said Avi a little uncertainly. "Onyweys, ah'm gonnae scrieve something oan yir T-shirt. Ye're ayeweys sic a braw bonnie wee souk . . ."

"Houts touts ah'm braw," said Alicia "But oan ye go, O boakin brither o mine, scrieve whit ye want."

Avi crushed a handful of bilberries with his fingers, in sheer desperation noticing how there still seemed to be as many berries on the hill as there were when they first burst in on the scene. He smeared them all over his hands so that his fingers turned black, sat down in front of her and began to write on her T-shirt, all over her chest and stomach.

"Are ye scrievin aboot wulves?" Alicia asked, and her voice betrayed her lack of interest—she was now lying on her back with her eyes shut. "Ah'm fadin awa wi faimish . . ."

"Aye" said Avi without raising his eyes—he was completely engrossed in what he was doing. "Thare ye go, aw done."

He stretched out his hand to her, and they both stood up. The nearby marsh gave off a tasty smell, like lunchtime in the Camp kitchen. Somewhere over there—where mosquitoes were twisting and turning their clouds round and round in the air—lay the track to the car. It was like going through smoke when they

braw: good   *souk*: someone who curries favour   *houts touts*: like hell

18

passed through the mosquitoes with their eyes half-shut. They stood for a bit beneath a sunbeam that bounced straight off the nearest bush, then continued their weary way along the path until at last they came out on to the road where the car was.

Kenzy and Faither were still there. Kenzy had her cheek pressed against one of the side windows; she was trying to grope for Faither with her hand behind her back, but he wouldn't let himself be found. His nose was pressed against the nape of Kenzy's neck, and his nostrils were filled with the scent of her yellow hair.

I wad na gie a button for her.

Right now the two of them were one person, and there was no place for Alicia and Avi between them.

Mally's meek, Mally's sweet,
Mally's modest and discreet;
Mally's rare, Mally's fair,
Mally's every way complete.

"Ah canna comprehend whit he's sayin," said Avi.

"But ah can," retorted Alicia. "Hing aboot, ah'll jist be a wee minuit."

She crept towards the car, which still had its doors open. She crawled on her knees on the side away from Faither and Kenzy, then quickly made her way back to Avi with a book in her hands—the 1939 road atlas of Europe. A real little treasure. Avi looked at his sister with admiration.

"Ye ken whit, Avi?" said Alicia. "Hou aboots we gang tae Bremen?"

"Aye, let's," he said. "But we huv tae gaither supplies. It's langtimes tae gang thare. Awfy langtimes. D'ye ken hou faur it's tae Bremen frae here?"

"Ah'll tell ye," Alicia thought for a moment. "Jist short o a thoosand kilometres. Whit instrument'll ye be playin wance we've arrivert?"

"The clavicle," said Avi. "D'ye ken humans an animals hae banes wi hales ye can blaw intae, likes o a flute?"

"Aye," said Alicia. "An ah'm gonnae touk a muckle drum."

"Bang oan the bass," said Avi.

"Bi touk o drum," said Alicia.

They took each other by the hand and returned to the land where the bilberries grow. They had the feeling that even more berries had grown while they had been away. Lifting their legs up high so as not to sink into the blue bog below, they set off in the opposite direction, away from where the mosquitoes were to where the bilberry kingdom came to an end. And very soon they were nowhere to be found; they weren't on the hill, not under it, not anywhere on the map, and not underneath it either. And all that was left for the man with the scarlet face and the woman with the short yellow hair to do was to ask the mosquito cloud where their legitimately acquired blood had run off to.

"Aviiiiiiiii! Aliciaaaaaaaa!"

"Thay've goat voices likes o they troop leaders i the Camp," said Avi and quickened his pace.

> A barefit maid I chanc'd tae meet;
> But O the road was very hard
> For that fair maiden's tender feet
> Her yellow hair, beyond compare.

It was then that Alicia burst out laughing. A lot of time had passed since she last laughed. And the forest started laughing with her.

banes: bones   *touk*: beat   *muckle*: big

2

The tractor driver had six fingers

The tractor driver had six fingers. Whether it was on the right hand or on the left hand Faither could no longer remember. He had five normal fingers, like all people have, with shiny black nails, hard as diamonds—and behind the hairy little finger there was another one, small, thin, pale blue, that protruded to one side, with a tiny nail, white and well cared-for. Faither could not tear his eyes away from this additional, bonus finger. It was apparent that the tractor driver was unable to move it. A useless, pretty, feminine finger. It had grown on the man's hand like a weed. Perhaps it wasn't a finger at all, just some kind of appendage. Faither struggled not to gawp at that sixth finger, but he did so all the same. He was hypnotised by it.

The tractor materialised before them on the road like a ghost and stopped, as if painted in the air, right in front of their car. The driver made no attempt to leave the cabin, but simply looked at Faither and Kenzy, and waited. Attached to the tractor was a long, empty trailer that had clearly been used to transport logs. Faither raced up to the cabin waving his arms; it was only then that the driver unwillingly got out, listened to Faither's hurried explanations of what was needed without showing any sign of interest, climbed back in and began to unwind a tow rope. The driver's gaze—malicious and mocking—was fixed only on Kenzy, not Faither, but Faither couldn't stop staring at the extra finger. Sitting on a tree stump, Kenzy stared intently at the forest; Faither didn't like it. He wanted to tell her about the finger. And he had a strong urge to ask the tractor driver how he contrived to exist with such a hand.

An say yon tractor driver wis gangin tae toun, he coud get his-sel oan the leet fir an operation. Yon extra pinkie wad be chapped aff, nae scaur oan the haund, an naebody wad gowp at him like he wis some kind o freakerie o nature. Tractor drivers likes o him gang up tae the caipital. They dawdle alang the main drag, dither roond wi folk doon the mercat, hae thair photae taen be-side moniments, sink a few hunner-gram shots o vodka wi beer at the worst dives. They ming o yon foostiness that's unscrubbit. Why does he no get yon stump cut aff? Too dear? Feart o sur-geons? (An ye, are ye feart o thaim? Wad ye allou yersel tae be gullied?) Is he jist puttin it aff the nou an the morn's morn, tae the end o life? Or is he proud o it oan the sly, since ye somehou must be different frae ither folk? Mebbe it's yon picture hingin i yon cabin o yer tractor that maks ye unalike? Maist tractor driv-ers hae pictures o scuddy women, but this one's goat photaes o black-belt karate fechters.

Perchance he's decided awreadies whit he's gaun tae dae. The morn's morn, while he's timmer hackin, he'll neck a shot o vodka, eat a wairm, sun-saft tomatae alang wi it, set yon digit oan the block, turn his ee awa—an it's aff! His eik-name's aw that re-mains.

"OK," said the tractor driver and spat on the palms of his hands. "Let's go. Let's dae it."

The tractor driver lit a cigarette while standing on the foot-board. The tractor began to puff and snort, then drove around the car, crushing bushes in its way. It took a whole hour to attach the car, turn it round and tow it to the nearest village. Faither said not a word to the tractor driver about Alicia and Avi, or about how he and Kenzy had spent several hours wandering around in the forest and, oblivious of the need for caution, had shouted

leet: list *scaur*: scar *mercat*: market *ming*: stink *gullied*: cut, knifed *the morn's morn*: tomorrow morning *scuddy*: naked *eik-name*: nickname

themselves hoarse while looking for the children, and then how the two adults themselves got lost and had to hunt for the car. The village mechanic who took just a few minutes to bring the untamed, dusty car back to life did not inspire Faither's confidence either. He no longer trusted anyone except Kenzy. She, however, sat in silence with a worried expression on her face. Her yellow hair, her black brows pressed into a frown, and her refined nose all revealed that she was afraid of something. This was in stark contrast to yesterday evening, when they were discussing for the last time all the details and possible traps, and to the morning once they, cold and steel hard in their resolve, had left the city. And to the night as well, when Kenzy was more tender than she had ever been. He clenched his teeth so not to give way to tears. She paid the tractor driver and the mechanic without a word, and once again they drove out on to the main road. It greeted them mockingly with all the road signs and markings that they knew so well.

"Hou much cash did ye gie thaim?"

"Whit weys does it mak odds?"

The farmstead where they intended to take the children, hidden in the marshes and not marked on any map, was still some ninety kilometers away. It was no longer feasible to get there, and there was no point anyway without Avi and Alicia, without the children for whose sake he had been working, living and striving. Faither and Kenzy were so tired by their wandering around the forest that they began to fall asleep; Faither hadn't noticed that his neck had been burned by the sun, so it was just as well that he couldn't lean it against the headrest.

Outside the car windows night was falling. The day was becoming shorter. Thay'd been hopin tae be at the fermhoose bi the nou. Tae've goat the fire goin, the bairns fed an couried in, singin their favourit sangs, aw thegither aside the loch. Faither's

courie: snuggle   aw thegither: all together

23

heid woud be lain oan Kenzy's laup. Thare'd be starns abuin, an the bairns' voices close to, richt bi his lug. An than … weel, he'd no as yet pictured tae hisself whit next.

"She's wabbit, her tummy's gey sair, ah'm awfy fu o care fur ma lassie!"

Or this one, about Ulysses: "Fa lal de lal de laling, wi aw their jibber-jabberin, But wha minds the bairns? Ayeweys ma laddie's wunnerin," Faither began singing to himself, expecting that Kenzy would join in. She didn't.

She was tired. It had been a hard day.

The moon came creeping out way off in the fake cheerful sky where it was still light. It followed them, keeping its distance but not falling behind. Jist wan heidlicht. The muin's lik a motorbike. Yon gadgie doon the forest wi yon saxt finger's likely tae hae a bike back o his yaird. It's deepest nicht, he's a heivenly biker wha rides aff intae drift mist an disappears aroon a corner intae day. He's pictured that well, hasn't he? The moon …

Accompanied by the moon, they reached a small town and crossed a bridge, cautiously caressing it with their headlights. September Seventeenth Street, Lenin Square[2]—and there wasn't a single Lenin anywhere to be seen. A Catholic church, an Orthodox church, the House of Culture. The bus station, where a lone minibus was standing. There was a fat bloke hanging around next to it; he glanced at them and continued watching out patiently for likely passengers in the early twilight. "Stap," said Kenzy.

He smiled at her and turned smoothly towards the Catholic church, from where a street led off to the outskirts of the town. Shuirly thare's somewhares roond here whare ye can buy petrol, hae wee bite tae eat, kip doon i the motor an wake up afreshed? Than gang back tae the forest, whare his damp wee footprints hae lang disappeared frae yon dry sprigs an sprots o fir tree? Nou

starns: stars   *wabbit*: exhausted   *gey*: very   *sair*: sore   *gadgie*: bloke thare'll be somebody rakin o'er thaim, shuvin thaim aside wi thair haund, or shoud that be foot? A body saxt-fingert, acht-fingert, twal-fingert …

"*Stap*, ah said!"

He stopped the car. Kenzy got out and put her rucksack on her back. Then she turned and quickly kissed him on the forehead.

"Ye shuirly huv tae recognise yersel it's no gonnae pan oot. Ah'm goin back hame. Ah'm sorry."

"Kenzy!"

"Ah howp ye find thaim, but ah canna dae this ony mair," and she ran across the street to the minibus. Faither started up the car and moved off as if on autopilot. He drove round the square, past the spot where a Lenin ought to be standing, next to the pine trees and the lone plinth. He went on driving round, wasting petrol and still with a smile on his face.

He turned the town round in his hands like a steering wheel. Just as schoolboys twist and turn pencils in their hands, murderers twist their knives, teachers their pointers or a traveller his feeble staff. And the town obediently joined the whirl. Roonaboot roonaboot roonaboot ye gang, gin ye gang oan, ye're aff.

The streetlightss were whirling. The porch railings whirled. The low fences whirled. The evergreens whirled with the shop signs that shone in the denser, more meaningful twilight. In the air he heard music, music solely for him, a four-four time tune that encompassed it all: a lullaby, some kind of jazz, the blues of a small town and Slavonic Bazaar.[3]

Second-Hand
Goods from Europe
Prestige
Plumbing Supplies

gin: if

Pet World
Laguna Café

Stuff that's awreddy used. Prestige. Stuff fur plumbers. Warld o Pets an Laguna Café. Shift up the gear. Pit foot tae gas, press haurder. Lauchin' gas that brings oan the giggles an hurls the steerin wheel free. Used café, warld o pets, prestige, laguna, used. Ill-used warld, fuckit warld. Hou coud she dae that? Hou coud she abandon him here, richt whan he needit her the maist? Whan he wanted tae be alane, she wis ayeweys thare, alangside lik a shaidae. Ye couldna shift her. But nou …

For a second he thought he saw Avi standing in front of him, caught in his headlights. Faither braked sharply, but it was only some kid, completely drunk and yelling something. Faither carefully drove round him and, giving way to a police van, turned into the neighbouring street.

> *Hey tutti taiti,*
> *How tutti taiti,*
> *Hey tutti taiti,*
> *Wha's fou now?*

He wanted tae get fou, pished. Pished likes o he'd niver been afore. Yon wey time woud unspeal,

> *Hey tutti taiti,*
> *How tutti taiti,*

so he woudnae think oan her nor ony ither body,

> *Wha's fou nou?*

---

shaidae: shadow   *fou*: drunk   *unspeal*: wind back

He drove at a snail's pace along the street; it bore the name of some character he had never heard of. The street was obviously not one that deserved bright lights. There was almost no one to be seen, except for a crowd that had gathered around the entrance to a restaurant called Emperor Paul. The women's dresses shone unnaturally white beneath the streetlights, and an unhealthy glow was coming off the men's Lycra shirts so that they seemed to be leading a quite separate existence from the trousers that were invisible in the darkness. Indeed, it was as if the women were surrounded by torsos, phantoms with chests unbuttoned. Through the wide-open mouth of the restaurant flowed the voice of a comic doing an opening act. A hysterical voice that caused slurping feedback sounds in the speakers and then flew out into the street and on to the courtyards of two-storey apartment blocks that stood stock still in the murk.

The car engine unexpectedly said something and fell silent. It continued to roll slowly along the street, and now it was possible to make out what was actually being said by those people who were having a ball inside the restaurant. Faither stuck his face out of the car window. Immediately behind the restaurant there was a building with a sign that said "Hotel," in darkness except for a single spot of light that came from a table lamp in the foyer. Next to the hotel were bare wooden notice boards surrounded by flower beds. It was into these flower beds that the wheels of the car gently glided. It came to a complete halt.

He paid a ridiculously small sum for a room—made even more ridiculous by the fact that he had just about enough cash on him for a week, no more. He shouda drove eftir yon minibus, cam alangside tae stapp it. She's mebbes hae some change o mind, she mebbe rues her abandonment o him here. Houaniver, he didna trust Kenzy ony mair, an he didna ken which road she'd taken. Tae the capital? Her parents? Mebbes tae Vilnia, yon's jist wee weys frae here.[4] The hotel receptionist, a woman of Kenzy's age, and indeed herself something of a parody of Kenzy, yawned and shoved the room keys in his direction—just as if she had made a move in a kind of table game.

"Want some loo paper?"

He looked at the receptionist with horror.

"I asked you if you want some loo paper? It's not included in the price of the room."

Landlady, count the lawin,
The day is near the dawin,
Ye're a' blind drunk boys
And I'm but jolly fou.
Hey tutti taiti …

"Naw!" he said, stressing the answer with a hand gesture, "Naw!"

It came out too emotionally, but he couldn't restrain himself. She shrugged her shoulders.

"Is thare … ony ither bodies here?"

"No. Just some people from Moscow. Your neighbours."

He remembered what the receptionist had said about loo paper the moment he opened the wobbly lock and switched on the light. A dim bulb shed its scant light on a depressing, cramped room, as yellow as the flowers that Margarita held in her hand.[5] The merry voices of the Emperor Paul's guests could be heard from beyond the pink curtains. By one wall there was a bed, made up military-style with well-scrubbed, mended and orphaned bedclothes. On the sheet there was a large, dark prison-coloured stamp with an illegible abbreviation. The greasy, lacquered wood of the bed gave off a feeble gleam, reminding the viewer that having a good sleep meant wasting precious working time. There was an office desk that had been skilfully knocked together from other office desks of varying ages and colours. On it was an ashtray of ideal cleanliness; you could get the urge to drown yourself in it. From a corner of the room a black television was glaring sullenly at Faither. "Do you want me to tell your fortune?" it asked.

"Switch me on," it commanded. "You're going to die," it promised. "You're already dead," it confirmed.

Hey tutti taiti ...

The room smelled of carefully concealed socks, patriotism and bleach. It gave off such an air of poverty, disrespect and despair that Faither was unable to bring himself to sit. He just stood there, frozen to the spot beneath the light bulb, inside which its exhausted slave—a tiny, puny, gilded homunculus—was dancing on hot coals. There was nothing pleasant about even feeling the lino under his feet. It had been laid crooked and crawled up the rotted skirting board like skin that had been hastily torn off a huge, sick beast.

Cog, an ye were aye fou,
Cog, an ye were aye fou,
I wad sit and sing to you,
If ye were aye fou!
Hey tutti taiti ...

A hotel to die in. Everything about the place was talking to him rapidly, all at the same time, voices vying with each other to get their word in first, voices of misery, of condemnation, of how nothing would come out right, of how there was no escape, not now, not ever. A hotel for those who have decided to depart this life. That's why toilet paper is "not included." What do you need toilet paper for, if you're going to kill yourself? Should the hotel perhaps provide waste bins and leave moist wipes on the table as well? The dead don't defecate.

This hotel and this God-left wee toun's a perfect spot for disenchauntit bardies an artistes tae while awa thair final nichts, thought Faither. No the ceety, amangst ease an yon perpetuel hurlie-burlie life o their tenements, whare decisions are ticklers; naw, hereaboots ye realise pronto yer life's been a failure an thare's nae point tae gangin oan. A haven fur folk wha's lost faith i thirsel. Ye coud envisage yon tae yersel: wakin up wi a huge hangover i this roomie

Landlady, count the lawin,
The day is near the dawin,
Ye're a' blind drunk boys
And I'm but jolly fou

oan some back-end o the year mornin whan the heatin's nae yet switched oan an the rain's scuddin the windae panes. Precisely here's whaur Howplessness bides an labours, keys tae aw these roomies tae haund.

Hey tutti taiti …

He bounded out of the room and went downstairs, where the receptionist was still sitting motionless under the light of the table lamp. It looked as though she had put the lampshade on her head. In the Emperor Paul he ordered some vodka for himself; there was some kind of celebration going on, maybe a wedding—any one of the guests could have been either the groom or the bride.

Weel may ye a'be!
Ill may ye never see!
God bless the king
And the companie!
Hey tutti taiti …

However, they sat him down and brought him so much bread that he could have used it to feed all the local pigeons. The salad was quite tasty, and after the first hundred grams of vodka, the cawing of voices flew off to the far side of his heart and ceased annoying him so much. He went out for a smoke, stood for a bit some distance away from a group of people that eyed him with interest but without hostility. He went back inside, sat down and ordered some more vodka. Strange, but he had managed to pass through the throng without touching anyone's elbow, back or arm, as if he had conjured up all these people in his mind.

"Fancy a wee bit skirt?" someone asked, bending over his ear. Again, just as he had done in the hotel, he gestured "no" with his hands without looking up to see who had spoken. He'd tae catch his breath an calm doon afore pickin up his glais agin. A wee bit skirt? He could weel imagine whit kind o lass yon meant. A lassie, chitterin wi cauld, faimisht, big een wi his spitten image i baith o thaim, staundin fou wi a glittie faiple.

> Your rosy cheeks are turned sae wan,
> Ye're greener than the gress, lassie,
> Your coatie's shorter by a span,
> Yet deil an inch the less, lassie.

He shoudna booze sae much, he's muckle things tae dae the morn; get cash, get the motor fettle'd up, return tae yon woodland track, than aff tae yon dark pairt o the wood whaur thare's nae addresses, nae walls, nae windaes. Search fur Alicia an Avi, airt them oot an feenish whit he wis minded tae dae: rescue his bairns. Wee bit skirt . . . lassie. "Lassie" is a puir ward, puir lik watter; a lassie has tae be somebody's tochter, either yer ain or some ither body's. "A wee bit skirt"—whit the Lingo caws craiturs wi false smiles an price tags hingin frae thair bubbies,

> Ye hae lien wrang, lassie,
> Ye've lien a'wrang,
> Ye've lien is some unco bed,
> An wi some unco man

a glittie faiple: a lower lip shining with grease   *airt oot*: find

she's a burd o the gemm, a product. Langage in general fankles y'up. Think oan an it's langage that's guilty o awthings.

Ye've loot the pownie ower the dyke,
An he's been in the corn, lassie;
For ay the brose ye sup at e'en,
Ye boak them on the morn, lassie.

He went back to the hotel and, shuddering at the inevitability of returning to his comfortless room, unlocked the door. Somewhere oan ither side o the wall, thay folk frae Moscow wis up an aboot; roonaboot thair parts, roon Moscow, it wis aw goin oan— yon Moscow metro runnin, yon Kremlin chimes chimin, folk gangin alang the pavements, clocks markin time. Whit are they fowk frae Moscow daein here, onyweys? Thay're drivin roun the forests, tryin tae find a simmer cottar's hoose fir thaimsel, scourin the locus. Dreadfu—hou can ye grapple wi Roushie? An it's perfectly possible thay'll be oot drivin the morn's morn an pick up twa bairnies wanderin alang the way: thay'll pit them i thair motor an flee aff wi them eastwards, lauchin at these taciturn, sunburnit bairns; each Ruskie motor's muckle likes o Siberia an unchancy likes o ignorance.

Faither grated his teeth. The vodka no longer warmed his insides, and he had no way of stoking the fire. The morn's morn. It's the morn's morn awready. Whit fur this useless wee toun woudna wake suiner. If anely time coud begin agin.

He lay face down on the pillow.

Your rosy cheeks are turned sae wan,
Ye're greener than the gress, lassie.

Whaur's yer tochter?[6] His thoughts of Alicia were light, but at the same time they oozed blood. The pain with which he gave

unchancy: dangerous

himself over to them was so sweet. Here he was, already allowing Alicia to create her own environment. He lay there, inventing a future for the girl.

And, gradually, there arose before him an image of a great city, somewhere abroad. He pictured Alicia—already quite grown-up, perhaps a student, beautifully but casually dressed Western-style in dark blue—standing on a hill overlooking the coloured tiles on pointed roofs. At her side there's a boy, at first glance a real foreigner.

Faither pictured them so clearly that he could hear their voices. Voices from the future. They were speaking a foreign language, but Faither could understand everything.

"Belarus," says the young foreigner, with puckered lips and a burr in his voice. "What did you do there, in your country? Do you have parents there?"

"Yes," nods Alicia. "My father and my brother."

"What about your mother? Why don't you say anything about her? Fine, don't say anything if you don't want to," says the boy, looking intently at Alicia. "What kind of things did you do in your country? What were you interested in?"

"At first I was silent and went to school. Then I was given therapy."

"Why were you silent? Do you mean that you just didn't like talking? You really don't speak our language very well yet, do you, Ali? Come now, don't be upset. Tell me, were you really silent? Why?"

"I wasn't silent with everyone," says Alicia. It was difficult for her to part her lips. "I used to talk to my father."

"Did he beat you? Or rape you?"

Fou lichtly lap ye ower the knowe,
An throu the wud ye sang, lassie;
But herryin o the foggie byke,
I fear ye've got a stang, lassie

he asks after a lengthy pause.

"No. We used to sing together."

"I'm sorry. I didn't mean to say anything bad about your father. But why didn't you talk to other people?"

"I wasn't allowed to. It was the Lingo. Everybody spoke the Lingo. My father said that we mustn't speak the Lingo. So it was better not to say anything. Everybody thought that I was a mute."

By now his face is very close to hers. He *leuks gey fey*, thinks Faither. He's reddy fur tae *faw* fur aw sorts.

"What happened next? What were you being treated for?"

"For my refusal to speak."

"Oh, what nonsense!" he exclaims with relief. "You and your endless riddles. Do you speak the Lingo now? Can you speak it?"

"Why should I?" Alicia is puzzled. "I'm talking to you now. What do we need the Lingo for?"

"OK, but what then? What happened next? Were you cured?"

"Then my father rescued us. We were driving for ages, then we walked through a forest and sang. And now I'm here."

"Stop it, stop playing around." The boy is becoming annoyed. "You speak our language well. You were top of the class by the end of the course."

"What I'm telling you is the truth."

"Listen, Ali, we're engaged, aren't we? And I really, really do love you ..."

"Right then," says Alicia, studying his face with obvious distrust. "I'll tell you something if you want, but I don't much like mentioning it."

"Are you going to tell me about the men in your life?"

"You can be really silly sometimes." Alicia is frowning. "There's nothing but sex in your head. No. It isn't about men. It's about something I once read when my father's things somehow reached me.

"I had a different name back then. And there were completely different people around me.

he leuks gey fey: he looks so naive   *faw*: fall

34

"My father forbade us to speak the Lingo. 'Yon langage,' he would say, and frown in the way I'm frowning now; he would drag out the 'a' sound of 'lang' with loathing. It was just like how they used to drag my brother by his ears in the Camp, and I had to chase after them and beat them with anything that came to hand—my legs, a chair, a bucket, a belt. 'Thaaaat Lingo ...' And we would stop talking. It was as loathsome to us as it was to him. I didn't find out who Neznaika was until I was sixteen.[7] It's possible that people did tell me, but my father wouldn't allow me to listen to them. I didn't know anything at all about Cheburashka; or about the blue railway carriage that rocks from side to side.[8] And who exactly Aibolit is I have only the vaguest notion.[9] I know he was a doctor, but I can't have the same attitude towards doctors as ... as ..."

"As what?"

"A doctor for me is someone different ... If he's a real doctor, he doesn't try to save you, he ... Anyway, do you know who Aibolit is? So be quiet. You don't have anyone like him. There's only been one real doctor in my life, and he was very kind. He could do anything, but he didn't have time to complete my cure. So that's how I came here—uncured. And at first it wasn't all that easy for me. But do you know that there in the Camp they gave us such good vitamins?"

"Food supplements? Drugs?"

"No, please don't interrupt. Now I think it's only thanks to those vitamins that I was able to stay here. To go to college, find a job and meet you.

"One day a package arrived for me from my home country. It contained my father's things. He kept a diary—the thought never entered his head to post on social media—it was his private diary; he simply wrote it on his laptop in a straightforward text file. Pretend that it was just a diary under lock and key that only I could see. And that's all. I read it. It was very interesting. Except ..."

"Except what?"

"I got the feeling that it wasn't me he was writing about. It was about some other little girl, and about a different country. Not the one I came from. He must have been in hiding."

"I understand," said her boyfriend, not really sure that he did.

"And there's something else—for some reason, there isn't a word in it about my brother. If you want, I'll read a bit to you. I always carry the text around with me. Would you like me to? True, it'll be a translation. But then translation is a way of avenging yourself on language for what it has done … Because there's no end to it, and because it's so powerful."

"I've lost you again. You can't say it like that in our language. It sounds strange. Avenging yourself on language. Ha, ha! Sorry."

"You might understand more if you laughed less. Just listen. It won't be easy, but I will try to translate for you."

Hey tutti, taiti …

3

Likes o maist lassies her age
she wisna that fond o her name

Likes o maist lassies her age she wisna that fond o her name. She confessed it tae me wee whiles ago at brakfast, her ee cast doon, an chowin oan a muckle cheekfu o peanut butter piece. Fur whitiver reason, ah'd ayeways jaloused peanut butter tae be hinnied, thanks tae yon hard nut brittle ah used tae hae such a penchant fir whan ah wis a laddie—it wis kent bi Francaise—"grillage." E'en the nou, ah eat somethin burnin hot an imagine nut bitties stuck atween ma teeth. Nou thay've startit wi selling peanut butter hereaboots. Ah'd absolute nae thocht as tae whit yon wis like. It's salty, likes o herring,

Clupea harengus,

i succar. She coud eat it tae a baund playin tho.

I could range the world around,
For the sake o' Somebody.

She's no daft.

We wis rattlin throu brakfast, as per usual. Music blarin oot the wireless. We ayeweys pit it up tae max whaniver we wanted a confab—only instrumental. It wis than she admitted hou she

jaloused: guessed   *hinnied*: sweet, honeyed   *tae a baund playin*: till the cows come home

wanted tae be kent bi something entirely ither. She wis gabbin throu moothfus, gabbin an greetin an ramshin aw at same time; she had tae say whit she wanted, but it wis terrifyin her tae say it, an whan ye swally yir wards, it maks ye feel less guiltfu o daein it.

O-hon! For Somebody!
O-hey! For Somebody!

It's somethin bairns alane dae. She niver yet mooted me whit name she found maist beautifu. Aye but ah'm her faither, ah hae nae need o her tellin me whit gien name is richt, yon's ma job. If yon wis up tae her, she woud certainly want tae be cried ... Weel, par example—Yaryna. Or Karyna. Or Aksana. Or Silvana. Bellanna. Crappi-Botti-anna.

O-hon for Somebody!

Ye coud really fankle up yer tongue. Whan ye mooth gien names likes o this, ye fairly realise first haund hou thay're no *Niaroo*, oor ain; ye realise oor sprach organs staund agin thaim; they dinna hae the genetic bent tae say these teuch notes. Thay're no adapted tae pronoonce such improbable, fremmit, coorse—

O-hey for Somebody!

Na, thay're no gien names: thay're solely suitit tae cawin dugs. Ah'm o'ercome whan ah think oan her—ma wee lassie, my Siamese Sia hauding a wunnerfu papyrus i her slender haunds, birlin doun the road like a Karyna blawin the ocarina, or a Bellanna wi wee bells roun her neck, or a Silvana dressed en soie. It's no gonnae happen. Ah've spoken.

greetin: crying   *ramshin*: chewing   *moot*: mention   *tae be cried*: to be called   *sprach*: speech   *teuch*: tough   *fremmit*: foreign   *cawin*: calling   *dugs*: dogs   *birlin*: running

I wad do—what wad I not?
For the sake o' Somebody.

Ah'm her faither.

Ah mind hou ah chose her name. It wis a matter o principle fir me t'ensure her name wad appear i her passeport precisely as ah wantit. Yon time we thocht—yersel an me—only yon way woud she, Sia, hae means tae convey her papyrus wi honeur, no wi fearfulness an no hidin frae onyone. Nouadays ah woud be mair canny. That day, houaniver, wi whit wis a floorish o righteous irritation, ah went tae the Registration Office brammed up fur a wedding. Fur Sia's wedding—aye, in certain manner, it wis shuirly her first haund-festin tae the warld.

I am my mammy's ae bairn, Wi'unco folk I weary, Sir.

An ah had tae look lik ah'd respectabeelity so they had tae tak tent o me an no jist simply cast me oot.

I'm o'er young,

ah even screenged ma teeth, likes o ah wis aff tae the dentist. Ah pit a tie oan. Ah trimmed ma neb birsies,

I'm o'er young to marry yet.

A youthfu faither, wi his purvey o cannon fodder an fresh ova, gangin tae Court o His Maijesty.

I'm o'er young, 'twad be a sin
To tak me frae my mammy yet.

---

brammed up: dressed up   *haund-festin*: betrothal   *tak tent o*: take notice of   *screenged*: scrubbed   *neb birsies*: nose hairs   *ova*: egg cells

Awthings are carefully thocht oot here. The Registration Office wis at one an same time a tapsalteerie babbie bath, a bride's cake an a burial moond. Here's whaur Death woud haund in reports, but only if yon death wis registrate fir oor district. Hereaboot a maisterfu midwife o papier wad tak delivery o babbies, provided they came frae oor district. Ither bodies hae ither pairishes.

Ah goat in jist afore closin time. The buildin wis recently re-decore'd: yon empie corridors pit me i mind o fallin rates o birth an growthiness; it smelt foostie—like plaister an the feenalitie o the grave. Ah jee'd open the door—she wis seatit belaw a roon signet o state lookin aw humpybackit—weighed doon w'it. She wis gien her feathers a wee dicht, waitin oan leavin.

> *I rede you beware at the hunting, young men,*
> *I rede you beware at the hunting, young men;*
> *Tak some on the wing, and some as they spring,*
> *But cannily steal on a bonnie moor-hen.*

"Sima?" she cast back at me. Plain as parritch she cared nae a flea. "Sita? Serafima?"

Sia, ma guidwife.

"Non. Ye didna pick me up richt. Si-a."

She sighed, pu'd oot a drawer, an lifted oot the Book.

"Listen. There are names on the list like these beginning with S. Sara, Sviatlana, Safia, Sniazhana, Stanislava, Stella, Suzanna, Serafima. There's Staglava, a beautiful Slavonic name. As you can see, the name Sya . . ."

> *Revered defender of beauteous Stuart,*
> *Of Stuaaaart, a name once respected;*
> *A name which to love was the mark of a true heart,*
> *But now 'tis despis'd and neglected.*

---

tapsalteerie: topsy-turvy *growthiness*: fertility *roon*: round *a wee*
dicht: a little tidying up *parritch*: porridge

"Si-a."
"... that name Sia's no on the list."

Tho' something like moisture conglobes in my eye,
Let no one misdeem me disloyal;

"Aye but thare must be ither leets. Onyweys, ma dochter hae only wan heid."[10]

A poor friendless wand'rer may well claim a sigh,
Still more if that wand'rer were royal

"Where did you get that name from?"

But why of that epocha make such a fuss,
Now we've the Hanover stem?
If getting George and his ilk was lucky for us,
I'm sure 'twas as lucky for them.

Ah coud read tae ye a bit Scrift o the Deid. Ah'm willin tae bet oan it fallin i yir locus o competence, whate'er yer daft gien name is, ye daupit coo.

But, loyalty, truce! we're on dangerous ground;
Who knows how the fashions may alter?
The doctrine today that is loyalty sound,
Tomorrow may bring us a halter!

Ye mak contribution tae yon scrift eftir aw. But naw, ah said none o that. In actual fact, ah said nothing.
"Folk dae come awa wi unco names ..." she said sadly. "It's the bairns as suuuuffer aw thair lives."

---

scrift: book   *daupit coo*: stupid cow   *unco*: strange

"Why mind at suuuuffering the nou?" an ah gied her as douce a look as ah wis able.

"It's wi them til thay're deid!" and—to add greater conviction to what she said—she rolled her eyes.

"She's no even a month auld yet. Whit death?"

"Use yer fantice!" she put the book back and slammed the drawer shut. "Sometimes folk dee, even frae oor district."

"Folk are jist like langages, but fur some raison ah feel mair vext fur langages," ah hummer'd. "See, ah'm no aboot tae name her onything lik Acacia nor Armoracia. An ah've nae mind tae caw her onything like 'Adolf Hitler.' Or ... och ... ah dinna ken ... 765Kh6422MND."

"Thare's instances o yon sort ..." she said thoughtfully. "But no inaboot oor district. If ye really want tae ken the maist popular name inaboot oor destrict ... Ah'll tak a wee look, jist ootae interest. Here we go: Marya, Stella, Aliaksandar, Zulfia. Thare's loadsae parents who've historical interest an fur them we occasionally mak exception. Maliuta, Messalina ... But as ah've awready tellt ye, fur oor district we've Marya, Stella, Ziamfira, Aliaksandar and Zulfia. Fur laddies it's Aliaksandar, fur lassies Zulfia."

"Ikhtiandar and Giulchatai," ah added, girnin.[11] "C'mon. Sia's a hamely name. Awmaist like Maria. Or the first syllable o Pius."

Auld Phoebus himsel, as he peep'd o'er the hill,
In spite at her plumage he tried his skill:
He levell'd his rays where she bask'd on the brae—

"Who's this Pius supposed to be? Some kind of ideological diversion?" The countenance o the Weirdwife o the Registration Office darkened. "Now you listen to me, this isn't a game. And, anyway, I'm going to be closing the office in five minutes."

douce: kind, straight   *fantice*: fantasy   *hummer'd*: murmured   *girnin*: pulling a face

42

His rays were outshone, and but mark'd where she lay.

"Yon's precisely why ..." Ah wis wheedlin nou.

"If you was a girl and they called you Sya ..." and she rolled her eyes again.

"Sia."

"Have it your way. Sia. How would you feel with a name like that?"

"Ah'd be prood," I said.

This Great Seal of State in feminine guise was quick to retort: "You would be teased."

Ah dinna back doon sae easy:

"Ah'd be fair chuffed tae ken hou."

"Well, for example ... Sia ... Sia ... Look, I've got to go. Sia ... What's this? What on earth gives you the idea that I'd take ... No, no, take it away this instant. OK, hang on a moment. All right, fine, give it here. Sia. Utterly crazy. Just fill out the form and be quick about it, since you're so insistent on creating problems for your daughter. All the same, there's something not quite right here ... Well then, there you are, it's all done. Poor child ..."

They hunted the valley, they hunted the hill,
The best of our lads wi' the best o' their skill;
But still as the fairest she sat in their sight,
Then, whirr! she was over, a mile at a flight.

***

Tho firstlins we wanted tae name her Phoenix.

Clear, simple an maijestic. An then Bennu—fir Bennu, yellae wagtail o the Nile, *Motacilla alba yarrellii*, goddess o rebirth. We thocht names fur her likes o she'd been a story character: we

prood: proud   *firstlins*: at first

deleted thaim, argied o'er thaim, tasted thaim oan oor tongue. Than ye found Sia. Sia—a short, prood name, likes o

> *Farewell, ye dungeons dark and strong,*
> *The wretch's destinie!*

yon goddess Sia wi whom yon papyrus scroll o maist importance o thaim aw be trusted. She must be keeper o the message—an oor message wis the Leid. Yon wis message we'd entrustit wi oor dochter, an she must bear yon through aw trials an tribulations that befaw her fur tae haund it oan tae future generations. Sia—yon's the cry o a bird aye fleein afore ye. So it was that yon Nile wagtail Bennu an yon goddess Sia wis melled intae wan body, wan gorblin, wan papyrus scroll held i the frailtie o her beak. Sia—ye moot yer cry, an aw bodies birl roon. Likes o they wis invoked, aw the gither wi a name o glamourie.

> *Then, whirr! she was over, a mile at a flight.*

Wha else woud e'er tak it intae the heid tae caw thair dochter Sia? Only a wumman whose man's name wis Ivan Ivanavich Ivanou. Ma faimily name's no Ivanou, an ah'm no Ivan Ivanavich by the by, but guid as. It's only ma gien name that's unusual; ma faimily name's mair hamely. It's aw the same tae me whit kind o patronymic she gets; oor Leid's naething likes o yon byganes. That aw came eftir, foisted oan us, exchanged, like swappin gless beads fur gowd.[12]

> *O would, or I had seen the day*
> *That Treason this could sell us,*

gorblin: unfledged bird   *ye moot yer cry*: you mention your name   *aw bodies*: everyone   *birl roon*: turn round   *the gither*: together   *glamourie*: magic   *byganes*: in the past

My auld gray head had lien in clay,
 Wi Bruce and loyal Wallace!

Sia. Oor toun's no muckle, albeit's a provincial centre. Thare's naething o much import tae occupy yer time hereaboots, therefore aw that's left's fir folk tae quately become dotterels *Charadrius morinellus*; find interest i Egyptology; howk up mass graves o sodgers killed frae Seicond Warld War; plant ginseng i the kailyard an follow football teams.

But pith and power, till my last hour,
I'll mak this declaration;
We're bought and sold for English gold—
Such a parcel of rogues in a nation!

Ah usually dinnae sup mair than a hunnert gram o vodka per day, but yon day ah'd no sleept fur the hale nicht afore, an ah wis i bit o a dwaum sat at the table. It wis dusk. Sia wis playin i the livin room, sippin purposefully frae a flask, wi an omelette tae feast oan. Ah heard her sing—saftly, lik we'd concordit—a wee lilt:

O can ye sew cushions? And can ye sew sheets?
And can ye sing ballooloo when the bairn greets?
And hee and haw birdie, and hee and haw lamb;
And hee and haw birdie, my bonnie wee lamb!

Heeo, weeo, what wou'd I do wi' you?
Black's the life that I lead wi' you;
Mony o' ye, Little to gie you.
Heeo, weeo, what wou'd I do wi' you?

---

howk: dig   *kailyard*: kitchen garden   *sup*: drink   *dwaum*: stupor

It wis a sang i the Leid, a lullaby fur somebody amang they few wha luve it, fur the only wee birdie i the warld as can quoth oor langage, an wi peacefu soond o yon ah fell tae sleepin. Ah wis wakened bi somebody ringin the front door bell. Whit ah wis maist feart o at such maument wis fur Sia tae disobey me an open yon hersel. Still a wee bit oot o it, still stottin' aboot i ma sunlicht reveries, ah fuffled tae the door jist as ah wis, hauf-asleep sportin ma trackie trews fur tae see wha wis thare.

It wis a neebour. Whit bluidy neebour wis it like eneuch tae be?

Ah kent aw the bodies wha wis bidin' thare. The flat o'er the landin frae us had a loon caw'd Basil wha wis ayeweys deein i some iverlestin fecht.[13]

> *Does haughty Gaul invasion threat?*
> *Then let the louns beware, Sir;*

rechts o me wis an awfy murky ditty. The wumman wha bidet thare hae registered anither dame she'd taen as her ludger wi the polis: the ludger'd straightweys goat hersel a man an set him up i th'appartement as weel.[14] A Cauld War wis nou bein fecht oan twenty squerr metres o livin room. Whit's mair—yon landleddy's

> *John Anderson, my jo, John*

an her ludger's

> *John Anderson, my jo, John*

swappit places awmaist every day. Meantime, yon twenty squerr metres were still four-cornered, an thare yet remained but twenty o thaim.

---

quoth: speak   *trews*: trousers   *bidin'*: living

O let us not, like snarling curs,
In wrangling be divided,
Till, slap! come in an unco loun, and wi' a rung decide it!

One o the appartements up the stair wis empie, anither occupied bi twa students, baith lassies. Thare's a university fur oor toun—nae jokes, aw honesty. Ae-times it wis technical college fur learnin chemistry. Yon wis oor verra ain kinky-mingeour.

Nane o ma neebours wad deign tae say "hiyah" tae me. Ah swear ah'd learnt them no tae. Insides o ilka muckle human body thare's a teenie wee inspector hunker'd doon, an wance Sia wis o an age whan it's permitted tae interrogate a wee human body (fur the maument withoot use o special gear), yon teenie wee inspectors started tae reveal thirsels: "Och ye puir wee thing, come oan noo, huv a wee gab wi me, come oan, say 'mammie daddie' gape yer tottie wee mooth an ye'll get this 'konfeta.'" Yon's a "sweetie" i the Lingo, "doucebit" i the Leid. Whitever ye're cawin yon, yon's some thingummy bairns are ordinarly presumed tae be willing tae sell faither fur. Folk started tae gie me the phone nummer fur some ower-specialist i Miensk itsel: "He's brocht sae mony an mony unweel bairns back intae the common weal o society."[15] He's brocht them back—oh aye, lik yon Pied Piper o Hamelin, yon jay pyot, *Garrulus glandarius*, has a sudden fit o remorse … Rideeculas! A neebour frae doon the sterr wance gied me a swatch o some leaflet he pits oot. Nou ah ken exactly whit his gemm is. He's an ower-specialist wha does mair than cure psychosocial troubles. Somehou he's a bane setter, or bane breaker, fur the resettin o tongue, tuith an thrapple. He descrives whit he does as puttin richt the pronoonciation o bairns frae the mountainous country.

Rusticity's ungainly form
May cloud the highest mind;

mingeour: something that produces a bad smell   *thrapple*: throat

47

But when the heart is nobly warm,
The Good excuse will find.

Oh aye, whit yon means is this couthie auld fellow from the capital wi his clever white lab coat's reddin oot whitever's left o' oor mither tongue; whitever oor langage uses tae haud oan tae itsel eftir it's awreddies bin dealt a mortal dunt—oor auld chaunt, somethin that aye marks us unalike incomers.

Propriety's cold cautious rules
Warm fervour may o'erlook;
But spare poor Sensibility
The ungentle harsh rebuke.

Ah wunner hou he maks yon "righting," oor miracle worker? A wee operation fur yer brains thru yer harnpan? Snip-snip! Raspin' doon yer teeth, a slight adjustment tae yer hyoid bane? Ah howp yon gars him brek oot i sweat, an he burns wi the Earl o Hell oan a banefire o his stinkin brochures, an they steek his "Great and Powerful Lingo"

Is there a bard of rustic song,
Who, noteless, steals the crowds among

richt up his backside.

Is there a whim-inspired fool,
Owre fast for thought, owre hot for rule,
Owre blate to seek, owre proud to snool,
Let him draw near;
And owre this grassy heap sing dool,
And drap a tear.

couthie: nice   *redding oot*: getting rid of   *dunt*: blow   *gars*: makes

Thare wis only wan raison fur ma neebours tae be ringin ma doorbell—whaniver some body dee'd i oor tenement. Fur some raison tho—naebody dee'd hereaboots; it wasnae the district fur it. It wis aboot five kilometre awa frae the chemical works. Oors wis the maist healthfu, green district o the toun. Folk bidin i this district clung fast tae it, never mind it wis the provinces. They didna want tae flit, unless thay'd be flittin tae Miensk. Or mebbes tae be somewhares fremmit, an "toot sweet."

Thare wis a Jimmy staudin at the door i his kegs. "Therr's a wee lassie cryin here?" he said wi a grin.

"Ah can assure ye thare's nae," ah bit back an tried tae shut the door.

"A wean's cryin. Ah hear it!" An Jimmy i the kegs clacht haud o ma door hannle an woudnae lat go. "Greetin fur a hale oor, so it huz. Whit the hell's goin oan in here? Whit ur ye maltreatin a wean fur, ye bad basturd?"

"An jist wha d'ye think ye are?" ah askit, calm as ah coud.

"Ah'm tellin' ye, ah'm yer nayburr frae up the sterr," said Jimmy i the kegs. He wis calmer nou an smilin awa agane. He wis twa heid higher than me, an broad-shoudert. He wis built like a gable end.

Nou he wis takin a keek at onything the open door let him see, gabbin at me aw the while. An it gied him a keek o helluva loadae stuff. Kind o whit's necessary tae permit certain conclusions tae be drawn. Empties staundin belaw the mirror like skittles—ah'd bin meanin tae get the monies back oan them suiner or syne. Yon Munro o clarty ashets oan the kitchen table—ah couldnae be fasht tae wash thaim, ah wis aye pittin it aff til the morn. Glittie scraps floatin oan bowls o unfeenisht soup. An the bairn keekin

---

toot sweet: tout de suite   *Jimmy*: bloke   *kegs*: underpants   *wean*: little child   *clacht haud*: caught hold   *twa heid*: two heads   *keek*: look   *suiner or syne*: sooner or later   *Monro o clarty ashets*: mountain of dirty dishes   *fasht*: bothered

oot frae her chambie, glowerin at the visitor withoot blenkin. Wi a swollen cheek.

She tellt me she'd fell.

"So ye werna greetin?" an he bent o'er her. He grinned, but nou it wis plain as parritch he wis makin tae ingratiate hissel wi her. He must've thocht he looked like a faither, or lawfu gairdian. His ee, houaniver, darted roon the flat, o'er Sia's airms an neck, o'er yon wee bit o her warld he'd managed tae keek ahint her back: her playocks, her bed, her lamp, her beuks. Beuks she'd no read, but that ah'd tae keep i the hoose i accord wi thair langage laws. An, nae doot aboot it, her chambie wis a cowp.

"She doesnae speak," ah said, howpfu yon wid hae guid effect an he'd bugger aff at lang last ...

"Aw, so *yur* the wan, ur ye?" He made hissel staund up an gied me his haund, that ah unwillint took. "The paw o yin wee tongue-tackit lassie? Aye, ah ken aw aboot ye. They don't huv much time fur yese, folk oan this sterr. Huz she been like yon fur a while?"

Ah hunkled ma shouders. Whitwey shoud ah responder?

"Ye've nae idee jist hou lang."

"Ah'm yer new nayburr." At this pynt he howked up his kegs. "Ah'll be livin' up the sterr from yese. Whit's yir name? Whit's hers?"

"Sia. It's a Egypt name," ah said, wi haste.

"Aw aye, ah ken. Like a name fur a cat. Ah've goat a sphinsk like that. They've aw got Egyptian names."

Yon's exactly hou he said it: Sphinsk. Like Minsk or Pinsk.

"Ur ye gonnae come up the sterr tae play wi ma wee pussy cat?" He lent doon tae Sia agin, likes o she wis blindit or deif. She kept up her glowerin o him wi n'er a blink o her ee.

"So who wis it greetin here the noo?" Suspeecion'd creepit back intae his voice.

chambie: room   *beuks*: books   *cowp*: mess   *tongue-tackit*: tongue-tied   *howked up*: heaved up

"Ah've nae idee." Ah hunkled ma shouders agane. "Awtho ah think mebbe Schnittke."[16] Ah liftit wan o ma empie CD casements aff the flair.

"It's richt dulesome musique. Ye maist likely thocht somebody wis greetin. It wis Schnittke. Music. Verstehen?"

He tried tae look likes o believin me.

"Aye aye so it goes. Like m'auld Granmaw Broon wid ayeweys say: 'A shnit i time saufs nine.'"

He quoth it, a proverb. One o the auld wans. Barely kenable wi his coorse, fremmit way o pronooncin things; sauf fur ma perfectly tuned lug, it wouda bin unpossible tae jalouse whit he said, but, aye, he'd quoth it.

"So yon's whit ma Granmaw Broon ayeweys used tae say. But aw that stuff dee'd oot yonks ago. It's no right these days, it's aw jynin the gither. Wan country, wan Lingo. Everythin's deein oot if it duznae waaant tae unite, or if it duznae waaant jist the wan Lingo. Sia, gie it tae me straight—d'yese get teased at the school an caw'd "Sissy"? She unnerstaunds me, ah can see it in her eyes, but she cannae say nuthin. She's like a wee dug. Och well, youse'll soon be speakin' in aw. When they high heid yins pit the pressure oan, we'll aw start speakin; "it's in the nature of our people." D'yese play baseball? Shame. It's wan of oor auld gemms from way back. "Lapta!"[17] We could huv a gemm wan o these days. Aye weel. OK, ah'm offski. An youse, nae mair schnittkering, capiche?" He grinned, took a haud o Sia bi the cheek, shoogled it a wee bit an used his fingers as if tae see whit stuff she wis made o, than he jeeg'd doon the sterr. Ah closed the door, held Sia bi the haund an led her intae her chambie. We set oursel jist the wey we liked tae be—Sia oan the sofae an me at her feet, lookin intently at each an each ither's ee. Twa elf-shot bodies i kingdom o draigon an castle. "He didnae scare ye too much?"

sauf fur: save for   *shoogled*: shook   *elf-shot*: (old superstition) shot by elves using invisible arrows

"Na," said Sia an turned awa. "But for why did he come here? He thocht ah wis greetin? Did ah get his Lingo richt?"

"Aye, but ah promise he'll no return."

"But whit fur does he think yon?" she whispert, an dove intae ma ee agin, whaur she swam like a flichtin o dust only tears may wash awa.

"Acause he's deif. Deif an dumm. Ah'm tellin ye, ah swear he'll niver come back."

"An whit did he mean bi 'nae mair schnittkering'?"

"We'll no concern oorsel wi yon," ah said. "It's only important fur us tae no forget whit ... Whit hae ah learnt ye we huv tae remember?"

"Ah've no forgot, but ..."

"We've a saicret, the twa o us. A saicret we fend. Dinnae forget yon." Ah straik'd her shoulders.

Gien me the nod, she leuked her books o'er—no thaim set oan shelves fir appearances sake only. Naw, the richt ones. Oor favorites.

"Nou ah ken whit body ah'm. Ah'm Alicia. Alec's fur laddies, but it's Alicia fur lassies."

An then she stairtit tae tears. Naethin left fur me tae dae but caw her wi name she wanted.

I wad do—what would I not?—
For the sake o' Somebody.

At least at hame.

4

Ah'm awa tae hunt oot something shairp

"Ah'm awa tae hunt oot something shairp," Avi said to her and
disappeared behind the trees. In his hand he held a long stick;
he had become obsessed with the idea of making it sharp, like a
spear, so that he not only had something to lean on while walking, but also something that he could use to hurl at targets.

Alicia was now alone, lying tummy down on the cool moss
with the road atlas open in front of her. Something tiny and
scared immediately clambered on her, found itself a nice, warm
groin and began running around her skin; it was just like the
light physical contact of another human that had broken free
and begun to live its own life. A sightless human touch that was
condemned to come into contact with other people. A touch that
possesses a myriad of ticklish little feet. Alicia had no wish to
brush it off. A touch like this does not live long; it dies as soon as
you make it your own. How did she know that?

Possibly from Faither.

She wasn't worried about Faither. He had his Kenzy. The
woman with the yellow hair. Faither had made a hole in something that seemed to both her brother and her inviolable, eternal,
immutable. It was his own fault that things had gone wrong. If
you are going to make a hole, you have to be prepared for everything to come crumbling down; from that moment nothing will
come right.

Something fell on her neck, and she covered it with her hand.
She spread her fingers wide—a slender stick insect was pretend-
ing with all its might to be just a stick. Alicia held it up to her
eyes; the stick shuddered, ran around her hand and landed on

her wrist. She blew it gently away. The gentle touch of another homeless wanderer in the forest. She took pleasure in turning the page of the road atlas. For the umpteenth time she examined the next page. She found the continuation of the route they were to take, and smiled.

She smiled at a squirrel that was watching her without blinking, as if Alicia had just told it a story, a terrible story ... You could read in its eyes what it was thinking: Should I believe what you're telling me or not? Oh, I can't be bothered. And the squirrel jumped on to a tree and tapped out a brief rapid melody of distrust on the bark, as if it had to check immediately, without waiting any longer, if the little girl was fibbing. The little girl Alicia who was unafraid of the hairy moss beneath her tummy. Moving, soft and green—like someone's sweaty belly.

"Ye've fund something," she said, only half-convinced, when Avi, fighting with tree branches, emerged from the thicket. His face was not happy. Avi made no attempt to sit next to Alicia; instead he stood right over her, swaying and leaning on his long stick.

"Aye ah've fund something," he said gloomily. "Ah fund a jocteleg. An it's no rusty."

Forbye, he'll shape you aff fu' gleg
The cut of Adam's philibeg;

"Gies a gander."
"Oan ye go," and he flung the knife down so hard that the blade cut right into the moss. The handle shone in the sun.

The knife that nickit Abel's craig

She picked up the knife, wiped it and rubbed the flat side of the blade on her wrist. This was another kind of touch. The touch of an owner.

jocteleg: pocket knife

54

He'll prove you fully,
It was a faulding jocteleg.

"Yon's braw," said Alicia. "An awmaist spang-new. Real braw. An leuk, some body's scrieved watchwirds i German. Makkit bi a body, makkit wi luve, makkit fur folk."

"Aye," said Avi. "An bocht short syne, i Swisserland."

"Ye dinna seem too chuffed." Alicia sat down and began using her fingernails to clean between her toes, where a large number of little black creatures had gathered.

"Ah've airt oot a chib," said Avi with pride. "But thare's mair tae yon. Yon chib wis i his pootch."

Avi took her into the depths of the forest so she could see what he meant with her own eyes: the knife had indeed been in a pocket. In the pocket of a man lying with his face in a muddy puddle, like he was drinking water.

Hear, Land o' cakes, and brither Scots,
Frae Maidenkirk to Johnie Groat's,
If there's a hole in a' your coats,
I rede you tent it:
A chield's amang you, taking notes,
And, faith, he'll prent it.

Right next to him was a bucket, half full of mushrooms mixed with pine needles and leaves.

Ilk ghaist that haunts auld ha' or chaumer,
Ye gypsy gang that deal in glamour,
And you, deep-read in Hell's black grammar,
Warlocks and witches,
Ye'll quake at his conjuring hammer,
Ye midnight bitches.

short syne: recently   *chib*: knife used as weapon   *pootch*: pocket

The man was dressed in a waterproof jacket, and there were fisherman's boots on his feet.

The blind forest was putting out feelers, some big, some small, all over his back and the nape of his neck. The man was drinking, and simply couldn't get enough. Judging by the way his fingers were pressing into the damp earth so that you couldn't see them any more, he must have been drinking for several days.

> *If in your bounds ye chance to light*
> *Upon a fine, fat fodgel wight,*
> *O' stature short but genius bright,*
> *That's he, mark weel—*
> *And wow! he has an unco sleight,*
> *O' cauk and keel.*

"Yon chib wis stickin oot his pootch," said Avi. "An thare wis bluid oan him richt here. Ah'm richt, ah'm ah no? Ah'm ah no, Alicia?"

She didn't reply. She watched the man drinking water. The water level remained the same.

"We're no gaun tae birl him ower oan his back," said Alicia.

"But ah want tae," said Avi.

"Non, we willna," said Alicia in a threatening voice, and showed him her grown-up claws.

"Gies back ma jocteleg," ordered Avi, looking around.

"It's no belongin tae ye," said Alicia. "Ye may whittle yer stick wi it, than pit it back whauriver ye got it."

"Whit if ah dinna?" shouted Avi, sounding almost as though he really was angry.

"In sicca case ..." Alicia thought for a moment.—"Drap! Tae the grund! Drap, y'eediot!"

He fell on the ground next to her, and just in the nick of time. A pair of squirrels with their front paws folded, they watched a tractor appear on the forest road that lay hidden a metre from them. It was towing a long trailer loaded up with logs. Lying on the moss and the bilberry bushes the children resembled mushrooms. This helped: the tractor driver didn't notice them. He looked straight ahead down the forest road; the only one to see it, soundlessly moving his lips.

The tractor trundled slowly past the spot where Avi and Alicia lay hidden, belching like a large fish in a cloudy lake, the long logs crashed together, the big wheels yowled as they forced the little ones forward. It took an eternity for the tractor to pass them. The racket was becoming greater and greater. It seemed like the tractor was driving straight over them. As if they were sitting in a pit. A wolf pit.

"Whaur'll ye find yon bane?" asked Alicia, as they picked their way through the dense forest. There were more mosquitoes here, and more sun, but less and less strength in their arms and legs. Yon's obviously acause we're takin vitamins, thought Alicia. She almost choked when she thought about the vitamins—juice, maybe even saliva, began to run down her chin. The earth was no longer calling them—but it was obeying them more and more unwillingly. Avi was hobbling along in an altogether strange kind of way.

"D'ye mean yon bane ah maun play?" asked Avi in his turn. "Weel, folk maun get thaim somewhaurs. Maun be some pairts whaur they growe."

This made Alicia think. Something was prompting her inside, making her feel that there was something not quite right about Avi's response. In fact, it didn't hang together. Whaur dae folk get banes frae? Whaur dae banes growe? An whan?

"Wis that carle oot gaitherin foostie-baws, *Agaricus campestris*?" Avi suddenly asked her. "Some body maun stickit him i the back. Some body he kent, acause o he war stickit i the back. Ah

---

carle: fellow *ootlander*: stranger *foostie-baws*: mushrooms *kent*: knew wadna staund backs tae ony ootlander. Same gaes fur yersel. I the Camp thare war only Tolik wha docht staund backs t'aebody he didna ken."

"Aye." Alicia stopped. Her head was spinning. "Yon carle wis a foostie-baws scaffenger.

He has a fouth o' auld nick-nackets:
Rusty airn caps and jinglin jackets,

Whit's mair, it's like eneuch he kent awthings regairdin foostie-baws an banes. But yon's aw we'll say aboot him the day. Nae-thing else. He didna exist. Ye get it?"

Avi, who had been listening to her with a serious look on his face, suddenly said, "Alicia, I think you're going to have a boak."

Sure enough, then she really did vomit. They both bent over and began to examine what had come gushing out of her. Alicia was really surprised. What she had puked up was all colours of the rainbow. The kind of rainbow that Alicia had once painted in school. A rainbow consisting of all the colours of the palette of a little child. "Therr's naebuddy gits rainbows like they wans Sissy's painted," yelled the twins on the front desk.

Whit she wanted tae say wis thay waur aw bawheids, an acause thay spake the Lingo thair bawheiditness meant thay woud n'er get a deek o rainbowes likes o hers; thay wad n'er sing sangs likes o hers an thay wad n'er hae a daddy likes o hers. She wanted to slap them with these words across the rosy cheeks that made them look like matrioshka dolls. But she couldn't speak. They have to know that she can't speak. So she carried on painting— roads, maps, bridges and a frontier patrol cutting through the undergrowth, and two children observing them, hidden behind the paw-like branches of spruce trees.

"D'ye ken a border guard dug disna yowl?" she said once, when Faither picked her up at the school gate and they went off to have a milk cocktail.

Faither looked at her in amazement, but very soon his astonishment gave way to understanding.

"Aye, ah ken."

It's tauld he was a sodger bred,
And a wad rather fa'n than fled;
But now he's quat the spurtle blade, and dog-skin wallet,
And tae the—Antiquarian trade,
I think they call it.

And she calmed down.

Now that she had been sick, she felt so light that she took hold of Avi's hand and pulled him along behind her. It seemed as though it took them no more than a few leaps and bounds to pass through a wood full of prickles—and quite unexpectedly they emerged on to the shore of a lake.

A long lake, which stretched its way through the forest like a serpent. A serpent with a slippery, scaly skin that was pleasant to the touch.

"A coble," said Avi.

"A coble," said Alicia.

It really was a boat, with only one oar which fitted in it like a quill pen fits in an inkwell. The boat lay on the shore right by a swampy quagmire—looking just as if it had floated up from the depths to lie in the sun for a bit. It was black; in the bottom of the boat water was rippling gently, filled with the sky, small fry and reflections. Avi grabbed hold of the side of the boat, dug his bare heels into the sand and pushed with all his might—and off he flew into the open space of the lake, together with the boat. He gave the impression of having done this all his life. Alicia caught up with them and, almost rolling head over heels, filled the boat with her knees.

"Are ye certain we maun gang t'ither side?" asked Avi, expertly sweeping the oar through the water. "Tae the shore o'er thare?"

It occurred to Alicia that she ought to tell him the truth. After all, he is her brother, and anyway he's deserved it.

"Lochs dinna hae ither shores," she said. "It's nae a river, Avi. Ev'ry shore o ev'ry loch's same as."

She could see that he understood her, and it made her feel all warm inside. Should she give him a kiss, or what?

"Avi, wad ye like me tae gie ye a kiss?"

"Na, ah woudna," replied Avi, turning a silly smile towards the sun.

"Fine. Hou aboot a sing-sang?"

This was an idea close to Avi's heart. Spontaneously they both started singing a song that they had never sung before, but even so they somehow knew it. Yon's acause we're brither an sister, thought Alicia. She was happy, for here in the forest an answer could quickly be found for everything.

To be honest, the first to start the song was Avi. Then Alicia joined in, for the words were familiar to her, and the music was sailing behind their boat. All she had to do was spot it in time, pick it up and then imitate it.

"J-i-i-i-st as soon as ah ..." Avi shouted, drawing out the first loud vowel so that it spread all over the surrounding expanse, then following it with a brief, decisive "as a."[18] He went on, wielding the oar in time to the rhythm and waving his arms in front on him: "cam born ..."

"Ma faither said ..." Alicia joined in and then they yelled in one voice:

"Things will be bad ..."

And now they continued singing in unison, so that the song flew ahead of them right to the shore—the shore that was always the right one, so it didn't matter to them where they landed:

"A-a-an shuir eneuch ...

He was not wrong."

"Ah-Ah-Ah wis mocked," words that the sun shouted to them, loud words that rose from the depths in their stead, words whistled by the cutting wind that lived in the very centre of the lake.

"*By Goad an Man!!!*" Avi and Alicia finished the song after them, spitting out the whole tribes of mosquitoes that had flown into their hospitably gaping mouths.

That's simply the kind of song it was. A loud song for singing in the open. A song for singing on a loch. A song of their very own. And now that other shore was already very close. Alicia jumped out of the boat, and the water came up to her neck. Then she seized Avi and dragged him in after her. He looked round in surprise and sank straight to the bottom.

I whyles claw the elbow o' troublesome thought;
but Man is a soger, and Life is a faught;

She had to catch him by his legs, and then use her feet to trample the sand down under the water. It was cold beneath her heels—strong, icy underwater currents were enveloping her legs, wanting to make her sit on their collective lap, embrace her and tug her down by the calves ...

My mirth and guid humour are coin in my pouch,
And my freedom's my lairdship nae monarch dare touch ...

Night was falling on the other shore. As a warning, the forest extinguished its little lights, closed up its passageways, switched on the intertwined trees' alarm system, flung on a cobweb shawl and fell silent. The forest left just one way open for the children—a path lit here and there by the distant, mean light of a star that was losing ever more of its strength. Yonce we'd the sonne, an nou we've a muckle starn—acause a starn pits ye i mynd o the bygane, thought Alicia. It gies oot its licht, an yon's eneuch.

This one path led them out to a marsh. Alicia noticed it at

sonne: sun   *the bygane*: the past

once, pressed a finger to her lips and pointed it out to Avi: at the very edge of the marsh something dark loomed large. They went round the marsh and stopped directly in front of the oddest cottage they had ever seen.

Alicia was the first to realise what the secret was.

"Get a swatch o that!" she whispered. "Read it aff!"

The cottage really could be read like a book. And examined like pictures in a gallery. Its walls were made up of cardboard boxes of all sizes and colours.

"Slodych," said Avi. "Kamunarka ..."

There was, however, more here than the products of the "Slodych" and "Kamunarka" factories. There were marshmallows, both in chocolate and plain, there were boxes that had once held doughnuts of various different kinds, packaging from candied fruits and halva. Avi, who was proud of his prowess at reading the Lingo, misread "scone" as "scorn," leaving him wondering what on earth could possibly be in it. Alicia thought that it might make a scone even tastier. Folk micht be o'er scornfu tae eat something that's sae sweet like, sae slither'd wi butter that it turnit scones intae forbidden fruit.

"Ah'm faimisht," said Avi, and looked shamelessly at Alicia.

"Whit?" Alicia turned to him. "Say that tae m'ither lug. Fur some raison ah'm no hearin ye wi this one."

"Whit lug?"

"Yon one! Keep mynd o't. Yon's important."

"Ma tittie's deif," said Avi. "Jist dinna thrapple me, awricht?"

But once again Alicia didn't quite catch what he said.

The cottage roof was made of condensed milk tins from Rahachou and Hlybokaye. Alicia thought hou braw t'wad be tae be set doon i the hoose oan some rainy day jist tae hear raindraps tappin oot some cheery airs fur ye. Instead of glass in the windows, cellophane from the Lasunak factory outlet had been stretched

* *swatch*: look   *thrapple*: strangle

across the frames. The tiny, narrow veranda was constructed out of boxes, which—if you could believe what was written on them—had once contained confectionery from Ukraine: "Crazy Bee" sweets, marvellously crunchy chocolate wafers and layer cakes from the Roshen company.

But here's the sorry part. All this packaging was empty. All you had to do was tap lightly on the boxes to hear that the contents had long ago been eaten. And no one had left even the tiniest piece for Avi or Alicia.

"Tak a vizzie an see whaur we've laundit," asked Avi, and Alicia automatically opened the atlas.

"We're no oan the cairt yet," she said. "We maun dae muckle walkin yet. Thare's nae weys they managed tae gorble aw yon daintees. Thay've semply shiftit the purvey inside fir no tae get it spylt wi rain."

By some auld, houlet-haunted biggin

"D'ye think we shoud gang in?" asked Avi.

Or kirk deserted by its riggin

He looked at the cellophane windows and hesitated.

It's ten to ane ye'll find her snug in
Some eldritch part,
Wi deils, they say, Lord safe's! colleaguin
At some black art.

"Aye, ye can."

cairt: map   *gorble*: gobble   *daintees*: delicacies   *purvey*: food supplied for a special occasion, e.g., weddings and funerals

Of Eve's first fire she has a cinder ...
A broomstick o the witch of Endor,
Weel shod wi brass.

They heard a rasping voice and turned their heads to face the direction it came from—to the forest that was by now in complete darkness.

Blind Chance, let her snapper and stoyte on her way;
Be't to me, be't frae me, e'en let the jade gae:
Come Ease, or come Travail, come Pleasure or Pain,
My warst word is—"Welcome, and welcome again!"

5

You risk nothing by substituting one word for another

You risk nothing by substituting one word for another, thought the Doctor. Of course, most people would not agree with that. Especially so-called poets. People are accustomed to hold the view that a word should be precise. People believe in style and in shades of meaning. At the same time they are themselves incapable of expressing correctly what it is that seems to them so important.

This is something that he liked to think about after lunch. This postprandial period was indeed the time when doubts faded away and only certainties remained. Food makes people self-assured. With words it's quite different. Words have meaning only within the confines of one language, and even then not always. In actual fact, the only important thing is how you pronounce the sounds.

That a general inability to read, or speak, with propriety and grace in public, runs through the natives of the British dominions, is acknowledged; it shews itself in our senates and churches, on the bench and at the bar.

Do you make correct use of the instruments that were given to you so you could talk? Words themselves are an arbitrary convention. In the place of each word there could just as easily be another one.

Substitute one word for another, clear one word away, or scrap it entirely. That's exactly what he does sometimes, and nothing changes. The office becomes no bigger, the white walls do not acquire a red tinge, that random fly does not start reciting poems, the table does not rise from the floor and hang above his head. His assistant—the one who insists on calling herself a nurse—is not at the moment thrusting a pig's head round the door instead of her own, curly-haired and eternally shiny. It's the hair lacquer that does it. She uses it far too often.

"D'ye whant a nice wee cup o tea?" asked the assistant. "Likes o ah eyways make fur ye?"

"No, thanks, no tea," he replied. "Please shut the door ... although, no, wait a moment ..."

He looked at her with interest.

"How did you say that just now?"

"Whit'd ah say?" she asked in alarm and smoothed her hair down. Now her hands are shiny as well. Sweaty, lacquer-covered hands that she's going to use to take a mug and pour the tea.

"Repeat what you said about the tea ... Come on in and shut the door."

"Ah jist whanted tae knaw whether ye whanted some tea," said the assistant quite at a loss, shutting the door.

"No, you didn't say it like that. Repeat that bit about the nice cup of tea."

"D'ye whant a wee cup o tea?" mumbled the assistant, hiding her eyes. The Doctor got up from the table and strode over to where they were hidden—these two hollows in her face, shining with something that had been smeared thickly over them. The eyes had leapt out, but obediently returned to their proper place when he looked closely at her lips. The eyes glanced at him. There was no depth to them. It would be possible to work with people like this.

"Say it again," he said gently, but with a note of authority in his voice. He took her by the chin.

"D'ye whant a wee cup o tea?"

"Once more."

"D'ye whant a wee cup o tea?"

"Again."

"D'ye whant a wee cup o tea?"

"Repeat it thirteen times."

My wife's a wanton, wee thing,
My wife's a wanton, wee thing,
My wife's a wanton, wee thing,
She winna be guided by me.

She looked at him so helplessly that the Doctor began to feel disgust. The only thing that marks the difference between her and an animal is her language, something that was gifted to her by some caprice of nature. A language with a capital letter. A Lingo great and mighty, a hope and bulwark. What does she need it for? How has she deserved it? How can this creature have possibly deserved such a gift—a gift that she mangles. Every day she mangles it, she wrecks it because she is incapable of using it correctly.

There is so much injustice in the world, and only doctors can put it right. Not politicians, not artists, not money. Only doctors.

"I told you to repeat it thirteen times."

And so she began. She was clearly keeping count in her head: one, two, three, four ... Making a huge effort. Afraid of losing count. An animal. The Doctor couldn't be bothered to count. It was a matter of total indifference to him how many times she said it. He could hear, and she couldn't. That's what counts.

"Fine," said the Doctor approvingly when she stopped. "You've already taken a course of treatment with me, haven't you?"

"Aye, five year ago."

She play'd the loon or she was married,
She play'd the loon or she was married,
She play'd the loon or she was married,
She'll do it again or she die.

"Well done." He smiled. "You know, yes, do bring me some tea ...

She sell'd her coat and she drank it,
She sell'd her coat and she drank it,
She row'd hersel in a blanket—
She winna be guided by me.

That was a good thought of yours. But first of all ..."

She stopped in the doorway.

"Repeat what it was you said about the nice cups of tea another thirty times. Come and stand here. Look me in the eyes, and repeat. OK, let's go."

She stood in silence. He turned away and then shouted harshly right into her face:

"Come on then! What did I say to you just now?"

"D'ye whant a wee cup o tea ... D'ye whant a wee cup o tea?" burbled the nurse. Meanwhile he was looking right into her mouth, where the bone of her shiny yellow teeth was glinting and her barely visible tongue was working furiously.

"We do not need a 'h' sound. There's no 'h' in want," he said gently, while she was still declaiming in a monotone what the Doctor had sentenced her to. "You're not trying. Keep the words separate. You just don't want to let your tongue do its work. Set it free. Or is there something hindering it again? Is that it? Open your mouth!" said the Doctor in the complete silence of the room—disturbed only by that wretched fly.

"Yes, that's it," said the Doctor and clicked his tongue. "There's a tumour growing again. It's still quite small. The bone has become enlarged. For the time being we'll do without surgery. Just keep repeating those words about the nice cups of tea, and try to exert some control over yourself. Not here!" he yelled when she attempted to start the exercise again. "Do it back in your room or, I don't know, on the toilet. I've had a bellyful of your nice cups of tea for today ... Anyway, bring me some tea. How much longer are you going to keep me waiting for it? And stop spraying me with that stinking lacquer. You're bringing all the flies in with you, they swarm round you like children."

The assistant drew her head into her shoulders and made a run for the door.

"Go! Get out!" the Doctor yelled at her. How could he do otherwise, since she clearly liked being ordered around. Now she's going to appear to him in his dreams for several nights ahead, offering him a nice cup of tea. The Doctor was well aware that she was in love with him. At times he thought that from the purely scientific point of view, it would be interesting to check just how much effect this blasted little bone—in reality, a tiny lump—has on human sexuality. It must surely have some effect. It had, after all, chosen a really good place for itself. In just the same way as any other piece of nastiness that can be an impediment to life.

Any word can be substituted for any other word, and nothing will be changed. She could easily be forced to repeat "Doctor, I want to have your children" two hundred times, and nothing would ever change. The "wee cup of tea" would now be this "cuppa," which that damned lump in the throat would turn into a primeval, animal growl or some kind of gibbering instead of a refined melodious utterance. What a pity it is that absolute pitch cannot be handed to these creatures in the form of ordinary pills. This filthy camp could then be closed down—at times, especially in winter, it reminded him of a cemetery, and in summer of a warehouse. Remove the logo, take away the fence, load all the equipment on a lorry, and next to it he would be riding a bicycle along the forest track, making it look as though he's got nothing to do with it, he isn't a doctor, just some random bloke who lives in the country.

She mind't na when I forbade her,
She mind't na when I forbade her,

I took a rung and I claw'd her,
And a braw guid bairn was she.

The Doctor took a look at the mirror he used with patients. God alone knows how many throats, tonsils, larynxes and tongues had been reflected in it. He gave himself a wink, and then pulled the kind of face that the local rustics put on when they want to show that they too have brains. If only he could free himself from all this and go off... Somewhere where there would be just the two of them. Only him and Pushkin. As pure as the first snowflake of winter.

Any word can be substituted for any other word. He reached up to the top shelf of the cupboard and drew out a book in a red binding. The book opened on the usual page. He frequently leafed through it and re-read it. This was a book he respected because it confirmed his thoughts about language.

So it was now. He spoke the words softly:

Today it is difficult, if not impossible, for me to say when the words "Belarusian speaker" first gave me ground for special thoughts. At home I do not remember having heard the words during my father's lifetime. I believe that the old gentleman would have regarded any special emphasis on this term as cultural backwardness.

And further (he had even ringed round this paragraph with a pencil, something that he normally never did):

Likewise at school I found no occasion which could have led me to change this inherited picture. At school, to be sure, I did meet one boy, a Belarusian speaker, who was treated by all of us with caution, but only because various experiences had led us to doubt his discretion and we did not particularly trust him, but only because he was too quiet; but neither I nor the others

*had any thoughts on the matter. Not until my fourteenth or
fifteenth year did I begin to come across the words "Belarusian
speaker" with any frequency, partly in connection with political
discussions. This filled me with a mild distaste, and I could not
rid myself of an unpleasant feeling that always came over me
whenever religious quarrels occurred in my presence. At that
time the language question seemed to be nothing other than a
question of religion.*[19]

The assistant brought in the tea. He ran his eyes over her and
only then shut the book. If he were to ask her anything now,
she would cringe with fright. She'll stutter. That's what they all
do here, cringe and stutter. However, he had never had a single
failure. Each one of them leaves here vaccinated and with the
strength to speak correctly. After all, speaking correctly means
that you think correctly. And live correctly.

He knew how the book went on.

*There were few Belarusian speakers in Linz. In the course of the
centuries their outward appearance had become Europeanized
and had taken on a human look; in fact, I even took them for
Russians. The absurdity of this idea did not dawn on me because I saw no distinguishing feature but their religion.*

There weren't many of them ... And they looked human ...

*The ignorant savage that weather'd the storm,
When the man and the Brute differed but in form.*

***

In the small town where he lived—at the time he was a pupil in
Year 6 of Middle School No. 1 and not yet a doctor—there really
were very few of them.

Four, to be precise.

Just one family. There was no one else like them in the town. Four out of ten thousand. Half of those ten thousand could not speak correctly. That half was ashamed of what the other half thought, but those four had no shame whatsoever.

He knew the father of the family—a grey-faced bookkeeper in the distillery. He was nicknamed "the Baptist." He didn't drink, he didn't smoke, he didn't swear. A few times a year this not very bright individual—who, even when judged by the modest local standards, had achieved nothing in life—would go out on to the square of their little town, settle himself near the Lenin statue on the stool that he had brought with him, and bring out a placard and an apple. Everyone knew what was written on the placard. The bookkeeper demanded that his daughter Masha should be taught in her own Leid, not in the Lingo like everyone else. People used to laugh, but the future doctor never did. Even then he was interested in why such a thing could happen. He looked to see if he could find in the face of Masha's father any features at all that would distinguish him from all the other citizens of this little town.

Back then the doctor was already very keen on biology. It was his favourite subject, and although he didn't like the teacher very much, he went to all her extra classes. The teacher knew little and he wanted more, and she also spoke incorrectly. He was always itching to put her right, but in some ways the doctor was heavily dependent on her for his future.

He looked into her mouth, at her false teeth, and wondered what there was behind them. Teachers are the kind of people who are permitted to utter sounds and speak words, and no one has the right to interrupt them. He was fond of listening to the military instructor. He wasn't a local; he spoke correctly, clearly and loudly, like beating a drum, but life in the small town was beginning to affect him badly. He made mistakes in pronunciation more and more often, speaking like the old women in the marketplace. This was physically painful for the doctor, just as if his arm was being twisted, or a pattern was being burned on his skin with the aid of a magnifying glass (one of the games they had in the school).

But where do sounds actually come from? How are they shaped? And what obstacles do they have to overcome in order to break out and be heard and uttered. From out of the mouth of the instructor came forth the Lingo, and the doctor really wanted to receive it in the way in which it deserved. He would wait impatiently for the end of lessons and go out into the playground drenched in sweat, trying hard to avoid the hostile gangs of boys who lived on the other side of the river. He would buy some ice cream, lick it and feel it filling his mouth and spreading across the pathway inside himself that was intended for the emission of sounds—and watch a police van drive into the middle of the square. Out of the van there emerged a group of yobs that his brother played football with.

The ignorant savage that weather'd the storm,
When the man and the Brute differed but in form.

"Howzit gaun, Granpaw Broon?" was how they addressed him, and the father of the little girl Masha would take out his apple and begin to nibble it. The yobs would roll up their sleeves, unbutton their damp shirts, and one of them would go up to Masha's father and kick out the stool from under him. Masha's father would fall to the ground without letting go of the apple. With an elegant movement of the leg another of the yobs would kick the placard down to the asphalt and trample on it, leaving holes in the cardboard. Meanwhile the first one smashed the stool with an equally effective move, just like a real karate expert. Then they took hold of "Granpaw" and his apple and shoved him into the van.

God alone knows what they did with him then. There were times when the doctor saw him hurrying to work all covered in bruises, but at other times there were no bruises, there was a spring in his step and he even looked cheerful. The local citizenry was accustomed to this—it was just like changes in the weather. Nobody took him seriously; he was seen as mad but harmless. Never once even had he been sacked from his job. All his life he had been a bookkeeper, and that's precisely what he went on being. Other inhabitants of the town weren't so lucky. There was one neighbour in particular that the police had been to see on about five occasions. The neighbour then vanished. People said that he was in prison.

The mother of the unusual girl Masha was a school teacher. But not of biology. Not even of chemistry and physics—in the doctor's school those subjects were indeed taught by one teacher, as were German and history, and preliminary military training and geography. Masha's mother taught the Lingo. True, she taught it somewhere on the other side of the river, not in his school no. 1. The doctor could not understand how anyone with such problems could teach the Lingo. It's just like having a deaf music teacher, or a PE teacher without arms.

One more thing: Masha had an older sister, but she lived in the capital and nobody wanted anything to do with her. She often came down at weekends, and then the whole family would go to the market, babbling away in that Leid of theirs. Four sick people. The bookkeeper, always neat and tidy, always polite and ready to go up to anyone to ask how they are, his wife, their elder daughter in her long dresses and the child Masha.

During lessons Masha never answered in the Lingo. She said she didn't know it, but nobody believed her. She always sat on her own, not because everyone hated her, but because there was nothing to talk to her about. What is there to talk about with a foreigner?

The ignorant savage that weather'd the storm,
When the man and the Brute differed but in form.

That's how everyone thought, except the doctor, who behaved like they all did but in fact never agreed with them. There was a lot that he wanted to talk to foreigners about. For example: what do they feel when they swallow words in such a funny way, when they lisp and bur? Whenever he heard foreigners talk, he always formed the impression that they were eating while talking. And their bellies were stuffed full of words. He was eager to share his observations with someone, but there was simply no one around who could understand him.

The ignorant savage that weather'd the storm,
When the man and the Brute differed but in form.

His brother liked pumping iron and was getting ready to go into the army. Or maybe he would join the police. He hadn't made his mind up yet. The future doctor was dreaming of becoming a Doctor. Or a musician. In his mind the two professions were of equal standing. He was attracted to both of them, but each time he drew back. He simply could not make a choice.

"He's got perfect pitch," said his father, when he once took the future doctor to a group learning to play the guitar. The doctor-to-be was not accepted on the course. He wasn't downcast. If the leader of the group was unable to speak the Lingo correctly, how could he play? What could he teach?

However, the future doctor kept his thoughts to himself. And he set his sights on Masha. He found her interesting. No, he had no desire to kiss her, or pull her hair, or look to see what colour her knickers were. What he wanted was . . .

Well, first off he wanted to have a talk with her. One day he happened to see her crossing the bridge over the river—a river so narrow that you could spit from one side right to the other—and followed her. She saw him and speeded up, but he didn't fall behind.

All of a sudden she stopped and asked, "Whit d'ye whant frae me?"

He began to burble something

The bonniest lass that ye meet neist
Gie her a kiss an a' that,
In spite o ilka pairish priest,
Repentin stool, an a' that

about upcoming tests and homework, and she started to believe
him, dropped her defences and began to respond.

For a' that an a' that,
Their mim-mou'd sangs an a' that
In time an place convenient,
They'll do't themsels for a' that.

He didn't listen to what she said. Instead he looked at her mouth,
which to him seemed very beautiful. Inside this mouth there was
a mystery.

Your patriarchs in days o yore,
Haed their handmaids an a' that;
O bastard gets, some haed a score,
An some haed mair than a' that.

She was glad that someone had started a conversation with her
simply because she was a classmate, and not because she was the
daughter of a barmy bookkeeper.

It was May, and they set off together along the riverbank. She
walked on ahead, waving her schoolbag, and he followed with his
hands behind his back. He hadn't taken any books with him—he
knew it all already and had successfully completed all the tests
the day before.

King Davie, when he waxed auld,
An's bluid ran thin, an a' that,

An fand his cods were growin cauld,
Could not refrain, for a' that.

He was the best student in the class, and she was the worst. Perhaps that was why she paid no attention to the kind of things he asked her about—things that could not possibly have been of any interest to him.

They began meeting by the bridge and walked as far as the first barrack-like building—there were rows of them on the other side of the river. He learned her Leid; it wasn't difficult, he had the ability to acquire languages. Learning German at school wasn't enough for him; he had taught himself English and, listening to the Lithuanians who used to come to the market, had even begun to understand them. Then there was Polish, which he spoke with an accent, but all the same spoke it better than the local Poles. That's why it took him only a week to start speaking Masha's Leid, but he only ever used it when talking to Masha; he asked her not to tell anyone.

For a' that an a' that,
To keep him warm an a' that,
The dochters o Jerusalem
Were waled for him, an a' that.

Masha cherished this unexpected friendship.

She was definitely not a bright girl. She had absolutely no aptitude for learning. There was nothing surprising about that—if you pronounce words wrongly, you cannot possibly comprehend what they mean on their own, let alone what they mean in complex combinations. He was really surprised that he had managed so quickly to get her sufficiently relaxed to allow him to conduct experiments on her.

"Hou d'ye feel when ye're speakin wi yer Leid?" he once asked her when they took the risk of going out on to the square together. What she said in reply was something that troubled him for ages:

"Whan ah try tae speak likes o ilka body, it feels lik a wee bane i ma mou's bein hurt, ken? But whan ah speak wi the Leid it doesnae."

It took his breath away. She said it so naturally that it couldn't possibly be a lie. And anyway, she didn't know how to lie.

"Can ye feel yon wee bane wi yer tongue?" he asked, trying hard not to betray the thrill of happiness that shot through him.

Masha stopped, swallowed and, with a look of the utmost sincerity, attempted to move her tongue around the corners of her mouth.

"Ah canna," she said, disappointed. "Onyweys, we're bletherin wi the Leid."

"It's because the way we're talking is not right, it's wrong and it's ugly!" is what the doctor wanted to shout. "Here I am pulling my face into all kinds of grimaces just for you, for someone ugly and stupid." But he held himself in check. Even at that time he was aware that, in order to speak correctly, he had to be able to control himself. To ensure that every nerve could reach all the corners of his body.

He smiled:

"Ye're lik a cherry. Aw roundit wi wan wee paip."

She blushed with joy, and he, feigning indifference, said:

"Ah bide near aboots. Cry in by fir a wee bit, gin ye whant. Thare's nae buddy else thare. Ma brither's i the gym, an ma paurents are awa tae the dacha."

She was confused. She looked at him as though she wanted to extract some kind of promise from him. She liked that bit about the cherry, he could feel it. And he knew that she didn't want him to leave her. After all, he was the only student in her year that she could talk to in her Leid. She looked on him as a friend. All the same, she was afraid.

"Aye!" she smiled without looking at him. "Let's awa. If ah'd

paip: stone of a fruit   *cry in by*: drop in

78

kent ye war aboot askin me tae yer howff ah wad hae brocht an antics film wi me. Ma tittie bocht it fur me. Hae ye seen *Jane the Ape* set oot i oor Leid?"

The doctor shook his head. He had seen *Jane the Ape* three years ago—a cartoon film for elementary school kids. It's quite ridiculous to think that he would watch it, let alone in this "dialect" of hers ... Pathetic: to think that that sister of hers with a man's face would bring her damaged films from the capital ...

"Anither while fur yon?" she said cautiously. "Aye?"

"Aye! But let's awa the noo!" said the doctor.

Sure enough, there was no one at home. They went in and sat on the sofa. The doctor gave her his books to look at, showed her the souvenirs he had brought from Lithuania: shells, magnets, postcards ... Meanwhile he simply watched her in silence while she wittered on and on, commenting on every single little thing, every shadow on the photograph.

"What a chatterbox you are," he thought to himself. "Who would have thought it? It's that bone that's making her babble like this."

She stopped talking at last. By now, evening had crept into the room. The brother was due to come home soon. He poured her out a handful of sunflower seeds. She shifted closer to the wall, feeling herself freer and more relaxed. This was precisely what he wanted. She thought that he would switch on something for her; she couldn't stand the silence any longer.

"Spiel sumethin oan, likka vizzeo mebbes. Eh?"

"Ah thocht ye dinnae leuk tae thingmies likes o yon," said the doctor gloomily, as he got up from the sofa and closed the curtains.

"Ah dae unnerstaund the Lingo," and she waved her arms around. "An let's hae a shot o sumethin! Or spiel a wee bit musique ... This is yer chambie, shuirly? We'll no be rilin' onybody, eh?"

tae yer howff: to your place   *spiel*: put on, play

He switched on some music, some sort of ballad, a CD that he'd borrowed from his brother, and sat down next to her feet.

"Ah'm eftir askin ye something," he said softly and looked her straight in the eyes.

She said nothing, just stirred slightly on the sofa and started cracking the sunflower seeds open.

> *How can I keep my maidenhead,*
> *My maidenhead, my maidenhead;*
> *How can I keep my maidenhead,*
> *Among sae mony men, O.*

"Y're ma freend, aye?" said the doctor. "Ye'll no refuse me, eh?"

> *The Captain bad a guinea for't,*
> *A guinea for't, a guinea for't;*
> *The Captain bad a guinea for't,*
> *The Colonel he bad ten, O.*

"An whit if ah dae refuse?" she asked, and pressed her lips so tightly together—as if there was a bitter taste in her mouth—that something stirred inside the doctor.

"We winna be freends ony mair," he said sadly. "Ah thocht ye trustit me …"

"Aye aye, aw richt …"

> *I'll gie it to a bonnie lad,*
> *A bonnie lad, a bonnie lad;*
> *I'll gie it tae a bonnie lad,*
> *For just as gude again, O*

"… ah *dae* trust ye," she said in the dim evening light. "Jist dinnae dae onything nestie tae me."

ah'm eftir askin: I want to ask

For just as gude again, O.

He gave a nervous laugh and immediately cursed himself silently for it. However, she didn't notice anything anyway. The doctor sat nearer to her and picked up a torch. Their faces were very close to each other. "Shaw me yer ..." he said in an unexpectedly hoarse voice. She froze. "Gape yer mou appen an shaw me yon wee bane i yer thrapple ..."

"Whit's this?" she felt the torch in his hand. "Whit's it fur?"

"Ah need it," said the doctor and switched it on. "Gape awa!"

"Ah winna!" She wanted to tear herself away but the doctor held her fast. "Ye *are* gonnae dae somethin nestie tae me! Ah dinnae whant it!"

The doctor thought that the best thing would be to let her go. It worked. At first she made a dash for the door, but then he heard her footsteps and felt her hand on his head.

"Awricht, awricht," she said with a long sigh. "Avaunt, avaunt— hae a vizzie."

He didn't see it, but he heard a moist, squelching sound coming from her mouth. He stood up and switched on the torch. The inside of her mouth was red and smelled of sunflower seeds. There were husks hanging here and there from her lips. The doctor began feverishly to compare his own mouth—one that he had studied almost to perfection—with hers, one so small, so mysterious. She was trembling. Saliva was beginning to collect in that shallow, dark mouth.

An auld moulie maidenhead,
A maidenhead, a maidenhead;
An auld moulie maidenhead,
The weary wark I ken, O.

The doctor felt no disgust. He was looking for the little bone. All

avaunt: go ahead

of a sudden the girl coughed. From beneath a flap of skin—so taut and scarlet that you could easily get the urge to pierce it with a needle—something pointed poked out and then disappeared again, something with torn epithelium at the tip.

"Ah hae sicht o't," said the doctor. "Ah hae sicht o the bane. Thanks, Masha. Ye maun gang awa hame nou."

She just stood there with her mouth agape.

"What?" he shouted. "Off with you! Go home!"

That evening he grabbed a bottle of raspberry liqueur, went down to the river and, for the first time in his life, got drunk. All on his own. He could see that little bone in the water in front of him, he could hear how the Lingo was being mangled by the feeble-minded kids of carpenters and farm labourers on the other side of the river. Then he stood up, leant forwards over the water and

The stretchin' o't

vomited

the strivin' o't

on to the cracked reflection

the borin' o't

of a moon

the rivin' o't

that had been granted permanent right of residence in the little town. Out of his body flowed all his lack of resolve and fear

And ay the double drivin' o't

together with his vomit. And the dull throbbing in his head was the announcement that his youthful, restless genius had emerged from the void

The farther ye gang ben, O.

6

Only a fool trusts the side of a completely empty road

Only a fool trusts the side of a completely empty road. A fool—
or the faither of two children, who are God only knows where
by now, and who he has to find. And find them before night falls.
That's the task he's set himself. So here he is now, slowing down
and directing the car towards the side of the road. The distance
between the car and the village girl walking barefoot by the side
of the completely empty road is becoming smaller and smaller.
The girl was like a paper bag blown along by the wind. It isn't too
late to drive away without asking her anything. Faither sighs and
rests his head on the steering wheel.

He first noticed the girl when he was still quite a long way
away, and speeded up automatically. Then he slowed down,
watching the girl in the rearview mirror. And that in itself looked
suspicious. It seemed to him that the girl too slowed down as
soon as she saw the car come to a halt some fifty metres ahead
of her.

It's aw wrang—a lassie gangin alane alang sic an empie road.
Awtho folk i veelages hereaboots dinna fash themsel ower much
wi quaistens likes o yon. Yon wey local bairns get sic a scantiness
o bairndom; an yon wey the paurents hae sic a lang adult life.
Acause sic a life stairts early, oan the grune verge, while ither
bodies zip past at full tilt wi pimped up motors.

So here he is, going to speak to her at any moment. He's going
to overcome his hesitation and speak to her. The road really is
absolutely deserted; he has the impression that they are being

fash: worry

watched—him in his dirty car and the girl walking on the side of the road—but only by the forest, and the forest won't say anything to anyone. They will chat for a bit, and then he'll carry on driving, he won't have learned anything, he'll be in despair like he was before, without a clear plan. And she will go on her way, walking along her roadside, from point A to point B. Talking to her is sheer folly. Because if anything happens to this pure girl, as pure as his folly, if she disappears, if she's found murdered or raped, and she tells her parents what happened, they're bound to find someone who saw him.

Who saw him stop the car, open the door and speak to her. And no one will believe that all he asked her was:

"Seen twa bairns hereaboots at aw, blaw-ins, bairns wearin breekums an white T-shirts?"

"Naw, ah've no."

"Thay're neem'd Alicia an Aviator; Avi's his tae-name."

"Therr's no such names, mister. Youse been oan the bevvy? Yer breth's hummin wae it."

"Non, awtho ah bouse'd up yestreen. Ah dinna sup that much. Mebbe twa hunnert gramme. An aw ah've done the day is greet. For why d'ye say thare's nae sic neems? Whit're ye cried onyhou? Zhanna? Aksana? Ah thocht as much. Thay're named Alicia an Avi. Hamelt names. Wan o thaim haudit a beuk. A verra auld beuk..."

"Naw, mister. Ah've no seen thems."

"Bi fegs, ah maun airt them oot. Aiblins thare's a growen-body wha's seen thaim, eh?"

"Naw, ah've no heard that neither. Ah knaw the hale load o thems roon here."

"Peety."

"Aye, bit whit d'ye whaaant thems fur, mister?"

oan the bevvy: on the booze   *yestreen*: yesterday evening   *hamelt*: native   *haudit*: held   *aiblins*: perhaps   *a growen-body*: an adult

"Wha? Alicia an Aviator? Ah luve thaim, that's whit fur. Yer hale life ye'll be airtin oot folk ye luve as weel. Y're jist o'er young yet. Jist a wee lassie gangin alang grune verge o an enteerly empie road."

"Wherr'd they wans live, mister, yon Alicia an Aviator?"

"Whaur d' they bide?" Faither looked pensive. "Thay're alive yet, aye. Ah believe it. They canna semply be disparu. Acause Alicia hae Aviator, her brither. Aye, he's younger than she is, but he'll help her. He'll no see her forsaken. Will ah gie ye a birl doon the road?"

"Naw, thanks. Ma mammy tellt me tae no get in a motor wi ootlanders."

"Aye, but we're no strangers ony mair. Ye ken muckle mair aboot me than ye shoud, Aksana-Snowanna. Ye ken mair aboot me than ony ither body i hale wide warld. O'er much. Ye'll gang hame an stairt tae tell yon unchancy mither o yours—things sic a body haed absolutely nae need tae ken. Than she'll get anither body tellt. An yon ither body'll get anither body tellt. An aw ma airtin oot maun be feenishit. Thay'll be airtin me oot! Ach but jist jump i the motor. Fur aw that."

Whaur d'thay bide?

A good question.

... Back then, an eternity ago, the two of them—Faither and Alicia—lived in the greenest part of the town, some five kilometres from the chemical plant. In a two-room flat—one room was Alicia's, and the other was for them both, their games, films, dances and whatever else they got up to. Faither used to sleep in the kitchen, on an old, clapped-out sofa on which there was no room for his legs, so he used to put them on a stool; it was as if he took them off for the night. It was a tight fit to squeeze into the kitchen because of all the empty bottles that lived there. A heap of empty bottles that he didn't at first dare to take out of the flat. The heap continued to grow to the point where he was afraid to be seen with them.

The reason for his fear: he was a faither bringing up his daughter on his own. And that was enough to arouse their suspicions—all those people who lived alongside them and kept an eye on Alicia and him through their all-knowing windows. A faither bringing up his daughter on his own was bad enough. But a faither whose daughter never speaks to a living soul was many times worse. Every second he could feel the interest in his unusual family. They looked at him oddly, as though they knew exactly what it was that he did with his daughter when he was alone with her. He could feel these crooked glances, these ambiguous smiles, this urge to spy through the keyhole to prove to themselves that everything was just as they thought. This certainty that where there's dark, there's also dirt.

For the moment, however, he gave them no cause. And they had no proof. He was equally polite to everyone, and he had developed within himself a way of skilfully avoiding awkward questions. He never let anyone into his flat but would always gladly come to the aid of any of his neighbours. This probably served merely to strengthen their suspicions. To them, that is what a real maniac, family rapist and freak must look like. They knew, they could sense with that blasted tribal intuition of theirs that something was not quite right there.

And they were right.

If only they knew what it was that he and Alicia did together when they were at home.

Talking together, singing, playing word games, reading—isn't this just the most terrible kind of perversion? No, it isn't, provided it's all done in the right language. And there is only one right language outside the house. The Lingo. The language of the majority. The language of all. The language of each individual. The language that is understood by the folk who look at you through your window and invent your life for you.

All the bottles that he had drained dry lived in the kitchen. Every evening he drank, every evening one two-hundred-gram miniature to accompany a simple supper, after Alicia had gone to sleep. It was an even more terrifying time for him when he was left to himself while she was falling asleep. Vodka drove away the shadows, vodka defended him from tomorrow, vodka gave him strength. Without his miniatures there was absolutely no way he could have coped with life; in each of them lay hidden his own personal servant, his bodyguard awaiting evening release. A tiny demon of resistance, a taciturn masseur with burning fingers and evil eyes. Very soon he was unable to live without vodka.

In addition to his army of phantoms, the kitchen was also home to his books. His beloved books. There was no longer any room to sit and have breakfast, just enough space for cooking, reading and sleeping. When he finished his evening vodka, he threw the dirty dishes into the sink. Only rarely did he do the washing up, so the sink was full to overflowing. It was a real work of art to add yet another plate to the pile. Outside the window the night was raging, twisting and turning the flat this way and that, like an idiot struggling to retrieve the coins from a piggy bank. Faither was smiling. They're bound to be found out one day, but Faither believed they still had a few years. Provided they're careful and don't draw attention to themselves, and Alicia continues to obey him, the outside world will not be able to do anything. The main thing was not to put a foot wrong, not to do what the world expects him to do.

Bottles and books. Above the sofa hung a portrait of the man who won a victory, a portrait of the bearded Jew Perelman who was born close to this little town with its chemical plant.[20] Yon Jew Perelman hae makkit a langage floorish. Yon Jew Perelman pruiv'd ye coud win throu. Yon Jew Perelman kent.

Faither disliked Jews. He disliked them with the ordinary dislike of an ordinary inhabitant of an unsuccessful country. In his dislike there was no aggression, but there was envy. For that reason Faither had a Jew of his own. Perelman, the serious Jew with the mournful eyes of a practising magician.

"Awthings that a body, e'en jist wan body, strives tae say . . ."

All of this can become a language. By either reviving it or creating it—but it can be done.

Only one person. Even if there is only one person. Faither would close his eyes and stop breathing, feeling the unexpected vast expanse of cosmic space within him. Just imagine: one person. A language needs only one person in order to become alive, whereas a dead entity cannot be brought back to life by one that is living. Jist wan body—yon's gey few. Maun creaution o yon body be unpossible task?

Wha'll dae it gin we dinna? That was the question he used to ask himself in his younger years. The question did not need an answer. Just one person—that was the answer.

Just one person. And that person is asleep on the other side of the wall. A little girl that he at first imagined and then created. A language that sprouted from his seed. Like a plant. Like water, like the dawn, like grass. A little mother-Leid-girl. A little bird-girl.

Sia, a wagtail from the Nile, with language in her beak.

He checked that Alicia was asleep and then returned to the kitchen and lay down on the sofa. Sometimes he masturbated just to stop himself going mad. He looked at the drops that ran through the grey hairs on his belly and thought that each of them could have become that "just one person," and all together they would have made an army which would change everything. Just one—that was also about him. That Jew Perelman was called the faither of a language. He too was the faither of a language, and that gave him the desire to carry on living.

That is how he lived beneath the portrait—for the sake of the Leid, in whatever guise it chose to appear to him.

At times he thought he was going mad. At times he simply wanted to get away, to open the door carefully, leave the flat and never return. The little girl Sia would wait for him, then she too would leave the flat and go to them, to the world, to the Lingo. At moments like that Faither would be overcome by rage and would start to roar quietly. Responsibility for the Leid began to slap him around the head. He would crawl from the sofa down on to the floor and start praying. And meanwhile the Jew Perelman would look down on all this from the filthy wallpaper with no hint of surprise on his face.

"Jew, tell me whit wey ye hae managed it," is what Faither wanted to shout at the photograph, but he knew he shouldn't. It's obvious what they would think.

One of the sides of the fridge was hard up against his head on the sofa, and at night it would rattle and shake. He would wake up and look at the alarm clock. He would get up and go to peek in on Alicia. Right from the moment she first appeared in the flat, he was obsessed with the idea that she might one night suffocate. And so every night he would get up to check that everything was all right. Alicia slept, and he would lean over and inhale the scent of her breath.

Oh yes, those nights. Right, he would look at the alarm clock and then go to look in on Alicia. Time passed, and Alicia grew in her sleep. Sia the little bird was training her wings on the far side of reality so that at one miraculous moment she could fly off and bring everything truly to life. Him, the Country and the Leid.

Before they left the flat in the mornings, they did their utmost to speak as much as they possibly could. He would switch some music on and they would chatter about everything under the sun—except school. Surprisingly enough, at that terrible time they always had something to talk about. So they talked and talked in the Leid, and rejoiced without shame at the way in which words came together so beautifully, how they flew from their mouths and wove nests in each other's eyes. They found delight in speaking.

For ahead of Alicia there lay silence. Eight hours of silence.

She didn't know that some people can suffocate in their sleep, but she did know what happens to people who speak in a language other than their own. This wasn't a ban—it was a necessary condition for survival.

Half an hour later they were right by the school. And at precisely the same moment as they approached the school entrance they were as usual joined by a woman—the psychologist Miss Edwardson. She bent down to Alicia and shook her hand.

"Hello, Sia. How are things?"

She pronounced her name correctly, and for this Faither hated her. Sia the schoolgirl was chewing a sandwich and looking at Miss Edwardson in the way you would look at a large dog. The sandwich was a cunning device of theirs. Previously Miss Edwardson had been fond of peering into Alicia's mouth, as if she wanted to find the cause of her problems there. However, even a school psychologist finds it difficult to peer into a mouth full of salami and baguette.

"I have the impression that she will begin to speak soon," said Miss Edwardson on one occasion, when Sia was running up the steps and Faither was preparing to return to his car. "I also have the impression that there are some things you are not telling me."

This was said in such a calm voice that Faither was really shaken up by it. He stopped and tried to make himself smaller by drawing his head into his shoulders, but he found sufficient strength to straighten up and turn his face to hers. Her bright eyes pierced right through him, just as if he were a schoolboy.

"What do you mean?" he asked with a smile which to his mind gave him away completely.

The Lingo cursed by God. The language of intrigues and fear, the language of humiliation and rape, the language of the kangaroo court where only the innocent are ever found guilty. "What do you mean?" Yon's the means o parsing a quaisten tae speel oot time an pu' yir shouders back up. "What do you mean?" A quaisten that means ye unnerstaund perfectly in whit wey y're tae blame.

"I have the impression that things are not so simple when dealing with you," mewed Miss Edwardson. "And Sia can feel it."

"Nonsense," and he made a dismissive, sweeping gesture with his hand.

"I have the impression that you do not want ..." she continued, noting with interest how his eyes were darting back and forth.

"What?"

"You do not want her to be healthy. You do not want a normal child."

To his horror he realised that he was blushing. She was in no hurry to leave, although the bell had already rung. She looked at him with all the tenderness of a policeman, finding pleasure in pricking him with her pure voice: "It is quite conceivable that you have become accustomed to playing the role of victim. And it's easier for you. It's easier when the child is sick. You are unable to imagine what your life will be like when she starts to speak, when she gets better."

"No, no," he held out his hand, palm forward, but this bitch with a university diploma had no intention of listening to him.

"Maybe, but it is perfectly possible that there's something else behind it all. Some secret. And I am definitely going to get to the bottom of it. I feel sorry for the girl. She's talented, you can see that at once, and she deserves to be happy in her own country. Even if that country isn't this one."

Without a word she went off towards the school door, above which there was a board that read "Welcome." Faither and Alicia often used to laugh together at the way that perfidious Lingo of theirs mutilates the real meaning of words: a "welcome guest" was originally a guest who was "well come," one that the host wished to see. How many hosts had there been over the years who were always glad to see guests who spoke the Lingo?

Faither followed Miss Edwardson with his eyes. Her legs in black tights, her fair hair cascading down over her shoulders, the way she held herself—exactly what you would expect from a fine filly in an urban environment, even in the capital ... Faither laithe'd Miss Edwardson—but he coudnae see past her.

Wanst he haed a dream o her. Oan parteecular occasions he thocht oan whit micht come o him shuvin whit she deserred in-tae her mooth.

She mind't na when I forbade her,
She mind't na when I forbade her.

Than whit langage wad she gab? Or mebbes she'd gab naething. But more than anything else there was in Miss Edwardson an inner strength that found expression in her wonderfully pure voice. The power of victory. Faither found it difficult to talk to her precisely because of that—her crystal-clear voice was impossible to imitate.

" ... Jist drap me aff here, mister," said the little girl, pushing on the door with her shoulder. He stopped the car so clumsily that he almost broke his passenger's nose. Outside the window there was a village, a freshly painted fence, and on the other side of the fence a man and a woman with buckets.

"Ye willna clype aboot Alicia an Avi?" asked Faither, but the girl was no longer listening. She had jumped out of the car and started to run towards the wicket gate. Faither drove off straight towards the chickens; cursing in French they scattered in all directions and Faither got the car stuck in a pile of something or other. Beyond the cottage where the little girl lived loomed the black shape of the forest.

That selfsame forest. The huge frontier forest that had swallowed his children. He had simply driven around the forest—that's all that had happened that day. He reversed the car out of the pile of whatever it was towards the pink-painted cross that

clype: inform

marked the beginning of the village. In that way he unwound the cottages, the chickens and the naked children who kept their eyes glued to his car—like they were trying to remember the number on his licence plate. He turned the car round and just managed to see out of the corner of his eye that the parents of the little girl had come right out of the house, and she was telling them something and pointing to the road with her finger.

POSTSCRIPT:

What Mum and Dad say, in Spenserian Stanza (Anon., 2020)

Dinnae ken aboot you, but ah'm famish'd.
Weel hou aboot a cairry-in the nicht—
Mebbes a wee Thailander McTavish'd?
Aye but you dae it acause ah'm pished ... *Richt ...*
Whit?! ... *Thur menu's awa tae minimised sicht!*
Maks nae matter, get yon MegaBanquet—
Yon's goat free juice! ... *Aw that an aw that's ... Mighty*
f###in me! Uise ma caird! *But whaur's it?!*
There! Therr! Thare! Oan the flair! THAAARE ye bawheidit
   ... Tit!

What Burns Then Said in Spenserian Stanza (1786)

But now the supper crowns their simple board,
The halesome parritch, chief of Scotia's food;
The sowp their only hawkie does afford,
That, 'yont the hallan snugly chows her cood;
The dame brings forth, in complimental mood,
To grace the lad, her weel-hain'd kebbuck, fell;
And aft he's prest, and aft he ca'd it guid:
The frugal wifie, garrulous will tell
How t'was a towmond auld, sin' lint was i' the bell.

How Robert Fergusson Concluded the Matter in Spenserian
Stanza (1773)

On sicken food has mony a doughty deed
By Caledonia's ancestors been done;
By this did mony wight fu' weirlike bleed
In brulzies frae the dawn to set o' sun:
'Twas this that braced their gardies, stiff and strang,
That bent the deidly yew in antient days,
Laid Denmark's daring sons on yird alang,
Gar'd Scottish thristles bang the Roman bays;
For near our crest their heads they doughtna raise.

7
Trying hard not to look at her teeth

Trying hard not to look at her teeth, Alicia and Avi came closer to the lady of the cottage, and she stroked their hair. What a pleasant sensation it was—just like being washed with water; Alicia and Avi had never had a Granmaw, and they decided that that was what they would call the woman. They did not say anything to each other, they simply decided, that's all, and each of them knew that the decision was mutual.

Although the lady of this candy cottage did look much too young to be a granmaw ... For some reason, however, that thought didn't enter their heads. A young woman, a bit on the chubby side, wearing a red top from a two-piece swimming costume and capacious shorts stitched out of a pair of men's trousers. She looked as though she had only just straightened up after digging in the kitchen garden. That in itself inspired a strange kind of confidence.

Ally bally, ally bally bee,
Sittin' on yer mammy's knee,
Greetin' for a wee bawbee,
Tae buy some Coulter's Candy.

It was her teeth that spoiled the impression. Pointed, blackened predatory shards that poked out from a plump upper lip, eager to tear at their prey, along with dark voids next to glittering gold crowns. The children's eyes were drawn towards this terrifying, mutilated mouth, so they tried to look lower. Down to her boobs that were swaying from side to side, as if they had been brought along for the sole purpose of being hung on the cottage alongside all the other tasty treats.

"Weans, ma bonnie wee *birdies*," said the lady of the cottage squinting. "Youz must be ferr famished."

"Non, we arena," said Alicia and looked sternly at Avi.

"Na," said Avi, but there was a note of regret in his voice.

"Is it langweys tae Bremen frae here?" asked Alicia as she opened the map. "We maun ken wither we're oan the cairt bi nou or no."

"It's awfy near, ma *bonnie* wee birdies, awfy near," said Granmaw, and her hollow mouth smiled. "Bremen, och aye, ah knaw aw aboot Bremen. Yon's wherr ah goat took fur tae dae forced labour. Therr's a helluva work therr. But things arenae bad ... Aboot ten year ago ah goat bit compensation seein as ah'd been an Ostarbeiter.[21] Aw payed in German marks so it wis. Ah changed it intae dollars an passed it tae ma granweans." There was something about what she said that wasn't quite right, it didn't hang together, thought Alicia, but she decided not to ask unnecessary questions. Meanwhile, the cottage behind their backs was calling out to them, drawing them in by means of its labels and pictures. It was as if the cottage was quietly sending out shivers of excitement in the early evening twilight, and both Alicia and Avi could feel the thrill—with their spines, the tips of their fingers, their heels, their tummies ...

"Virtue in a humble cott," quoted Avi, looking round respectfully at the candy confection cottage.

"Ah knaw *nuthin* aboot virtue," said mutton-dressed-as-lamb Granmaw. "Ma hoose is in the toon doon by, an this here's ma holiday howff. Ah put it aw thegither oan ma pension an whit ah could scroungey ... see it's like yon bonnie auld sang: 'Ah put it aw thegither wi junk jist lyin aroond, an yon hoose that ah built wis the best that ah foond.' Aye but therr's nae ways youz mind that, eh? Youz ur awfy young."

"Y're no chauntin it richt i the Lingo," said Avi with a frown. "Here's hou ye maun chaunt: 'I put it together out of what was lying around, and the house that I built was the best place I e'er found.' Nice rounded vowels in 'around' and 'found' and there's a 'd' at the end of those words by the way, and don't forget your 'g' after 'n' in a participle."

"Who's a wee smerty pants, then!" and Granmaw broke into another smile. "Wherr did *you* get tae be sae brainy? An ye soond like ye wuz born back o beyond. God awmichty knaws hoo come suchlike comes."

And, with no shame whatsoever, she opened her mouth wide. Alicia and Avi turned hastily away.

"Right, wherr d'y come frae, weans?"

"No registrated, nae fixed abode, we live bi God's guid grace alane," said Avi, recalling Faither's books.[22] "Na, sairiously, we're frae ..."

"Yon's ma brither," said Alicia, and seized Avi by the hand to stop him saying anything else. "We maun win a locus oan the cairt, syne we'll wark it oot oorsel."

"Bruthur?" Granmaw's smile made her look even friendlier, but she suddenly squeezed her lips tight shut and that somehow made her frightening. By now it was totally dark in the forest and impossible to read the labels on the cottage walls. "Youz dinnae look the same. Bru*uu*thur, eh ..."

She looked intently at Avi and then reached out and touched his cheeks.

"Ah hae ma doots," she said in the same rasping voice that she had used at the start. "Things ur a wee bit complicated wi this wee man ... Ferr do's aw the same, if youz want him tae be yir bruthur, let him be yir bruthur. Youz ur ferr famished, and youz'll huv tae keep up yir strength if youz ur gonnae make it tae

chaunt: speak in a stylised manner

Bremen. Therrz nae buses the night, an furst wan's away eight o'clock the morn. Ah'll take youz tae the stop, an youz can kip doon here wi me the night. Ah'll feed yese, hae a look at yirsel!

Ally bally, ally bally bee,
Sittin' on yer mammy's knee,
Greetin' for a wee bawbee,
Tae buy some Coulter's Candy

Poor wee Jeanie's lookin awfy thin,
A handfu' o' bones aw coverd wi skin

—y're baith like skelfs! Naw, skellytons!"

"The ward is skeletons, nae skellytons," said Avi, and it seemed to Alicia that he was about to bite Granmaw—either on the hand with hairy fingers that were bending this way and that as though they were talking, or on the breasts. Alicia could see that Avi was very, very, very hungry.

"An whit aboot yon daintees that wis i the boxes—whaur's thay?" asked Avi and licked his lips. He turned eagerly towards the cottage.

"Therr's a wee bit o this an a wee bit o that left," said Granmaw readily, and signalled to them to follow her. "We'll get yese a wee bit this an a wee bit that. We'll feed yese up,

Noo she's growin' a wee double chin,
Frae eatin' Coulter's Candy

otherwise it's a long, long wey tae yon Bremen o yourz, it's likes o goin tae the moon, yon's a faur-aff warld, yon Bremen: youz'll need tae change see*ee*veral times, youz'll need tae huv euros an a hale loadae thingmies as weel ..."

skelf: splinter; small, thin person

They came up to the cottage. It had a weird shape unlike any-thing that could normally be found in a village. In the darkness it resembled an alien spaceship. Granmaw opened the door:

"Come oan in, therr's no much room, it's ma holiday howff, aye, plenty fur me, but we'll fun some room fir youz two, ma bonnie wee ..."

She let them go on ahead.

"Ah'll jist pit the light oan ..."

Somewhere to one side a little bulb lit up and pinned their shadows to the ceiling. There was a table standing next to the wall opposite, and on the table was a kettle.

"Jist a wee bittie mair," said the rasping voice behind Alicia's and Avi's backs. They took one more step forward, and the floor suddenly gave way beneath their feet.

The first to tumble into the black hole was Avi. He fell on to something soft, but then Alicia's bottom came to rest on his neck and knocked him right down into the depths of a pit lined with rotten straw. The light was now way above their heads, but down here it was cramped, like being smothered with a blanket and left to suffocate, and it was dark. The result was that Alicia, while waving her arms around, hit Avi in the eye.

"Use your eyes!" Avi yelled. He was annoyed; back in the Camp he used to love using the Lingo when he wanted to quarrel. And Alicia quite unexpectedly recalled her life in the Camp with such clarity that she felt a pang in the pit of her stomach. Worst of all was that she remembered about the pills. At once her body began to buzz, and in her head she could hear the Call of the Camp Bugle. They had forgotten to take the tablets, they had forgotten to take their medicine!

Coulter he's an affa funny man,
He maks his candy in a pan,
Awa an greet to yer ma,
Tae buy some Coulter's Candy.

This was the most terrible, the most irreparable thing that could have happened. For this a real medieval punishment could be inflicted on them! Back there in the Camp the tablets had made them want to dig themselves into the ground, and now here they are, beneath the ground, and there are no medicines, nothing's making sense, none of it holds together, it's not working out right.

"Use yer ain!" said Alicia rudely, in an attempt to calm down, to soothe the gnawing sensation she felt inside her and to stifle that damned bugle in her head. It worked. She could feel that Avi had also got himself under control and was now looking at her with respect in this straw-strewn murk.

Whit tae dae? They knew that this was a question which they should never ask aloud; they just knew, without coming to any kind of agreement. Alicia knew, and Avi knew. If they were to utter those words, nothing would come right. All the same, Alicia wanted to say them, not even to Avi, nor to that ring of light above their heads, nor to herself, but to whoever it was who had conjured up everything that was happening to them. Someone was drawing circles around them, and breaking out was more difficult than they had thought.

All they had to do was get on to the map, and then they would find the way.

"We maun mynd oor atlas," said Avi in the darkness. "We durna forget it whan we're oan oor wey."

"Ah'll hae mynd o't,"

When you grow old, a man to be,
You'll work hard and you'll sail the seas,
An bring hame pennies for your faither and me,
Tae buy some Coulter's Candy,

said Alicia and stroked him on the knee. "Awa an let's sleep. D'ye think ye can?"

"Aye," and Avi's voice sounded so sleepy, just as if all he had been waiting for was her suggestion.

Feeling how soft Avi's body had become, Alicia cuddled up close to him and shut her eyes. It seemed to her that barely a moment had passed, but when she opened them she could see that the bright cloud of morning had been forced into the cottage above them. It brought with it the scent of fog and cold.

"Avi," she called out, retrieving her arm from beneath his T-shirt.

"Whit?" His voice sounded as though he hadn't been asleep.

"Will ye no tell me whaur ye cam frae?"

"Ah'm yer brither," said Avi, picking at something, either on his toenails or on the ground around him.

"Ah'm no daupit, ah ken ye're ma brither," said Alicia stretching. "But whaur d'ye *cam* frae? Firstens ye werna thare, than ye waur—as ma brither; an eftirwards thare waur aw ither things, we waur i the Camp. An nou we're tummelt i this cowp. But d'ye no hae *ony* mynd o whare ye cam frae?"

Avi thought for a moment and said, "Jist same as ilka body. If ye hae a name gien tae ye, if ye get caw'd bi some wird or t'ither, it means that ye endure."

"But fur aw that, aw laddies are no ma brither," said Alicia, sitting up. "D'ye no unnerstaund, tumshie heid?"

"That's acause thay're no aviators," retorted Avi with certainty.

There was a certain convincing logic in these words that made Alicia slide her hands once more under Avi's T-shirt and go to sleep.

Granmaw fed them in the morning. They could hear her footsteps as she came up to the cottage. They remembered what her mouth looked like and thought that it would not be a bad idea to clean their teeth. They decided that, when they moved on, they

daupit: stupid   *endure*: exist   *tumshie heid*: turnip head would look for an orchard and eat an apple each. That's what the dentist in the Camp told them: if they suddenly find themselves without toothpaste and toothbrush, they can eat an apple. But, of course, that was only in an emergency.

Granmaw entered the cottage, and a flood of wet, slimy little fishes rained down on them. Some of the fish were still alive, wriggling beneath their feet. Avi picked them up, and they slid out of his fingers right on to Alicia.

"Get wired in, ma bonnies." They heard Granmaw's youthful laughter from above. "Ah've jist caught thum. Fry thum, bile thum, whitiver yese waaant ... Whit's that, yese've loast yir appetite? Nae bother, it'll be back. Ah've ran ootae dinner stuff, but wance they've brung some ah'll gie yese breed. Here's wee bit o whit wis lyin aroon fir the noo, stuff ah've goat in the hoose, therr it is ... ah liked it at lest ..."

Avi responded by shouting up at her, "When you are talking in the Lingo you should say, 'Here's a little of what I had in the house.'"

Granmaw raised her voice, "Shut it, ya wee nyaff, awa an bile yer heid, greetin face. They've stuffed his heid wi stuff, an noo he's aw gallus. It's no hairm tae *ye, ye* dinnae need tae eat; but yon sister o yourz is gonnae peg oot. Look efter her."

The fish were dying. Their scarcely visible bodies lay twitching, and Alicia felt as though she and Avi were sitting in the water; they had dived into the lake and were now pressed one against the other right near the bottom. And now they couldn't get back to the surface. The air in their lungs was running out, but she wasn't afraid. Living was possible even here, underwater. The one who really knew no fear was Avi. He behaved just as though he could manage to escape from the pit at any moment and continue on his journey. Continue towards the map, and then be on the map. Through forests, along roads, across lakes,

nyaff: brat   *gallus*: bold, daring, unmanageable

over the treetops, up hill and down dale, stepping right through the horizon. He simply doesn't feel like it. He's waiting for all the air to leave him—so it doesn't hinder him walking, doesn't drag him down to the ground. Air is a dead weight.

"Air is a deid wecht," said Alicia.

"A deid wecht hinging roon aboot yer neck," said Avi. "Tak it aff—naw, ah willna. Tak it aff—naw, ah willna."

Coulter's Candy, a penny a lump,
'At's i' stuff tae mak ye jump,
If ye jump you're sure tae fa',
Coulter's Candy, a penny fur a'.

"Ah'll tak it aff," said Alicia and placed her hands on his neck.

That evening they were given half a bucket of water—water from the lake that seemed to them to be even tastier than the water in the Camp. Granmaw poured it down to them in a fine trickle, and Alicia and Avi took turns to hold their open mouths beneath it. Granmaw could, of course, have lowered the whole bucket, but she didn't—and Alicia knew why. Because then she and Avi would have seized hold of the rope, or of the wire, or of the stick on which this oh so tasty bucket was swaying—and they would have pulled it down, and now they would have had something in their hands.

A weapon. Hope. Love.

"Whit tae dae, eh? Whit tae dae?" Granmaw said over and over again, sitting on the edge of the pit, and as if repeating a question that the children had asked, although they had asked no such thing. "Ah'll pit ma thinkin cap oan. Come tae that tho, whit's tae think aboot? You, hen, ah'm gonnae sell. Jist no the noo, ah'll shift ye later. Ah'll sell ye tae yon paramedic fellae, an he'll reset ye tae somebody else. Goad anely knaws wherr, but

hen: girl

therr huz tae be places wherr kids likes o ye'll be snapped up fur experiments when folk ur huntin oot some bane or ither. Yon paramedic'll shell oot a hale loadae cash fur a body likes o *you*, hen. An as for *you*, brains trust, ah'll make ye intae ma dug. Ma auld dug's deid, drownit. Ah caw'd him Paulie. Ah goat him when he wis still a wee puppy. Therr wis weekenders here back then, aw the wey frae Moscow. Haud oan ... wherr's yon bluidy place Moscow ...?"

Granmaw fell to thinking.

"D'ye think yon Moscow o yourz is oan the map?"

"Thare's nae sic a ceety," said Avi loudly, and Granmaw swore.

"You dinnae exist either, ya bampot." Granmaw bent over the pit. "D'ye reckon yur hur *bruthur*? *Some*body's *grand*wean, ur yese? Some kinna bruthur, y'ur ... Y're no entitletit tae open yer gub, so y'ur no. Ah've nae notion the noo who y'ur, but ah'll touch the bottom o it, ah will, never ye fear. Clarty wee shite, he disnae knaw Moscow!"

"It's folk wha hae inventit Moscow," said Avi in a calm, even voice. "Likes o they inventit God Awmichtie, or Auld Nick. Moscow is a mythic place whare aebody gabs the Lingo. But thare's nae such thing."

"Oh aye, they wans speak wi the Lingo?" muttered Granmaw, but then calmed down. "Therrz nae Goad Awmichtie an nae Moscow fur him ... You ur a Right. Wee. Goadless. Heathen. Who's yir mammy then, ya wee heathen? Ah'm gonnae huv youz two oan yer knees prayin every single Goad-given day. An youz'll baith be oan yer knees scrubbin the flair o ma wee churchie. Ah've goat an orthodox churchie o ma ain ben the forest ... pity ah cannae fix up tae get the perr o youz merrit therr."

"Hae us *mairit*?" asked Alicia, lying flat out on the bottom of the pit. She felt as though the pit was getting deeper and deeper, and above her—in the foul-smelling stink of the rotten straw—

---

bampot: idiot   *gub*: gob   *aebody*: everybody

clinging on to the walls of the pit by their fingernails there were other Alicias hanging—lots of Alicias, who opened their mouths but were unable to say anything.

Little Annie's greetin' tae,
Sae whit can puir wee Mammy dae,
But gie them a penny atween them twae,
Tae buy mair Coulter's Candy.

"Damn right, ah'm gonnae merry the perr of youz tae wan another," said Granmaw with satisfaction in her voice. "Therr's some guid reason fur the baith o youz goin erse over elbow in tae same pit. Ah need a guid, solid "peasant" faimily. Wan that'll stay oan the land, wan tae contribute tae the hoosehold. An, of course, goes withoot sayin, wan tae aye be fruitfu …"

Granmaw glanced down into the pit and bared her teeth.

"Youz'll present me wi a great-grandson, an then ah'll sell ye tae the paramedic. An that wan'll be replacement fur ma wee Paulie. By the weys, whit am ah supposed tae caw youz weans? Ah forgoat tae ask youz, ah've nae memory, nae memories left tae me …"

"Ah'm Aviator," said Avi. "An this is Alicia."

"Misbegotten wee ally bally bastuuurrrds!" And Granmaw shook her head.

"*Aviators* they wans caw thur weans! Ah'd get the social services tae strip they wans o their parental rights an lock the load o they wans up toot sweet! Hoo aboot that then, Lucia? D'ye want tae merry the wee man? Why d'yese no say somethin? Okey dokey, ah'll gies ye sum mair watter. An sum cocoakey bu'ur—ah've jist fund sum, youz'ur welcum tae it. Therr yese go,

Here's auld Coulter comin roon

catch!" And a lump of butter fell on Avi's head

Wi a basket oan his croon,

followed by a steady stream of that selfsame fragrant lake water that gave off a pungent aroma of forest, freedom and dead animals.

"Ah'll fix yer waddin' up the morra!" said Granmaw. "Therr will be no winching. Therr will be no lumbers. Therr will be no nookie aforehaund, because ah'm *tellin* youz, OK? Ah'm *tellin* youz! Kin youz hear whit ah'm *tellin* tae youz weans?"

Then they just lay there for a long time cheek to cheek, their faces covered by the now thoroughly damp road atlas. Neither of them knew what a wedding was. Neither of them knew what they should do when a Granmaw starts to order them about. Probably they should obey. "But whit aboot Faither?" asked Avi. Then they began to discuss who was more important: Faither or Granmaw. Alicia was all for Granmaw.

"Awricht, ah dinna want ony argie bargie wi ye," said Avi at last. "Ah jist want ye tae no be eatit by yon wulves, *Canis lupus*. An whit d'ye reckon tae yon wumman wi the yellae haar: wha's she?"

"Ah've nae idea,"

Mammy gie's ma thrifty doon,

Alicia's voice came clearly through the dark. "It's like eneuch she's a brand spanken new Miss Edwardson."

"Aiblins she is," agreed Avi. "But she's no Mither, is she?"

"Ye're richt daft"

Tae buy that Coulter's Candy,

said Alicia and fell asleep at once—just as if someone in the pit had picked up a slender white candle and blown it out.

winching: wenching, trying to attract females   *lumbers*: one-night stands

8

The little letters were like a horde of flies that had come to settle on the piece of paper

The little letters were like a horde of flies that had come to settle on the piece of paper. The Doctor had the urge to chase them off—then nothing would happen, there would be no bad news to start the day, and he wouldn't have to make any decisions.

"Those poor children," said the Doctor, stroking the piece of paper with the palm of his hand. "It's the little girl that I feel so sorry for. She's made a marked improvement, and now look what's happened. Poor children."

"Nothin but ructions," said the caretaker. "It's aye yon wee schilpit wans gie us maist grief. Ah've goat a report done fur ye …" A new set of letters now lay on the table right in front of the Doctor; they too looked like tracks left by flies as they fussed around the paper. Anti-hygienic letters.

At that moment he recalled another sheet of paper. Far from this forest, in a totally different life.

… That particular piece of paper was pinned to a display stand. On it there was a list with exactly similar minute letters. Nowhere near as short as today's. A very long list.

The list began at eye level; to read it right to the end, you had to either squat on your haunches or make a low, respectful bow.

The Doctor did neither one thing nor the other.

He simply took two steps back and read the list right through again. And then again.

schilpit: pathetic

His name wasn't on it. His eyes once more ran the full distance from Afanas'eva I. R. to Yakhantovich P. A. He read the list like a poem. Barygin, Brysevich, Gul'mukhamedova. His name ought to be listed between Brysevich and Gul'mukhamedova. But it wasn't there.

It meant that he hadn't been given a place in the Medical Institute. It meant that Barygin, Brysevich and Gul'mukhamedova— not forgetting about Afanas'eva and Yakhantovich—would be studying for seven years. Then—until they reached the age of seventy—they would be pulling the rotted teeth of complete wastrels who were both deaf and dumb, writing them sick notes and prescriptions for aspirin, setting the ridiculous bones that these jelly-like creatures had no need of, making incisions into their filthy skin—skin that had died because of the contempt in which nature held them. And not one of these would-be doctors would ever attain the realisation that that little bone is where a start has to be made. That little bone in the mouth, the size of a cherry stone. That little extra bone that people can't spit out, and are thereby condemned to fall ill and suffer, condemned to be no more than flesh. Just flesh. And his discovery will remain forever his secret.

It meant disaster.

The Doctor stood alone in the midst of the huge city, in a white shirt with the sleeves rolled up as if he was about to undertake some hard, physical work. He was nearly eighteen. Milling around him were creatures just like himself: half-familiar, faces that he had studied during the previous week, and—like blood flowing from an open wound—that ceaseless chatter that he could not bear to hear; when they tried to pronounce the "g" sound, they breathed garlic in your face, their "r" was rolled like an animal's roar and as hard as the wooden seats in the suburban trains, they chomped and munched all their "sh" and "ch" sounds as if they were chewing lumps of pork fat. It was July, and boiling hot. The girls' legs suddenly grew longer, and the boys' sweat left white, greasy-looking smudges on their T-shirts. The Doctor managed to take a sly glance or two into the girls' open mouths. It was there that his future lay: behind the teeth, in the spittle that they left on their cigarette filters. Almost everyone here was going around with an inflamed ulcer in their mouths. A little bone that was suffocating them—and no one would admit it or seek help. The Doctor looked at them and was so excited that he wanted to seize them by their bare, suntanned arms—all of them at once—and yell: "Spit it out! Feel it with your tongue, work it loose. Tear it off and spit it out! Then go home and—as best you can—make music with your voice."

Music that was given to you for God only knows what reason. The Music of the Lingo.

They had dictation yesterday. They were read something by Lermontov. What could these rustic savages possibly understand of Lermontov and the great literature of which Lermontov formed part—all these types called Brysevich and Barygin—if they couldn't even say his name correctly? Their speech articulators—all twisted up cobra-like by this little red bone—had abandoned all responsibility; they produced the wrong sounds in all the most important places. There where the sound needed to be forthright and decisive, it came out all rounded and rolled away into thin air. As if some kind of fear of actually speaking lived in their mouths, as if they were afraid of uttering words right to the very end. The speech of the orally challenged—and their whole brogue is like that. Mealy-mouthed, incoherent and misshapen attempts to speak.

He could cure them. But his name was not on the list.

He was given an excellent mark for his dictation. He failed biology.

The Doctor walked to the station and bought a ticket for the bus home. The bus talked and talked, like pus oozing out of an open wound. His hope lay inside their mouths.

He donned his headphones and, unnoticed by anyone,

switched on his Dictaphone. They were all hopeless, these patients of his, returning from the symphonic music of the capital city to a domestic cacophony in which they could talk as they liked, not as they should. No, wait, there was hope. He had been making a thorough study of them and some time ago noticed that there were times when music would break through the mouths that had been so badly disfigured by that lump. He was interested in finding out if there was any correlation between the purity of the way they spoke and what it was they were talking about. Take that man over there with the shaven head—the one with a vaguely familiar face and a belt he's holding tight in his hand; he's obviously just been demobbed after completing his military service. He's tipsy, he feels relaxed, but there's a hard, tenacious look in his eyes, the look of someone who has done time. When he's talking to the old women about what's been happening while he's been away, there is no music to be heard, it's all mumbo-jumbo, but when he talks about himself, he makes an effort, he shapes the sounds inside himself, there's some animal instinct that makes him realise how a Human Being should speak.

By proper use of his tongue and the Lingo. Not the little bone that has stuck in his throat, not out of habit, not with milk and not with pork fat, not with pears from the orchard or tomatoes from the kitchen garden. Not with his granddad's ciggies and not with his miserable childhood. Just by proper use of his tongue and the Lingo.

In the autumn the Doctor was himself called up for military service. It was just as if he had changed places with that freshly demobbed bloke on the bus.

In the local military registration office sat a woman with a man's haircut, in soldier's boots, with legs shaped like a pair of riding breeches; she peered into the Doctor's mouth and announced, "Fit." "Can't you see?" he wanted to shout out. "Isn't it visible to the naked eye that I'm too healthy? That I was lucky and the lump didn't grow in size? That I've been spared? Maybe it's because my parents always wanted to move eastwards, where people know how to call things by their proper names and therefore know their true value? Or maybe it's because I've read all the books—the great books of a great literature—that I think can be understood only if you control your breathing and let all the sounds run on a leash that you hold firmly? Pushkin, Tolstoy, Lermontov, Chekhov, Nekrasov, Dostoyevsky. Those writers who nurtured the Lingo in people, who nurtured in them the music of the Lingo by recording it on human membranes. A heritage that here, in this godforsaken country, has been allowed to rot, in the belief that people can be left to speak in any way they want. That everything in the world is to do with language. That everyone can have their own mother tongue.

"Can you not see that I already am serving?" he wanted to say. "Serving the Lingo."

"D'youz huv somethin tae say tae me?" asked the woman, thumping her boots on the floor. There was a pair of scissors sticking out of the pocket of her white coat. It was with these that five minutes earlier she had threatened to cut the balls off of a schoolmate of the Doctor's. For trying to make a fool of her by complaining about his heart. "Whit hert?" she asked. "How d'youz knaw wherr a man's hert is?"

"D'youz no whant tae say something tae me, squaddie boy?"

The Doctor was confused. The woman impatiently pressed her arms against the table. The arms were hairy, like tropical plants.

"Awright then, repeat efter me: Sarge, the regimental colours huv been torched!" she ordered, looking at him with suspicion straight in the eye.

"Sergeant, the regimental colours have been set on fire," the Doctor repeated humbly.

"Ayc OK," and she gestured approvingly with her hand. "He's fit an weel."

But he hadn't repeated the sentence she wanted. He pronounced these stupid words in a quite different way. And she didn't notice. She didn't notice the music, didn't hear the Lingo. Just as she doesn't notice the little bone in her own military-uniformed mouth.

That same little bone. The tiny bone that you could spit out if you wanted.

He devoted himself entirely to chemistry during those dusty and hopeless months before call-up. It's just as well that an opportunity arose—and quite unexpectedly.

One evening soon after his inglorious return from his crusade to the capital city—an evening so quiet that you could even hear the blood trembling in your ears—the Doctor was out on the street and chanced to meet his old school chemistry teacher, the Chemist. Together they went back to the Chemist's place; they sat out in the yard and the Chemist fetched some of his homemade booze. The Doctor observed him with interest: there was something not quite right about the Chemist. Hidden in his eyes, once so full of authority, there was now some sort of kind-hearted, unclouded, harmless and absolutely untreatable insanity: like all teachers, the Chemist regarded his own subject as the most important of all the school subjects. The Chemist talked to the Doctor as an equal, like an adult; he argued with him, tried to prove things—and the Doctor could see that this was a man with the chin of a lion and the speech of a swineherd. He was unable to hear the sounds that were coming out of his own mouth ... The Doctor asked him for the keys to the school laboratory—and went on calmly spending time there right up to September, conducting experiments with a variety of substances.

This was risky—the laboratory supplies were running out, and the shortage could well arouse the curiosity of the school administration. Anything that the Chemist was unable to explain to him, the Doctor sought on the internet—and with every day the feeling grew in him that the alchemy of language was yielding up more and more of its secrets. He needed to understand the imperceptible connection that existed between mental state and the kind of language that he could hear everywhere: the level of purity of the sounds produced by these creatures depended not only on the situations in which they found themselves, but also, for example, on their stress levels, on their pathetic little pleasures, and on the extent to which they were free to give vent to their instincts.

There was plenty of work to be done! Whenever his compatriots' inner calm is disturbed, whenever their eyes are shining hysterically, or when they've been generously plied with Buckie from the kind monks down south, just like when the earth is well watered, they all talk quite differently from when they enter the Register Office, go to a parents' meeting in their children's school or attend a cultural event. Even the Chemist himself, when asked by the Doctor for a consultation on compounds and reactions, burst into such pure nightingale song that the Doctor at times forgot that in fact there was a patient standing before him, and that they both found themselves in a country dominated by a nasty, stupid little bone. However, all the Chemist had to do was to start talking about local news, about everyday run-of-the-mill matters, about stuff acquired and stuff stolen—and he was transformed into an ordinary cripple who was being suffocated from inside by his linguistic handicap.

They got together almost every day. The Doctor made sure that the Chemist had plenty to drink; he quickly became intoxicated, just as science demanded. The summer rolled like a windfall apple down the sandy path that leads to the garden gate; they sat in the garden in front of the open door of the Chemist's garage, chewing on sun-warmed tomatoes. From inside the little garage, the Chemist's Zhyguli kept watch on the Doctor with its round, unblinking pupils—the eyes of an assassin.[23] The Chemist was talking about how to catch fish, and about how the school headmaster had ended up in hospital after drinking too much raw spirit ... He spoke just like all the locals, and the Doctor looked into his mouth—as a faithful pupil would—and thought about how he had saved the poor fellow from the uselessness of his random bits of knowledge. Autumn came, the school laboratory was empty. On the first of September the Chemist hanged himself, in that very garage.[24] People said that he was ill, that he could no longer put up with the pain. But the Doctor knew the real reason. It was the Leid. Nothing else. You couldn't say anything to the world in the Leid. It thirsted after purification. But it was too late. The Doctor was lucky—he was assigned to the frontier troops.

That is how he started living in the forest. And this was the first forest in his life.

The forest compelled him to look at himself from another angle—as if it had kicked him all alone on to a sunlit clearing.

On one occasion he was with a detachment patrolling through a dense part of the forest, when they came across a barbed-wire fence. It was impossible to go around it; there was no end to it; it disappeared in the forest—that's the right word; it was just as if the fence was a direct continuation of the forest itself, as if it was growing directly out of the ground. They had to climb over it. On the other side of the fence, they found what was either an empty sanatorium, totally devoid of people, or an abandoned Young Pioneer camp. The wind, clearly in charge here, had sorted out the window frames and the doors, and a brilliant homespun patch of moss was spreading over the steps leading up to the buildings. A sports ground was rusting away in the middle of the buildings; at one end there was a stage neatly strewn with pine needles, as if they had been deliberately scattered there just before the people departed. There was a smell of rotten potatoes in the canteen. They reached the entrance gate along a barely visible overgrown path. Above it hung a sun of iron, peeling and spattered with bird shit. "Bluidy hell ... It's likes o 'Little Ray of Sunshine' concentration camp, ken?" joked the sergeant, with a note of sadness in his voice. He spat on the ground.

The forest had long ago taken control of this place. The wind dropped all of a sudden, and they began to feel uneasy. Their voices sounded dead, the sounds trailed off into nothingness; the air didn't hold them, and it didn't send them on either. Like receivers that had been switched off. It was then that the Doctor was struck forcefully by a sense of what isolation was—a way of purification. If he were to be abandoned here on his own for a week, he would either go mad or come to comprehend something really important. And what if the linguistically handicapped were to be left here? There would be nothing for them to waste sounds on. Everything superfluous would disappear into the void, into the pine needles, into the sand; it would fly off into the broken windows of the camp barracks.

And music would sound forth.

Meanwhile, the forest was waiting for them to leave. The forest was growing angry. It was a frontier forest, and no one wanted to start a quarrel with it. And so they left, shutting the entrance gate behind themselves.

Back at base, he at once turned his attention to a simpleton with a beetroot-red face called Bannock. For some unknown reason, Bannock had taken a liking to the Doctor right from the start and would always be coming up to him with tales of his life on civvy street. This was a dubious friendship—everyone made Bannock the butt of their ridicule. He was as daft as a brush with no bristles, and as naive as a child. He was the only one there from a village—clodhopper Bannock, Bannock the numptie. And "the Bannock 'Donald, Where's Your Troosers?' Arse."

That is what they called him in the base, just to see Bannock's little eyes begin to dart to and fro in panic, his hands shake and his face blush so furiously that you could half expect blood to come pouring out of his ears at any moment. And all because Bannock was unable to say the word "Private" like everyone else; instead, it came out with a heavily rolled "r," "Prrrrivate"; the bone in Bannock's throat—and the Doctor's thoughts were totally preoccupied with it—was probably as fat as a leg of lamb, and the Doctor really wanted to have a look at it. However, caution held him back. The Doctor strove not to be noticed, something he managed to achieve throughout the whole period of his military service. There was hardship here aplenty, but it was bearable. There weren't many people around; the forest governed everything. The Doctor followed the simple rules, asked for nothing extra, obeyed those who had to be obeyed—and secretly kept a close watch on Bannock. And then he dared to take a step. He began to slip a potion of his own devising into Bannock's food.

So Bannock fed himself into the trap. Right on to the tip of a scalpel.

One day when they had sat down for a short rest in a forest clearing Bannock said, "Awa the noo and all my faithful chum, your brain's big enough to fill my lum! I've just come down from the Isle of Skye, and yon Lingo's what I need och aye!" There was no one to see them. They weren't supposed to sit down, but they did and stretched their legs. The Doctor had the odd feeling that some unknown force had thrust him and this saddo together into the epicentre of bird twitter and slanting slices of sunshine, and this twittering was pure speech, the crystal-clear language of birds. And the birds would not have suffered Bannock to linger in their presence; they would have pecked him and driven him back to where the humans are. He had another thought as well: the inability to pronounce sounds correctly inevitably means the inability to hear them. Bannock cannot hear the magic of the forest, Bannock has crossed the line. Bannock asks his stupid questions at precisely the moment when there is music in the air. That is why people like Bannock have to be treated.

"And?" said the Doctor offhand.

"Mebbes you micht be tellin me where," Bannock shifted right up close to the Doctor. "One can be learnt how no to swear? You know, like you an oor bonnie sergeant? Awa the noo! Where is one learnt to ditch this rant?"

lum: chimney

"I don't know." The Doctor turned on his back and stared at the sky.

"It might only happen in the ceety, hoots! That would be such great peety," Bannock was fixated on the idea. "Although—d'you know, Doctor, I've heard some folk there speak the Leid and claim it's no the death o yon interlocutor; but then they're awa learnin' their lads and lassies it, which I'm sure you'll agree soonds awfy like pure *Braveheart* shit."

"I really know nothing about it." The Doctor tried to make his voice sound as calm as possible. "I'm not interested in politics."

"Ochone ochone!" Bannock was clearly upset. "Misery on my granny's heilan hame! I must forever hang my head in shame! Condemned to be a heuchter-teuchter blether, when all I want's to escape oor weather!"

"There are loads and loads of people like you there," said the Doctor. "And they manage. What difference does it make how you speak?"

"There was a soldier, a Scottish soldier, but e'er in *Brigadoon* he's portrayed," and Bannock gesticulated with his arms, "and by yon Central Belt betrayed."

"Well, once you move to the city, you won't even notice how you start speaking like everyone else." The Doctor rose to his feet. "Let's go."

It was not until the evening, when he heard the others making fun of Bannock yet again, that the Doctor sidled up to him as if quite by chance:

"I've read something about tablets that help you speak correctly. I can get some. I'll write to my mates and they'll bring them."

A week passed. Bannock was now undergoing a full experimental course of treatment. He asked the Doctor in private if

ochone: alas   *heuchter-teuchter*: (contempt.) pertaining to the Scottish Highlands

he could notice any improvement. The Doctor turned his eyes away and mumbled a few words about there being something of the kind. And that they were not laughing at Bannock so often. Bannock believed him. The Doctor, however, was waiting for a reaction.

What happened then was something that the Doctor could not possibly have reckoned with.

One night Bannock ran off. He ran off with a Kalashnikov and the Doctor's food supply. Bannock they never did find. They did find something else.

They found three dead soldiers, murdered while they were playing cards in a forest clearing. Their bellies had been ripped open, and all three corpses were displaying their trumps to the sun. Sated flies were buzzing around above the bodies. Not far from the base they found their sergeant, buried up to the waist in the ground—horrifyingly, headfirst. The legs were hanging in different directions and swaying; this in turn stirred the unravelled laces of his boots—the sergeant used to boast about these boots; they came from NATO. From the side, the sergeant's legs resembled a blind creature with long ears that had stopped right there and was now desperately demanding something. A twenty-man-strong group was immediately despatched to comb the forest. It was only in the evening that Bannock's uniform was found, covered in blood, by a lake where surprised fish were splashing around. Apart from the Doctor, no one ever learned about the last item that was found. Among the things that had been stolen from him, the Doctor discovered a scrap of paper with a verse scrawled on it. A verse which the Doctor took as a sign—a verse of thanks, a verse of recognition.

I've seen the glory, I've told the story, You gave me speech. You shoved it down my gob. You understood. The sergeant was a slob. Yours aye, B.

Yours aye, B ... They never did find Bannock. They found a boat full of blood; in it there was a side cap with a little star. They found Bannock's boots—the size was the same. They found footprints—the tracks of a frontier guard making his way barefoot along the lake, across marshland, towards a dry spot; trailing behind those tracks there was a set of bloody footprints, as clear as if they had been painted on. The Doctor told no one about the poem that Bannock had dedicated to him. No one was ever to find out about their conversations and the treatment. Investigators spent a long time interviewing Bannock's fellow squaddies. The Doctor told them everything he knew, everything he ought to have known, and then they left him alone.

The Doctor kept hold of that piece of paper. It was now inside his desk, in the drawer where his working notebooks and his books on orthoepy were. Today the Doctor remembered it, took it out and reread it.

You gave me speech. You shoved it down my gob.

Bannock was probably ashamed of what he had written back then.

He was always ashamed. The Doctor folded the piece of paper and returned it carefully to its place.

… When darkness fell and the Camp grew quiet—all that could be heard occasionally were the stern voices of the troop leaders— the Doctor switched off the lamp, stretched and removed his lab coat. He left the building through doors that only he knew about and stopped in front of the wire mesh fence. He stood for a bit, inhaling the nighttime scent of the spruces; their daytime scent was quite different. It was only at night that the spruces began to live. It was only in the evening twilight that the forest was prepared to talk to him. The Doctor shuffled some pine cones around with his feet. Perhaps that was a mouse running past. Or maybe a squirrel hurrying home for the night. Predators still ruled in this forest. The forest was huge—like the world.

He went up to the fence and lifted the wire in a place that only he knew. One of the troop leaders looked out from behind a tree and respectfully hid himself again to allow the Doctor to pass.

The Doctor walked along a path flooded with the light of the full moon and turned next to a special bush, stopped and stood for a moment to flick off some cobwebs on his sleeve.

"You are already here," he said sternly. "And you didn't even say 'good evening.'"

From among the trees came a guilty-sounding groan.

"Come on, show yourself." There was a distinct note of authority in the Doctor's voice. "I want to be sure that you are really here. Not everyone is so ashamed of their face. I always told you that the main thing is the voice. As for the face ... Believe me, there are no handsome men left in this fucking country."

A figure emerged from between the spruces, bared his brilliant white teeth, gave a brief howl and disappeared.

"Well, good evening to you, Bannock the arrrrse," said the Doctor maliciously. "Now listen. There are two of them: a girl and a little lad. Fifty kilometres to the north. You'll recognise them at once."

A groan came from among the spruces.

"The quicker, the better," said the Doctor gloomily, lost in his own thoughts. "The girl is more important. Now tell me, just before we part ... I want to be sure that you understand correctly. Who are they?"

"Poor children just come down from the Isle of Skye, no very big and awful shy," replied the tightly packed spruces.

"Good lad," and the Doctor put his hands in his pockets. "Poor children."

9

He who seeks: what does he fear?

He who seeks: what does he fear?

Most of all, of course, he fears finding.

And Faither really was afraid. The forest could palm him off with some other kind of Alicia. The forest could make her unrecognisable. It could do with her what people had not managed to do.

Faither did not believe that Alicia and Avi could return to the Camp. None of the forest roads that he had driven over in recent days could lead the children out to the right path. On the day of the children's escape they had covered their tracks well, changed routes, made huge loops on busy highways, thwarted the logic of traffic junctions and used minor side roads wherever there was a direct, straightforward road to follow. Anyone following them would have thought they were headed south, because all roads going north ran up against the frontier. To return to the Camp, Alicia needed a map. And that is what she and Avi didn't have.

Provided, of course, you didn't count the old atlas.

Only today Faither discovered that that yellowing, pointless atlas from the 1930s had disappeared out of the car. He fumbled around in the glove compartment trying to find a knife—he was dressed up like someone going out to collect mushrooms. On a Sunday morning the forest demanded some play-acting. What's more, he had already been stopped by a police patrol on a country road, either by chance, or because the car had been noticed after so much driving around; hundreds of people had seen him, however hard he tried. All the roads inside the forest formed a circle; today he was going to start searching again at the place where he had given up yesterday.

His fingers came into contact with the knife, and he realised that the children had taken the atlas with them.

At one time Alicia and he used to love lying on the floor together, examining the roads marked in the atlas. Touching them with their fingers, driving towards each other and meeting, crossing frontiers and escaping from war. And they loved coming up with cars—the wonderful cars of the twenties and thirties, certainly not the dull monsters they make these days. They had a book about old cars—and they both had their own favourites: convertibles, landaus, a car like Kupala's, a car like Stierlitz's . . .[25] "Tae get ahint the wheel o a motor like yon wad be mairvelous!" said Alicia, and he promised: "Aye, we'll shuirly dae that. Sometime we'll drive tae a place whare we needna ayeweys haud oor wheesht. Whare oor Leid maun be regarded a langage humaine lik onyither. Whare the Lingo's no gien a special place. Whaur ye dinna tak bairns frae parents acause o the langage they spak. Whaur we're no obliged tae be ayeweys joukin aboot. Thare's a special garage thare fu o auld motors. Ye pay thaim cash an ye can drive aroun aw day. Ye choose the motor ye want, ye get ahint the wheel an awa ye go. Ye maun jist retour yon motor same day." Alicia looked at Faither, and her eyes gleamed like two headlights in the fog of the room. And then Faither used to pretend to sound a car horn by pressing lightly on the palm of her hand: toot-toot, too-oo-oot! It's no wonder that she didn't want to part with this well-worn volume.

She's probably sitting with Avi somewhere beneath a tree, and they are studying it together and tracing the roads with their fingers. Avi was Faither's hope. Avi had to know what to do.

Clutching the knife tightly in his pocket, Faither walked on through a stand of birches that soon gave way to a mass of fir trees. Here it was darker, but nevertheless the forest surprised Faither with the number of people there were. People loomed

ahint: behind

among the trees like buildings and came towards Faither with their eyes cast down. People with buckets large and small, jars, baskets ... The forest which now surrounded him—the forest he hoped this time to merge with completely, where he wanted to sink into its mossy floor and there find at least a trace—this forest was beginning to resemble a city street on a Sunday morning, throbbing with passersby who seemed to be drunk on some unknown potion. Faither stubbornly headed for where the darkness was thickest, but at the same time strove not to appear as though he was in a hurry. Foostie-baws. Ah'm oot gaitherin foostie-baws, *Agaricus campestris*. Here, in this country of his, that's like a confession of faith. A foostie-baw i yer haund's lik a wee cross roun yer craig. Ah'm rangin fir foostie-baws. Fact is, ah only need a couple. Ah'll skive thaim aff an cart them awa. An this forest'll ne'er hae sicht o me agin. Naebody here'll be seein us agin.

Whatever happens, Avi will know what to do. Fall to the ground like a tree so that Alicia can cross a swamp. Transform himself into a hiding place if there are search parties out looking for her. Serve as a shield to ward off any blows that are, of course, intended for him, her Faither, but which are as usual aimed at the child. Be a key for her if there are any doors that have to be opened. Be a sledgehammer for her if a wall should suddenly grow up before his Sia. Be a sturdy rope ladder if she ever has to climb out of a hole. Be her deafness if that Lingo of theirs comes to assault her on all sides like poisonous smoke, full of alien, stifling sounds.

He ought never to have left her on her own. It ought to have been like it was before, in their past life, when Alicia emerged from her school, so lonely and open to every danger. She seemed so light as she came down the steps of the school entrance and out into the street, as if she were transparent. The other children knocked into her with their elbows, but she never looked round; it was like she floated across the schoolyard. She stood out like a clear word in the midst of mindless babbling.

Out she would come on to the pavement and stand, as she always did, by the newspaper kiosk that was closed for lunch. Faither would hurriedly go up to greet her, each time with a heavy heart. She never once sought him out with her eyes; she simply stood there, staring into space. Her eyes spoke, and only he could hear and understand what they were saying.

There were times when he had just got out of his car and at a distance could see adults stopping in front of her and looking with disapproval at her old dress and clumsily knotted pigtail. Sometimes they tried to strike up a conversation with her and she would slowly raise her eyes up to them. They were struck dumb by the look she gave them, and, obviously deflated, rapidly melted into the crowds on the busy street. She stood there quite alone, alone in the whole wide world. His heart bled for her at the realisation that she is the world, she is the purpose of the world. She and the Leid that lives in her feather-light childhood.

Once he had come within a hair's breadth of an accident. It was as if the sky itself had got lost in the huge wheel that suddenly appeared from somewhere up above, winding around itself the view from the side window, the street, the chestnut trees and the lampposts. In a flash he realised that he would be the next to be caught up by this centrifugal force bearing down from the right. With a final inhuman movement he managed to twist the wheel like he was turning himself inside out. The car struck a brick wall which scraped the whole of the left side. The whole business ended with nothing worse than a lot of cursing and some cosmetic repair. He had been on his way to collect Alicia and was two hours late. She was standing on exactly the same spot next to the kiosk. He kissed her on the forehead that was so cold he could have been kissing a statue.

"Ah'm sair vext fur ye," he said to the forehead.

And he realised that she had been standing here singing. To herself. The songs of solitary Sia.

At that very moment the thought struck Faither for the first time: the day will come when he will be unable to come to collect her. He will be somewhere stuck out there in that frantic rushing around outside the car's right-hand window.

She'll be standing here for such a long, long time, singing the songs that only she can hear. Sooner or later though, someone is bound to turn up who will take her by the hand and lead her away. That someone will begin to creep closer to her code and intercept the message that was never intended for him.

"Ah'll gie ye awthings," he used to say at night, listening intently to her breathing. "The only thing ah canna gie ye's a brither. Ah'd be hauf wumman tae gie wan tae ye. Ah'd be wi bairn the nicht (an no mynd it tae be terrifyin, stiflin) throu spauldin ma self, thru welcomin m' ain shaidae tae bide inside o me. Ah'd mak him steidfest, an he'd be wi ye, he'd pertect ye an the Leid stowed insides o ye. But ah canna be wumman, e'en fur ma wee Sia . . .

"Ah'll gie her awthings," he used to say to the Jew hanging on the wall. The Jew Perelman. "Only thing ah canna dae's gie her a brither. But ah dinna hae the richt tae *no* dae that. *O thou, my elder brother in misfortune, By far my elder brother in the Muse* gie's a help-haund, Jew. Thou thruive, an sicweys an thus y're brither tae me." Sia's Faither could do any number of things, *With tears I pity thy unhappy fate*—go mad, die, hit the bottle, renounce her. But he was aware he had no right to do any of them.

And that, presumably, is how Aviator appeared.

***

In the town there was a market ringed by upright concrete slabs, with serried ranks of marquees and stalls that looked for all the world as though their owners had been rounded up and forced to come here, and were therefore all selling the same thing; in this selfsame market, in summer when wasps like gold rings crawled

the nicht: tonight   *spauldin*: splitting open   *pertect*: protect   *thruive*: thrived

between the fingers of the fruit and veg vendors and in winter they had piles of trousers for sale that felt hard as if they had been made out of tree bark, and slap-bang right in the middle of it all there was an old chap with a nose like a stuffed bird's beak who day after day laid out his wares for sale.

So, what did he sell, this old bloke? It would be easier to ask what he didn't sell. You really could buy anything from him the world had to offer—as long as there was room for it on his little folding table. Here was a man who seemed to be without problems of any kind: none with history, none with time or geography, and certainly none with languages—he spoke all of them. And all because his name was Aron Abramovich Hillel; it's almost impossible to faze anyone with a name like that. Or with nasal hair like that either; in Aron Abramovich's case, the hairs reached right down to his upper lip.

Whenever Faither and Alicia paid a visit to the market, they would walk past his table standing beneath a homemade awning. Faither always felt a strong dislike for the old man sitting there with an expression on his face that showed he had not a care in the world.

So, one cold autumn day he and Alicia came up to Aron Abramovich's table, but Faither was quite unable to broach the subject he wanted to talk about. Instead he at first bought a tin of paint and a pair of scissors and walked away, dragging the obedient Alicia behind him. Only then did he go back to the table and clear his throat to gain attention. Aron Abramovich's nasal hairs began to tremble.

"Now what kind of little girl do we have here?" he said pensively. There was a cunning expression on his face when he looked at Alicia. "Oy, but it's one of mine. Little girls like her I sell for a hundred thousand apiece. She must have fallen out of her box. Give her back, please. I'll sell her for two hundred."

Alicia said nothing, but was trying very hard to understand what on earth was going on.

"I'm telling you, she's one of mine," muttered Aron Abramovich. "My little girls always keep shtum. They only ever talk at home when no one can hear what they're saying. A very convenient model. And the main thing is, it doesn't get in anyone's way."

Faither grabbed Alicia by the hand to tear her away, but she continued to stare straight at Aron Abramovich's nostrils and the thick red hairs protruding out of them that were all aquiver like tongues.

"You know what can happen with little girls like that? They start saying something when you're out on the street, and then shame you in front of people." Aron Abramovich was beginning to babble. "Wait a moment, my little girl's lost something. Look, it's fallen out of her mouth. Let's put it back in place."

He deftly placed a neatly unwrapped sweet in Alicia's mouth. Her lips closed round it, as if it was exactly what she had been waiting for.

"I need to talk to you," said Faither, feeling sick and fearful. "I need *a thing* ..."

"*I don't sell things singly.*" Aron Abramovich cut him short. "*Put in a wholesale order. This table can accommodate any amount of any thing. It's just like your mouth—it can hold all the words there are, but not just any one particular word.*"

So it was that they left empty-handed. Faither didn't know how to talk to this weird, none-too-pleasant man. A week later he came back again, but this time without Alicia. He ambled round and round the table, sometimes making wide circles and at other times coming in closer. Aron Abramovich didn't notice him, or at least pretended not to. At precisely six that evening Aron Abramovich gave orders to some suspicious-looking types—all of them like him—to clear the table, and then made for the exit. Faither, trying hard to stay out of sight, followed.

At first it was easy for Faither to go unnoticed. Aron Abramovich was walking along Lenin Street where there were always lots of people, then he turned into Soviet Street and came out on to Chemists' Square. From there he started up Uritski Street in the direction of the private housing sector.[26] He kept an even, unhurried pace, but with sudden jerky movements that made it seem as though he was getting ready at any moment to fall face first on the pavement. Faither hid behind trees and tried to look as though he was waiting for a bus at the empty, leaf-strewn bus stops. Or else he had to stand stock still, peering into other people's gardens, a piece of impudence that infuriated the dogs. Aron Abramovich turned left into an alleyway, and Faither made up his mind that the right moment had come. It took him three steps to catch up with Aron Abramovich's shadow; the man himself had already managed to creep into a dark passageway between the houses. Faither was just on the point of calling out to Aron Abramovich, when he suddenly realised that he had disappeared. As if he had never been. *O thou, my elder brother* ... Utterly confused, Faither looked all around. The dogs were pulling at their chains and barking as if they hadn't seen another human being for ages. The street was indeed completely empty and there was no light burning anywhere, although it was beginning to get dark. "Go, go, go" is what Faither seemed to hear the dogs yelling at him. All of a sudden, his legs felt like cotton wool and his heart began to weave a terrifying void around itself. Feverishly he started looking around for a spot where he could sit down for a moment. He knew the feeling would soon pass. It had to.

The scarcely audible sound of movement in the distance caught his ear, and he moaned "Aron Abramovich!" He knew that he could not bear any more of this tension and fear.

But no response came. Behind his back he heard the clacking of heels. Someone was coming straight for him with arms outstretched—long, long arms, the length of the street. Faither covered his face with his hands. *With tears I pity thy unhappy fate! Why is the Bard unfitted for the world, Yet has so keen a relish of its pleasures?*

"Is it you who lost this?" a woman's voice said. Unexpectedly appearing like a pale ghost from out of the half-light, a figure clacked on past him. Faither could make out that it was a young woman, one of the types who work up at the office of the chemical factory. He looked cautiously all around and then turned his gaze to the ground. Right next to his feet, on the very spot where only a few moments ago Aron Abramovich had been walking, there was a packet. Faither picked it up, tore off a corner and pushed his finger inside. The packet was full of wet clay. Like a mouth full of words that should under no circumstances ever be uttered.

This clay, which Faither brought home and hid on the balcony, was the forerunner of certain events. For a long time he didn't dare go anywhere near it. And when he did, those events started happening, one after the other, bad events, and there was no end to them.

"I need to talk to you," said Miss Edwardson to him one Monday morning, when he, as he always did, brought Sia to school and kissed her goodbye. Sia went up to the school door: you could see the decisiveness of her back and the stubbornness of the nape of her neck. Here was a girl who could overcome anything, a girl firmly locked within herself. Miss Edwardson watched him with sadness in her eyes and, raising her eyebrows in invitation, said:

"Let's have a talk in my office. It's serious."

Faither knew what it was she wanted to talk about. *Weel-mounted on his grey mare, Meg, A better never lifted leg, Tam skelpit on thro' dub and mire, Despising wind, and rain, and fire;*

"No time," he said rudely. "I've got to go to work."

"I won't keep you long," said Miss Edwardson calmly, looking him straight in the eye. "It's to do with your child. And you don't really have a job to rush off to, do you? You're a taxi driver, I think. And at night you don't do what you ought to be doing. I can tell by your eyes. You just want to get some sleep, don't you?"

And so he gave way and let himself be led up the stairs like a sheep to the first floor. *She ventur'd forward on the light; And, Wow! Tam saw an unco sight!* Those black tights and the skin that shone through them with a dull glimmer! *Her cutty sark, o' Paisley harn, That while a lassie she had worn, In longitude tho' sorely scanty, It was her best, and she was vauntie.* And that hair, falling over her shoulders in waves as if they were underwater! He was hypnotised by them. Taxi driver ... Hmmm, she must have found out somehow about his illegal bit of work on the side. The one thing she didn't know, though, was that he, a graduate of the philological faculty of the university, was a very bad taxi driver. He very rarely picked up any fares. It was as if his car gave off a disastrous smell of defeat, and potential passengers could sense it. *Ah! Little kend thy reverend granie, That sark she coft for her wee Nannie, Wi twa pund Scots ('twas all her riches)*

Her office was well aired, and there was a distinct odour of perfume and coffee. He was amazed at how clean it was. Cleanliness was something to which he was unaccustomed. And that voice! That pure voice! *Wad ever grac'd a dance of witches!*

"You reek of drink, by the way. Are you a drinker?"

"Is there anyone in this town who isn't?" and Faither gave a wry smile. He spoke the Lingo with a heavy accent. *But here my Muse her wing maun cour, Sic flights are far beyond her power;*

"And you smoke as well ..." Miss Edwardson's pure voice rang clear in the crackling whiteness of this ideal room, *To sing how Nannie lap and flang, (A souple jade she was and strang)* just as the very air itself seems to ring on a bright winter's day. "Tell me, what is it you and Sia do together when you're at home. And at what time does she go to bed."

And how Tam stood, like a bewitch'd, And thought his very een enrich'd The words came out of Faither's mouth in a somewhat confused manner because they were all mixed up in his head.

What he related was the story he had concocted with Sia—a brief account of those "scientific recommendations" that he had been given over the years by teachers and other specialists, all of them so anxious about "our poor little girl." They advised him to spend more time with his daughter in the fresh air, they prescribed cold baths, they persistently reminded him that Alicia should make friends and paint human figures. Faither's gloomy voice went on to talk about how they go to the park after school, how they go to the country at weekends, how they do physical exercises together in the pine forest near their flat. And then there are the wall bars that Alicia has at home, and she has a little friend called Liuda, and the two of them paint whole crowds of funny, jolly compatriots holdings bunches of daffodils and wearing flower crowns.

An five tomahawks, wi' bluid red-rusted;
Five scimitars, wi' murder crusted;
A garter, which a babe had strangled;
A knife, a faither's throat had mangled,

he wanted to add, but refrained. All this was pure fabrication. Alicia spent the whole time at home, and she didn't know anyone. Faither and Alicia together listened to music, read old books, painted only animals, and taught her dolls their language. Nothing else was possible. She was a messenger on a mission, and he was her bodyguard. He, her faither, had the task of protecting Alicia and the Leid from the poisonous Lingo, and that poison was everywhere.

Even Satan glowr'd, and fidg'd fu' fain,
And hotch'd and blew wi' might and main:

It seeped into all the pores of the town, it was spoken by all the seasons of the year: the one right language, the one pure language, the one great language, the only healthy language.

"Why is your pronunciation so bad?" asked Miss Edwardson, frowning as she placed a cup of coffee in front of him. "After all, you were born in the capital, you studied there ..."

Here, in the confines of a locked office, Faither was well aware that his words did sound uncouth, that he was unable to cope with that blasted Lingo. Usually, after leaving Alicia by her school he would sit in his car and try once again to tune himself into the Lingo, to switch off within himself all the little lights and knobs of his native Leid, and that's how it would be until the evening when Alicia and he once again crossed the threshold of their fortress and shut the door.

Today she had caught him unawares

(For monie a beast to dead she shot,
And perish'd monie a bonnie boat,
And shook baith meikle corn and bear,
And kept the countryside in fear);

and had deliberately brought him to this room where everything is heard exactly as it is pronounced. Where the only thing to be heard is the truth.

"I speak just like everyone speaks in this town," he said with a guilty smile on his face. Miss Edwardson shook her head:

"No, you don't. I can hear perfectly well that you are trying to talk like everyone. Believe me, you're not very good at it. You're clever and very devious."

And she lowered her eyebrows in sorrow, only in the very next moment to fix him with her steely eyes: "Your daughter doesn't hear pure language being spoken at home. And she doesn't want to listen to it in school. It's really noticeable, especially when there's a chance to observe her during group activities. Perhaps you don't quite understand me ..."

"Why maun ah unnerstaund ye?" he shouted in his thoughts. "Y're fremmit. Y've nae richt tae be unnerstood. E'en the grund ye stap oan willna unnerstaund ye."

"What is there to understand?" he said cautiously. "I'll try to do more drawing with Sia.

Till first ae caper, syne anither.

Drawings of people."
Drawins o hures.

Tam tint his reason a thegither.

"Sure, Sia doesn't speak," Miss Edwardson declared solemnly, drilling into him with her eyes. "But here the point lies in the fact that she does write. And in what she writes. Here, take a look at this. Maybe you really don't know what is going on in her head. But this—this whatever you call it!—amply demonstrates the kind of monstrosity of a language, if you can call it a language at all, that she hears in her head."

And Miss Edwardson, without letting the piece of paper out of her hand, allowed him to read a few lines written in pleadingly red-coloured pencil. He swallowed it avidly. This was written by Sia. His very own Alicia. He read it as if it was a letter written from prison.

"The little girl and the peech.

Once there was a little girl sitting alone in an empty room, and on the table laid a peech. The peech spoke a tung of its own, and the little girl couldna understand it. But she wonted very much to talk to it, and then she putted it in her mouth and started chewing it. And the peech stane jumpt right into the wee girls mouth and stayd there. An artist who by chans lookt in at the window drew a picture of the seen. The little girl tryd to spit out the stane, but she couldna. And so she dyed with the stane in her mouth. But she didna fall, because the heavy peech stane kept her on the chair. And everyone thought that she was alive alive alive."

hures: whores

"Where did she get that from?" asked Miss Edwardson in a hushed voice. "And what sort of language is this?"

"Well, you can understand it, can't you?" muttered Faither. "And as for the language ... It's her language. Her own language."

"There's no such thing as one's 'own language,'" Miss Edwardson stated slowly and clearly. "There is a language that society uses. For some reason that is not the language that Sia hears in her head. What's more, Sia ignores the language that she can hear people speak. And I suspect that you encourage her in this."

"She is seeking a language that will be natural for her," whispered Faither.

"People do not get to choose a language. A natural language is one which will help her become a full member of society. She will always lag behind in her development if she continues to use the language that she can hear in her head, the horrendous hotchpotch that her unfortunate brain produces—not, I might add, without some help from you. Oh yes, and by the way, here's one of her drawings. It's your portrait. Take a good look at it. That's how she sees the place where she lives."

She held out a sheet of paper that had been torn out of an exercise book. In the middle was a painting of a man all coloured black sitting above some kind of icon in a black frame. Sticking out between his legs there was something elongated, huge, straining—there was no telling whether it was a bottle or a penis.

"This is you. Can you recognise yourself? That's the kind of person she sees at home."

"There are all sorts of things she could have drawn."

"Maybe so, but she did this drawing. She could have gone on drawing some more. She was really keen."

"Where did you get this drawing from? Was it a special task that was set in class?" asked Faither, lowering his eyes.

"She did the drawing in the toilet. She locked herself in. It took us quite a while to find her."

"What you're saying is that this drawing wasn't something she was told to do in class. Is that right?"

"What difference does it make?"
"Ye stealt it," said Faither.

And roars out "Weel done, Cutty-sark!"

"What? What did you say just then?"

And in an instant all was dark.

"Ye stealt it. Ye chored it frae ma wee lassie. Stealt, nae dout aboot it. Yon's aw yir pedagogie: dippin yir digits intae some ither body's pootch, intae thair saul, intae thair mooth."

"You're saying some very odd things there. Are you all right?"

The bell rang. Without a word Faither bounded out of the office. Just as he was closing the door he thought he saw a look of almost physical pleasure on her face.

A week passed. It occurred to him that he had given up keeping the diary that he had started so long ago. The diary was not about his life with Alicia, but concerned a completely different Faither and a completely different daughter, living alone in a completely different country and awaiting rescue, but there was a nagging feeling inside him that he ought to hide it. He put it among Alicia's old toys. Who is ever going to bother to rummage around in children's toys?

By now Faither and Sia were arriving late for school every day. Faither had no wish to once again come face-to-face with those steely eyes and the hair that suffocated him in his dreams. But things were not that simple. One evening, when the two of them were playing chess together on the sofa, the thunderous ringing of the doorbell resounded in their private sky, right above the chessboard.

Outside the door was Miss Edwardson. Faither opened the door slightly and looked out. She was standing there soaked; the

chored: stole

raincoat she was wearing made her look so slender that you could easily get the urge to break her. There was such an intoxicating scent coming from her hair that Faither couldn't help going out on to the landing, but keeping his hand on the door handle—just in case.

"Good evening," said Miss Edwardson, giving her luxurious hair a shake. "There's something I have to talk to you about. Please open the door. I hope that Sia is at home."

How well she can pronounce her name! There isn't a single one of the others who can say it like she does. The bitch must have been practising hard.

"Why?" asked Faither exhausted.

"We're conducting a survey of the conditions in which our children live at home, and so, of course, I decided to call on you."

"First off, you should have w-w-warned me," and Faither's Adam's apple was working furiously. She interrupted him sharply: "So that you could evade any kind of responsibility? So that you could fool those idiots from the school by constructing a neat little Potemkin village in this stinking hole of yours, a hole where that poor little girl is dying because of your obsession? Open the door and let me in. I want to see Sia."

"Non, ye durna come in." Faither felt that his voice had become firmer, but Miss Edwardson burst into laughter. "You can't even talk properly. You're drunk, like you always are. Do you understand that you could be stripped of your parental rights?"

"It wasna ye wha gied me yon richts, an it's no fur ye tae tak them awa." The look she gave Faither flattened him against the dirty landing wall, but he still resisted; he was prepared to strike her if she managed to get past him into his home. "I can hear the drink talking when you speak," she laughed. Any minute now she's going to try to get in—and he'll grab her by the hair, pull her down to the dirty floor and then—darkness, non-existence, happiness, silence.

But she didn't do anything except simply sweep her hair from her forehead and smile:

"Listen, I just want to help. I know how difficult it can be to raise a daughter alone, without her mother. Not that I've had any experience, of course, but my empathy is sufficiently well developed. I feel very sorry for you. It's obvious you can't cope. Let other people help you. That'll be better for all concerned, and especially for our Sia. Incidentally, why did you call her that?"

"Awa hame," and Faither gestured with his hand. "I'm not going to let you in. Ah'm no gonnae let ye in. Dinna even try. Ah canna bear tae hear yir mongrel Lingo ony mair."

"You're delirious," she said and stretched out her arm. He leapt back.

"Dinna lay a fuckin haund oan me!"

"Don't swear," said Miss Edwardson gently and licked her lips. For a split second Faither blacked out and then he hurried back into the flat and bolted the door. He knew that the neighbours had seen everything. He knew too that Miss Edwardson was standing very close, leaning against the door a mere finger's breadth away. And she really did start talking, somewhere very, very close:

"Open up, Daddy, otherwise things will go very differently for you. I've already had a talk with the neighbours. What they told me is absolutely horrendous."

"Awa an screw yirsel," said Faither softly, but expressively, and then went back to Alicia, where the sky above the chessboard had once again cleared and there were no more claps of thunder. And Sia won the game.

After dropping Sia off at school a few days later, Faither was driving slowly along the high street behind a bus when he saw Miss Edwardson in the same raincoat. She was walking at the same pace as the car, noticed him and waved as though nothing untoward had happened. This finally finished him off. He stopped the car, got out—and now here they are in a café, and an excessively sweet cake is stuck on the roof of his mouth, and the clinking of teaspoons has announced the coming of the dénouement.

"I'm on holiday," said Miss Edwardson. "You're in luck, you have a reprieve. Think about it."

Then came vodka, and the town park, and the car that didn't want to start. And there were the steely eyes that gradually became simply grey, and in this greyness he just wanted to be himself.

"You have to tell me everything. I'll find out anyway."

On the next day she was talking quite differently. On that very same sofa where Faither and Alicia loved playing chess together. Alicia was already in school, and in a low predatory voice Miss Edwardson was uttering words which it was impossible to make out. Seizing her hair and pressing her head into the pillow Faither answered her, and the fuzz on the nape of her neck stood upright as if ruffled by the wind. Choking on his own saliva, he thrust his tongue into her and she became the Leid. And then he fell asleep.

Faither well remembered that morning. He woke up and groaned without opening his eyes. He felt as though the whole town was standing on his belly. And then he heard voices close by. Very close.

"This colour would go very well here, don't you think, Sia?"

He jumped up quite naked, exactly like he was on the drawing that he'd been shown in the school by this scary woman with legs in black tights, legs that he so wanted to bite right through and let the blood come oozing out.

"Now let's draw a ... a ... you know what I mean, something that would be hanging down, like dogs do when they're hot ... What is it we've drawn on him?"

Alicia answered—and in her voice there was joy such as he had never before heard from her:

"A tongue!"

Miss Edwardson was sitting on the floor, dressed in that same raincoat of hers. And in front of her sat Alicia, looking at an array of pencils laid out like a fan.

"So here we are, already friends," she smiled. "And, as we can see, Daddy is a little mistaken. We're speaking just like everyone does, and no one's died yet. Oh well, never mind, daddies can sometimes make mistakes too. That's right, isn't it, my little ray of sunshine?"

"Aye, that's richt," said Sia, looking intently at Miss Edwardson with eyes once so deep, and now childish, foolish and empty. "Paw, see whit we're drawin? Aye but guess first whare ah'm tae gang this simmer?"

He couldn't remember if he had struck Miss Edwardson at that moment. More likely he missed. Anyway, she left of her own volition, slowly retreating towards the door, step by step, touch by touch, each one of which she was obliged to leave here, and word by word—words that he didn't listen to, so great was his hatred of himself.

"What you're doing to her is a crime," she hissed, moving backwards towards the doorway. "You're condemning her to a life among demons. Among monsters! There is no 'Leid,' there hasn't been for a very long time, and indeed there never was one. There is no Leid, but the demons remain. You feel comfortable with them, but you are making her a cripple."

He raised his arm, she screwed up her eyes

And flew at Tam wi furious ettle

"A Pure Language will restore her to life," she sang.

But little wist she Maggie's mettle—
Ae spring brought aff her master hale,
But left behind her ain grey tail;

And her hair wound itself around her head.

The carlin caught her by the rump
And left poor Maggie scarce a stump.

"No other way is possible. Children must have a clear, pure voice. Children are Life, and your Leid is death."

"Ah'll slauchter ye."

"No, you can't," she laughed. "Your Leid isn't capable of doing even that. It's dead. You put your daughter in a grave and don't let her escape from it. But we're going to put that right. We're going to put it right very soon, aren't we, Sia?"

She never came again, but Faither and Alicia did start receiving letters with official seals and coats of arms. He didn't read them. He just threw them on the floor and trampled on them. His trampling was so enthusiastic that Alicia gladly joined in, and together they launched into a kind of wild dance for two. Other people came, more and more often, banging on the door, waving wads of papers, threatening them with the courts. There was no question of Alicia going to school. They didn't leave the flat any more or open the door to anyone. There were people shouting by the door, repeating something about a law, the Language Law, always languages, languages, languages. It was all beginning to sound like delirious blathering, or a prayer in the Old Lingo. A phrase got stuck in Faither's head: "Thou shalt become an astonishment among all nations." Thou shalt become an astonishment? Ridiculous bloody language. No more concessions, no more games.

Whenever the yelling and banging on the door became unbearable, Faither and Alicia would begin to sing. They sang all the folk songs they knew—about the rose, about the little cottage made of goosefoot, about the knight on horseback, and about the three sons. The louder the demands to enter made on the other side of the door, the greater the number of holes that appeared on their clay whistles—that's what they called their voices now.

"Ye sing sae braw."

"Jist same weys as ye, Faither."

One day the door did come open wide. Just before it did (there was an almighty crack, and it was obvious that the lock wouldn't hold), Faither went out on to the balcony and looked down at the street through the dirty window. There was nowhere to run to, and so he said a prayer and sat back down.

And then there was an explosion in the front hall. In an instant the flat was full of people; it was as if a sack full of Christmas presents from a doll factory had burst above their heads. Faither and Alicia were sitting on the floor examining an atlas, and people were running around saying something, but what Faither could not understand. His Lingo had run out. Someone seized Alicia by the arms, she made no attempt to escape. By now booted feet were tramping all over the flat. The balcony door squeaked, and a man in a cap went out cautiously into the piles of rags and empty bottles and the fog that had penetrated during the night.

"Hang on!" he shouted. "There's another one out here!"

For a second complete silence reigned.

"Another child!" And the man in the cap brought from the balcony a little boy, a bit shorter than Alicia but wider in the shoulders.

A completely naked little boy.

"Is this your child?" a woman in a fur hat asked. Her tone was threatening.

Faither nodded, but that wasn't enough.

"Is this your little brother?" Alicia was asked, and she gave a nod too.

"What's your name?" said the menacing woman, but someone called out from behind her back:

"Just put some clothes on him!"

"You bastard," said the policeman, looking at Faither and twisting his arms behind his back so you could hear the bones crack. "Types like you ought to be done away with."

"I've already told you: don't shnittker. There's no need for any shnittkering here!" Faither turned round when he heard this voice, and saw that a neighbour was looking through the open door of the flat. It was the same neighbour who at one time thought that he heard Alicia crying. Ridiculous. Faither had never heard his daughter cry.

An sicweys, Jew, hae the maiter endit.

There were children standing behind the neighbour's back, a

whole brood of them. Children who could speak, who did not have to hide from anyone. It would be interesting to find out if this made them happy. Children who were born just like that, without a mission. The children were looking at him with interest; in their huge eyes there was neither hatred nor disapproval. And the little boy who had been found on the balcony looked at them. He was just like any normal little boy, but all the same there was something that didn't quite fit. As if he was the son of a foreign spy, or simply the son of a foreign tourist.

"What's your name, sonny?" asked a young lady with a camera that was pointing straight at the boy's face.

"Ah'm an aviator, but ye may cry me Avi," the boy said and looked sullenly at the team of medics—three young male nurses and a drunken woman doctor with a Gladstone bag who had no idea how to approach him.

"Ah'm an aviator, but ye may cry me Avi," the boy said again, this time behind Faither's back. Faither was being led out of the room. Avi said the words clearly, in a way that Faither would remember. And remember he did. Morning, fog outside the windows, the smell and noise of strangers in the place where he had been happy, fuss, rustling of papers, pencils strewn all over the floor, dirty footprints on the floor, words, words, words. And the childish bass voice of his son—a son who was so familiar, as if he had always been living with them here and had read the same books.

> Now, wha this tale o' truth shall read,
> Ilk man and mother's son, take heed:
> When'er to drink you are inclin'd,
> Or cutty-sarks rin in your mind,
> Think! ye may buy the joys o'er dear:
> Remember Tam o' Shanter's mare.

cry: call

10
Youz'll huv the best waddin o yer puff

"Youz'll huv the best waddin o yer puff," said Granmaw bending down over the pit, and she cackled. Then she looked suspiciously at Alicia:

"He's no been feelin ye up, huz he? He didnae try tae gie ye a lumber durin the night, eh? *Eh?* Ah'm no sure, yir T-shirt's aw fankled. Jist watch it, hen, it's aw gonnae get done right guid an proper—the wey it's ayeweys been."

Granmaw had started preparing for the wedding early in the morning. For Alicia she plaited a cornflower crown, and found one made of straw for Avi. And for both of them she made a whole sack of nettles ready. They couldn't see the nettles, but Granmaw was providing a loud commentary on everything she was doing from her place on the very edge of the pit. They were agasp with alarm at what they heard, and meanwhile hunger was squealing in their tummies, and the voice from above was pressing down on them like a saucepan lid:

"Ah'm gonnae dress ye aw up wae jaggie-nettles; ah'll stitch yer claes masel. Best quaaality medicinal jaggies they ur, thay'll pit aw that daftie stuff right oot yer heids. Aw yer skin's gonnae come aff whance yese stairt crawlin aroon doon therr scratchin yirsel oan the groond. Ah really luve it, whan skin's jist aboot tae peel aff. Whan ah wis young ah goat psoriasis. Wee scunners likes o youz turnit thur backs oan me: ah gied them the dry boak, an they shoutit, 'Who's goat the scalies? Who's goat the scalies?

jaggie: stinging   *scunners*: loathsome objects   *dry boak*: retching without vomiting   *scalies*: scabies

You've goat the scalies!' Right, weans, noo it's *yoor* turn tae huv the scalies, an ah'll jist watch!" Granmaw burst into a fit of either laughing or coughing, it was impossible to tell which. The thought occurred to both Avi and Alicia simultaneously—after all, their thoughts also found themselves side by side in the same pit—that it is not always a Good Thing to have a Granmaw.

"Folk doontoon therr think ah dee'd yonks ago," Granmaw went on. "An thay'd no be wrang. So faur as thay're concernit, ah did dee. Ah torched yon but 'n' ben ah hud doontoon. But it wisnae empty. Therr wis an auld hoor insides. Ah goat hauld o some wumman unner a brig an ah shoudered her back tae the but 'n' ben. Yon weys they aw thought how it wis me in therr. Except but it wisnae but. Ah'd scarpered tae the forest, an the forest cured me pronto, see? Ma skin's pure dead brilliant noo. Goat the green eye fur it hen? Eh? *Eh?*"

"Ah've the feelin that Granmaw's goat a ferr fantice," said Alicia. "Whan ah wis gangin in the schuil, ah sairly wanted tae be imaiginative. Acause gin ye use yir imagination thare's nae need o a carte tae gang tae Bremen."

"Granmaw's goat imagination awright," agreed Avi. "The only thing is she doesna ken whit tae dae wi't. It's like as ah wis gien a jocteleg an dinna hae haunds tae haud it wi."

"Ye'd hae a mooth," said Alicia. "A mooth wi teeth. An ye'd clink up yon jocteleg wi yir teeth tae cairve onything ye wanted."

"Ah coud dae it wi ma teeth onywey." Avi sneezed and continued to look at Alicia without blinking. "See—thay're muckle shairp."

He opened his mouth wide and Alicia drew her index finger along his teeth, as if they were the blade of a saw.

"Haud aff wi bletherin doon therr!" yelled Granmaw from above. "Yer gladrags ur gonnae be reddy the noo! Ah'll pass them aw doon tae youz, an yese can pit them oan straightaweys."

but 'n' ben: cottage   *brig*: bridge

"An if we dinna?" asked Alicia, turning her head up towards the light, in which there was a fine petal dust floating.

"Then I'll let the punishment fit the crime," sang Granmaw after a moment's thought, as though she was singing a line from a song. "Youz'll be gettin *nuh*thin tae eat nor drink until such time as yese pit them oan. Youz huv goat tae be quite the wee chatterboxes doon therr, eh? Eh? Nivver mind, youz'll be getting yir weddin prezzies soon enough. So shut it, gitface. Youz ur gonnae be gettin a loadae ma big fuckin jaggie needle, an then ye'll haud yer fuckin wheesht, ya wee neds! Eh? Eh? Eh?"

Granmaw once again leant over the pit and stretched out her hand so that her fingers blocked the light, that selfsame light that Alicia and Avi could see from the bottom of their grave. The needle really was a big one—long, fat and made of bone. It was a special needle for making clothes out of nettles or for showing to children who are sitting underground and need to get to Bremen. Granmaw's fingers also looked like needles—elongated, yellowish and with sharp pointed nails at the tips.

"Youz can listen tae the wireless," Granmaw decided, pleased with the effect her needle had on the children. "Ah'll fire it up fur ye cuz it doesnae dae fir youz young wans tae be bored oot yer skulls noo, does it? Eh? Ach, whit a wee stoatir o a bride y're gonnae be, eh no? Youz'll be dishin me up some rerr cuts of meat, eh no? Grab a lugfu o they tunes fur grannies oan trannies in single ends an buts 'n' bens! Shuggle yer wallies!"

After a few moments some music did indeed start playing; Granmaw had placed the receiver right on the edge of the pit. "It's a variety show," she said in a respectful tone. "Exactly whit we're needin fur a great day like the day!" The variety show, however, very soon came to an end, and was followed by a very interesting programme about language. Both Alicia and Avi pricked up their ears; this was the kind of subject they liked. What's more,

stoatir: stunner   *shuggle yer wallies*: (lit.) "shake your false teeth"

147

the programme reminded them of the Camp. The voice of the presenter even began to sound like the voice of their troop leader. It was as if the Camp had caught up with them and had vowed never again to leave the brother and sister.

"As you know, our Russian is the language of good, honest people," the radio asserted.[27] "From days of yore the Russian language has been our sole harbinger of hope. It has been our mainstay. And the people protected their language as best they could. Each individual realised that it was the only treasure capable of offering hope, even at times when ..." Alicia and Avi were on the point of arguing about what all this meant. Days of your Russian? And what's a sole harbinger? Avi thought that "harbinger" must be something to do with "harbour," and "sole" is a fish, so it might be a place where they sell fish. And wasn't a mainstay something on a ship?

"Na, yon canna be richt," said Alicia, although she was by no means certain. She had made up her mind that she wasn't going to give way to him, even if he was right. She had no intention of agreeing with him. Avi, however, wasn't looking for a quarrel.

"Whan ah hear the Lingo, or whan ah gab the Lingo, ah hae the feelin o something unco," said Avi. "Likes o yon press i the Doctor's bureau, dae ye hae mynd o that? Yon whare he keepit yon mooth-airns he uised tae appen up yir mooth wide, wide as y're able. Ah hae nae dout thare waur shuirly something suspeecious thare."

Alicia shrugged her shoulders. It wasn't very pleasant to be reminded of those gags. It was like something icy being put in your mouth. The gags stretched your mouth so much that your teeth, nose and even your jaws began to hurt. Before she arrived in the Camp, Alicia had never imagined that she could open her mouth that wide, but there was no way of resisting those gags. The gags made them say "ahhh," the roundest and widest "a" sound that a

mooth-airns: mouth gags

human could ever utter. A hairy hand was thrust in between the gags and started doing something, although what they couldn't feel; before the gags were inserted, they had been given tablets. The tablets were so tasty that there were children in the Camp who begged for gag-time, just so as to get their reward before the procedure.

Meanwhile the programme had ended. Alicia and Avi were disappointed: that good, honest people spoke the Lingo was no secret. They also knew that they too could become good, honest people—they simply needed a little patience and to remember to take their tablets. Black ones, blue ones, ones so white they were almost transparent—through their gel coating you could see something like a beetle—and especially the brown ones.

"Ah'm faimisht," said Avi. "An ah'm gonnae eat a wirm richt nou. Yon wan!" And he threw something long, wriggling, cold and terrified into Alicia's shorts.

"Awa! Awa w'it!" she squealed.

"Willna!" and Avi burst out laughing. At that Alicia threw herself on him and started strangling him. And up above them there was music playing again, the kind of hectic, stomping music which made it seem as though the whole Camp was now out of breath after running up to see what it was that Alicia and Avi were doing that would justify the troop leaders in handing out truly medieval punishment to each member of the troop.

It turned out not to be a worm. Just an ordinary lump of earth.

"Whit does clart taste like?" wondered Alicia out loud. "Ah'm gien it a shot."

"Naw," said Avi with conviction. "Naebody gangin tae Bremen eats clart. Forby, ye're a lassie. An it'll gie ye the boak."

"Daft wee Avi," said Alicia calmly. She put a lump of earth into her mouth and began to chew. "It tastes likes o ... o ..."

It was difficult for her to say exactly what it tasted like, that

clart: dirt

lump of earth. Salty, perhaps? No, not really. Quite honestly, it reminded her more than anything of how Avi's skin tasted when you gave it a lick. For some reason, though, Alicia was ashamed to tell him that. She listened intently to what was playing on the radio up above—right at that moment someone was singing about "strawberry lips." Alicia was already thinking about telling that cheeky so-and-so Avi that earth tastes like strawberry lips, because he was waiting for a reply. All of a sudden her head started going round and round and she fell right to the bottom of the pit. She just managed to say one word, "lips," before she lost control of her eyes; they closed like the doors of a bus, hissing, slamming shut, resistance is futile, mind your fingers. Weird, she couldn't sit up, but she couldn't sleep either. Avi said it was just the earth doing this, but Alicia knew that the earth had nothing to do with it. All she wanted ever so much was to breathe, to be able to see something other than the dark, cold walls of the pit. And to have a bite to eat. Those bilberries, for example. Those wonderful bilberries that they had stuffed their mouths with, as if they had stolen them from someone who had turned away and pretended that he hadn't noticed what was going on …

Alicia didn't know how long she had been asleep, or indeed if she had slept at all. If she had slept then it must have been the cold and silence that woke her. The radio had suddenly gone quiet, and the silence was bitingly sharp, like ice. Both she and Avi had the feeling that the whole of the magic cottage had been pervaded by an arctic chill, and that this chill had now found them; it had penetrated the very crust of the Earth and was reaching with its tentacles down to the deepest roots. It was as if winter had struck.

Up above them Granmaw swore, and there was a distinct note of fear in her voice.

"Ah huvnae bluidy feenishit! Ah huvnae feenishit wi sewin yer bluidy claes, wee wans!" she howled. "An therr's gonnae be a hale loadae bluidy guests at yer waddin. Jist sit quiet doon there, ye bluidy wee buggers, an dinnae open yer gobs or else therr willnae be time fur youz tae get hitched, an in *that* case aw hell's gonnae brek bluidy loose. Sae be bluidy quiet!"

Alicia made a feeble hand gesture to Avi and, holding his hand to the side of his mouth to make the sound carry further, he shouted:

"Soon as ye gie's meat we'll dae whit ye want."

"Yon's the Spectator! The Watchie Man!" yelled Granmaw. There was a note of panic in her voice; she sounded like a bird at night. "Mr. Spectator Watchie Man's come fir a visit. Mebbes it'll be OK. Please tae Goad. Hunker doon an git yer back intae some serious praying. Ah'll pray too. Goad'll nae abandon us Orthodox Christians."

"Guid day tae aw youz in this hoose!" announced the unknown guest. "May Goad speed tae yir aid!" The radio was still playing and the guest sang along—

Oh we're no awa tae bide awa,
We're no awa tae le'e ye,
We're no awa tae bide awa,
We'll aye come back an see ye!

"An same tae you, Mr. Spectator Watchie Man," came Granmaw's voice in reply. "An hoo's yer health, son, eh?"

"Whit sort o health does a man hae these days?" asked the mysterious Mr. Spectator Watchie Man. "Nae body takes care o us. Therr's the stress, the burdens we bear, the general mess we're in an jist the sheer vulgaaarity of it aw. An for why? It's cuz wummans run the world.

As I was walking doon the street,
I met wee Johnny Scobie,
Says he tae me, "Could ye go a hauf?"
Says I, "Man that's ma hoabby."

"Huv ye a wee dram fur me?"

Just a wee deoch an doris,
Just a wee drop, that's all,
Just a wee deoch an doris
Afore ye gang awa,

sang Granmaw, hurriedly. Then came a gulping sound and the crunching of a cucumber. Alicia pictured the cucumber—firm, bitter green, handy size like the handle of a knife. A bitter green sweet bumpy-skinned fragrant get-the-juices-flowing-in-the-mouth cucumber.

"Huv ye heard that some weans huv shot the craw frae a pioneer camp?" asked Mr. Spectator Watchie Man. His voice sounded as though he didn't really care. "Therr's a couple or mair o them."

There's a wee wifie waitin in a wee but 'n' ben.

"Fancy that eh?" said Granmaw despondently.

If you can say "It's a braw bricht moonlicht nicht"
Then yer a'richt

"... Ach, naebody keeps an eye oan the weans nooadays, they're jist left tae thur ain devices, so they ur. Yon's why they scarper," *ye ken.*

"That's whit ah'm *tellin* ye," said Mr. Spectator Watchie Man with a sigh.

Now I like a man that is a man;
A man that's straight and fair.

shot the craw: scarpered

"Wummans dinnae keep an eye oan thur weans, instead they go an stick thur nebs intae things wherr they shouldnae. In tae politics, in tae newspapers, in tae Space.

The kind of man that will and can,
In all things do his share.

"Even in tae the theatre. The theatre's a total disaaaster. Therr's nae theatre any mair.

Och, I like a man a jolly man,
The kind of man you know,
The chap that slaps your back and says,
"Jock, just before ye go …"

An therr's some wee wumman's even goat hersel in tae a high heid yin position in the local administration. So *ah'm* thinking they willnae even huv the Gaiety any mair. Pity really, therr wis a brammer of a troupe therr."

"Goad above, Mr. Spectator, whit troops ur ye talkin aboot?" squealed Granmaw, almost jumping out of her seat. "It's aw right and proper roon here, Christian-like. We dinnae need nae troops."

"So y've nae heard aboot the weans?" said the Mr. Spectator Watchie Man with even greater indifference.

"Naw, ah've no came across them," said Granmaw. She sort of crossed herself.

"Ferr do's, pour us anither dram, wid ye?" said Mr. Spectator Watchie Man. He drank it down and took another bite out of the cucumber.

Of a' the friens that ere I kenned,

a brammer of: a really good

There's nane like Johnnie Scobie,
His hert is leal, he's true as steel,
An' a hauf is aye his hoabby.

Turn yer erse tae me," he said, heaving another almighty sigh. This was followed by coarse, heavy breathing and hough, hough hough,

> houghma
> > houghma
> > > houghma mamamamamamama
> > > > houghmagandie!

Some loose earth fell to the bottom of the pit, right on to Avi's head. Alicia took him by the hand and he twisted his face as though he was about to sneeze. He held it in, good lad, and as a sign of her approval Alicia squeezed his nearly frozen fingers.

"Phew," said Mr. Spectator Watchie Man. "It's a good joab ah dropped in oan ye. Otherwise ah woudae bin jiggert withoot a wumman's tender loving care. Ye knaw it yersel, wummanz aw ower the shoap ur wantin tae be heid bummerz. Oor Gaiety Theatre fur instance—ye might jist as well bury it the noo. Ur ye gonnae get a wumman tae gie money fur theatre? Right then, shaw me the noo."

"But ah've awreddy shawn ye everything, Mr. Spectator."

"Here, gonnae no mess wi me? We're baith o us Goad-fearin, ur we no? Messing aroon wi folk's a sin. Especially when yer dealin wi men. D'y think ah dinnae ken ye? An this—whit's this here? Whit is it, eh? *Eh?* Ah'm *askin* ye!"

Now it was Granmaw's turn to heave a sigh, such a deep one that Alicia began to feel sorry for her.

"Well noo, it's a big jaggie needle," said Mr. Spectator Watchie Man. "Y're fixin up anither wedding, ur ye no? An ye didnae invite me. Yese really ur a stupitt wumman, eh? EH? Ah bet nine-

---

houghmagandie: fornication   *heid bummerz*: top dogs

teen tae the dozen y've nivver set foot inside of a theatre, huv ye? Ah'm right, ahmn't ah? Whit's mair, y've been sittin in a bed of jaggie nettles, an y're stung aw ower yer erse. So, gies a gander o *whit y've goat therr.*"

Once again Alicia and Avi could see light up above them, and within the circle of this dim light there appeared the face of a man who was smiling down at them in such a friendly manner that the two children hastily turned their faces away and now looked at each other with something amounting to horror.

"Weanz," said Mr. Spectator Watchie Man in a wooden voice. "Weanz. Wance again. Good day tae youz, weanz. Huv youz ivver been tae the Gaiety?"

"Aye!" said Avi in a way that sounded like a challenge. "Aye, we hae been, an mair than wanst!"

Although Avi had never been in a theatre, and Alicia somehow knew that. She had never been in a theatre either, but she could well imagine what it was like. A long time ago, before the Camp, she and Faither had played theatres with something that had a very strange name: Batliejka.[28] She even had a thought that her brother could have had a name like that, but she wasn't too bothered about it. "So Granmaw wants tae jyne the perr of youz thegither, does she?" Mr. Spectator Watchie Man asked without taking his eyes off them. "Granmaw's fu o't it whan therr's loads o weanz aroond. But me, ah'm no sae keen."

Suddenly a pocket torch appeared in one of his hands and a pair of glasses in the other. Of the opera variety.

"The aulder wan aye—she's a typical wean," said Mr. Spectator Watchie Man sorrowfully. "Ah can sense whit sortae odour she gives aff. Like a Dudarau play that's flopped.[29] It's no Shakespeare, but aw the same ... But whit's *that* next tae her?"

"Ah dinnae quite unnerstaun *him* either," Granmaw put in hastily. "But he'll dae tae replace ma puir deid wee Paulie."

"Forget aboot yer Paulie," frowned Mr. Spectator Watchie Man. "Whit a thing tae think of—turnin weans intae dugs. Y've nivver been in a theatre an therr ye go, tryin tae play aroon wi the mysteries o metamorphosis ...

There's a good old Scottish custom that has stood the test o'
*   time,*
It's a custom that's been carried out in every land and clime ...

"Pour anither dram."

Mr. Spectator Watchie Man settled himself with his legs dangling over the edge of the pit, and downed another shot. This time he bit into a piece of salami; the heady aroma wafted down to the two children.

"The lassie ah'll tak wi me," said Mr. Spectator Watchie Man, putting the opera glasses up to one eye. "Ye huvnae yet drained aw her blood. An yon ither wan, yon thingummyjig, ah dinnae need. Jist caw canny—it might maulicate ye. Y'd be better aff burying it here."

"Ah dinna think he's goat much o a fantice," whispered Avi, and Alicia nodded in agreement.

"It speaks!" exclaimed Mr. Spectator Watchie Man who had been watching closely what was going on in the pit. "It should let oan tae us wherr it comes frae. Weanz dinnae knaw how tae tell the truth, right enough. Quite frankly, they dinnae knaw how tae talk. Weanz arenae folk. Y'can dae whit the hell ye like wi them, ye can even make them believe how their maws an paws ayeweys tell the truth. They're that obedient. They're the only beings in the world that aaactually believe langwidge. But langwidge is theatre. It's aw relative, nane o it's real. Weanz knaw wan langwidge only—the langwidge of their parents."

If ye can say "It's a braw, bricht mooonlicht nicht"
Ye're aw richt, ye ken!

"Naw! Non! No!" shouted Avi. "I can speak the Great Lingo!"

"Only those who can speak the Lingo have the right to speak at all," said Mr. Spectator Watchie Man in a didactic tone. "An nae yellin up the back! Ah'm auld-fashioned an ah like order. An ah'm a man. An yon's how ah like brief, clear answers. So, who ur youz, *eh*?"

And at that moment Mr. Spectator Watchie Man as if by accident dropped the unfinished piece of salami out of his hand. Alicia's eyes lit up. Avi held their road atlas tightly in his hands.

"Ah'm Aviator, an yon's ma tittie Alicia," proclaimed Avi. "We're gangin tae Bremen an we hae lost the road. We maun win someplace markit oan oor cairt. Thareaneftir we'll mak oor ain Niaroo wey."

"An wha's ye?" asked Alicia without raising her eyes. She was hypnotised by the salami, but she didn't dare pick it up. Who knows what there could be on a piece of salami that a man with no imagination had bitten a chunk out of?

"Wheesht," ordered Mr. Spectator Watchie Man and looked at Alicia. It was only then that she noticed how very red his eyes were, like the brake lights on Faither's car. "Why is it that weans willnae nivver *haud their wheesht*? Even in the *theatre ...*"

Mr. Spectator Watchie Man heaved a deep sigh, but then his voice sounded a little kinder.

"Ah ... D'yese want tae knaw who ah am? OK then, ah'll tell youz. An efter that ..."

And so Mr. Spectator Watchie Man embarked at a leisurely pace upon his tale.

***

There was a time when my work involved the removal of unruly children from cinemas and theatres.

Unless you have succeeded in mastering this inestimable skill in good time, you had better avoid going to the cinema or theatre altogether. Although what kind of ability was it really? What kind of skill? No, it was a real martial art from the Orient. A duel on the very edge of the abyss. Psychological combat that demands the maximum mobilisation of the organism.

Now I do not possess that kind of martial skill in the necessary degree, but nevertheless I am a real aficionado of both the cinema and the theatre. It's simply that I entrust this matter to the professionals. However, there are fewer and fewer of them, and the number of children and teenagers continues to grow. As the statistics show, the country is for the first time since independence experiencing a veritable baby boom. And that is just the beginning. People have developed a sense of confidence in what tomorrow will bring, and have started having children and taking them to cinemas, theatres and similar places of entertainment. Now about this confidence in the morrow ... If they do have it, then let them take their offspring to tomorrow's screenings and performances. But, oh no, they insist on taking them to whatever is showing today, exactly to the one where you are going. "Clear off to McDonald's! That's the right place for you!" is what you want to say to these self-assured fellow countrymen who have decided that they can cart their kids off to wherever the urge suddenly takes them.

And so it is up to individuals who prefer to teach themselves to attain the wisdom of how to resist this mass attack.

Of course the best solution would be to remove every child from the building before the start of the screening or performance. But more often than not, they are accompanied by adults whose reaction to such a prophylactic measure may be unpredictable.

In the good old days it was all so simple. You could grab a kid by his ear and drag him to the door, and everybody would look at you with approval. The kid wouldn't say a word, he'd put up with it and his ear would fill with blood, just like your eyes, stern yes, but just. You would be filled with an incredible strength. Even if you're nothing but skin and bones, at this moment you'll have the feeling that you're strong and supple, and you'll be aware that the ladies are looking at you with interest. You are a protector and a saviour, and you did this! And when you've removed the little yob and at last let go of his ear—which he grabs hold of as if it was a Big Mac in his local McDonald's—then you realise that the applause you can hear from the auditorium is not solely intended for the actors. That the success of the performance is in part thanks to you. A tiny fragment of your labour, unpleasant but necessary, the kind of task that is so often undertaken by individuals who are not indifferent to their surroundings.

In those good old days you needed no word of thanks. You would simply return to the auditorium, pleasantly excited, with your hand on your heart. You would face the stage, and your whole body would show that the unfortunate actors on stage should not be deprived of attention. In your place any one of them would have done exactly the same, and you—well, you are only a spectator, no better than anyone else.

But this was by no means the end of your triumph. After the show you would be approached by a limping old lady—one of those who sold programmes and checked tickets—and she would look you in the eye and utter in her slightly grating, kind voice:

"Thank you, sonny."

"No worries, luv," you would say with a cool shrug of your shoulders. You could see behind the old woman the figure of a young lady, obviously a teacher who had brought that brat from a brood of other people's kids here to the theatre. The young lady would look timidly at that stern face of yours and say quickly:

"Please forgive me, I'm so grateful, that little boy Kasperovich, he's from a difficult family, he's growing up without a father."

And she herself was open like a rose, her cheeks were blushing bright scarlet, her hands were trembling. And you would draw yourself up and stand before her, inaccessible and majestic, and say in a stern voice: "You should look after those who are in your charge. After all, you are a professional!"

That's how things were in the good old days. And this Kasperovich or Kazbiaruk or whatever his name was would look up at you with respect while he rubbed his ear. Then the producer of the play would come up to you together with the theatre director, and they would invite you to the first-night party, given that you had saved the première, and off you would go hand in hand with the young lady teacher to the basement where the table would already be laid and a fragrant scent would be gently wafting from modest nibbles. From there things could go any way you liked. It all depended on your imagination.

... This all happened in one of those old Minsk cinemas which still occasionally show films and draw in their audience by means of real hand-painted posters.

True, there was one particular film for which posters like that weren't produced for some reason. The film dealt with old age and loneliness. Of course it would have been possible to paint posters, but then could they have been used to draw people in to see the film? I doubt it. Right in the middle of the screening there was sex. The screen was large and so there was a lot of sex. An elderly couple were in love and oblivious to the rest of the world. Flabby skin, sagging bellies and breasts, scars left by operations, the liver spots of old age, kilos of flesh that still wants to live but which no one wants to buy. And this covering the entire screen. Old age as long as a feature film, and an expanse of loneliness like a brick wall. But there were kids in the audience. And these kids kept roaring with laughter. Throughout the whole film.

***

Mr. Spectator Watchie Man sighed.

> *So we had a hauf an' anither hauf,*
> *And then we had anither,*
> *When he got fou' he shouted "Hoo!*
> *It's Carnwath Mill for ever."*

"They wans thought they wur nivver gonnae dee."
He fell silent, drank straight from the bottle that Granmaw

had been using to pour shots for him and pulled a pill out of his pocket. Alicia and Avi could both hear Granmaw snoring close by.

Mr. Spectator Watchie Man looked down at Alicia and said to her: "Ah'm gonnae throw a ledder doon an then y're gonnae come wi me. Ah cannae be bother'd tae teach ye how tae pronounce sounds properly. Verra soon ye'll become jist a sound yersel. That's aw *Wumman's* fit fur.

We wandered doon the street again
We cleekit unco cheery,
When John got hame his wife cried "Shame!
I see you're enjoyin' your hobby."

"Youz make yir sound, an then youz disappear. It's no painful. They simply remove youz oot the auditorium, and the show goes on."

"Ah'll no be aff tae onywhares!" said Alicia.

"She'll no be aff tae onywhares!" said Avi.

"Hoo! She'll go awright," said Mr. Spectator Watchie Man, and his eyes shone bright red. "An yon *thingummyjig* therr"—to Avi—"yon *thingummyjig* therr will haud its wheesht. As it staunds, yon *thingummyjig* has awreddy spoilt the performance fur mony a jolly chap that slaps your back."

"Ah willna go," repeated Alicia.

Mr. Spectator Watchie Man burst out laughing. "Jist think oan it like this: y're gonnae be merrit tae me." He spread his trembling hands wide over the pit as though he was warming them over a fire. "Youz wur preparin tae be merrit the day, werr youz nae?"

"Ah willna go! Ah want tae bide wi ma brither!"

"Wae yerr bruther? Something tells me that yir Paw wuznae completely honest with yir Maw." By now Mr. Spectator Watchie Man was shaking like an out-of-order drinks dispenser. "Wae yir bruthur indeed! Ur y'gonnae tell me how he's goat the same blood as you? Ye're gonnae come wae me an keep me warm!

That's aw! Otherwise ah'll droon the perr o youz alive."

At that moment Alicia made a scarcely perceptible movement of her hand, like putting a finger in her ear to scrape out a lump of wax that was stuck there. And all of a sudden her hand was holding a pill—a tiny, black pill like a ripe, tense, self-assured bilberry.

"Bletherberry," said Avi.

And that is indeed what it was. Alicia passed the pill to him, and he seized it with his lips straight from the palm of her hand and swallowed it greedily. His Adam's apple lurched and fell back into place like a living thing. Avi clicked his tongue in satisfaction.

"We maun speak!" whispered Alicia. "We can dae it! We maun speak sae puirly, sae puirly likes o jist us twa!"

Avi corrected her: "Sing, nae speakin!" And together, their voices trembling yet resolute, they launched into a song they had learned in the Camp:

With purest voice and laughter gay
We sing out loud all the livelong day:
Cheap, reap, gene, sheep!
Clean your teeth before you sleep,
Your voice is pure—you've got the knack:
Say it right, you'll get no flak!

A rope ladder let itself down into the pit of its own accord, unwinding like a snake to the sounds of a fakir's pungi. Standing on the very edge of the pit, Mr. Spectator Watchie Man suddenly gave a pathetic groan and started shrinking. At first he became as small as Alicia standing on tiptoe. Then as small as Avi if he was wearing shoes with heels. Then as small as Alicia if she was bending forwards to tie up her shoelaces. Then as small as Avi if he was bending forwards to bite Alicia on the leg.

Our Lingo is our Sun that shines so bright,
Our mouths are windows that let in the light,

With no stupid accent we can speak,
Ugly sounds no damage wreak,
Sill! Seal! Will! Wheel!

Mr. Spectator Watchie Man had shrunk to the size of a cat, and Granmaw was snoring away somewhere in a corner and had heard nothing. They even felt sorry for her—she had missed it all! Avi started scrambling upwards; behind him Alicia climbed happily, grabbing hold of the rope ladder's disobedient rungs. All the while they kept singing:

Our Lingo now is span and spick.
Climb with us up to the peak:
Boot! Bout! Beak!
Bake! Bone! Bark!

They reached the surface in the middle of the cottage. By this time Mr. Spectator Watchie Man was no bigger than a worm; he was wriggling helplessly on the very edge of the pit, and kind Avi kicked him in. After Mr. Spectator Watchie Man down hurtled Granmaw, who was now equally tiny, just like a little fruit gum.

Oh we're no awa tae bide awa,
We're no awa tae le'e ye,
We're no awa tae bide awa,
We'll aye come back an' see ye.

Very soon there was not a living soul in the cottage.

We'll aye come back an' see ye.
Just a wee deoch an doris, just a wee drop, that's all.
Just a wee deoch an doris, afore ye gang awa.
There's a wee wifie waitin' in a wee but an ben,
If you can say it's a braw bricht moonlicht nicht ...

After all, that dark, stinking pit cannot be regarded as a cottage. Any other children who found themselves in a pit like that might have forgotten where they were going.

But not Avi. And not Alicia. *"Then ye're aw richt, ye ken!"*

11

Of course he could recall them—
he had a good memory for voices

On auld worm-eaten skelf, in cellar dunk,
Whare hearty benders synd their drouhty trunk,
Twa chappin bottles, pang'd wi liquor fu',
BRANDY *the tane, the tither* WHISKY *blue,*
Grew canker'd; for the twa war het within,
An' het-skin'd fock to flyting soon begin:

Of course he could recall them—he had a good memory for voices. The Doctor took a fastidious look at the photographs: totally unmemorable faces they had, both the boy and the girl. Anyway, children in general are all alike, until they are subjected to punishment and upbringing. You can remember a child only when it starts crying. It's only by their voices that you can tell them apart. And the voices that these two had were exactly what he needed. A difficult case. Almost clinical.

"Goodness me, how it's all been neglected," said the nurse at the time. She was standing behind the odd couple: a girl, skinny as a bird's leg, with ugly, pimple-like eyes, and a boy, for whom the Doctor felt a strange instant loathing.

"Be quiet," and the Doctor looked at her in such a way that she recoiled in alarm. "For God's sake, shut up."

The nurse, visibly upset, turned around and put her hands in the pockets of her gown. Then he sacked her. Too much initiative.

It was a sunny winter's day and a little noisy in the Camp. He had to close the office windows. The boy was looking at his surroundings with interest, but the girl was simply staring at the

Doctor. It struck him later on—she was staring straight into his mouth. As though she was waiting to see what he was going to pull out of there.

Sia. Only someone very sick, possessed by the demons of the Leid could think up a name like that. Someone without the Lingo.

"Do you understand me, Sia?" the Doctor asked.

The little girl made no movement. He would have to encourage her with a smile,

"Do you understand our language?"

"A little," she said at last, keeping a close eye on the Doctor's lips. He licked them and turned to the boy.

"What about you? Did anyone teach you to speak?"

"Ah'm Avi," said the boy.

"Yes, I know," nodded the Doctor. "But we can't call you Avi. Avi isn't a name. And, by the way, neither is Sia. I think that the name Gleb would suit you. And as for your sister…"

"Alicia," said the boy and pointed at his sister.

"Alicia?" The Doctor smiled again. "Well, that's beginning to sound better. More human. So, you do understand me, right?"

"Y're baith guid bairns, but y're no weel," he went on. "Ah'm a doctor, ah unnerstaund wha hae whit as regards ailments. Nae need tae greet nor tae think shame—tae be unweel's no blamewirthy. Ye maun imaginate a great muckle factorywark whare they mak wheeriorums, playocks. Comprenez? Hae yir Paw tauld ye whit a factorywark is? Guid. Nou, some o yon playocks are shaped a wee bit wrang.

BRANDY
Black be your fa! Ye cottar loun mislear'd,
Blawn by the PORTERS, *chairmen,* CITY-GUARD;
Ha'e ye nae breeding, that you shaw your nose
Anent my sweetly gusted cordial dose.

wheeriorum: thingummyjig

They want fir some pairts. Bodies workin there either forgat aboot them or went a bit easy-oasy tae mak playocks richt. An these playocks that waurna quite richt waur dispatchit tae shops an folk startit tae buy thaim. Some bocht braw playocks. An ithers—you twa, par exemple—bocht playocks that didna wark richt, acause they got shapeit aw hashie.

> BRANDY
> *For love to you there's mony a tenant gaes*
> *Bare-ars'd and barefoot o'er the Highland braes*

Yon's whare ah interpone—ah pit playocks tae richts. Savvy?"
Alicia furrowed her brows.

> WHISKY
> *But ye maun be content, and mauna rue,*
> *Tho' erst ye've bizz'd in bonny madam's mou'—*
> *Yet I am hameil, there's the sour mischance!*
> *I'm no frae Turkey, Italy or France*

"Folk's no playocks," she said. "Playocks may blether ony language ye crave. But folk maun spak a langage that willna kill thaim. Man, y'coud chowk wi spakin a langage that's nae yir ain."
"Wha tellt ye *that*?"

> BRANDY
> *Wanwordy gowk! Did I sae aften shine*
> *Wi' gowdin glister thro' the chrystal fine*

The Doctor bent down to the level of her face and put a hand on her shoulder. The girl's eyes showed no interest at all, just as though she was saying things that were obvious. The sky is blue, snow is cold, water is wet.

hashie: carelessly

"Ma faither o coorse. Anely he knaws the richt Leid. Oor Leid."

WHISKY
Alake! The by-word's o'er weel kend through oot,
"Prophets at hame are held in nae repute."

BRANDY
Wi' cairds like thee I scorn to file my thumb,
For gentle spirits gentle breeding doom

"Nae dout yir paw lues ye verra much," the Doctor said gently. "Regaird me. Or yon dame thare ... the nursie ... Or the bodies wha brocht ye here. Are we aw chowkin? Tak me par exemple, ah'm nae chowkin. Au contraire, ah feel braw an it's near dennertime. Ah'm fair chuffed wi that. Hae a keek oot the windae. Ah dinna think onybody oot thare's chowkin. Or am ah wrang?"

BRANDY
Frae some poor poet, o'er as poor a pot,
Ye've lear'd to crack sae crouse, ye haveril Scot!

Avi and Alicia did go over to the window and looked out so seriously that the Doctor decided to note it down as an example of an inadequate reaction.

"Yon dinna pruiv onything," said Alicia. "Thay may've chowkit awreadies, an whit we're seein's jist inertia."

WHISKY
Braw days for you, when fools newfangle fain,
Like ither countries better than their ain.

lues: loves

"Hoots! Yir faither's learnt ye some fancy wirds richt eneuch!" The Doctor laughed. "Ma tochter dinna ken wirds likes o yon, an she's aulder than yese."

BRANDY
For you nae mair the thrifty gudewife sees
Her lassie kirn, or brize the dainty cheese.

He was lying. He had no daughter.

"Yir Paw was richt aboot one thing tho. Forsuith, folk maun chowk if they canna pronoonce soonds clearsome. An if thay're conceitit w'it, it's as weel tae scrub thaim aff aw thegither. Here i the Camp we seek t'airt oot the puir voice insides o each body, sicweys we can aw spak *Our Great Lingo* clearsome. If ye listen tae ma helpenders an the troop heidsmen an dae whit thay've tellt yese, if ye appen up yir mooths wide whan y're tellt, an keep them clampit whan ye huv tae keep stumm, than naebody'll iver, iver agin mak a mockerie o ye, naebody'll caw yese *coofs*. Ye'll begin t'unnerstaund whit ony kyndly body can unnerstaund. Aye but yon'll dae fir the nou—ah've the neb o a dug an ah've the ee o a gowden eagle, *Aquila chrysaetos*; ma neb's tellin me dennertime's kicked-aff, an ma ee's perceivit that the ersten troop's awready set aff fir the canteen. Yese'll be faimisht as weel. The cuisine's rare here i the Camp. Auld Vasya maks it. Ye'll like it that much yese'll be lickin yir fingers."

"Ye shouldna lick yir fingers," said Avi suddenly.

WHISKY
Sair dung wi' dule, and fley'd for coming debt,
They gar their mou-bits wi' their incomes mett

"Yon's clarty. An biting yer nagels as weel."

coof: fool, simpleton   *ersten*: first

"Ah hae a hunch yer Paw forgat t'expliquer a few things tae yese," smiled the Doctor.

BRANDY
I shall yet on bien-tables stand,
Bouden wi' a' the daintiths of the land.

"Braw. Aff yese go, nursie'll tak yese. We'll hae sicht o a anither twice weekly. An nae mair o yon langage o yir Paw's. Anely puir, clearsome Lingo. Awtho, jist haud it a wee minuit ... Yese look gey weary. OK, we've had our fun, and that's enough. From now on we're going to try to speak properly. So start singing me a song. Any song you know!"

Jist as suin as ah cam born,
Ma faither said: Things will be bad ...[30]

"Whaur'd ye get that sang frae?" asked Alicia as they followed the nurse along the sand-strewn path towards the main building.

"Frae Faither, o coorse," said Avi. "Whaur else?"

Truelins, whaur else wad he win't? thought Alicia. She had been wondering a great deal recently about that long wrinkle that had appeared on her forehead—just like the one Faither has. The wrinkle just didn't want to go away. Alicia had tried to clear it up—after all, who wants a dash-type punctuation mark on their forehead? And in the Camp it had become a habit to try to make the skin on her forehead smooth by stretching it out right by her hair. The wrinkle still wouldn't go away. It might grow paler and unwillingly merge with the rest of her skin, but all she had to do was release her fingers and back it would come, as though she hadn't done anything.

During their next meeting the Doctor started talking to them about their mother.

"We've nane," said Alicia.

"What do you mean, 'We've nane'?" The Doctor pretended to be astounded. "Where is she then? Has she died?"

"You can say that."

"Are you afraid of death? Try to answer in the Lingo, as purely as you can."

"I am a little," whispered Alicia. She looked round at Avi, but he was examining some scissors. When they first met the Doctor, those scissors weren't in the office.

"Say it again," the Doctor asked. "Please."

"A little bit," said Alicia.

"Can you say it like this: … Like a bird …"

Alicia couldn't hold back a smile.

"Try again. Are you afraid of death?"

"A very, very little."

"Don't be afraid. And you're already beginning to speak a little clearer! You and your brother … er, Gleb—it is Gleb, isn't it?—you must be very tired. You're like little birds that someone desperately needs. Out there, beyond the Camp walls there's a variety of phantoms and other vicious nasties hunting for you. In reality they don't exist, but for as long as you're sick, they'll seem real and they're going to torment you. You know what phantoms are, don't you? But inside the Camp you're safe. We all help each other in the Camp, and the troop leaders are here to protect you. Do you like it here in the Camp?"

"Yes," said Alicia. "The tablets are tasty."

"What about you, Gleb?"

"I am Avi," said Avi. "What is the 'it' here in the Camp that you are asking about? I like to sing."

"No, no." Alicia corrected him. "He's asking if you like being in the Camp."

"Don't worry," and the Doctor gave them an encouraging smile. "While you are making an effort, no phantom is ever going to dare stick so much as its nose in here. And now, Alicia, come over here and open your mouth as wide as you can. A bit wider.

Imagine that you have to put a whole apple in your mouth. You're going to feel something a bit cold ..." He knew how to talk to children. He himself had no idea where he learned it. Back there in the forest, in the blue forest where their base was and where special training courses and even master classes were laid on for them every day, they weren't taught how to talk to children. Everything was done there to gear them up for war. Adults against adults. A war of the pure voice against babbling. A war of music against superfluous noise.

***

Later on, he would come to recall that day frequently and realise that nothing happens by pure chance. His bus could have come on time, and he would have gone off to the railway station, and from there would have returned to the dusty little town where he lived. There he would have become a school teacher or got himself a job at the distillery that produces all the benefits of sweet, strong, cheap booze. But Fortune favoured him and took him under her wing. After finishing his military service he spent several months in the capital, living with distant relatives: cold little room, cold food, cold smiles, the poor relation; have you found a job yet? And he almost gave up. He was standing at a bus stop with a sports bag, and he had just enough money for a ticket. Already balding, already putting on a paunch. The line of his lips had finally straightened out, like it was set in stone. Here he was, standing and looking at his reflection in a shop window. He never did dare make another attempt to get into medical school, and now the exams were in full swing, and here they were again, the same girls who had failed the last time round. The only difference was that this summer was colder.

No bus came for ages. The Doctor, tired of looking at his depressing reflection, started studying the notices stuck on the bus stop. Nothing interesting there. A crowd was beginning to gather at the stop, and the Doctor felt as though he was surrounded by loonies. There wasn't a single person there who could pronounce sounds correctly. And yet, here we are in the capital ...

At that moment a lad in a kind of paramilitary uniform came to stand next to him. The Doctor automatically made way for him when he drew a small notice out of his rucksack and deftly stuck it on the bus stop that was already covered in scraps of paper. He glanced at the Doctor and went on his way. Dozens of eyes watched him go with total indifference, put their fingers up to the new notice, and then stared at the road again. The Doctor, however, read it from beginning to end. Because there was no bus in sight. Because there were more and more people crowding round the stop. Because he had nothing else to do.

The notice invited everyone to take part in a course entitled "Pure Voice."

"We invite all our friends ..." it said, but there was a charge for attending, not a large sum of money, but serious enough for the Doctor all the same. In his pocket he had exactly the same amount for his ticket. The course promised to assist participants to determine what was clean and what was dirty within themselves. The notice wasn't exactly clear. There were quite a lot of notices like that all around the city. There was some foreign doctor of unheard-of sciences, the author of unheard-of bestsellers who had brought happiness to the capital with his lecture on the topic "How to attain a true understanding of your innermost being and become rich and successful," or you had nudists seeking members for their esoteric group, or else there was a medium sending out invitations to all those desirous of reading the Tarot cards with her. But this time there was something serious. And as for the name—the Doctor had the unpleasant feeling that something had been stolen from him that belonged to him alone. And then there was that sign in the middle. The sign of the Sun. The sign of purity.

So he stayed on, and went at the appointed time right to the very edge of the city. At first it seemed as if they were making a fool of him. But then he went to the second and the third sessions. It was just as well he did. Each time he listened to discussions of the pure voice and the oral hygiene of correct pronunciation, he had the distinct feeling that there was something he wasn't being told, that there was some secret. At the third session all the superfluous visitors left, all the random individuals who asked stupid questions. The Doctor stayed, and then the real learning began. He had never before heard such pure language as he did here. Only those who had gone through a whole selection procedure could talk like that. The Doctor was soon to find out where that selection took place.

And so it was that he found himself once more in a forest.

They were handed uniforms without identification marks and allocated spaces in huge canvas tents. Seated at oak tables the instructors taught them a thousand different ways of compelling people to say what was necessary, and, more importantly, how they should say it. Officially this was called psychotraining, but it was actually little short of wild animal taming. There were a thousand ways, and no one knew that the Doctor had discovered the thousand and first. He was in no hurry to share his secret right away; in fact he was anxious to keep a low profile. He listened carefully, took copious notes and was never late for practical exercises—interrogation sessions that sometimes lasted from daybreak until late at night. They used to question collective farm workers that they had managed to catch in the forest. These peasant types never complained, willingly opened their mouths wide and put up with everything that was demanded of them, including experiments that involved high voltage.

Time flew by fast. It was as if no more than a single night had passed from the time when the Doctor first saw that notice on the bus stop to the moment he was standing in the rank of course graduates to receive his diploma. He was rated the very best of the students on the course—the first time in his life that anything like that had happened to him. People with the right connections gave him all the necessary references—and now, here he is, the Doctor, someone no one wanted to see in the capital only three years ago, sitting in the office of the Minister for Public Health and looking out of the window. There was the capital spread out before him, its mouth gaping obediently, and he felt that he could do with it whatever he wanted.

But he had no need of the capital. At one time it rejected him, threw him out on to the scrap heap of life, but now it was he who—with a sense of justice restored—rejected the capital.

BRANDY
But here's the brouster-wife, and she can tell
Wha's win the day, and wha shou'd wear the bell:
Ha'e done your din, an' lat her judgement join
In final verdic twixt your play an mine.

The Doctor watched as the Minister, a generously proportioned woman with a tall hairdo, read his letter requesting that a former pioneer camp now written off the books be placed at his disposal. Any minute now she'll give her official approval, and then he'll be able to get on with the job he's decided to devote his entire life to.

True, this grande dame of the Health Directorate was in no hurry. Her lips moved as she read; perhaps she was afraid of missing some hidden meaning, or perhaps she was simply not used to reading such long letters. She's the only woman in the Cabinet. The maternal figure to all the children of the country, the only female in the ministerial harem that belongs to the President Himself.

"Fine, ah'll approve yer request," she said, lifting her eyes. "Ah can see y're really *experienced*. Ma heartfelt thaaanks ur goan tae youse oan behauf of aw oor dear wee chuldren an aw the paaarents. We really dae huve tae care fur oor chuldren, nane will argie wi *that*. Youse knaw how we did awa wi the Leid *so long ago*, bit we stull canna learn tae speak proper, like normal humin be'ins. We bring shaaame oan oor State."

"Yes," said the Doctor. "We do."

It's not only the state he could help. He could be of personal assistance to her too, the old biddy with the blue cheeks and the hairdo like a wedding cake on the top of her head. How deeply embarrassed she must be when foreign visitors come with their pure voices. And what fear she feels when she has to make a speech or give an interview. If she but realised what exactly he could do for her, then she would be the one who would probably have to request an appointment to see him.

"Gude," she said, and stamped the letter with her mark of approval.

LANDLADY
In days o yore I could my living prize,
Nor faush'd wi doleful gaugers or excise;
But now-a-days we're blyth to lear the thrift
Our heads 'boon licence and excise to lift:
In lakes o BRANDY *we can soon supply*
By WHISKY *tinctur'd wi the* SAFFRON'S *dye.*

"Whit ur youse gonnae caw this ... this estaaablishmen? Cen're fur Urthuepic Urthudontics? Ur Cen're fur Lingusurgery? Ur sumethin else?"

LANDLADY
Will you your breeding threep, ye moungrel loun?
Frae hame-bred liquor dy'd to colour broon!

"The name is something I'll come up with," he said. "After all, we're dealing with children here. There's no hurry."

So FLUNKY braw, whan drest in master's claes,
Struts to Auld Reikie's cross on sunny days

"Gude. Youse see tae it then. Gie't a year an wu'll hae a look at yur results. Good luck, Doctur!"

"Many thanks." The Doctor bent down and kissed her puffy hand. The expensive watch on her wrist gave him a quick flash of farewell.

LANDLADY
Bumbaz'd he loups frae sight, and jooks his ken,
Fley'd to be seen amang the tassel'd train.

12
Yon's yir ain hallucinations,
an ye maun get thaim sortit yirsel

Yon's yir ain hallucinations, an ye maun get thaim sortit yirsel. Faither sat on the edge of a tree stump and thought: Something like that should be written into the Law on Marriage and the Family. He, the faither of a very unusual little girl and an even more unusual little boy, had cynically broken many of the provisions of this law after tearing through the paper walls that surrounded it.

> *I sing his name and nobler fame,*
> *Wha multiplies his number.*

And had irrevocably crashed out of a world where such things as marriage and family exist.

Yon hallucinations o mine—sae near, sae dear tae me, wi the Leid likes o me, wi bluid likes o me, thae hallucinations in breekums ... It's guid t'hae simmer the nou, the bairns willna be stivent. Nae sae guid's nae winter—winter wad'ae left thair trodmerks, winter wad'ae drove them tae fun herbourie i warmth o whare folks bide, it wad'ae bin facile t'airt them oot. When he was forcing his way through this endless forest where the roads had no ending, where they seemed to drown in dense thickets, there were times when he thought he could see Alicia and Avi in the distance, on higher ground. There they were, floating along hand in hand through the forest and over clearings that looked like circus rings.

Great Nature spoke, with air benign,
"Go on, ye human race!
This lower world I you resign;
Be fruitful and increase."

Then he would run to them and put his arms around trees and even weep.

"Here, on this hand, does Mankind stand,
And there is Beauty's blossom!"

He needed to have a good cry now, because when he eventually finds them they mustn't see a single tear on his face. After all, none of it was his fault until he let them go away from the car on that nasty, illogical, chaotic day.

He was sitting on the tree stump with his legs stretched out; he took a swig of vodka and called Kenzy. He called her number several times a day.

The hero of these artless strains,
A lowly bard was he.

He was really missing her. Kenzy would be bound to think of what needed to be done. Kenzy knew how to talk to people as well as follow tracks on the ground. She it was who back then noticed the trampled bilberry bushes. But even Kenzy wouldn't be able to negotiate with the forest the release of those ...

He sought a correspondent breast,
To give obedience due.

Those children who were sick in the head.

He felt the powerful, high behest
Thrill, vital, thro' and thro'.

Those wretched little ingrates that he had foisted on the world.

Propitious Powers screen'd the young flow'rs,
From mildews of abortion;
And low! the bard—a great reward—
Has got a double portion!

At moments such as this he was struck by bouts of real rage. Rage at the way the world was made. Rage at forest and fortune.

Auld, cantie Coil may count the day,
As annual it returns,
The third of Libra's equal sway,
That gave another Burns.

Faither realised that Alicia was not to blame for anything.

With future rhymes, in other times,
To emulate her sire—
To sing auld Coil in nobler style,
With more poetic fire.

And that was her main offence.

He was given a comparatively mild punishment. All they did was terminate his parental rights. As though those rights were like a driving licence. What a joke! They—the progenitors and judges of their own children—were the ones who had cooked up this weird name for such a terrible punishment. Termination of parental rights... As though such rights could ever be terminated. The thought occurred to Faither that a punishment like that was a sort of castration in reverse: first you engender the children, but then you are held incapable of engendering these selfsame children who by now have been running around for quite a long time.

"Kenzy," he said aloud into his unheeding telephone, "Kenzy, y'maun retour. Ah hae need o ye. Yir hair, yir bonnie yellae hair hinders ma sairch fir the bairns. Come awa back—fir ma sake, fir sake o the Leid, fir sake o message the yellae Nile wagtail, the *Motacilla alba*, maun pass oan—ye ken, ah tellt ye aw aboot it mony's the time. Ah realeese y're afeart, ah respect yir fear. Aye but ye maun retour. Kenzy. Ah've loast haud o masel."

Mixed in with the rage, the self-pity and the fear for Alicia there was dread, hardened and painful, that Kenzy would give him away.

To tell the truth, he didn't know what she was capable of. There was a time when there was no Kenzy. She had appeared in his life by chance, like love. And the fact that he had taught love to speak his Leid meant nothing.

Once he had officially ceased to be Alicia's faither, there was nothing left for him to do but leave their little town; the story of Alicia and her faither was common knowledge, and there was so much hatred surrounding him that he was unable to sleep. He felt as though the fluids coming from this hatred were seeping beneath his blanket and paralysing his body.

Here lies Squire Hugh—ye harlot crew,
Come mak your watter on him,
I'm shuir that he weel pleased wad be
To think ye pished upon him.

So he sold their flat and bought himself a studio on the outskirts of the capital. He returned to the place from where he had once fled with the little girl who was to become Alicia. At that time he thought he was going out to the people. Closer to the forest, to his native land, to his Leid. He had had to hire a bus to transport all his stuff.

Now he took only what was really necessary. Alicia's toys. The world's only Belarusian-speaking doll moved to the capital.

ah've loast haud o masel: I've lost hold of myself

To be honest, it wasn't even a studio, but just half of a small privately owned house close to a newly built metro line. With its own entrance and rotten floorboards. On the other hand, no one knew him here. He had to find a job to earn a living. And to organise Alicia's escape. They may have taken away his parental rights, but Alicia they couldn't take. He promised himself that he would find out where they were keeping her—all these Misses Edwardsons, these neighbours, teachers, doctors, these lawyer types, these aliens who had lost their Leid and with it their mind and soul.

He took any odd job he could find in the capital, and began to set money aside. He stuck notices up all over the place, the paper stuck to the concrete together with his fingers. He tramped across the city as a courier for a variety of dubious firms. He did the homework for young retards with empty eyes. He swept the boulevards. He looked after old people. With them he could relax and speak the Leid, and they could understand him, these stinking old people, except that the topic was always the same: they asked him either to kill them or to make the TV louder.

And he continued to keep a diary. Writing was something he was good at. If anybody asked, he would say that he was writing a novel. All kinds of novels are being written these days.

But writing didn't save him. He was overcome more and more often by waves of such total despair that he froze one step from the abyss known as resignation and recognition of defeat.

Then he met Kenzy.

***

That autumn he managed to fix himself up with a job on a newspaper that was far from being the most popular. The newspaper brought him in a regular income and the opportunity to quite legally fish around for bits and pieces of information, like where children end up when their faithers have been castrated after the event. However, the newspaper stole his time. Faither was in a hurry, but the newspaper wasn't. It didn't exactly burn with desire to keep up with the events of the day. Somehow Faither found bound collections of past issues of the paper in the editorial offices, and this filled him with enthusiasm. He discovered that the paper had at one time been published in the Leid. These bound volumes that were no longer of any use to anyone held the truth about what the Leid had once been, and what it had become. This truth had been written by people who had no concern for the Leid. They probably didn't even speak it. They could only write it.

Faither would hand in for correction his hastily written lines on the kindergartens that factories had built for their workers, on the Spartakiad of the Peoples organised by the transport sector, on the latest news of the House of Culture (that still, after all the changes, bore the name of one of Stalin's odious henchmen), and then would hide himself away behind an old cupboard and pore over the bound collections of newspapers. He read them like they were a novel.

The newspaper, almost a daily, had been coming out since the end of the 1940s. It was spring when he started to read through the back issues, because he hadn't learned of their existence straightaway; by November he had reached only as far as the 1960s.

These back issues, all bearing the aquiline profile of the Leader of the Peoples, would wrap themselves in dark raincoats, give off the sweetish aroma of petrol, and breathe cheap chypre perfume into the face before submersing themselves in the glacial depths. The people in them were generous in both their cursing of others and their own swearing of oaths of fealty. First names were replaced by the three letters "Com" for "comrade," used like initials—the same for all. Sombre yellow pages with the faces of newly defunct heroes of labour, written-off gods and officials without end. Detailed letters of complaint that were coming more and more to resemble denunciations, from readers who still believed in what they read in the newspapers. This was a newspaper that gave the full names of idlers and saboteurs right down to the last letter—no "names changed" here. This reality that had disappeared—it was truly frightening how much it had come to resemble the reality of today, like the squeaking of an old cupboard behind your back. Yesterday had become today, and there was no sign of tomorrow. His love affair with the bound volumes of old issues of the paper would have to come to an end in the 1990s; that was where the afterword begins, something that nobody ever reads.

There were times when the editor caught Faither at his favourite pastime.

"Reading those bound volumes again, eh?" he said with no special malice in his voice; he felt a certain sympathy for Faither. "OK, then. Bit of a bounder, are you?"

Faither wasn't insulted. The editor was an old man. For him, Faither was a person without a past.

On that particular day Faither was in a hurry to hand in all his material for the paper before lunch. It was a Friday, and ever since the morning all his colleagues had been bored and in a bad mood; there is nothing more intolerable than waiting for Friday evening, a time when work slackens off for a while, anaesthetised by the thought of tomorrow. During the lunch break Faither had bought himself a bottle of cheap plonk and hidden it in his desk; now he was waiting for all the others to leave. He even encouraged them by setting light to their soul's desire: to go home as soon as possible. This he did by assuring them that he had heard from the editor that none of the bosses would appear in the office for the rest of the day; the next issue of the paper had already been signed off for printing.

Faither was itching to be left alone, to go over to his cupboard, uncork the wine, and delve into the bound volumes. He simply had to know what would turn up next. There's nothing more boring in the world than a newspaper—with or without drawings—but to his surprise Faither discovered that any newspaper, even the dullest of them, could over time turn into Literature with a capital "L," just as dung turns into fuel. The most important thing is not to be in a hurry. Not to look in a newspaper for something that it has not yet become. To wait and turn the pages, reading whatever is printed there in small type. And to learn to read whatever is printed in invisible type.

At last his colleagues (Faither affectionately called them zombies) began to leave one by one; the working day was coming to an end, albeit slowly, by small droplets, by the bits of ash that fall off cigarette stubs little by little. Until finally there were just two of them left in the editorial office: Faither and some old biddy who was afraid that the editor would phone and make a note of who was still slaving away and who had already fled the scene. Then the two of them would get a bonus and all the others would have their pay docked for taking time off. She, the biddy that is, was beginning to suspect that Faither was playing a game of his own. The thought seemed to have occurred to her that he had fooled them into thinking he was privy to some secret information and really wanted to collect for himself all the bonus payouts for loyalty in the workplace. And so a kind of competition began, to see which of them could outsit the other. By a happy chance someone phoned her from home. Something had happened. She hurriedly put her coat on, ready to run out of the office ...

"Keys!" Faither reminded her; whoever was last to leave had to lock up the office and switch on the alarm downstairs. She turned back and started rummaging around in her handbag. The keys had fallen on to the floor. He bent down to pick them up, but by the time he had straightened up again she had disappeared. Opening his bottle he watched the zombiette through the window; she raised her zombie umbrella and made a dash for the tram. Something serious must really have happened at home.

He went over to the cupboard and opened one of the bound volumes. He wasn't threatened by anything unexpected for the next couple of hours. If he wanted he could stay here right into the night. And read and read. He got down to his collected back runs (oh yes, that's right, he had long ago come to think of these bound volumes as his own, and he dreamed of somehow taking them home—no one would ever notice anyway), he picked them up them gently and slowly, drawing out the pleasure. It was raining outside. He had the delightful feeling that now he could do something that wasn't allowed. He placed the keys next to him—the keys to all the offices. He poured himself some of the golden-coloured wine into a coffee mug. On the anniversary of the Great ... Com. R. draws attention to ...

Someone was coming up the stairs. Faither could clearly hear footsteps resounding in the stairwell. No, it couldn't be anyone from the management; they don't tread so lightly; they're afraid of their authority draining away on the steps, and they certainly weren't the overburdened, fussy footfalls of his beloved zombies. Faither tried to picture to himself who this late visitor could possibly be. Could it be Comrade R. who has come back from the past? He's slipped out of the old newspaper, finds himself all of a sudden on a street which he has no difficulty in recognising, and now here he is, quickly climbing the stairs to the editorial office to complain that no one has changed his work clothes for ages.

O gie the lass her fairin lad,
O gie the lass her fairin,
An something else she'll gie to you,
That's waly worth the wearin;

Faither was in need of love. Not the kind that lasts a year or only a month, not the kind where you just take everything that's offered. No. He needed the kind of love that the Leid gives, the kind that is given once and lasts forever. He needed the love of an accomplice.

It was a woman of quite extraordinary beauty. The kind of beauty that can make people say about a woman, "No, she is not for you."

Syne cowp her ower amang the creels,
When ye hae taen your brandy,

The kind of beauty encountered only in a book or a film. But that was what she was really like. A beauty that could only be imagined, or what? There aren't women like that.

The mair she bangs the less she squeels;

imagined, wet and beautiful,

an hey for houghmagandie.

She lowered her umbrella, greeted Faither and even gave her name. Her first name. That was so intimate. Like an earlobe.

Then gie the lass a fairin, lad,
O gie the lass her fairin,
An she'll gie you a hairy thing,
An o it be na sparin.

Dozens of Faither's acquaintances with the same first name flashed through his mind, winked at him and faded away, mortally insulted. Thousands of words rose up in his head, only to disappear the next instant: the Leid, the Lingo, words that are whispered drowsily into the pillow, words that are licked off hot skin, words that are said in the heart, as if you're having an injection. Faither coughed and his own name flew right out of his head.

"I was here yesterday. I came about the urgent care centre, the editor promised to raise the issue at the next ... What do you call it?"

Faither instantly fell in love with urgent medical care centres. He was truly grateful to old Pete of the care centre at the factory for existing in this world; Pete of the hairy ears, the reek of booze that he gave off, the garlicky eyes and the sergeant-majorly jokes.

"Editorial board meeting."

"... And I left my gloves here." She smiled. He hadn't seen any gloves in the offices, and he couldn't recall that the topic of urgent care centres had ever been raised at yesterday's meeting; he was seeing this woman for the first time in his life; yesterday he had sat at his desk the whole day working on some daft council report, but that couldn't possibly be the reason why he hadn't noticed the miracle that was now brightening this dismal office and the corridor behind his back, and all the rest of the wretched world around him. It's simply not possible that she could have existed yesterday, or that she would still exist tomorrow. She's of the here and now, freshly made, she's risen like a blonde Venus out of the foam of Friday, out of the slush outside the window, and the rustling of bound volumes of old newspapers.

But he had to find those gloves. He was ready to give up his life to find them. And all the maps. And all the castles. That's how easy it is to betray yourself when the time comes.

"We'll airt them oot," he said gloomily.

"What did you say?"

"Thay'll turn up." She'll be awa ony minuit, an yon'll be end o't. "Thay canna jist be disparu. Thay're aw honest, the bodies wha labour here. Thay'd hae mair mynd tae chowk oan thare ain gubbins than lay a finger oan anither body's stuff."

"You have such a strange way of talking. Have you just come up from the country?"

Her smile was even wider. Now it was a smile for him. For him alone. The witch knew exactly what she was doing to him.

"Wee drap vino, mebbes?" Faither asked even more gloomily. It sounded a bit vulgar. But sod it, he was always like that at work.

To his surprise, she didn't refuse. He poured her out a brimful. She took a tiny sip. Yes, now it's all going to come to an end. He thought of the game he had quite recently started playing. Most probably out of desperation and loneliness—the only things it is impossible to withstand. Whenever he was in an empty space somewhere—in the library, in a shop, in a room, in a corridor, or even in a carriage on the underground—he would shut his eyes and wait for someone to come in. He would sit with his eyes shut and tell himself: Gin it's a wumman-body, ye'll tummel tae l'amour. He would hear the doors open. The women who entered the torture chamber of his game were invariably his mother's age. He only ever encountered the elderly. All he had to do was stop playing the game and immediately some angels in short skirts would come and sit next to him, little demons of unimaginable pulchritude. Sent to mock him.

Yes, it'll all end, right now. But there was such warmth emanating from Faither's evening guest. It was as if she had been searching for him, looking everywhere in the city, beneath all the balconies, until she found him at last.

"D'ye no hae a notion tae gie yirsel some heat wi this?" begged Faither. "Begged" is the right word. He sounded like a supplicant.

Once again she just wetted her lips with the wine. He took her by the hand. OK, that's it, it's all going to finish now. Get her out of her mind with drink, push her flat on the table, right on top of the old newspapers, show her who's boss, lift her up, tear her clothes off, strangle her, force yourself inside her, go to sleep next to her, and let tomorrow look after itself.

"D'ye bide hereaboots?"

"No, quite a long way away ... Is this where you work, your office?" she asked pensively, as she cast her eyes around the shabby old furnishings of what could only be described as a storeroom.

"Na na, aw that's here's auld jurnals an stuff ... jist craperie. Ma bureau's doon the wey."

"What do you mean by 'craperie'? What's in this cupboard? Can I have a look? Do you ever wash them? These cups here?"

She freed her hand and opened the cupboard, and, of course,

tummel tae l'amour: fall in love   _doon the wey_: down the corridor

she started sneezing immediately. And in a jokey kind of way, as if she was doing it on purpose. Faither was struck with a sudden urge to poison her with this dust. So that she too would be unable to tear herself away from these collections of old newspapers, so that she should sit at his side and leaf through them. To make it so that she might understand him. To make her a part of himself. An accomplice. She drew her fingertips across the table. "Thare's wee bit chocolate thare," said Faither, without taking his eyes off her. She opened the drawer.

"Where?"

"That means thare's nane."

It was then that Faither went over and put his arms around her.

"Is that to make up for the chocolate? What long fingers you have," she said. Now she was becoming really personal. The cupboard with the old newspapers squeaked its approval, and a timid burst of applause came from the balcony.

"Fingers fit anely fir pianae," Faither pulled a face, and his voice trembled.

"A masseur's fingers more like," and she smiled again. "You could earn some good money that way. Haven't you ever tried? There are a lot of old ladies in this city. Who, if you touch them in a certain way with fingers like that ..."

What is she talking about? And how did she guess? About old age, the thing he feared the most, old age that he had so often won for himself in that stupid game of his. He had no right to grow old until he was certain that the message would be delivered.

"Ye've goat this awfy bonnie ..." he said, and with two fingers grasped whatever it was hanging round her neck. A little piece of faded dark red cloth.

"What's 'awfy bonnie'?"

"This yin here, ah dinna ken hou ye'd caw it."

"Oh, that ..." she said in a voice devoid of any interest.

"Wait." All of a sudden she halted the persistent, rude movements of his hands with a slight frown, a look that suited her well. "Where's the toilet?"

"Gang oot o here an birl left, thare's only fower rooms." Faither gave his explanation hurriedly. "Awbesit thay're lockit, tak the checks, here."

She took them, smiled at Faither once more and left the room. Pouring himself some more of the plonk, Faither heard her stop in the corridor. Then something really rather droll happened, something absolutely irredeemable. He realised that she was locking the door to the room where he was, leaving him alone inside.

There were four keys on the ring. Faither was left on his lonesome with his old newspapers, the cupboard, the old typewriter in the corner and the shabby table on which stood a bottle of Massandra and a mug inscribed "Moscow forever." A gift to the editorial office from Russian colleagues.

She had simply up and locked him in.

But cowp her ower amang the creels,
An bar the door wi baith your heels,
The mair she bangs the less she squeels,
An hey for houghmagandie!

"Whit a bitch," he thought to himself tenderly. He sat and listened to her methodically fiddling with the locks and doors in turn, walking around the editorial offices, opening and shutting drawers and shuffling papers. Anyone else in his place would by now have worked out what was worth carrying out of the building. Computers—six in all, a printer, a scanner, telephones, sundry other petty items, none of them of any use. The safe beneath the bookkeeper's desk. A variety of awards for participating in media shows: the artificial gilding on the Golden Pens and the Silver Letters that had been lacquered to look like the real thing.

And the new furniture. But Faither couldn't be bothered to list

awbesit: albeit   *check*: key

it all. He was in her power and he liked it. He stepped out on to the balcony, the old balcony, lit up a cigarette and poured himself some more wine.

The newspaper offices were on the second floor. He could have phoned the police or even one of the bosses, he could have yelled out for someone to come up and catch the criminal, but there was no one on the street and Faither didn't want to spoil the evening by having an extra unwanted human around. And as for her ... She knew full well that he would never do any such thing. She had seen right through him from the very start. He flicked his dog-end into the rain and went back to his table. She was still in the building. He could hear her footsteps in the corridor, he could see how the wet marks left by her shoes between the door and his table were gradually disappearing, and he sat there drinking his cheap wine, and for some reason he felt fine. For the first time in many, many years. And then he dozed off with his head on the old newspapers, and dreamed of Comrade R. and old Pete—all three of them naked, sitting in a cold bathhouse. They were consoling Faither, whipping their birch twigs and saying that she would return, she was bound to return. "Wha, Alicia?" asked Faither, and they shook their heads, "Non, thare's naethin yese can dae aboot yon."

In the morning, when some policemen came with the editor—straight from his little place in the country, dressed in a tracksuit bearing the state coat of arms—and Faither was freed from captivity, it turned out that nothing had been taken. Absolutely nothing. Faither stood out on the balcony for a bit with a taciturn, angry policeman.

"So why in hell's name's she done this?"

"She wiz oan the prowl fur sumthin," the policeman answered unwillingly. "Or mebbe no. Punters dae helluva weird stuff sumetimes. Therr wis this heidcase oot the 'burbs, torched his ain hoose! So we sed tae him, why d'ye dae it? An he sed 'Nae idea. Ah jist waaanted tae.' No right in the heid. Jist like hur. A burd waaants sumthin aw o a suddin, but whit the hell it is she waaants she's nae idea."

Faither liked the answer.

He ran across her a month later—in the metro. He followed her, keeping up with every step she took and shoving his face into her field of vision: come awa, tak cognisance o me, dinna be wasetfu o time. Thare maun be an seicont spiel. Ye hae plichtit. She tried to get away, she hid herself in the ladies loo of a big department store and didn't come out for ages, maybe a whole hour. But finally she did emerge, tidying her hair. She tried to get past him—a proud, innocent Venus. He blocked her way. They descended the stairs to the street in silence.

"So, are you going to hand me over to the police?" She smiled. "Masseur's fingers."

"Non." He shrugged his shoulders. "Whit fir? Jist hear me oot."

And so they began to talk. To meet in the frozen parks and talk. And drink ice-cold plonk in his flat.

"There's something I want," she said. "I don't know what it is myself. I just want something odd to happen. Very odd. I want things not to go as they should."

He talked to her for hours on end. He read books to her. He read his diary aloud. And by the summer they were already speaking his Leid. But they spoke it so that no one else could hear them. He told her about the wooden flutes of the past, the fairy tales that no one tells to children any more, he talked of victories and castles, of grandeur and great sorrow. He showed her a whole continent on which she lived and knew nothing about.

"Ye maun be the queerest thing's happent tae me."

Kenzy had changed a great deal. They met up once, and at a distance he didn't recognise her; her hair was yellow like the sky above the capital when the sun was about to go down on it for the very last time. This was the time when he told her about Sia,

spiel: act   *ye hae plichtit*: you gave a solemn promise

194

the little Nile wagtail in the form of a little girl, and the message that had been entrusted to her.

Kenzy's eyes shone with horror.

"Whit befaw Alicia's mither?"

"She's nae here ony mair."

"Is she deid?"

"Ye micht say as much."

"Is Alicia alike wi her?"

"Alicia's alike wi naebody. Or she coudna deleever the message."

In the early days of summer, the time of year when bureaucrats start going on their holidays, Kenzy paid a visit to one particular state body—and thanks to her (all she had to do was get herself lost among all the separate offices) they learned of the existence of a not exactly well-known camp in the forest where they toughen up and treat orphans and children whose parents have been declared reverse castrates. So it was that right at the beginning of summer Faither and Kenzy together started to hatch plans of escape.

He didn't notice it straightaway, but Kenzy had undergone a great change. It was as though some kind of restless spirit had taken up residence within her along with the Leid. In some kind of strange fever with her voice halting and stumbling, she sought to tell Faither that there were times when, sitting on a trolleybus battling its way across the city whirlwind, she would look out of the window and see two children holding each other by the hand, walking straight through walls of snow. There were times when she dreamed

O, an ye were dead, guidman,
A green turf on your head, guidman,
I wad bestow my widowhood
Upon a rantin' Highlandman

befaw: befell

—and the dreams seemed so real that she still felt pain between her legs—that she had given herself over to twelve warriors in turn, and each one of them, before withdrawing from her, writes a word on her belly with a finger still encased in armour, and the word's burning on her skin, and she wants to say the word, but she can't, she smears cream all over herself, but the word is still there. The words were all very different—and Faither was pleased that they were all old, forgotten words that he had revealed to her.

> There's sax eggs in the pot, guidman,
> There's sax eggs in the pot, guidman;
> There's a to you, and twa to me,
> And three to our John Highlandman.

It had been a long time since Faither had experienced such joy of discovery. Among the personages that peopled Kenzy's dreams at night and appeared to her in broad daylight—daylight so bright that it hurt the eyes—there was one that gradually came to occupy pride of place: a green-eyed warrior with long, blond hair. He looked like a real Aryan. Kenzy said that he had revealed his name to her—the knight Sir Nowers.[31] Faither listened to her stories of him with the greatest of pleasure, and at length this Sir Nowers became an ally in their struggle. Oddly enough, Faither never felt any jealousy when he heard how in her dreams Kenzy lays her yellow-haired head like a field of wind-ruffled wheat on his shoulder of iron so she can stroke his breast where the chill of his armour yet lingers, how she wraps her legs round his carved oak limbs.

> A sheep-head's in the pot, guidman,
> A sheep-head's in the pot, guidman;
> The flesh to him, the broo to me,
> An' the horns become your brow, guidman.

Sir Nowers the knight related to her tales of his glorious victories, using strange words that could not be found even in the oldest dictionaries. One fine day, the first day of summer, Faither and Kenzy agreed to await a signal from Nowers. For some time now he had become their oracle; without his approval they could not begin the operation for the liberation of Sia and her brother. Every day Faither waited impatiently for Kenzy to tell him about her latest dream, but for the time being Nowers the brave and wise was silent.

With each day Kenzy was becoming more and more transparent. She now knew what she wanted. And this desire as it were lifted a veil from her—there was no past any more, no experience, no perplexity, no feeling of senselessness. Kenzy now stood out against a background that had been purged of all superfluous colours—his Kenzy, his accomplice against the world, a willing martyr in defence of the Leid that they now shared between them, and there was no less of it because of their sharing. Just as Alicia had need of Avi, so he, Faither, needed this woman, whose life had been given meaning by him.

She wrote a letter to a German Slavist who, according to Faither, was the last specialist in the world who regarded their Leid as still alive. She dared to take a step that he himself had been dreaming about for years.

What was the point of their writing to him? It's simply because they had seen him one evening on the television: this Slavist, Herr Günsche, was giving an interview on the First National channel. What he was saying would not please Miss Edwardson or any of them.

"I am of the opinion that it is too late to revive this 'Leid' of yours, and for that reason I would not waste time on doing something that has no chance of success." Herr Günsche spoke the Lingo correctly—very correctly, even—making mistakes only in the word stresses. "But then the accent ... this 'brogue' as some people call it—it is very recognisable, it could bring you all together better than a stillborn Leid, which, as we know, was an artificial project. To the best of my knowledge there is not a single child for whom the Leid has been native since birth. And no adults either. Except for graphic artists and writers."

At this point the ruddy-faced presenter butted in: "Yes, our state is doing a great deal in this direction."

"But the accent is still there. Like a fly in amber. Preserve it, and it will replace the whole of your Leid. If you really do want to create a nation of your own in this day and age, you should raise aloft the flag of your accent. It is the only thing that distinguishes you from others. There is nothing else. Nada, nix, nil."

"But we do not want to be different!" The presenter smiled. "Everyone in our country dreams of speaking the Lingo properly. Even writers!"

"I too fail to understand what you need a dead language for, but the accent—on this point I cannot agree." The German shook his head. "It is beautiful. It lends colour to your pure Language. You know, too pure means too dull. You have to add some spice. You know, it is at times attractive to hear people speak with a slight stammer, or make their 'r' sounds in the back of the throat."

The presenter laughed good-naturedly. The professor also gave a smile.

"The language you speak must surely have some sort of individuality! In general, what we consider to be a language is these days a Big Question. Why not think of it as pure Lingo, but with your accent? Phonetic peculiarities, yes. Even in the former Yugoslavia..."

Faither and Kenzy were no longer listening. They sat there gobsmacked in front of the television, trying to make sense of what they had just heard. Was the distinguished professor trying to make fools of them? Faither agreed that the accent was the straw at which it was worth clutching. But was it enough to be left clutching a dry piece of straw in your hand, when it could lead you to an ear of corn and so to the Leid of the poet Kolas?[32] It was frightening just to think about it.

Kenzy found a way of contacting the Professor, and wrote to him, saying that he was mistaken—because there is one little girl. A little girl who very soon will be left without even an accent. Kenzy sought his help, but he never replied. Perhaps the contact address was wrong. Perhaps she should have written in English. Herr Günsche didn't look like a man who could speak their Leid.

But Kenzy could.

Kenzy.

Sing round about the fire wi' a rung she ran,
An' round about the fire wi' a rung she ran:
Your horns shall tie you to the staw,
An' I shall bang your hide, guidman!

The woman who had betrayed him. Faither hid his face in his hands. His body, however, wanted more, and so he fell on to the moss and burst into tears. And the forest could hear his sobs. He felt no shame in front of the forest.

Lang may she stand to prop the land,
The flow'r of ancient nations;

In the end, a forest is just that—a forest, whatever the poets that no one reads have to say on the subject. Their beloved poets.

And Burnses spring, her fame to sing,
To endless generations!

13

Yon sonne must shuirly slauchter me

Yon sonne must shuirly slauchter me, thought the writer Mike McFinnie to himself.[33] He stopped, pulled out a hanky and wiped the heroic sweat from his brow. Words like that always entered his head in his native language. After all, he was a Writer and it was permitted. He had started out early that morning to beat the heat. He took a tram—quite empty at this time of day—to the bus station, where he boarded a share taxi which over a two-hour journey managed to shake his insides out. The driver was someone he knew; he dropped him off where he wanted—by a roadside pole that had pushed its way up between birches and pines. It was nearer from here to his dacha than from the bus stop. The tarmacked road wound on, but Mike McFinnie plodded off straight into the forest. There was such a sense of security and calm in the forest that Mike McFinnie enjoyed picturing to himself how well he would work at the dacha. "It'll be like lying on Abraham's bosom," he said aloud.

And Edinburgh and Glasgow
Are like ploomen in a pub.
They want to hear o' naething
But their ain foul hubbub …

There were clouds of dust whirling above the narrow rural road on to which he emerged from the forest. All he had to do now was follow the road for about two kilometres, go up a hill and then plunge into a wooded area, where he would find the lonely dacha that he had recently bought for a song. And it was here, as he was walking along the road, that the heat finally hit him, taking its revenge for his cunning ruse of the morning by gently cooking him on all sides in its frying pan. It was pushing him downhill and then forcing him to climb upwards again, panting for breath. And he obediently trudged on, like forcing a way through melted fat.

He had drunk all the water he had with him while he was still in the taxi. There seemed to be no end to the road; the writer was waiting in torment for the moment when the hill he so longed to see would throw itself at his feet, and just beyond the hill there lay ahead of him three whole days that he could devote entirely to work and the well with its wonder-working ice-cold water that could restore you after the heaviest of benders.

Be't whisky gill or penny wheep,
Or ony ither lotion,
We 'bood to ha'e a thimblefu' first,
And syne we'll toom an ocean! ...

Then there was the inspiration that he had so carefully saved up for when he was in the dacha: after all, when he was at home it could be stolen, because, firstly, there could well be people who are jealous of him, Mike McFinnie—and secondly, in the city there were lots and lots of things he had to do, some important, some not very. And what's more, out here there were berries and mushrooms, a good book with naked babes,

Noo Cutty Sark's tint that ana,
And dances in her skin—Ha! Ha!

I canna ride awa' like Tam,
But e'en maun bide juist whaur I am.

I canna ride—and gin I could,
I'd sune be sorry I hedna stood,

For less than a' there is to see
'll never be owre muckle for me.

Cutty, gin you've mair to strip,
Aff wi't, lass—and let it rip!

and his fashionable folksy embroidered shirt—all Mike McFinnie had to do was put it on, and he would sit down to work
and, most importantly, feel that he was a real man. And there
lay something else in Mike McFinnie's sports bag (which, so it
was said, had belonged to that great writer Mr. Don Keyes himself[34]): a story, but not just any old story, it was about the war. A
story that was penetrating and deeply moving, and with it Mike
McFinnie hoped to reconcile everyone; he loved it when he was
called a writer who stood above all the squabbles and intrigues,
and who used his authority to help find compromises.

The haill warld's barkin' and fleein',
And this is its echo and aiker,
A soond that arrears in my lug
Herrin'-banein' back to its maker

And lastly: his wife would not be at the dacha.

It's a queer thing to tryst wi' a wumman
When the boss o' her body's gane,
And her banes in the wund as she comes
Dirl like a raff o' rain.

His wife was someone Mike McFinnie really hated. Inspiration and his wife were not compatible with each other: his wife
pulled him down to ground level,

Like a thunder-plump on the sunlicht,
Or the slounge o' daith on my dreams,

Or as to a fair forfochen man
A breedin' wife's beddiness seems,

and Mike McFinnie was a poet. A poet who had only recently begun to write prose. He had discovered the prose writer within himself; it was like what happens when you open a book and—hey presto!—find some money you'd forgotten about, thirty whole dollars! And this particular prose writer turned out to be fierce, rancorous, awkward and extremely talented. And apart from that, this prose writer wanted to be up to the moment—and Mike McFinnie was trying not to stand in his way.

"Why are you burying me in the ground?" he had shouted at his wife. "I'm going to show these jumped-up little nyaffs how to write!"

"All your life you've been writing about the land," she replied. "You don't know how to do anything else! Open your eyes! The land is the only reason they like you, Mike!"

Animals, vegetables, what are they a'
But as thochts that a man has ha'en?
And Earth sall be like a toom skull syne
—Whaur'll its thochts be then? ...

There are certain important matters that require explanation at this point.

When he was contemplating the kind of work that lay ahead of him over the next three days, he did not have in mind what people who are far removed from literature might have thought.

The work that preoccupied his soul—a soul so sensitive to beauty—centred on a large, deep pit which he had dug at an appropriate distance from the cottage that was still not yet ready for human habitation. Mike McFinnie had planned to fix the place up with a privy over the summer. The privy that the previous owner had used was now in a parlous state. There was a risk attached to trying to use it. There were draughts from below and from the sides, and from the top as well. The whole construction threatened—right at the most pleasant, intimate moment—to collapse on its owner and bury him beneath the ruins.

What forest worn to the backhauf's this,
What Eden brocht doon to a beanswaup?
—A' the ferlies o' natur' spring frae the earth,
And into't again maun drap.

And so at the beginning of the summer Mike McFinnie dismantled the old privy. He set aside half of the wood to use for heating, and the other half he threw as far as he could away from the cottage, where there was already a pile of various odds and ends. The old, rotten floorboards also flew out in that direction. The pit latrine was now bare, open to the weather and other people's eyes. And, as it turned out, it was full to the brim. Generations of our ancestors must have been going to the site to heed the call of nature, thought Mike McFinnie to himself as he stood on the edge of the pit. Some were lucky, some weren't. And the earth would take it all—hope, caresses and flames.[35]

As the worms'll breed in my corpse until
It's like a rice-puddin', the thistle
Has made an eel-ark o' the lift
Whaur elvers like skirl-in-the-pan sizzle.

In his rare free moments, he had line by line sketched out his plan for the new loo. He had gradually acquired materials, bought planks for the clapboarding in the nearest town and come to an arrangement with a tractor driver for him to transport it all to this quiet, secluded old farmstead. On baking hot days the privy pit gave off an odour of hoary antiquity. And on each occasion he visited the dacha, Mike McFinnie would never cease to be amazed at just how well this antiquity had been preserved. He even thought of inviting a mate of his who was a local history buff and archaeologist. Just think of the layers of history that they could dig up!

A spook o' soond that frae the unkent grave
In which oor nation lies loups up to wave
Sic leprous chuns as tatties have
That cellar boond send spindles gropin'
Towards ony hole that's open.

The work promised to bring him that long forgotten delight in creation. And Mike McFinnie was very happy at having three days torn out of the greyness of his everyday routine. Everything stood ready for him in the dacha: hammers, nails, pliers. Mike McFinnie could not bear plagiarism. He did everything himself, with his own hands.

The story in Mike McFinnie's bag was, it should be said, not his, but by someone else. Mike McFinnie was a writer whose work had earned the respect he deserved, and so he no longer needed to write anything.

I was an anxious barrel, lad,
When first they tapped my bung.
They whistled me up, yet thro' the lift
My freaths like rainbows swung.

Now he had to read what other writers had written and choose whatever was fit for publication in the great literary journal of which he, Mike McFinnie, was Chief Editor. Our writer was a little upset by the need to read several dozen sheets of paper over the next three days. So he decided to do it like this: first he would tackle the most boring material, the story, and early tomorrow morning he would get down to the work that sent such delicious shivers up and down his spine.

Young writers had respect for Mike McFinnie. But Mike

McFinnie was not a young man, and moreover he had been eaten by the woodworm of his creative achievements.

Abordage o' this toom houk's nae mowse.
It munks and's ill to lay haud o',
As gin a man ettled to ride
On the shouders o' his ain shadow.

When he finally reached the farmstead, he no longer had any strength to read or write. He got out his keys but decided to have a little sit-down in front of the door. He plumped himself down on a wooden bench, by which there stood a table carved out of a single piece of wood, and retrieved the manuscript ... Non. Th'morn. Mike McFinnie opened the door, had a swift drink and a bite to eat and went out to cast his eye around his estate.

The last time he was here, he had covered the pit with a plastic sheet. And now, solemnly, as if he was unveiling an expensive statue, he drew back the by now mucky piece of sheeting from the place where the pit was, took a quick satisfied glance down at it and then looked up at the sky. The heat by now was at its most intense. Mike McFinnie returned to the shade, sat on the bench, rested his head on his hands and tried to imagine what It—his privy to be—would look like.

Blue. The top would be painted in the national colours (red and green), and on each wall there would be a portrait of some prominent national figure. It was a pity that there were only four walls, and a multitude of national figures. Lots of talent, that's what we have in this country, thought Mike McFinnie. And, of course, there will be quotations. And among them (why not, hasn't he deserved it?) a four-line verse from one of his own poems.

I'll ha'e nae hauf-way hoose, but aye be whaur
Extremes meet—it's the only way I ken

To dodge the curst conceit o' bein' right
That damns the vast majority o' men

And so he sat there with his head resting on his hands—at one time there was a photograph of him in exactly that pose in all the poetry anthologies. Mike McFinnie knew that young people remembered and respected him. Not long ago a young chap had turned up at his place. They had talked about the Leid. Good lad, that one.

"Son, the thing of utmost importance is tae luve yir countrie," Mike McFinnie said as the lad was leaving. "And nationalism—don't touch it, it's gey fause and pernicious to boot. It maks nae matter what lingo you choose to love your country in—the haill warld's barkin and fleein of course and lingo its echoing shadow. But the land doesn't ask. It takes what you give her, and oor thistle's to the earth as the Man in the Mune's the moon, poor chap..."

The lad had gone away happy. Mike McFinnie had even signed a book for him.

"T'ane young eagle fr'ane Auld Yin."

The signature was dashing and youthful, as if he was signing a receipt in a bank.

There were tools neatly laid out in front of him on the table. Pliers, screwdrivers, hammers, saws—and a whole family of nails, all arranged by size, big down to little, all well made, strong and with a mighty grip, like a row of young sons. Over the next two days he'll be able to get a lot done. By the end of the summer the privy will be up. A sight to please both the eye and the aesthetic sensibilities. What a sight it'll be!

The heat had become simply unbearable. The yard floated and melted in the hot air, the dry bushes had turned completely brown. There was a smell of cooked paint and scorched sand—there were two heaps of it that had been lying here since the

t'ane: to a   *fr'ane*: from an

208

spring; the writer had as yet no idea what he needed it for. Mike McFinnie screwed his eyes up. The oak table at which he sat, feeling a strange weakness in his legs, stood in the shade of a straggling apple tree that the previous owner had planted, and Mike McFinnie thought to himself what a good idea it had been to buy this decrepit farmstead and at last get down to some real creativity.

His legs really did seem to have switched off. He had no desire to move; all he wanted was just to sit there until the evening, by then the heat would have died down. Mike McFinnie sat numb, staring intently at some incandescent mirage and waiting idly for the first breath of cool air to drift over from the forest, and for the sky to turn from bluish to grey and merciful towards all who had the good fortune to have been born beneath it.

And then quite suddenly, in the thick, stifling air that shifted and shimmered as if caught in a kaleidoscope, there appeared the ghostly outlines of two little figures. They seemed to have come from nowhere and were now walking through the yard in the direction of Mike McFinnie. He waved his arm in an attempt to rid himself of the stupor, but it didn't go away. He tried to stand up, but his legs were heavy, and he sat back down on the bench.

Two children—a girl and a boy. Dressed in unimaginably dirty T-shirts and shorts, and their skin was also filthy, so it was almost impossible to tell the difference between it and their clothing. Village kids, thought Mike McFinnie with relief. How neglected they are; nobody looks after them, just like it was one hundred, two hundred years ago. When you think of what's been given to people—education, electricity in every home, paramedics in their villages, the Lingo, passports, pensions—and they still don't look after their kids any better than they used to. Mike McFinnie himself was from a small country town, but had been living in the capital ever since he was a young man and entered the philological faculty of the university. There were little kids like these two running around the little town where he was born, mud and muck up to the knees, unwashed, unkempt and with filthy words on their tongues—but Mike McFinnie was from a family of high-ups, and thought of himself as a city dweller. There was no doubt that these two were from some collective farm somewhere. They're wandering about here instead of helping their parents. Mike McFinnie had written ten books for children and had translated another ten from ten different languages, but he had never really known how to talk to children.

The children were coming in his direction without taking their eyes off of him. When they reached the table they stopped. Now they're going to start bombarding me with questions and begging me for something. Mike McFinnie winced, but then gave them a friendly smile:

"Greetings, my young friends! How's it gaun, guys?" He was trying.

"Hullo!" It was the girl who spoke. "Coud ye tell tae us whaur the road is hereaboots, maister?"

"We maun fin oorsels oan the cairt," added the boy in a hoarse voice, and sat on the edge of the table. Black fingernails, hair looking like it had been smeared with lard, strong, tenacious arms, muscles working beneath the skin that are just waiting to burst forth and do something. Don't expect anything good from this one when he grows up. And there's something not right about the girl either.

In ony brat you can produce.
Carline, gi'e owre—O what's the use?

You pay nae heed but plop me in,
Syne shove me oot, and winna be din,

—Owre and owre, the same auld trick,
Cratur withoot climaeteric! …

The eyes are wrong, they look depraved. Felons, thought Mike McFinnie, but said happily:

"Hout tout! Yese spak oor native tongue! Oor Leid! It's not often we come across children, bairns, weans, likes o youse. Yese must be young writers, shuirly?"

"We're gangin tae Bremen," said the boy. "Ah'm Avi, an yon here's ma tittie Alicia. We want tae get oan tae the cairt an mak oor ain wey. Whit gave ye mynd o us bein scrievers?"

"I can smell a writer a long way aff," and Mike McFinnie sniffed the air. "Hoots, I'm a writer mysel."

"Wow!" said Avi. "But is thare a road hereaboot? *The real Mackay*, ah mean tae say?"

"Weel-a wat there is!" Mike McFinnie replied hastily. "It's o'er therr. You may even win a shared taxi therr."

"Gangin bi taxi w'ither folk?" Alicia's eyebrows shot up. "Na, na, yon's nae fir likes o us. Taxis likes o yon dinna gang tae Bremen, we daurna dae that. We're unweel. Ye see that, aye? Y're scriever richt eneuch?"

"Aye," said Mike McFinnie, and for some reason once again rested his head on his hands. "My name is Mike McFinnie. Children used to read my poems i the schuil."

"Oor paw's a scriever in aw," said Alicia. "Ah reck he is. Ah hae mynd o yon time whan he uised tae scrieve something almaist ev'ry day fir his diary. A diary's whan ye scrieve somethin, but dinna exheebit it t'onybody. Whan ye scrieve fir yirsel alane. D'ye scrieve fir yirsel alane as weel?"

"Naw." Mike McFinnie laughed. "I scrieve for everyone."

"Whit fir?" Avi was quick to ask the question.

"Well, acause I'm a writer." Mike McFinnie laughed again. "Some people go to schuil, like you par example, and writers scrieve books."

hout tout: good heavens

"We dinna gang i the schuil," said Alicia. "We hae, but latterlies we war ta'en aff tae the Camp."

And she pointed to the forest that was behind her back listening attentively to the conversation.

"D'y hae onything tae eat?" she asked. "We're ferr faimish'd. We hae waulkit the forest day an daily syne three days."

"Yon I misbelieve," guffawed Mike McFinnie. "There arenae no weans like that."

"Whit kynd are thare?" she asked. "Thare's teeps o bairn who spak the Leid? Tell us whaur thay bide, maister."

"Come along now, it's a wee bittie early for youse to be thinking about such things." Mike McFinnie was alarmed. "The Leid again ... You'd better hae a wee wash first. And you'll find something to eat thru by in the kitchen. There's a pan loaf therr and some cold pressed sliced ox tongue. And you can take an apple each. You go ahead and grab some purvey, and I'll just sit me doon here ..."

> Gin my thochts that circle like hobby horses
> 'Udna loosen to nightmares. I'd sleep;
> For nocht but a chowed core's left whaur Jerusalem lay
> Like aipples in a heap! ...

The children made for the farmstead, holding each other by the hand. This also raised Mike McFinnie's suspicions. He tried to stand up to retrieve his phone and call to the proper authorities, but the children suddenly appeared before him as if they had risen out of the ground.

"D'y hae mynd o the Granmaw?" said Avi, looking hard at Alicia. "This pits me i mynd o her."

"D'you think he's the Granpaw?" asked Alicia. "D'y think we'll feenish up i yon pit agane? An yon mannie wi the reid een en retour?"

reid een: red eyes

"Aye," said Avi with certainty. "Jist hae a leukie. Granmaw haed muckle needle an chizors. Growen-bodies ayeweys hae somethin shairp. Faither, Granmaw, the Doctor. This wan in aw—it's awreadies laid oot oan the table."

Mike McFinnie remembered that his phone was in the bag. In the bag by the door. In the same bag as that stupid manuscript and his plans for the privy and a lot else for these three wonderful days.

"Sae whaur's the pit here?" asked Alicia. "Close tae the but 'n' ben? We daurna gang i thare."

"Pit?" Avi glanced around the yard. "Whit's this here?" He ran over to the pit and pointed it out to Alicia.

"Ah dinna want tae gang thareawa," said Avi.

"Aye, that's it, richt eneuch," said Alicia sadly.

And at that moment Mike McFinnie felt that his stiff, numb legs had somehow been tied to the table. This was Avi's doing. He didn't wait for Alicia to finish what she was saying and decided to take preventative security measures.

"Weans, bairns, what are you doing?" yelled Mike McFinnie. "You're wee felons, that's what you are. What do you want from me?"

"Ah dinna ken whit 'felons' are," said Avi. "Thare's 'melons.'"

"Mebbes we're melons," said Alicia. "But y're no goin tae pit us in tae the pit, maister."

"Espeicially likes o that yin," said Avi.

Mike McFinnie said nothing. He bent his head low and began to examine the even furrows in the surface of the table. He had never known how to talk to children. He had two of his own, but they had grown up a long time ago and it was already about ten years ago that they had last been to see their father. Perhaps they'll come to his funeral. With his sons he spoke in the normal Lingo; they laughed at his Leid and at his books. And here are

hae a leukie: have a little look   *chizors*: scissors

kids who can natter away in the Leid. As if they were high on drugs.

"Whit in the name o the wee man are you doing this for, bairns?" groaned Mike McFinnie. "End of the day, gemm of two halves, I did show you the road on to that, whadyamacallit, that word that's like the word for 'red carded' in the Leid. And youse may cairry oot aw the cold sliced pressed ox tongue, and the pan loaf. What else ur yese efter? You're good children. Leave the big Auld Yin in peace. You have a maw, don't you? And a daddy?"

"We dinna hae ony daddies," said Alicia sternly. "An we hae nae mither either."

"What do you mean?" Mike McFinnie was horrified. "Where is your mummy? Has she died? Is she deid?"

"Ye coud say yon," Avi announced in Alicia's voice. "Oor mither . . ."

And he glanced helplessly at Alicia for support.

"Oor mither wis kilt," said Alicia with a sigh. "Faither tellt me aboot it. Na. Amaist kilt. She wis hoondit awa frae the Leid."

"That sort of thing doesn't happen," said the writer Mike McFinnie. "Perhaps she was chased oot of her Hame'll Dae Me? Or oot of the kintra? End of the day such things do happen in a gemm of two halves, unfortunately."

"Non, she wis hoondit awa frae the Leid," said Alicia, but there was a note of uncertainty in her voice, and now it was her turn to look at Avi, but he was busy examining the tools. "An yon's why she jist aboot dee'd. Amaist dee'd. Mither uised tae sing sangs."

"In the Leid, presumably?" There was a note of confirmation in the writer's question. An odd little family. "Was it your maw who taught youse to speak the Leid so braw?"

In ony brat you can produce.
Carline, gi'e owre—O what's the use?

Hame'll Dae Me: home will do me

"She haed a wee lump i'er mooth in aw." Alicia's voice became more animated. "Aftwhiles ah think she couda been i Camp. But they dinna accept growen-bodies thare. Th'auldest thare's Ginger o the ersten troup."

"What camp is this?" asked Mike McFinnie.

"Maks nae recks," and Alicia dismissed the question with a wave of her hand. "Mither used tae sing an her sangs waur beautifu. But folk wanted ither types o sang. Ae day, whiles she sang her latest sang—an her maist beautiful—folk startit oan scrievin aboot her. Mither sang o emptie rooms wi naither doors nor windaes. She sang o beasts hirl'd frae tapmaist flets o heich buildins. She sang o weemen bluidy atweesh thair thees an the bairns yon haar o early morn taks awa w'it. An folk hae nae fondness fur likes o yon. Thay want cheerfu sangs concernit wi cantie stuff."

"Yon wis only teep o sang we sung i the Camp" said Avi. "Aye an we'd tasty peels in aw!"

"An nestie wans!" said Alicia. She was a stickler for fairness.

Mike McFinnie broke out in a cold sweat. Impossible in this heat, he thought, but then added to himself, almost impossible. If you can almost die, then everything becomes almost impossible. This sun is going to kill me. These children are going to kill me.

Your acid tongue, vieve lauchter, and hawk's een,
And bluid that drobs like haill to quicken me,
Can turn the mid-day black or midnicht bricht,
Lowse me frae licht or eke frae darkness free.

"Sicweys, folk startit oan tae scrievin 'the hale truith' aboot her," Alicia continued, looking over at the forest. "Sayin hou she war a seekenin auld hure. Hou she bare affrontit awbody wha'd lugs. Hou she wants the nameliheid but her innerside's emptie

maks nae recks: it doesn't matter   *atweesh*: between   *thees*: thighs
haar: mist   *cantie*: cheerful   *peel*: pill   *nameliheid*: fame

215

an she's useless tae awbody, likes o a haar. She soonds likes o a banshee whan she sings. Her neb's likes o a witch's. She scrieves aboot menstruation but withoot ony wird aboot her countrie. Her cunt's o mair import tae her than deegnity or grace. She's tairrible as daith, an folk think shame tae be seen oan the street wi her ..."

"She must have ... *tholed* a lot," said Mike McFinnie.

"Aye," said Alicia as though she didn't really care. "Than some body scrieve'd sayin, 'Awa frae oor Leid! Fuck aff!' Yon's whit he pit oan the web. An mither went unweel."

"Was it her hert?" asked Mike McFinnie as sympathetically as he could.

A spook o' soond that frae the unkent grave
In which oor nation lies loups up to wave

"I don't think I've ever heard of a chantie likes o yon."

"Mebbes acause ye war solely i the Camp," said Avi, also sympathetically.

"Non, it wisna her hert," said Alicia. "Mither stairtit tae hoond hersel awa frae the Leid. She war gey fond o yon sic folk, an she tellt Faither hou she maun tak tent o thaim. Houiver, she coudna hoond hersel awa frae the Leid aw o a sudden. Naw. She stairtit daein it bit bi bit. She'd skive skin aff hersel an thraw it ootae the windae. Consequaintly ah fund thaim whaniver Faither took me fir a daunder up the road. It wis simmer, likes o the nou, an yon slives o skin wis warm. Faither tellt me aw this. Ah hae amaist nae mynd o Mither."

"What happened then?"

"Than jist Faither," said Alicia hurriedly. "Yon's richt, is it na, Avi? But Avi's no goat much memory o Mither. He wisna thare."

thole: suffer   *skive*: pare   *daunder*: walk

216

You pay nae heed but plop me in,
Syne shove me oot, and winna be din,

—Owre and owre, the same auld trick,
Cratur withoot climaeteric! ...

"But there isn't such a big difference in your aaages." Mike McFinnie made an effort to smile. Out of the corner of his eye he watched Avi pick up the tools, run his finger along them, put them to his skin and secretly try them for taste on his tongue. It was apparent that he was listening intently to Alicia, as though he was hearing what she had to say for the first time.

"If y're a scriever, read somethin tae us," asked Alicia. "Faither ayeweys used tae read a loadae o stuff tae us afore we beddit doun. Various teeps o fairy stories. Ah'm nae wrang, am ah, Avi?"

"Belarusian and Ukrainian stories," said Avi.

"German and African stories," said Alicia.

"Japanese stories and stories o Indes folk o Latin America," said Avi.

Alicia didn't remember any Indians, but she nodded her head so enthusiastically that Avi felt like pouring something on her. Because he too wanted to nod his head like that.

"Fine," said Mike McFinnie. "But with one condition. I'll declaim you something o interest, but you will then untie me, tak what e'er you need and bugger aff. OK? Ferr do's? Final whistle?"

"If we lowse ye, ye'll jist hurl us intae yon pit," said Avi. "Naw, ye maun read, an we maun penser. But dinna read onything o'er lang."

And Mike McFinnie cleared his throat and read these ghastly children a short poem about a stream:

O burnie rinnin roun ma tree;
Ye're makin me pense oan cups o tea;
Oan yir banks (they maun be bings o bannocks);

Or by yon banks (gey sma' but pris'd lik Tunnocks)
Are braes wha lead us t'ane braw 'n' muckle pairty;
Haw! Jimmy! Rin an fetch yir daddie!

He had written it a long time ago, and in former times it was in all the anthologies.

"Ah ken yon!" Alicia nodded her head and her cheeks reddened. Even Mike McFinnie thought that this made her more like a human being. "Ah ken yon! Faither read it tae's!"

All the same, it was obvious that both Alicia and her brother were disappointed. Mike McFinnie read another two verses, and again the children recognised them and yawned.

"Why nut somethin an ither body's yet tae read?" said Alicia and looked the writer straight in the eye, right at the spot where Mike McFinnie himself had never yet ventured.

"Read us a fairy story," said Avi and he sat on the table with his legs dangling.

"But I don't write fairy tales," said the writer. "For bairns, weans, I only wrote poems. Ten beuks of them, and I've translated yet anither ten beuks from another ten languages."

"D'ye ken ten langages?" the children asked almost in chorus, and their eyes lit up. "Wow!"

"Well, no, I don't," said Mike McFinnie.

But in this huge ineducable
Heterogeneous hotch and rabble,
Why am I condemned to squabble?

"But you dinna have to know languages in order to translate from them."

"Oh, yon's like gabbin i the Lingo!" said Avi, hitting his feet against the bench in approval. "Ye maunna ken yon tae gab wi yon. Ye maun hae mynd tae jist keep oan wi the peels. An hae mynd o yon thingmies tae keep yir mooth prappit appen."

"Read us yon thingmy i yir baggage," said Alicia. "Ah see it keekin oot."

"It's not mine," said Mike McFinnie as if he didn't want to admit it.

"Wha's it?"

"It was written by another scriever. He said it's about the war."

"Maks nae maiter! Yon's rerr if it's aboot the waur. Thare maun be bluid flowin, an shootin. Oor laddies! Hände hoch! Oan w'it, read!" Avi was overjoyed. He ran to fetch the manuscript and handed it to Mike McFinnie, who then smoothed out the sheets of paper and placed them on the table. The text was completely unfamiliar, and Mike McFinnie was nervous.

"Bronia," he said. "Bronia."

The haill warld's barkin' and fleein',
And this is its echo and aiker,
A soond that arrears in my lug
Herrin'-banein' back to its maker.

And he raised his eyes and looked blankly at the children.

"Bronia?[36] ... What kind of nonsense is this? Och aye I get it. Stress on the first syllable. It's a name. A female name. Short for Bronislava. Good God, the things they think up these days ... Well, OK, ferr do's." He cleared his throat and began to read.

"It was dark in the dugout. The wood-burning stove—a good invention it was, although it seemed so old, from way back in the days of the civil war—had never given off any smoke before. It usually got the temperature quickly up to sauna levels, and in the evening you often had to open the door to let some fresh air in and drive the dry, stuffy air out. But now the warmth was all blown away the moment you opened the door.

"There was an early snowstorm raging outside, as vicious as

rerr: great

219

the war itself, or a sudden, unexpected enemy attack. It wasn't a noise that the forest was making—it was actually groaning with a myriad voices, loud trumpet blasts, the howling of an injured wolf, the sobbing of thousands of children. The wind could not break down the wall of trees, so instead hurled itself in rage down from the sky against the earth, through the treetops, weakening among the branches, then some of its currents burst with special force in at the "windows"—the gaps left by the pines that had been felled for the construction of the camp—and raise up whirling clouds of biting snow. At times the wind would make such an assault on the dugout and on the chimney that the stove would puff out flame and smoke through its vents . . ."

"Shall I carry on?" Mike McFinnie once more raised his eyes

"Aye," nodded Alicia.

"Oan w'it," said Avi.

And so Mike McFinnie continued reading aloud. He really did want to find out what was going to happen next.

14
The damn thing won't burn

"The damn thing won't burn," muttered the commander through gritted teeth, and unwillingly rose from his camp bed.[37] Dryzhuk got up after him and pulled Sidarau by the leg; he started kicking, still drunk, sleepy—his eyelids were stuck down—and with a green fog covering his eyes.

By the stove there was a blackened, cold kettle hanging on a nail, with its squashed spout pointing downwards. Three rifles were leaning against the wall, and very soon each one of them in turn was seized by powerful manly arms. Dryzhuk was the first to clamber out of the dugout, followed by Sidarau, grabbing hold of the snow-covered bushes. Last to emerge into the early morning snow, spitting on the palms of his hands, was the commander.

They made their way over to the other dugout and listened. Just like yesterday, they could hear a monotonous, barely audible mumbling.

"It's a job that's got to be done," said the commander. "Let's get on with it."

The commander offered the sentry a cigarette. He took it, began puffing avidly and moved the freshly made wooden cover of the dugout to one side, allowing the snowstorm to burst in and drag out into the light of day a feeble old woman dressed in rags. She screwed up her eyes and shifted her gaze from the sentry to the commander and back again. She finally fixed her eyes on the commander's face and stared at his red, frostbitten forehead beneath his fur hat. The old woman's nose emitted a hoarse whistling sound.

"She's falling to bits, but she did ID the boss at once," thought the commander approvingly, giving her a shove in her bent back. It was like pushing a dead aspen tree.

"Right then, Bronia," he said. "We're off. That's right. Soon everything'll be all right. We'll get your bones nice and warm, and you'll be sleeping long as you want at last. Come on."

The old woman obediently set off walking.

The commander placed Dryzhuk ahead of her, with Sidarau behind her. He himself walked alongside her, his rifle slung over his shoulder barrel downwards. He also had a Walther tucked into his Sam Browne and a sheath knife—a trophy of war—sticking out of his right boot. To one side hung a couple of heavy, handy grenades. It's a job that's got to be done.

They left the camp and, with snow up to their knees, made their way through a forest glade. What a storm, and it wasn't the end of November yet! Up ahead the commander could see Dryzhuk's back, straight as an axe. Behind him Sidarau was giving off the occasional belch while carefully watching where he put his feet. The three men were taking the old woman towards the shallow gully that cut through the pine forest. It was completely buried in snow, and it could be found only by someone who knew the scarcely visible landmarks—a fallen tree with a trunk that looked like an aerial bomb and one of its ends sticking out above a powdery covering of silver ice that still bore the shadows of night.

The old woman trudged on between them, swaying unsteadily as if she was in a cage bumping along a rough road. To the left of her there was no guard, just majestic tall pines standing stiff on parade. But the old woman wasn't going to make a run for it. She was already finding it difficult to move her legs—they were so heavy, like they had stones crammed into them. Through the rags you could see her flabby skin, now blue with cold. The storm had been tearing at her grey hair, blowing it in clumps all around her head. "Hou auld's she?" thought Sidarau. "Aichty, ninety?" She wis awreddy an auld wumman when he cam intae the wurld.

An noo wur takin her aff tae warm up thae crumblin banes o hers fur the last time; she'll faw doon intae yon snaw, while me, Sidarau, we've goat langwhiles yet tae live. We micht even see end o the waur. Therr'll be folk, weans, passin bi this gully. Gaitherin berries an foostie-baws. Eatin bilberries, pittin wild strawberries i their mooths. If it wis ayeways winter ye'd nivver let the weans come here—jist think oan whit they'd see! Sidarau knew exactly what. But as it staunds, summer'll dae its work. Therr willna be a trace o the auld yin. She'll hae rot awa, wizzent an black as the Yerl o Hell's waistcoat ... aye an yon kettle back at camp. Her speerit's aw that'll be left. The forest weezes oot auld yins likes o her, an yet folk imaigine it's reekin jist ozone an pine needles.

"Noo if ah jist grabbed this auld yin by the heels," thought Sidarau. "She'd faw face doon intae the snaw, an aw her duds wid ride up ... The commander willnae allow's a keek o nuthin but snaw. Therr's gonnae be a hale loadae snaw this winter, an we'll be seein mair than enough o't, so staunds tae raison we maun grab haud o chances tae colour it puir guid an red ..."

There was still about a hundred metres to go until they reached the gully. Snow clung to their legs in the way that prisoners condemned to death would grab hold of them. The commander felt that this was the right moment to cheer up his little company: "What's up, Bronia? I suppose you're freezing, right?" he said in a deliberately loud voice, so that even Dryzhuk turned and looked at him intrigued. Don't look at me, keep looking ahead, thought the commander. The one thing we don't want is for this piece of filth to escape.

"When you were working for the enemy, you were warm, weren't you, Bronia?" the commander said sharply, addressing his subordinates rather than the woman. "When you were boiling spuds for them, and there was all that lovely steam rising from the saucepan, it was all so nice and cosy then, wasn't it?"

Dryzhuk looked round to see how Bronia would react to the commander's words. She blushed and looked pleadingly at Dryzhuk, as if she was promising him something. Dryzhuk straightened up the rifle on his shoulder and looked away.

"Yon's some perr o cheekbanes she's goat oan'er tho'," thought Dryzhuk. "Likes o some queen o the Orient.

"Ah'm ferr vext fur that yin. Noo if oor commander were tae gie awa somethin mair aboot 'er ..." When Dryzhuk heard what he said about the enemy and the potatoes that gave off such a wonderful smell, something inside him ...

"Shall I go on?" asked Mike McFinnie in a trembling voice, not raising his eyes.

"An thay aw speak oor Leid?" asked Alicia timidly.

"Weel, yes, they are our folk," said Mike McFinnie firmly. "What other language should they spak?"

Avi looked doubtfully at him, but said nothing.

"Aye, read oan." Alicia gave permission.

When Dryzhuk heard what he said about the enemy and the potatoes that gave off such a wonderful smell, something inside him stirred, and for a moment he felt good: the fine needles of justice had begun to prick his anaesthetised conscience. But there was a need for a continuation; the steam from those enemy potatoes was evaporating away into nothingness. And the commander had apparently decided to arouse in them a thirst for revenge in small and clearly defined doses, like stoking the stove with firewood.

What is there to say? That's why he's a commander.

Whit kin o age is she? This was a question that started Dryzhuk pondering as he looked furtively at her still youngish face. Forty? Fifty? She could be his mother. And of all of a sudden he felt a craving, such a craving, like nothing he had ever experienced, for this woman behind his back to put her arms around him and kiss him. Just like a mother kisses her son. It had been a long time since anyone kissed Dryzhuk. Well, with the exception of Sidarau, of course. Whaniver Sidarau's been oan the bevvy, he tries tae get a lumber aff ony body. Dryzhuk once had to warn him: "Try that wan oan again, Sidarau, an ah'll blast yer fuckin baws aff." Sidarau tried to justify himself by saying, "Ah'm wan o yer best pals, am ah no?"

Let's go. Face front, raise rifle, aim fur commander an bang bang bang he's deid. Then get Luger oot pockit o padded jaiket, aim fur Sidarau—right atween they bluidshot ees still bleazy eftir aw the moonshine he's chored. Then hot foot it tae yon gully. Proceed tae faw intae this queen, this mither. Pit ma heid oan her knees so's she can stroke ma hair that's unnerneath ma bunnet, richt doon thru ma harnpan intae ma brains so's she pits me back intae the earth unner the snaw we've trod tracks thru like lines oan palm o yer haund. The camp wud get fundit. Fundit at top speed. Whit's yon tae me? Doesnae matter.

"So, Bronia." The commander had started talking again, twirling his handlebar moustache. "You've gone all blue. Even if we did—and here I'm speaking purely theoretically—even if we did let you go, any surgeon would turn you into a doll without arms and legs. And anyway, war doesn't deal in theories. I'm right, aren't I, Sidarau?"

"Aye, aye, Sir" muttered Sidarau, not for an instant taking his eyes away from those rosy heels. They weren't at all blue; they reminded him of rosy cheeks in the snow.

"You see? Sidarau agrees with me," the commander blurted out into the frosty air. "Now think for a moment, Bronia. When you were in that nicely warmed Army HQ—warmed, incidentally, with our firewood—when you, a Young Communist, were translating documents for our enemies, when you were using that wretched Leid of yours by indulging in a bit of collaboration in their nice warm beds, when they gave you a nice fur coat as a bonus for betraying your country—did it never occur to you that winter would come with a vengeance?

chored: stolen   *fundit*: found

"So now talk to the people, tell them why it was you were so warm. Aren't you going to say anything?"

"If it wisnae fur the waur, ah'd mairry a body likes o her," thought Sidarau, poking Bronia in her slender back with the barrel of his rifle not only to earn the commander's approval, but obviously also to somehow touch her skin with something—her skin so smooth, so softly vellus-haired that he wanted to kiss it. "They'd aw hae the green eye fur me, but ah'd be the wan tae suffer maist," he thought sadly. "Wi a body likes o her fur a missus, ah'd be chowed up wi jealousy aw the bluidy time. Naw naw, she's gonnae get whit's comin tae her. Dunt her right intae yon gully. Aye but she'd be a total brammer tae get unner the covers in aw, but ah'd *definitely* get totally chowed wi jealousy," thought Sidarau. "Say ah caught her at it wi some fud, ah'd get the auld haund grenade oot—an … How come Dryzhuk up therr keep's turnin roon? Huz he goat the hots fur oor wee Young Communist lassie'n aw?"

"Bronia, you yourself ought to know that you're guilty!" The commander was lecturing the prisoner for the last time. "You were laughing fit to burst with happiness, weren't you? When our enemies, those blasted fascists, bought her—this little bitch, I just can't go on any more—when those bloody fascists bought her a bike. She sold her homeland for a bike! Your dad, where is he exactly? He's at the front, that's where! And your mum! She's a telegraph operator in Moscow! And as for you … Your mates told me how you sang to the sounds of an enemy mouth organ, yes, that's what they said, you sang songs to the sound of a bleedin' mouth organ of theirs! And meanwhile, in the backyard our boys were being shot. And so go on and get a bit frostbitten, get really cold!"

The commander said no more, just took off his gloves and cleared the spittle from the corners of his mouth that by now had

dunt: drop   *fud*: arsehole

turned to ice. He did the same to his moustache. His whole face was icy. He watched the little prisoner trudging between Dryzhuk and Sidarau, stepping so slowly and so deep into the snow that they kept colliding with her. The gully was now very close. Make a turn by the stand of firs, and there it is. The commander thought of his little daughter with the cornflower blue eyes. Somewhere a thousand kilometres away in the evacuation, she was sitting and writing him a letter. What happiness it would be to sit her on his lap, press his stubbly cheek to her and take her tiny hand in his.

"Dryzhuk!" shouted the commander. "Can't you see that you've got to turn off here? Where the fuck do you think you're going?"

Dryzhuk stopped to get his breath back. It was difficult walking in this snow. So much of it had been dumped on the ground that it reminded him of what happens when a young private has to sit on the loo after returning to his unit from home leave and his mum's cooking.

"Sidarau!" The commander walked resolutely in the direction of the fir trees. He had already spotted the trunk of the felled tree; he could see the gully, full to the brim with snow. "Take her. Pick her up, you dopey sot!"

Sidarau grabbed hold of the tiny body and carried it to the fir trees. It yelled and wanted to eat. He gave it an icicle from off his sleeve to suck. Dryzhuk followed sullenly, using his rifle as a walking stick.

They were soon standing on the edge of the gully.

The commander once again checked the landmarks to make sure that they were in the right spot. Sidarau handed the tiny body over to Dryzhuk who placed it in the snow. They stood for a bit, puffing at their cigarettes.

"Now," said the commander. "Now." Reluctantly Dryzhuk threw his cigarette into the snow.

The commander gave him a piece of advice: "Khvedar, think of the enemy."

Stupefied, Dryzhuk looked round. The commander had never called him by his first name before. He took his rifle—clumsily, just like a townie would take a scythe—raised it and thought how he could do with some tea at that moment. Even if there wasn't any sugar.

For several minutes Mike McFinnie sat in silence. It seemed to him as though the words were hanging in the air.

And when he finally did raise his eyes again, he saw that those ghastly children were watching him with hatred.

Mike McFinnie tried to smile: "How *thrawart*. How could one write likes o yon? Ochone ochone and michtie me, this teep o thing maun mak no gree …"

The children moved closer, and Mike McFinnie had the feeling that something unpleasant was about to happen. But what exactly his lazy intuition refused to acknowledge.

"An ambiguous story," uttered Mike McFinnie in a hollow voice. "Did you grasp the gist of it at all? It's not exactly one for the weans. In fact, I think that bairns ought not to be allowed to read yon teep o stuff. But you did ask!"

Alicia and Avi said nothing, and in their eyes there was still that same hatred.

"Och but weel, if one or two things, quite unnecessary things, were to be cut out," suggested Mike McFinnie in his professional writer's voice, "then, maybe … It's richt braw that you dropped by, I have at least done some work."

And he started laughing. But his laughter seemed so out of place that he choked.

"Well, ah'm no the one who scriev'd it," he said in hope. "Ah did warn youse!"

"Aiblins," said Alicia, "Granmaw wis richt aboot yon pit."

"Aboot us, non. Aboot yon pit, aye," said Avi. "We maun dae wi this yin whit we done wi Mr. Spectator Watchie Man."

thrawart: perverse, contrary   *gree*: favour

"An wi Granmaw," said Alicia. "Itherweys, some ither puir body'll huv tae read yon."

Avi got down from the table; the purposeful way he did it was so menacing that Mike McFinnie had a fit of hysteria.

"What do I have to do with it? We had an agreement!"

"Yon," said Alicia, pointing at the manuscript, "we'll tak it wi us."

Then Avi untied Mike McFinnie's legs, but the writer remained seated on the bench as though glued to it. He showed no signs of wanting to get up. Not bothering to think about it for too long, Avi seized both the writer and the bench and dragged them to the pit. Meanwhile Alicia pushed the manuscript under her T-shirt, and its sharp edges scratched the skin on her tummy so pleasantly. Behind her back she heard a short sharp splash, and then there were some shouts, but what it was that the writer was yelling was already of no interest to her.

As they went up the hill, they could see Mike McFinnie running in the direction of the forest, from where they had emerged to make their way into his yard like a pair of ghosts a few hours earlier on this fatal summer's day, in a country where it is not so easy to find your way on to a map, unless you yourself are a road. In fiercely blazing heat, when good parents would never let their children go outside without something on their heads.

15

At nine o'clock they took a roll call and then turned the light off

At nine o'clock they took a roll call and then turned the light off. And while the roll call was going on, each child had to state their name. Tolik always tried to give his name loudly, he was so afraid of stumbling over it. That's what the troop leaders ordered. If they didn't do that, you never know what might happen: one of the boys might be dead, and he would be counted as if he was alive; there had been cases like that (they were called Incidents). And then the troop leaders would have problems. The troop leaders didn't like it when they had problems and Incidents. Then there really would be the Middle Ages in the dormitory blocks. And every boy and every girl in the Camp knew what the Middle Ages meant, but none of them better than Tolik.

It's the Middle Ages, for example, when they drag you out of bed, tie you to the window with your back to the outside world, drop your trousers and place a torch on the window ledge.

The window is open because it's summer. And insects are attracted to the light. For some reason they're very interested in your backside, and that's where they drink your blood. There were some who did not yet know what was meant by Middle Ages, and they crapped themselves with fear when they were being tied to the window. By morning they were plastered all over not only by mosquitoes, but by other insects as well.

Besides wanting to scratch your backside till it bled, you also felt very ashamed. All through the night eyes had been fixed on you from the neighbouring barrack block, dozens of eyes, white in the night, bright like fireflies. There were tablets that made the whites of the eyes go vivid in the darkness, like milk. They were good for frightening the girls—provided the girls themselves didn't also have these dazzlingly white eyes that seemed to have been cut out of paper.

Sometimes you could be standing by the window until seven in the morning, when the first troop of girls would go by to get washed. And then so many people would be passing by your naked backside, and all of them able to recall it down to the tiniest detail. True, nobody could see your face, and it's not easy to recognise someone by their backside. That, however, didn't save you: everyone knew who in the block they had to thank for the Middle Ages that night. And everyone knew who to thank whenever the Middle Ages happened to all the blocks.

The Middle Ages for everyone: even if just one of their number was to blame for something, the whole troop was forced to say a prayer all night.

For instance:

"Tolik is a good comrade of ours, we respect him and are always ready to come to his aid."

And everyone had to repeat these words a thousand times. And then another thousand. The child who was to blame—Tolik for example—did not have to say the prayer. He could sleep, or read, or simply listen to the others assuring him of their friendship.

And that in itself was quite difficult.

These were all the Middle Ages of summer, but there were ones in the winter as well. Today, Tolik had no wish to recall them.

In general, Tolik disliked remembering anything, because everything he had been taught was very quickly being forgotten. And that lump in his mouth was growing again; it just didn't want to get any smaller for some reason, despite the best efforts of the poor Camp Doctor. Tolik wanted to help him so very much, and he even thought up a way of doing it. But no one wanted to listen to him.

Tolik couldn't really understand why. He didn't crap himself any more when he was tied up, so that no one had to clean up after him. Even so there wasn't a single child who wanted to talk to him. Maybe that's because they were afraid—afraid of being infected. Tolik spoke badly. He did everything badly. Tolik had no friends. True, the Doctor told him that he was Tolik's friend, but for some reason Tolik didn't believe him. Somewhere he had found out—and he knew that he had known it since he was a small child—that a friend does not insert a gag into your mouth while holding a pair of scissors. The Doctor was a kind man, but being kind doesn't make him a friend of someone like Tolik.

Usually there were twenty-five boys here. Twenty-five boys and twenty-five beds. One boy—one bed. This Tolik could understand. But since a short while ago there had been twenty-five beds and twenty-four boys. And Tolik knew why. Except he mustn't tell anyone. The troop leader pretended that there were twenty-five boys, the same as the number of beds, and nobody said that there was a mistake and twenty-five minus one was twenty-four.

At the time when Tolik was still going to school, he could count considerably larger numbers of people and objects. He could—an it's the truith, it's truithfu', is it nae, Mither?—solve puzzles which even university professors couldn't. So it was decided to devise a special programme of study for him: he would spend half a day in school, and half a day in the centre of the city, in a huge, echoing hall with a glass board. But then there was a problem (or Incident, as the troop leaders say)—when he was brought before the professors to see if he really was so intelligent, he was incapable of saying what all these complicated things were. It became clear that mathematics has a Lingo of its own—as a young professor said. And its Lingo is unique. And Tolik's mum didn't know this; she had only the vaguest notion of what mathematics was. What else could you expect from her? She simply hadn't taught him the Lingo that the professors spoke. That's why Tolik was quite unable to say anything to them then. And that's how he ended up in the Camp.

Whenever he was going off duty the troop leader would always carefully straighten up the blanket on one of the boys' beds. The girls said that the Camp Director himself had told the troop leaders to do this. So that they, the boys and the girls, should feel as though they were at home in the Camp. "What rubbish," said the boys back then. Just girls' games. How could it be in the Camp like being at home? In the Camp it's a hundred times better! At home nobody gave them tablets like they get here. At home all the medicines are bitter. Bitter and nasty, and they make you want to throw up.

"They make a vomit begin," said one of the boys in their troop back then, trying to speak the Lingo. And they all agreed, although they knew that that wasn't the way to say it.

In their troop it was Tolik whose blanket was usually straightened up by the leader—and the blanket fell on the ground every time. Tolik would get out of bed to pick it up and receive a blow on the head. The troop leader's hand was very solicitous. Their troop leader was so solicitous about the head of one of the girls that she began to bleed. That was one of the stories that the girls told them—they always know everything, but you shouldn't believe them. How can blood come out of a person's head? If that story was true, everyone would come away from the Doctor covered in blood. But it was never like that—the mouth just hurt from the metal gag.

The group leader would then leave, reminding them about the Middle Ages. The light outside—Tolik's best friend—looked in on their room. Tolik was very fond of talking to it as he lay in bed with his blanket drawn right up to his eyes. The light knew a great deal about Tolik. And it never told on him; it knew how to keep secrets. The light knew, for example, that Tolik had once stolen tablets from the troop leaders who had taken them for themselves, although they were supposed to hand them to the children. He wanted to return them to the Doctor but ate them on the way. By the time he reached the sick bay, he was really high; he had his arms twisted behind his back and told in no uncertain terms never to go there again, that he wanted to kill the Doctor and that from now he could expect a Middle Ages session every day.

Once, on a quite ordinary, unmedieval night, the outside light saw Tolik climb out of the window and dig a hole. Then he got into it and covered himself with earth right up to his neck. All Tolik needed to do was make a simple device. He reckoned that what was needed from him in the Camp was his head, so there it is, he's left them just his head. That's where the tumour was, not in his belly or his heart.

Tolik also knew a thing or two about the light. But he kept his tongue behind his teeth—as the Doctor used to say. He re-membered what friendship was. Friendship is the ability to keep secrets. The light was silent on the topic of Tolik's secrets. And Tolik kept quiet about the secrets the light had.

For instance—it was right beneath this light that the troop leaders had been solicitous about a girl from troop no. 1. They had in turn been solicitous between her legs. Everyone in the dormitory had pretended to be asleep. At the time no one looked out of the window except Tolik. Modern folk are afraid of the Middle Ages; they think that they haven't ended yet. But that light in the middle of the night—that's exactly what the Middle Ages are. It's switched off in the daytime, but at night it shines. That's what Tolik thought, but nobody wanted to listen to him, in case he infected them.

The troop leader disappeared and the light shone, like the eye of a wolf, and close by you could hear the noise of the forest. And it was here that the most interesting thing of all was just beginning.

The boys began to tell stories that they had heard from the girls—and although you shouldn't believe what the girls have to say because they only pretend to know everything there is to know in the world, you can at least listen to them.

Everyone knew that in the forest surrounding the camp there lived all kinds of different beings. Of course, they could never get inside the Camp—but there are times when these beings come too close, and then you have to be really careful to avoid being involved in an Incident.

One of the stories was about a man who sometimes appears; he comes up close to the wire fence and offers sweets, and then turns himself inside out.

"Whit does yon mean?" the newbies would ask.

"Meanin what, is that whit yese mean? Ither ways roon. Insides ootsides." And then in the Lingo, sort of: "Learn the bleedin' Lingo. Then you'll understand."

Everyone was keen to know what happened when a man turned himself inside out, but all those who swore that they had seen him couldn't offer an explanation. Perhaps they didn't want to. Obviously, the sweets he had were tasty.

There was another story about a soldier who goes around the forest very close to the Camp. Perhaps he's a sailor, not a soldier. Or maybe even a policeman. Anyway, his name is Bannock the Bogill. Nobody knows why he's called that. Once he was seen by a boy from the third troop—the boy was nearly cured, they were about to discharge him from the Camp, but after encountering Bannock the Bogill, he couldn't speak at all. He couldn't speak properly, or improperly, and he couldn't even moo like a cow either. So they really did get rid of him from the Camp. They said his time there had come to an end. To each his own time in the Camp.

"That's because each person has their own individual period of childhood," explained the Director. Nobody understood what that was supposed to mean. And then a girl asked the Doctor and he calmly said that some people become adults earlier, and some later, and there are some who never grow up.

The Doctor went on: "If everyone became an adult all at the same time, just imagine what chaos would ensue. Just think for a minute: if all the children in our Camp were to go for lunch at the same time, what would happen?"

That was something even Tolik could understand. It was very easy to imagine what would happen if more and more boys and girls tried to pack themselves into the canteen that could hold no more than twenty-five. First troop, then the second, the third, the fourth, the fifth ... They would all have to sit on each other's laps, and it would be impossible to raise a spoon to your mouth— there would be pushing and shoving in such a tight squeeze, and there wouldn't be enough food, plates or spoons to go round.

On the next occasion the girl (now speaking the Lingo, sort of) asked the Doctor: "You said then that there are children who never become grown-ups. But are there children who become grown-ups at once, who were never little?"

And then the Doctor told her that there are such children, and even in the Camp there are some. The Doctor added that it all depends on the parents when childhood begins and when it ends.

There was a lot of storytelling at night. About the girl called Melanie whom they nicknamed the Melon, that she was really the Director's daughter. And that this Melon goes off into the forest at night, and there she catches worms and snakes. And then she throws them into a big cauldron of soup in the kitchen, when the cook—old uncle Vasya—goes outside for a smoke. And that's why the Director asked that Doctor of theirs to make a right Middle Ages for the Melon in the morning whenever she escapes into the forest at night to catch all them creepy-crawlies. And then in the morning, when you could hear the fat Melon yelling and mooing—after all, what are you going to be able to say when you've got a metal gag stuffed in your gob—the boys and girls would say:

"Serves her right!"

Nobody liked the Melon. But they didn't try to do anything to her, probably because then they would have to answer to the Director.

True, there weren't many who were afraid of the Director—

maybe only the newbies. The Director seemed a harmless sort of bloke, but nobody wanted to get into trouble with him. Anyway, he was hardly ever seen inside the Camp, and whenever anything had to be said at line-up, he used such incomprehensible words that he couldn't be understood even by those who already spoke the Lingo almost correctly.

The troop leaders punished them for telling stories like the ones about Bannock the Bogill, the Inside-Out Man and the Melon. Rumour had it that the Director himself had ordered them to do it. Their kind Doctor, when he spoke to the boys and girls, frowned crossly and explained:

"It's all the fault of your illnesses, of those nasty lumps and bumps, those scabs and warts all over your bodies. It's those tumours and tiny bones in your heads that create them. Our Camp must be purged of them! A pure voice that speaks correctly—that's the best way of ridding yourselves of these fantasies."

Tolik liked the Doctor very much. He couldn't call him a friend, because how could you have a friend who works in the sick bay? But if every boy and every girl in the world has a daddy, thought Tolik, then it's that Doctor of theirs that he would like to be his daddy. That same Doctor who is trying so hard to make sure that Tolik leaves the Camp healthy and with a pure voice. And then, who knows, it will be possible for him to return to mathematics. And then, if they put him together again with that young professor, he'll listen to him and say:

"Well done, Tolik. You're a real tonic."

Or:

"Well done, tonic. You're a real Tolik."

And so it was today: when the troop leader closed the door and switched on the friendly, conspiratorial light outside, Tolik laughed quietly as he pulled his blanket up. He had such an interesting name. In the Lingo a tonic was something refreshing and pure. Almost like a voice. Tolik was very fond of the Doctor—and wanted very much to help him.

However, the Doctor said that Tolik still had a tumour that

was too big, and it was unlikely he would be discharged soon. That the treatment he had been receiving had not yet been a complete success. It may not even be possible to discharge him the following summer, said the Doctor. Tolik was upset, not only for himself. He felt very sorry for the Doctor.

And that's why today, when all the stories had been told and everyone in the room had settled down to sleep, Tolik decided to put his idea into practise. The idea was simple and logical. Like the mathematical puzzle that even professors, even the oldest and greyest, had once been unable to resolve. But Tolik could.

When it had become completely quiet in the room, and all that Tolik could hear was snuffling and snoring, he opened his mouth as wide as he could. No one else in the troop could open their mouth as wide as he had learned to open his, because he had trained hard during the Doctor's examinations. Whenever the metal gags were inserted, he always tried hard to help the Doctor by forcing his mouth open as wide as possible.

He lay for a bit with his mouth open. The outside lamp winked at him:

"Come on, Tolik. You'll be a tonic."

Somewhere in his mouth there it was. The little bone, the tumour, the lump that was the reason why he couldn't speak with a pure, clear voice, so that people could understand him. Including professors of mathematics.

He lay still a little longer, and then he slowly began to insert his hand into his mouth. The whole fist. It was so good to feel the cool breeze from the open window on his spit-wet wrist.

He used his fingers to feel for that tumour, that little bone, that nasty little lump that caused so much trouble for his Doctor. It was difficult for the Doctor to reach it with his instruments. But Tolik got to it. Tomorrow the Doctor will insert the mouth gag, peer into Tolik's mouth, and ... No, Tolik didn't want congratulations or presents from the Doctor. He simply wanted the Doctor to be amazed, to smile his kind smile, and say: "Well done, Tolik! I always knew that you would be a tonic!"

Tolik tried to feel for the tumour with his fingers, but for some odd reason just couldn't locate it. His fingers wouldn't fit inside his mouth, and anyway he felt as though he was going to be sick at any moment. He had to hurry. Tolik pushed his fingers even deeper inside. The lump was playing hide-and-seek with him, and he was beginning to get angry. He clenched his fist still tighter—and then his fist suddenly grew to such a size that it filled his entire mouth. As if the saliva had made it swell.

"How deep I've pushed my fist in," thought Tolik. "Just a bit further and I'll be like the Inside-Out Man. I'll turn myself inside out and look to see where that lump has disappeared to."

His fist advanced further down and at last became wedged against some kind of tube that was slippery but too narrow. In his mind's eye Tolik could see the outside light; it was shining on him so comfortingly, as if inviting him to go off somewhere with it. Somewhere where all the Toliks of the world are always a tonic.

And then there were several lights. They went on multiplying and multiplying, like in mathematics. And Tolik felt that he really was off on a journey somewhere, travelling through the air. He realised that he would never return to the Camp. And so off he went on the way to where that outside light was pointing. That very first, kind, all-knowing light.

Ane Flyting:
The Fate o Puir Tolik (or Tonic)

Parties tae the flyting being
CALVINIST *(Elizabeth Melville, Lady Culross)*
and
JACOBITE *(Carolina Oliphant, Lady Nairne)*

CALVINIST
Och is my hairt of stone or steill?
It cannot brust in two.

I can not knaw quhat fear I feill
my saull is blinded so.
I am so tossed to and fro
my hairt is lyke a hell,
I feill a falss confused wo:
the caus I can not tell.

JACOBITE

Bonnie Charlie's now awa',
Safely owre the friendly main;
Mony a heart will break in twa,
Should he ne'er come back again.
Will ye no come back again?
Will ye no come back again?
Better lo'ed ye canna be.
Will ye no come back again?

CALVINIST

Sall I not find releif at lenth?
How bitter is my stryfe!
How sall I stryve without my strenth,
or live without my lyfe?
I sie my secreat sinis ar ryfe,
yit can I not contend.
O wisched death quhair is thy knyfe
that sould this battell end?

JACOBITE

English bribes were a' in vain,
An' e'en tho' puirer we may be;
Siller canna buy the heart
That beats aye for thine and thee.
Will ye no, etc.

CALVINIST

O slouthfull saull, O blinded beast,
quhy wereis thou so fast?
O fuill thou wold be gone in haist
now quhen thy grace is past!
Wilt thou not byde a bitter blast
for thy redeimeris saik?
Thy cair on him he bidis thee cast:
quhy is thy faith so waik?

JACOBITE

Sweet's the laverock's note and lang,
Lilting wildly up the glen;
But aye to me he sings ae sang—
Will ye no come back again? Will ye no come back again?
Will ye no come back again?
Better lo'ed ye canna be,
Will ye no come back again?

CALVINIST

O sall I live or sall I die,
and live no more in paine?
Or sall I ficht or sall I flie,
and lat my saull be slaine?
O sall I not from sin refraine
so long as I have braith?
O sall I spend more tyme in vaine
and heap up double wraith?

"There is," says Professor Masson, "a real moral worth in all the songs of Lady Nairne, and all have that genuine characteristic of a song which consists of an inner tune preceding and inspiring the words, and coiling the words, as it were, out of the heart along with it."

16
Iver haed bit gless i yir mooth?

Iver haed bit gless i yir mooth? Naw?
Ye ken whit ah'm oan aboot, tiny wee bits o gless, crushed lik y're awa tae pit thaim i the soupe.

Scots wha hae wi Wallace bled

Ye dinna unnerstaund richt awa whit's amiss, it's jist saund crinching yir teeth—but aw the same ye canna spittle thaim oot, so ye keep up wi chowin lik thare's a body wha gars ye tae. Ye canna help but chow,

Scots wham Bruce has aftimes led:

it's habit coupled up wi periodontal muscular reflex—

Welcome to your gory bed

—thare's naethin ye can dae aboot it.
In fact it's a sair fecht tae compel yer jaws be absolutely still, es-peicially as ye maun live i the age o chewing gum an betel leaves.

Or to Victorie

Ye may uitilise yer haunds tae remove some bits o the gless, providit thay're free, or dunt thaim wi yer tongue oot thru yer

gars: forces   *sair*: hard   *dunt*: push

243

lips, thegither wi wee bits o flesh, pith o mandarine oranges, wee beastie *Carabidae* dregs o sairly filter'd coffee, paips o yon grapes ye haed yestreen an guidness alane kens whit else; aw mixter maxter'd wi yer rosy-teeng'd slavers so ye maun dicht yer digits oan yer breeks. Firstlins tho, ye maun spittle oot soond o yon deevilish chowin.

Unpossible houaniver tae rid yersel completely o sic finely grund gless i yer mooth: thare's ayeweys bitties catchit i yer gums, bitties belaw yer tongue, bitties atween yer teeth. Swithly yer mooth fills wi bluid. Pyne? Weel, no pyne tae mak ye want tae screich, naw, mair like a blameless bawhair's lost i yer mooth. But insteed o pyne thare's panshite—jist dinna swallae! Than frantic attempts tae figure whit nummer o times y'actually swallae'd afore ye'd caught oan tae whit jist happent.

Nae howp,

Now's the day and now's the hour

—ye maun swallae onyhou. Yon teenie pieces o gless slowly gang doun intae yer stamack likes o wee wattersubmergit bombs, like diamants forcit doon gullet o an auld miser. Once it happent tae me ... Oh aye, the hale load o them hee haw'd!

See the front o' battle lour!

Nou ah'm feart o gless jaurs wi siller tops. Jaurs o brine'd daintees—thay're aquariums fu' o flesh-eatin fishies. Ev'ry time ah rip the lid aff a gless jaur wi an opener, ah glimpse teenie wee splinders o gless fawin insides o't; lyin tap o brine'd tomataes, gherkins or plooms: hidin' awa i thair moisty faulds o skin ...

See approach proud Edward's power ...

dicht: wipe   *swithly*: indeed   *bawhair*: testicular hair   *panshite*: panic
siller: (lit.) silver, metal

244

Wee, wee loast-frae-sicht-pairls i murks o seerups an sauces, bidin thair time.

Sicweys hae the Leid raxed inside o me.

Faither wanted to say all of this then, in court. He prepared himself carefully, sought the right words, but didn't say them. He signed all the pieces of paper that they needed. What he wanted was to leave the court room as quickly as possible, cease existing on paper, once again don his painful skin and again become deaf and dumb. But no, he was forced to traipse from office to office, presumably in the expectation that he would confess to something else as well.

He wanted to demand an interpreter—some bloke in a leather jacket turned up, sat next to him and proceeded to drill through Faither's ear with his eyes. The bloke was silent the whole time; he said not one single word throughout the hearing. Which, we must suppose, is also a kind of interpreting.

He once read about a father who had tipped a bucket of boiling water over his son. He had done it accidentally but was taken to court all the same. Even now Faither agreed that this was right and just. Parents are responsible for every time their hands tremble. For every time their bodies itch, for every time their bodies commit treachery.

While in one of the corridors of the courthouse, Faither thought he saw Alicia and Avi on the other side of a glass door. They were walking hand in hand, as though they had been placed in a glass jar, and all he could do was observe them bobbing up and down—or smash the glass. When he came out on to the street, there, right in front of the courthouse, was a woman pulling a little boy along by the arm. The boy was yelling at the top of his voice, demanding something in his childish, herbivorous tongue. She was frowning hard but not giving in; skinny legs in little coloured trousers were rolling around on the asphalt. She reminded Faither of a beautiful predator who had just hunted

raxed: reached

down some small animal and was now hauling it off to its lair, looking around with suspicion at the nosy people watching her. The little boy was in an uncontrollable fit of hysteria, rather like death throes. Faither walked past, simply unable to take his eyes off the scene. The woman seemed to look at him with envy. He was free and she had to obey her instincts.

It was like this woman here: she had just removed the lid from a glass jar in which floated something dead, mummified and wet. She too was subject solely to her instincts. All women resemble predators

Chains and Slaverie!

Even the woman who had become Alicia before disappearing; she too had always wanted blood, she had floated away on blood, she sang about blood.

... He had no idea how he had arrived at this cottage. He had simply emerged from the forest, like coming out of the cinema in the evening, and found himself in the yard. The cottage was blue, the carved wooden window surrounds were painted yellow, there was underwear trembling on the washing line, and looking very much like it there were white net curtains leaning timidly out of the windows down to the flower bed, just as though they were trying to pick themselves some tulips for a painting. The woman was drawing up a bucket from the well as if she was turning the handle of an old gramophone: and indeed there were jazzy notes coming up from the well, some piercing, some tremulous. The bucket itself began to clank like a drummer's cymbals, and then the wooden cover of the well began a brief solo.

And now here she was, feeding him, although he hadn't asked her to. He didn't even know what her name was.

Wha will be a traitor knave?

He just wasn't interested, and she didn't ask about his name either, and somehow this was a great comfort to him. Sausage, potatoes, a hundred grams of vodka. And then this whatever it was—menacing, marinaded, mangled.

"Whit's yon? Tomataes?" asked Faither, watching her plunge her plump hand into the glass jar. From it the hand pulled out two slushy, smiling heads; the heads jumped onto his plate, and juice began to run everywhere.

"Aye, tomatoes," she confirmed at last and gave him a puzzled look. "Oor ain. Niaroo. Get wired in!"

It was several days since he had last eaten, and still he didn't feel hungry. The tomatoes lay in front of him, and Faither could not understand what the point of them was. They were simply objects that needed to be used, and used correctly, in order to stay in this cottage for a little longer. He liked it here. Here nobody asked him anything, here all was quiet, here nobody would start looking for him. This cottage was as safe as a burrow.

How nice it would be if the forest brought Alicia and Avi to a place like this. Any minute now the door will open and they'll come in. He could see it all so clearly that he began to tidy his hair.

"*Wire in!*" Faither heard the lady of the house say again. He used his fingers to pick up one of the heads, sweet and a little rotten, and began to chew.

Wha can fill a coward's grave?

He couldn't taste anything. He moved his jaws and his mouth filled up with pickling juice that began to flow down his chin. Something crunched beneath his tongue, and a burning sensation ran across it.

"Therr's bluid aw ower yer chaft," said the woman. "Bluid!"

chaft: jaw

"It's gless," said Faither, and he spat out on to his hand everything that was in his mouth. "Yon's story o ma life."

"It cannae be, it's no possible," said the lady of the house pitifully. "Ah jemmied yon jaur that carefu! Come oan, gob it oot!"

He smiled.

"It willna help."

He stuck out his tongue and drew a finger across it. There really was blood on his finger. He sucked it and then ran his tongue across his teeth. The lady of the house brought him some water to rinse his mouth out with.

"Is it yir gums mebbe?" she said. "Ah've got same problem with ma gums, they bleed off an oan. Ah should go an see the doc, but ah'm feart."

Wha sae base as be a Slave?

Hearing the woman's voice, a little boy came running from the next room and stood shyly in the doorway.

Let him turn and flie.

Faither greeted him: "Hullo. Come oan o'er here."

The boy went over to him. He was about Avi's age, and Faither wanted to tell him about it.

Wha, for Scotland's King and Law,
Freedom's sword will strongly draw.

"Ah hae a laddie caw'd Avi," said Faither. "D'ye hae a tittie?"

"Naw," said the lady of the house. "That wan's m'anely wean. He's aff tae camp the morn, on holidays."

Free-man stand or Free-man fa

"Ah can gie ye a lift," said Faither. "Ah've a motor. Ah dinna ken whaur it is; somewhaur i the forest, lik eneuch."

Let him follow me.

"Yese need tae get a move oan while it's still daylight. Whit yese here fur enyweys?" asked the boy. "Huv yese come tae see sumbody?"

"Dinnae hassle," said the lady of the house with mock severity. She roared the words out lazily, like a well-fed animal. "Folk come here tae dae aw sortae stuff y're too wee tae knaw aboot. Loadsae folk come here. Frae Minsk. Even aw the way

By Oppression's woes and pains

frae Moscow. They buy up cottages fur thur summer hols. Ur yese a writer then? Yese talk like one."

"Non," said Faither. "Yon's hou ah cam here—en vacances. Let's awa." And he took the boy by the elbow. "Let's awa an tak a wee daunder.

By your Sons in servile chains

we willna gang o'er faur."

"Go faur as yese want." The lady of the house was clearing the table away. "He's no that much o a wean."

They went out into the yard. Except it didn't seem to be the same place. Something had changed, something that he couldn't put a finger on. When Faither first arrived in this place, he felt weak and incapable of doing anything except recollect; he felt it was offering him some kind of salvation—the end of the road. But now, watching the boy hanging on to the fence and swinging his legs in the air, looking at the nape of his neck, grey as the forest around them, at his head, close-cropped as if it was a target to be struck at, Faither suddenly felt so uneasy that he wiped his feet with revulsion on the grass. As though the mud hadn't stuck to his trainers back then when he was wandering around the forest, but had appeared on them just now, while he was sitting at that table covered with a cloth that looked like men's underpants, eating tomatoes from the hand of the mistress of the house.

"Whaur's yer paw?" asked Faither, going over to the boy.

"Paw's away tae the hospital," answered the boy readily. "Yon's why maw wants tae pack me aff tae camp. Thataweys it's easier fur her tae visit paw. We dinnae get concessions, so maw's hud tae gie the doc some cash."

"Whit's amiss wi yer paw? Let's gang tae the forest."

So they set off to where the first, sparse fir trees were growing, towering over faded clumps of plants that Faither didn't know the names of.

"Paw chopped his finger aff," said the boy loudly and with obvious pleasure. He clearly liked talking to this stranger. "Paw hud an extrae finger, ken? A sixth wan, right here. It wuz weird. He went yon ways,

We will drain our dearest veins,

that he jist chopped it aff wi an axe. Seein that he didnae get tae the hospital straight aff it went aw infected. So's he jist tipped that voddy he makes hissel o'er it an wrapped a wee rag roon it. He reckoned it wud heal up aw by itsel."

But they shall be free!

"Ah see." Faither looked back to work out how far they had come from the cottage. "Y're aff tae the holiday camp the morn, richt?"

"Uh-huh," the boy sighed. "The morra. How come yese talk aw funny? Whit's a holiday camp? Ye dinnae talk likesae roon here."

"D'ye want tae gang tae camp?"

"Aye, it'll be dead good fun therr, ah'm right am ah no?" said the boy politely. "Ah'll get a chance tae see loadsae peeples. Ah dinnae get taken tae places aw that much. Like, we've been up tae Minsk wance. Tae the circus. Aye, they took uz oan the bus. Or else we jist go doon the toon tae We Arra Peoples Palace oan Hogmanay. Will yese gies a lift in yir motor right enough?"

"If ah can airt it oot," said Faither hastily.

Lay the proud Usurpers low

"If ah find the motor an some petrol. Come awa o'er here."

He pulled the boy by his sleeve so as to get him to hide behind a grey and unremarkable pine tree that Faither felt he could trust.

Faither began to talk in a low voice, stressing every word: "Noo listen. Rin. Richt noo. Rin awa tae the forest. Ye've no tae gang tae the camp, d'ye unnerstaund? The folk thare mak bairns likes o ye intae harnless, tongue-tackit beasts o unmynd. *Fir the rest o thair lives.* Whit thay cairve oot o ye, ye'll n'er get back!"

Tyrants fall in every foe!

"Whitweys d'theys howk it oot?" The boy looked at him with wide, staring eyes. He had been listening, but hadn't yet fully understood what was going on, and Faither was in a hurry to din what was most important into the boy's young and still silly head:

"Jist likes o yon! Wi chizors! Likes o cuttin circles frae papier! Thay'll flay ye alive! Thay'll turn ye tae creeminal likes'd slauchter his ain mither. Thay'll tak awa awthings ye tresure. Thay'll mak a dunderheid o ye wha's nae idea wha he is nor whaur he's frae. Aw yer life ye'll speak wi yon Lingo. Yon robot Lingo. Tak it frae me. Ye maun believe me.

harnless: brainless, stupid

251

Rin, win yir freedom while ye can!"

"But Maw said ..."

"Thay've cairved awthing thay coud oot yer maw awready. An thay'll dae likeweys wi yer paw. But ye maun be sauf! Tak leg! Rin!"

"Wherr tae?"

"Dinna be daft—intae yon forest! The forest, laddie, the forest! Hae ye no a hidey thare? Whan ah wis wee ah ayeweys haed a hidey. Aye an noo ah'm a man-body ah hae wan yet. Here y'are bidin' cheek b'jowl wi the forest an ye've nae place tae hide awa? Rin, rin an n'er be retour!"

"But maw sed it's jist a nice wee pioneer camp."

"Yer mither's nae clue as tae whit passes thare. Tak leg, ye daft wee laddie! She's awready goat her doutes whaur ah'm concernit. She's jalousin ma gemm's up ... so dinna staund here bletherin, RIN!" And Faither shoved the boy's shoulder so hard that he fell, then jumped up with his face twisted in an expression of the deepest youthful resentment. He must have been thinking of how to escape, but Faither gripped his arm so tightly that the boy swore.

"Awa! Vamoose!" By now Faither was in the grip of blind rage at this little brat he had decided to save at any cost. "Skeedaddle awa tae the forest, doozy zombie!"

Faither let go of the boy's arm and gave him a swift kick. Only then did the boy run off. Home, of course. Who could have doubted it? Faither caught up with him, and together they fell to the ground. He roared and grabbed the boy by the neck:

"Gaun yersel! Tae the forest! Scarper! Pronto!"

He ran through the forest, fighting through the branches. He could feel the fir trees clearing a way for them. The trees did not want to touch the man running with a boy. Faither ran on with no idea of where he was going, squeezing that thin arm. It no longer mattered to him if he was holding anything other than the child's arm. That's all there was—the arm held tightly as if Faither was going to wield it to ward off enemies, the sound of loud sobbing behind his back; there was the forest, there was a goal to reach. They ran for a long time, until Faither fell face first into the moss. But he didn't let go of the hand.

Let us Do—or Die!!!

17

Ane weygait sign oan yon road indiques jist a wee while tae the bus stop

Ane weygait sign oan yon road indiques jist a wee while tae the bus stop. This was something that Alicia knew, although she had no idea how she knew it. It was just that a road was to her like a book, and that's how things were in books.

It was a strange sign, one that neither Alicia nor Avi had ever seen before. Two vertical black lines within a red triangle, one straight and the other bent.

"Yon's the Raidō rune, it means 'the wey o th'ongae,'" said Alicia, trying to walk so as to keep half a step in front of Avi.

"Bletheration!" said Avi. "It's mair like yon Marcomannic rune name o Hur."

Alicia didn't want to argue. They had slowly overcome the hill, and now walking was much easier. They had even started to sing a song—the one that, as Faither had said, was all about how bad things were going to be, but there were such wonderful sounds coming from the forest, and their singing on the roadside was more like plain, ordinary shouting, so they fell silent without reaching the end of their song.

The sun hung over the road, all the time retreating as if it was continually taking photographs of them, clickety-click, click, click; they could already see these solar images of themselves on this exposed film of a summer afternoon that unrolled in front of them and spread beneath their feet.

weygait sign: road sign   *wey o' th'ongae*: the way forward

"Here's anither!" Alicia ran up to the next sign. "The Sonne! Yon's the rune Sonne sign!"

"Wrang again." Without showing any interest, Avi walked past the road sign, and now he was in front, so Alicia had to catch him up and adapt the length of her steps. "Yon's Hagalaz mair like. 'A muckle hale o hailstanes.'"

"An Hagalaz tae you!" said Alicia, looking at her brother with disdain.

At long last they came out onto a proper road, and that gave them strength. True, neither of them knew if they were now on the map. These endless road verges made them feel quite uncomfortable—it was much jollier in the forest. The cars coming towards them brought them winds from unknown regions—but all Alicia wanted to do was go off to one side into the forest and conceal herself behind a solid wall of trees that would welcome her like old friends.

The sun thought for a bit and hid behind an almost transparent light summer cloud. And then they caught sight of a bus stop.

Although, maybe it wasn't one. Right on the verge there was a small, three-sided, pink building with a bench inside. On the bench sat an old lady in a black headscarf; she sat motionless, as if she was dead. Her eyes were riveted on something, and Avi tried to make out what exactly she was looking at, but couldn't.

Beyond the little concrete building the verge continued on and on, with occasional poles and road signs. It was the same on the other side of the road. Between the two sides lay the asphalt, eaten hungrily by the wheels of huge lorries. The air shimmered above the asphalt and spread across it like hot snakes; looking through them was like looking through tinted glass.

The old lady got up from the bench. Unexpectedly the fat snout of a bus appeared on the road. Its doors opened and the old lady clambered inside. It was quite amusing to watch her almost invisible feet shuffle up the steps.

a muckle hale: a whole load

"Let's awa," said Alicia.

"Let's awa," said Avi. "Mebbes we're awready oan the cairt. Folk oan the bus maun ken."

And so they climbed on board behind the little old lady in black. Once at the top they found at the steering wheel a man dressed in a bright coloured shirt, fat like his bus. Out of his shirt protruded huge hairy arms; the steering wheel looked like some sort of fruit in the paws of a monkey.

"Awright then, wherr youse two weans aff tae?" asked the driver. The look he gave Avi was hostile.

"D'ye mean us? Yon wey," and Avi pointed forward with his arm.

"Dinna lee," whispered Alicia and then in a loud voice she explained:

"We maun gang tae Bremen."

"Huvin a bit o a giggle, ur yese? Mebbe ah should drive yese tae Moscow? Right tae the Kremlin? Any bawbees oan yese, kids?"

"No registrated, nae fixed abode, we live bi God's guid grace alane," mumbled Avi, but then a woman who was fidgeting impatiently on the front seat grumbled: "Let the weans oan, whit ur ye goin oan aboot money fur?"[38]

"Okey dokey," said the driver and shut the doors. The bus, as stuffy as a school changing room after a PE lesson, moved off, grunting and groaning. It proceeded along the road at an unhurried pace, bumping and bouncing over the potholes as it went.

"See whit he's got thare," whispered Alicia. "Thare, whare he pits the cash. Richt thare!"

At last Avi saw, lying next to the driver, a greenish, folded, well-worn map.

"Ah've thocht on," said Alicia. "We can pit it thegither w'oor..."

Right at that moment a pile of papers fell from her hands on to the floor, and the whole bus surged forwards to help her pick them up.

lee: lie   *bawbees*: money

"Thanks tae ye, thanks tae ye," Avi repeated.

"Thanks tae ye," said Alicia. "Thanks tae ye, mistress. Thanks tae ye, kind bodies."

"Sae polite, they weans," someone said approvingly. "Their parents brought them up right well."

"Ah'm no sae sure aboot that," retorted the driver. "Aw ah ken is they're mingin'—stinkin' like swine."

"Haw! You! Take a gude lang look at yersel!" This was the woman who had persuaded the driver to take them on board; now she was defending them. "Rain or shine we huv tae open aw the windaes in this bus ivry time you let-aff!"

The whole bus roared with laughter. The driver blushed and put on his dark glasses.

"Coud ah hae a len o yir cairt a wee minuit, maister?" Alicia asked him, once all the papers had been gathered together.

"Whit?"

"This cairt here," said Avi, pointing with his finger.

"Y're pyntin wi yer finger agin," said Alicia. "Aye, yon one. We'll jist haud it up tae oors, see if they confeer, an we'll gie it back toot sweet, will we no, Avi?"

"Aye aye, OK then," he muttered. "Jist dinnae forget tae haund it back. An sit doon! Get up the back o the bus. Thataway ah dinnae huv tae tolerate yese mingin' here."

They seized the map and ran right to the back of the bus. But the map wasn't right. None of the roads marked on it matched any of the roads in the atlas. The driver's map wasn't correct—in the centre of it was the capital city of their country, and they simply couldn't find such a city in their road atlas.

"Nae maiter," said Avi. "The thing o maist import is that yon road gangs forrit."

They spread themselves out on the soft seats and looked out of the window. All they could see was that selfsame forest running past them.

coud ah hae len o: could I borrow

Up ahead the driver was talking in a low voice to someone on his mobile. Beneath their bottoms the engine was straining and howling, puffing out its hot cheeks. It grew quiet in the bus. People were beginning to doze; Alicia and Avi also felt that their eyes were sticking together. Alicia leant her head on Avi's warm shoulder, and placed her hands on his bare knees, all covered in scrapes and adorned with mosquito bites. His knees were cool to the touch, and Alicia was seized by the urge to kiss them. She suddenly felt so ashamed that she shuddered at the thought. Avi didn't notice anything.

"Ah'm wunnerin whare we are?" said Avi. "If Faither waur tae phone us the noo, whit wad we tell tae him? Or yon wumman, yon wi the yellae hair."

"Or Mither," said Alicia. "But thay willna ring. Whit wey maun thay ring us? Richt intae yer lug? Ring, ring, hullo, whare are yese?" And she fiddled a little with one of Avi's earlobes, like ringing a bicycle bell.

"Aye but aw the same, whare are we?" said Avi. "Mebbes we maun demander."

"Non," said Alicia. "Folk'll jalouse we're loast. Thay'll stairt offerin tae gie's a haund, an thataweys we'll n'er get tae Bremen."

They sat for a moment in silence, trying to drive away the heavy sleep brought on by the bus.

"Whare are we?" murmured Alicia. "Whare are we? But ah tak mair o a conceit in '*Wha* are we?'" And she looked suspiciously at Avi.

"*Wha* are we?" she repeated, half rising from her seat. "An *wha* are *ye*?"

"Ah'm yir brither," Avi answered patiently.

"OK, fine." Alicia rested her head on Avi's scabby knees. "Thare's twa tribes: the *whau*raweese an the *wha*aweese. Or thay're twa craiturs daunderin roon the globe, aw high an aw low roads left ahint thaim."

craiturs: creatures

"Yon's fandabidozi," laughed Avi. "You're *wha*aweese an ah'm *whau*raweese!"

"Musik tae ma lug!" Now it was Alicia's turn to laugh.

Satisfied with themselves, they adopted their previous positions.

Meanwhile the bus had turned off the old road onto a new one, and soon they were driving through a small town.

"September Seventeenth Street," read Avi as he stood up. "Is it autumn awready, an we've no noticed?"

"Ye can be awfy daft, Avi," said Alicia and stretched her whole body. "Yon's a day o celebration fir beardie men tae kiss aw thay men wi nae tache nor beard."

The bus swayed, sneezed and stopped beneath a low-hanging shelter, where there was a row of old women sitting with their suitcases.

"We halt here fur ten minutes," announced the driver, annoyed. He lit up a cigarette.

"The shops hereaboots've braw names," Alicia laughed and turned Avi's head in the direction of red-painted boards attached to some peculiar-looking constructions that resembled huge dumpsters made out of pieces from a Meccano set.

"Liliana, Alinta," they read aloud in chorus together and looked at each other in delight. "Tofilia, Lukerya."

"Ah want ma name tae be Alinta," said Alicia. "An ye'd get caw'd Lilian. Lilian Avi."

The doors opened to admit the thin, awkward and somewhat despondent figure of a policeman. He scanned the interior of the bus with his eyes and marched smartly to the back where Alicia and Avi were pulling faces at each other.

"OK, kids," said the policeman. "End o the line. Follae me, an dinnae try nuthin daft unless yese want beltit. Goin' oan a big

thay: those   *tache*: moustache

long journey?" He signalled that they should go ahead, and then followed them with the dispirited gait of a man who had been thoroughly ground down by the heat.

"So, as ah wiz sayin tae yese, yese goin' a long ways?" he repeated as he put them in a police van.

"We're gangin' tae Bremen," said Alicia proudly. "Whit, is yon forbadit?"

"Oh aye, talkin thataways ur yese?" The policeman was surprised. "OK, yese'll be at the copshop in a wee minute, an then yese can huv a wee blether."

The van sprang into life with a few nervous jolts and then bounded off along the narrow streets of the town. In less than five minutes Alicia and Avi were sitting at an old desk that looked like it had come from a school—there were scribblings all over it. Opposite them sat another policeman, short, with a big head that was tilted over the desk as if it was heavier than the body. They listened to what the head had to say:

"Yese ur gonnae tell uz wherr yir parents ur, ken? Whit's the gemm—aw oan yer ainsome doon the frontier zone? Get ma drift? Yese'll tell uz whit the gemm is aw oan yer ainsome ..."

Alicia and Avi said nothing, but just looked at him with no fear at all. Indeed, there was nothing frightening about him, this young policeman in a uniform that was too big for him. Alicia even smiled at him. That really confused him, and he began to fidget on his chair.

"Ferr do's." The policeman had clearly given in. "Oor inspector fur juveniles is gonnae be here any time the noo. Afore he turns up ah'm gonnae huv tae teach yese a few wee life lessons. Wi ma belt. Then the inspector's gonnae speak nice tae yese. Why d'yese huv tae make life sae complicated, weans? Eh?"

He took hold of his belt buckle. He gave it a rub. Then he rubbed it again. Then Avi, who had been following his actions with fascination, asked, "D'ye cairry a jocteleg?"

"Dinnae mess wi me!" The policeman was becoming angry. "Ah'm bein nice tae yese. Fur the last time, whit ur yese doin oan yer ain ..."

"We're no alane," said Avi. "We've a faither. Ah jalouse *ye'd* caw him 'Paw.'"

"Therr ye go, that's soundin mair like it." The nice policeman smiled and stopped fiddling with his belt. "Whit's yer Paw's name, wherr's he bide? We'll gie'im a caw an yese can trot aff hame."

"A Paw's a Paw." Avi shrugged his shoulders. "Whit for maun Paw be name'd? Ilka body's anely a Paw. Am ah richt or am ah richt? Or mebbes ye've aicht Paws?"

The policeman's jaw dropped in surprise, and Alicia hastily intervened:

"Ah'm Alicia, an this is ma brither Avi. We're gangin tae Bremen, but whan it comes tae findin oor way on tae the cairt, we hae nae howp at aw. Gie's a haund, an the Awmichtie'll no abandon ye."

"A sect." The policeman nodded his head. "Right enough. OK, sit here fur a wee whiley in the station an mebbe yese'll come tae yer senses."

The policeman led them out of that dismal room with bars on the windows into another where there were also bars on the window, but at least the window looked on to the outside world. You could calmly watch people walking along the street, and pigeons pecking around under their feet, and a small water truck slowly creeping up on a group of schoolgirls who had gone off somewhere for a surreptitious cigarette and were ineptly puffing out the smoke. You could even make out what the street was talking about—and it was talking about things that Alicia and Avi could not fully understand: about how there's going to be a concert today, and actually there's a fête in town, and there's been dancing in the park since the morning ...

The policeman locked the door and went off, leaving them

alone in this empty room, in which there was only a dirty bench and walls painted light green. They took an instant dislike to the walls. Alicia soon unravelled their secret. Whenever you shut your eyes, the walls make a very slight movement, and the room becomes smaller. These walls were alive; they moved closer when you weren't looking at them.

"Let's no blink," suggested Avi. "An thataweys they canna dae onything tae us."

Alicia agreed, but somehow she just couldn't stop herself from blinking. Her eyes filled with tears and started itching. They played the game ten times, because Avi wanted to show her that it was possible not to blink, and Avi won the game ten times in a row.

He really could sit without blinking. It was as though he had a special gag in his eyes, like the ones the Doctor used in their mouths. Alicia felt like crying with jealousy.

Right then a key scraped in the lock. The door was flung open, and in the doorway loomed the figure of the short policeman with the big head.

"Right," he said. "Shift yersel. Yer Paw's here."

They went back to the room with the school desk. In front of them stood a man in dark glasses, with a face overgrown with stubble. He was wearing military uniform without epaulettes or any other distinguishing marks. On his feet were tall combat boots. He looked like a fisherman, or a hunter, or someone going out to collect mushrooms. Something like that, anyway. And he was holding his hand by his mouth as if he was about to whisper something in your ear at any moment.

"Ur these wans yer weans?" asked the policeman.

"Mine. Aye. Yes," announced the man in military uniform. His voice sounded hollow. "We're off now. Follow me."

"Youse should see efter they weans better." This was the policeman giving his lesson of the day. "Sign yer moniker oan dottit line. An here in aw. Aye'n ah've goat sumthin else tae tell youse.

Gie they weans a good leatherin' when ye're back in the hoose. Providet yer religion says yese can, ah should say. Ah wud dae it like a shot if they weans wur mine, so ah wud."

"I will. Aye right," said the man, looking somewhere off to the side, and still holding his hand by his mouth, so that it was difficult to make out what he was saying. "I will. Aye. Right."

Alicia and Avi obediently headed towards the exit, but the man seized them by their hands—Avi by the right hand and Alicia by the left hand—and dragged them along, as if they were trying to resist. When they were already in the corridor, the policeman's voice stopped them:

"Haud oan a wee minute!"

All three of them turned. "An gie them a good scrub! They're bluidy needin it!"

The man nodded and dragged Avi and Alicia out onto the street.

There, in the shade of a chestnut tree, stood a little van. Vans like this one have recently appeared all over our country: on their well-worn sides they bear the logo of some long-defunct German firm, a no-longer-valid telephone number and an advert of indiscernible content. The man pulled the children to the tailgate of the van and opened it. Inside it was dark and cold, like in a pit, and the floor was covered with thick brown stains.

He looked around and pointed his finger towards the centre of the van: "In we get and we keep our mouths shut."

"Pyntin wi yer finger . . ." began Alicia, but this unknown daddy simply grabbed her round the waist, and she literally flew into the depths of the van. Avi came flying in after her; he even rather liked acrobatics of this kind. The tailgate slammed shut, and Alicia and Avi found themselves in complete darkness. Another short sharp clanking sound—and the van grunted maliciously as it began to move at a snail's pace over the cobblestones, then gave another grunt as if it had a throat to clear, and away it went. Alicia and Avi felt with their foreheads the speed with which it lurched forwards and started driving fast through the streets.

"His teeth hae leuk o needles," said Avi. "Ah wunner whit wey he maun kiss his wifie, Lucky."

"Aiblins her teeth be likes o threeds," said Alicia.

By the way the engine was talking, and the way the wheels kept in time with it, they soon realised that the van had left the town behind. It had also become much colder, and draughts were blowing in at them through the gaps, however much they tried to find a comfortable place to sit.

"Did ye read whit's screivit sides o this van?" asked Avi.

"Schröder & Son, Emergency Plumbers, 24 Hours Call-Out, Installation of Baths and Toilets, Pipe Replacement," declaimed Alicia in a voice that was both serious and concerned.

"Aye," and Avi shuffled up closer to Alicia.

They didn't travel for very long; the van shuddered and stopped. On the other side of the thin walls, they could hear the deafening sound of birdsong. It was the noise of the forest, from where wafted the scent of pine needles and earth. The tailgate opened, and sunlight once again blinded the children's eyes. They pressed themselves against the side of the van, but this unknown daddy flung the tailgate up as far as it would go, so that light flooded inside. Through the rectangle in front of them, they could once again see the forest; it was like seeing it on a cinema screen.

"It's wunnerfu," thought Alicia. After all those buses, police cars, vans and offices. And another thought suddenly entered her head: If ah war a warwulf, ah'd escape tae the forest early mornin, an no the nicht. She had no idea where the thought came from.

"Good," said the man, gritting his teeth, as if in agreement with Alicia's thoughts. "Good."

Then he removed his dark glasses, and beneath them there was nothing, nothing except smooth skin. True, two eyes had been drawn on the skin, but so badly—with an ordinary ball-point pen—that Alicia at once felt ill at ease.

"What is wrong with your eyes then?" Avi had decided to show off his knowledge of the Lingo.

"They have become overgrown," said the man, baring his needle-sharp teeth. He was no longer holding his hands right by his mouth, and he spoke the Lingo with such a pure, expressive voice that Avi was quite overcome with envy. "All those tablets I took. Yes ..." He looked at Alicia with his badly drawn eyes, and she recoiled in fear. The badly drawn eyes were unblinking; they gawped at her arms, her knees, the bare stomach that peered out from beneath her filthy T-shirt that had long ago turned blue, green and black.

"Good," repeated the unknown daddy. "You, boy, I'm going to take to the Doctor, for some emergency treatment. You, girl, out you come."

He took pleasure in enunciating the sounds, as if he was eating sweets. Alicia didn't move—and then the daddy jumped into the van, tore her away from Avi with ease and threw her onto the grass.

"Rin Alicia, rin, *rin!*" yelled Avi, but Alicia's legs would not obey her. There was a bang—the unknown daddy slammed the van tailgate shut, and Avi began pounding on it, but to no avail.

The man seized Alicia by the hair and dragged her off towards the trees. She, of course, started screaming because of the sudden pain, pain so severe that it became all there was: Alicia stopped being Alicia, she simply became a box full of old rubbish. Everything turned into old rubbish, except that pain.

"Tasty," said the unknown daddy, leaning her up against an oak tree. "Dirty. Tasty. It's good they didn't wash you."

For a moment, Alicia felt gratitude towards this man in military uniform—for making the pain go away, for the fact that his inhuman temperature was rapidly falling to zero, for being able to feel her head and her body again, and to see the forest and hear how the birds concealed in the branches above her all joined together in furious song. But this terrible, humiliating gratitude faded as though it had never been, and in its stead there was only hatred.

The man's face was very close, and she could feel his breath.

His mouth was open, and there was a smell of herring coming from his needle teeth. The badly drawn pupils of those badly drawn eyes stared unblinkingly at Alicia's wide open eyes, and out of those badly drawn pupils gaped a void irresistible and unyielding.

The unknown daddy began slowly to lower himself to a position where he was squatting on his haunches. He probably didn't hear a thing because his needle teeth suddenly began to ring like a peal of bells, not very loud at first, but the sound intensified, until it was like the buzzing of mosquitoes. But Alicia heard it—the van began to groan and shudder, and the sweet smell of exhaust fumes reached her nostrils.

In her mind Alicia could clearly see Avi sitting in the darkness of the van: he's spread out his arms and legs as wide as he can, as if he's holding the steering wheel in his hands, and his feet are pressing down on the pedals. Now Avi's hand is lying on something invisible that's grown right by his leg. Avi's lips form a sound: vroom, vroom. And then Avi begins to murmur a driver's song to himself:

"Hold the wheel firm, driver!"

The rear wheels of the van turned to have a look at Alicia and the unknown daddy who was now squatting in front of her. The van started up, turned round, stopped and then headed at speed straight for the unknown daddy, exactly like a bull in a bullfight. The unknown daddy at last glanced round and even managed to straighten himself up: the badly drawn eyes on his smooth face looked indifferently into the void from which the snub-nosed van was flying straight at him. Alicia felt—or even saw, because at this instant sight and hearing had changed places—how the van caught the unknown daddy on the bridge of its nose and sent him flying. He fell but was still in the path of the enraged van. Then the van drove right on to the unknown daddy with its round legs, first the front ones, and then the rear ones, and without stopping raced on ahead straight into the pines and crashed into a mass of intertwined trees. It bellowed one last time and fell silent.

"Ah jist coudna get a grip o the steering wheel!" Alicia could hear Avi's voice. "Bide an wee minuit. Crivvens! An nou it's no stairtin up."

Alicia found the van keys in the unknown daddy's pocket— she was trying hard not to look at the badly drawn eyes, but their merciless, empty gaze drew her to them. She would have liked these eyes to know what pain was, and then to be able to cover them up with something. But those eyes had no wish to obey Alicia. They just looked—that's all there was to it.

She bit her finger in an attempt to throw off her utter bewilderment, and ran off to open the van. She had once read somewhere that cars can blow up if they crash into something. Avi jumped down, all happy and smiling, as though nothing had happened— but she didn't want to see those badly drawn eyes again. What she wanted was to go off into the forest where she could be silent, where she could choose for herself what to see and what to look at. Avi didn't argue—in the last few minutes he had become really tired. More tired than he had ever felt during the days since their escape from the Camp. So they grasped each other by the hand—as firmly as they possibly could—and fled away from this terrible place.

"D'ye ken whit yon wis?" asked Avi when he got his breath back.

"Aye," said Alicia. "Bannock the Bogill."

Without saying a word, Avi jumped over a tree that was lying flat on the ground and gave her his hand.

18

A dark dark car in a dark dark city
on a dark dark avenue ...

A dark dark car in a dark dark city on a dark dark avenue ...

In actual fact, though, the city was not at all dark. Every time the Doctor travelled up to the capital, he was amazed by how much brighter it had become. There was once a time when its avenues at night were indistinguishable from any alleyway in some provincial town, but now the capital city was like the fabled Singing Fountains. Multi-coloured, seductive, full of sounds and light effects. Even the buildings on both sides of the city's main avenue were joining in the game; the radiance of the city had at last acquired its own pure voice after so many years of murky mumbling—like a burned-out light bulb.

He had no liking for official meetings. In general, the Doctor was very reluctant to leave the forest; he liked waking up with the birds and listening to their conversations, which could so easily—provided you wanted to—be noted down in the real Lingo. The people he had cured were also birds: they flew to freedom from the Camp to build nests of their own. Of course, the Doctor never shared such observations with anyone—they were much too intimate for that. And then there's that wreck of a language they call their Leid; it's caused by banal pathologies of the oral cavity. So with the Leid it's all the other way round: it's fit only for jotting down the coarse, garbled, primitive noises made by hulking, great, brainless mammals like pigs, cows ...

"And other goats," the Doctor said aloud to himself. The driver turned round, thinking that the words were addressed to him; the Doctor, embarrassed, stared out of the window at the dead-straight avenue flying past. Maybe it's worth preserving, that Leid of theirs, for the purpose of reproducing basic animal sounds. The sounds of lust, hunger, repletion and aggression— that's all the Leid can express. Birds have access to an incomparably wider spectrum of emotions. Birds can sing just for the joy of it, as they did this morning when he, the Doctor, got up to prepare for today's meeting. It is only when people want something that they speak.

No. He didn't like being here. He felt at home in the forest, in his humble little room on the first floor of the administrative block, in the sick bay. There he felt he really could be who he was—a grey cardinal, the Salazar of paediatric surgery. He knew what his responsibilities were and how he needed to speak to people. Here in the capital other people spoke.

And speak they did, it has to be admitted, with no talent for it and no knowledge of what they were speaking about.

He could cure all of them—those people he was obliged to present his report to. They all had tumours the size of a fist in their mouths. They reminded him of wild boars, cows and canine bitches decked out in expensive suits and dresses from the best boutiques of Europe. The Doctor felt disgust and pity for them—with the addition of a professional interest. And now these pigs, cows and bitches ...

"And goats." The word suddenly entered his head again. Why was it stuck to him so firmly?

"Haw! *Gait!*" he said, savouring the word with his lips. The word was in the Leid; it excited him so much that he did up all the buttons on his coat to calm himself down. The driver once again looked at him questioningly. It did indeed look as though the Doctor was getting ready to leave the car at any moment.

"Shall I stop?" asked the driver, anxious to please his passenger.

gait: goat

"No," said the Doctor, "but please repeat one more time what you just said."

"I simply asked …" The driver wanted to justify himself. He was a driver the Doctor didn't know. Each time the Doctor came up for one of these meetings, he was given a new driver. They have strict rules here. A pity they can't talk properly. Unlike this lad at the wheel today. They could learn a thing or two from him.

"Everything's fine," the Doctor reassured him. "Just repeat …"

"I asked if I should stop," said the driver sadly. "I thought …"

"Thank you," the Doctor nodded his head. Such pure pronunciation of the Lingo. It was immediately obvious that the young man had grown up in a family that was concerned about linguistic hygiene. The parents must have kept a close eye on him. As a boy—destined one day to become the driver of a dark dark car—he may even have been tapped on the tongue by them whenever he came back from the village at the end of August after spending the summer with his grandparents, bringing the local rustic accent with him. And there's the result. A pure voice.

Well, almost pure. There were a few errors that the Doctor could have put right. There is something in this country—something diffused in the very air that people breathe—that prevents people from speaking properly. Some chemical element that makes the tumour grow with such speed that surgery is unavoidable if it isn't tackled in time.

Then he again remembered the meeting.

The continued existence of the Camp depended on these porcine types and the bovines with gold teeth.

The meeting was attended by all kinds of people. With every single person present he had to be attentive and welcoming, he had to know each of them by name, with each one he had to have a laugh or share a whispered rumour. The forest would quickly clear their heads. There was no place in the forest and in the Camp for anything superfluous. There were only children—and the Doctor. True, there was also the Director, but he didn't interfere too much: the Doctor would give him a special mixture of tablets, two red and one black, and these, in conjunction with the moonshine that the troop leaders lugged in from the neighbouring villages especially for him, produced the desired effect. The Director would appear in the morning, bestow his vacant smile on all around, burble a bit of drivel and then disappear into his office.

In principle, the meeting went off well. All those porcines and bovines signed whatever he wanted them to sign. They didn't want to undergo any treatment for themselves; in fact, everything about them showed that they couldn't care less about their particular ailment—but they are thinking about the children, hypocrites that they are. The Doctor was dreaming of the day when those children would grow up. And then the whole country will at last speak with a pure voice, as it truly deserves. This will mark a return to the place where it belongs: within the Empire of the Pure Voice, where each sound is expressive and has real meaning.

Where everyone can hear one another, where no one will be ashamed or afraid to open their mouths before others.

And even if they hadn't signed—those bigwigs of both the male and the female varieties ... If they had refused ... In that case the Doctor had his own methods and his own people. Well, they weren't exactly people. But that was something the Doctor didn't like to think about. What difference does it make who they are? They're in the forest. And they obey every single order he gives them. Because he gave them what no other doctor could—a voice. As pure as the forest air.

And that was a miracle. The Doctor believed in science—but he also believed that there could be no science without miracles.

There were bigwigs at the meeting that the Doctor's elderly parents would once have seen on television. But they couldn't have seen all of them. For instance, that man from the Committee we don't mention:[39] for the most part he remained silent, interjecting a few remarks of his own occasionally—quite pertinent, in the Doctor's opinion. He was the kind of person no one would have seen on television. The post he held needed no publicity. Yet here was the Doctor sitting next to him. He alone, this frequenter of important state committees—along with some colonel from the Ministry of Defence—possessed a more or less pure voice. Well, it was quite obvious they weren't from these parts, although they had already picked up some of the local speech defects, like their "g" sound—not hard as it should be in Russian, but more like "h." And that problem with the vowels ... That's the first stage. All the others at the meeting were in the final stage. And yet they wanted the country to have a pure voice?? The Doctor could not understand the logic. However, for as long as they were his allies, he really didn't care.

The children will grow up.

The wheel will come full circle.

The tumour will be a thing of the past.

And then there was still the Writer. Someone unknown. The Doctor had been a little concerned. The previous Writer, McFinnie or whatever his name was, had successfully carried out the task he had been entrusted with—creating in the eyes of the general public a negative image of the tumour in the mouth. McFinnie served as a living example of the inability to create anything interesting with this tumour in the mouth. But McFinnie, so they said, was in hospital. A psychiatric one.

My loving lasses, I maun leave ye,
But dinna wi' your greeting grieve me,
Nor wi' your draunts and droning deave me,
But bring 's a gill:
For faith, my bairns, ye may believe me,
Tis 'gainst my will.

Even the classics are brought low by the demon drink.

Fortunately, it became evident that this new chap was no worse than McFinnie. He listened carefully to comments and jotted down what was required of him, and then read a few of his little verses. If the Doctor hadn't known any better, he would have thought that McFinnie himself had written them. It turned out that his pupil had. The pupil of the poet McFinnie.

Right at this moment the Doctor sensed his customary temptation stirring among his memories. The Doctor was unwilling to admit to himself that this particular temptation was still alive within him. Whether or not he yielded depended on so many delicate factors that he himself could never say with certainty how things would turn out on each occasion. The car stopped at traffic lights. Alongside was a sporty, low-slung Mazda. On the back seat there were people drinking champagne.

And the Doctor dared. He had restrained himself only once before when he was in town for a meeting. On that occasion he had had a headache. But now he was full of strength.

"OK," he said with a smile. "Turn here. We're going to the hotel. Wait for me, and then I'll tell you where we're going."

With a mysterious, slightly smug look on his face, the Doctor flung himself back on his seat.

In the hotel, he got undressed and stood for a moment in front of the mirror, naked. A naked Doctor. A pure voice. He mouthed:

> *O black-ey'd Bess, and mim-mou'd Meg,*
> *O'er good to work, or yet to beg,*
> *Lay sunkets up for a sair leg;*
> *For when ye fail,*
> *Ye'r face will not be worth a feg,*
> *Nor yet ye'r tail.*

Goats. Gaits.

He pulled on a pair of fine linen trousers, walked over to the wardrobe and stood pensively, feeling the temptation inside him grow stronger, filling him up, coursing through all his veins. He stood with his eyes closed. Then he opened them and burst out laughing.

"Pourquoi pas? Why not indeed?"

Whit wey shoud ah no, whit wey shoud ah no?

he chanted as he put on a snow-white pure cotton shirt embroidered by a well-known seamstress, the mother of one of his patients. A rectangle of red Belarusian ornament ran vertically downwards from the collar, and a waistband held the embroidered shirt in place.

He continued to mouth, then whispered, but getting louder and louder:

Three times the carline grain'd and rifted,
Then frae the cod her pow she lifted,
In bawdy policy well gifted,
When she now fan,
That death nae longer wad be shifted,
She thus began:

"Whit wey shoud ah no, whit wey shoud ah no?"
He took particular pleasure in rolling that heavily aspirated "w" around his mouth. Dirty, primitive sounds made their way easily into his body by deceiving him with their fake naturalness. The Doctor began to feel dizzy, and his cheeks burned at the mere thought of a tiny, but nevertheless sweet, transgression. He's allowed one wee sin today. He's allowed one once a year. Just one teensy-weensy time a year he's allowed anything. He is the Doctor after all.

He donned a jacket over the embroidered shirt, but as soon as he arrived at where he wanted to be, the Doctor left it in the car. It was a café in the centre of the capital. With a spring in his step, the Doctor entered and was at once swallowed up by the crowd.

Here no one paid any attention to his shirt, or to the Doctor either—until he secretly gave a signal to a grey man lurking quietly in a corner, drinking coffee and observing beneath long eyelashes the dirty dancing in the middle of a space that was already packed to capacity. Less than a minute passed before one of the sofas was freed up and the Doctor found himself seated in the middle; on one side there was a boy in tight trousers, the kind a ballet dancer might wear, and on the other a timid brunette—there were flashes of red and green lights running over her breasts. The Doctor said something to the boy, who took fright and fled.

"Whit d'ye dae?" asked the brunette, stroking the Doctor's hair.

Whane'er ye meet a fool that's fou,
That ye're a maiden gar him trow,
Seem nice, but stick to him like glue;
And when set down,
Drive at the jango till he spew,
Syne he'll sleep sown.

The Doctor inhaled the scent of the café, its sweat and its twilight, and sipped a cocktail from a tall glass that resembled the male sex organ.

"Ah mak voices puir," said the Doctor, smiling at this joyous, sinful darkness.

"Is yon even possible?"

"Some folk hae the hang o miracles."

"Oh aye, an who learnt yese t'dae yon?"

"Maks nae maiter." The Doctor took her hand and bit one of her fingers. "If ye really maun ken, ah'll quo ye the name by whit he's cried, the body ah haud tae be ma dominie—Jesus Christ."

"Oh aye." She wriggled her bitten finger beneath his shirt. "If youse'r a doctur, gonnae cure me?"

hae the hang o miracles: can work miracles   *dominie*: teacher

When he's asleep, then dive and catch
His ready cash, his rings, or watch;
And gin he likes to light his match
At your spunk-box,
Ne'er stand to let the fumbling wretch
E'en take the pox.

"Whit kind o mediciner am ah? Ah'm a hoormeister, yon's whit ah'm," thought the Doctor. But he wanted to say it aloud so that everyone could hear.

"Ah'm a hoormeister," he yelled, but no one paid him any heed. What a thrilling word, a startling word to roll around in the mouth.

"Jesus spak a deealect," said the Doctor. "O an unricht, befylit langage. An thay crucifee'd him."

"Yous blether nae problem wi the Leid." The finger with the long nail pressed on the skin, the finger needed a doctor urgently. "Therr's no many in this dive knaws 'crucifee'd.'"

Cleek a' ye can by hook or crook,
Ryp ilky pouch frae nook to nook;
Be sure to truff his pocket-book;
Saxty pounds Scots
Is nae deaf nits; in little bouk
Lie great bank notes.

"Thare's rules o cleanliness," said the Doctor loudly, above the noise of the music. "If ye dinna screenge yer teeth day an daily..."

"Why don't we find oot jist whit sortae doctor y'are?" she said, leaning over him. "We've plenty time. As much as ye want. But whit wuz it ye said jist the noo concernin Christ?"

To get amends of whinging fools,
That's frighted for repenting-stools,

hoormeister: whoremonger   befylit: befouled

277

Wha often whan their metal cools,
Turn sweer to pay,
Gar the kirk-boxie hale the dools,
Anither day?

"Ah've graduated frae the philological faculty o the university, so ah'm well qualified tae spraff oan topics likes o yon.
"Ah've awready expleen'd yon,"

There's ae sair cross attends the craft,
That curst correction-house, where aft
Wild hangy's taz ye'er riggings saft
Makes black and blae,
Enough to pit a body daft;
But what'll ye say?

said the Doctor in his didactic voice. "Christ's wirds anely becam holy wance they got moot wi a puir langage, a langage whare maiters o sic maument coud be pit an haundit oan."

The Doctor finished his cocktail and closed his eyes. He'll return to the Camp tomorrow. And no one will ever find out where he was tonight. Just as always, he could feel something in his mouth—something alive, growing, straining, vibrating—a small spot that he could control and play a risky game with. He had to do it today, otherwise he would forget the taste of struggle.

"D'ye huv weans?" Her fingers were cold, her fingers knew well what the sultry heat of the capital was like. He mentioned this to her, using such words as he could find, and these words sounded so vulgar that he wrinkled his forehead with happiness.

"Durty beast."

Wi well-crish'd loofs I hae been canty,
Whan e'er the lads wad fain ha'e faun t' ye,

spraff: talk

To try the auld game taunty-raunty,
Like coosers keen,
They took advice of me, your aunty,
If ye were clean.

And she bared her teeth. "Aw the same … d'ye huv any?"

My malison light ilka day
On them that drink and dinna pay,
But tak' a snack and run away;
May 't be their hap
Never to want a gonorrhea,
Or rotten clap.

"Aye, twa," said the Doctor. "A laddie an a lassie. The lassie's caw'd Alicia, she's kent as Sia an aw, an the laddie's caw'd Avi."

"D'they ken whit y're aboot here?"

"Non, o coorse non." The Doctor was beginning to pant with desire.

My bennison come on good doers,
Who spend their cash on bawds and whores;
May they ne'er want the wale of cures
For a sair snout;
Foul fa' the quacks wha that fire smoors,
And puts nae out.

"Daft wee lassie."

And then, at long last, he relaxed and allowed her to lead him into the depths that were as red as an open mouth.

19

He arrived here in the evening, from the direction of the petrol station

He arrived here in the evening, from the direction of the petrol station. He remembered the road well. First there'll be gardens, then two-storey apartment blocks, set out neatly like piles of boxes in a warehouse, there'll be two churches, one Catholic, the other Orthodox, exploding upwards into the dull grey sky and comparing each other's crosses for size, then there'll be a Lenin waving an arm from the square. The round, intolerably round square.

Second-Hand   Goods from Europe
Prestige   Plumbing Supplies
Pet World   Laguna Café
The Emperor Paul

And there it is, the hotel.

"Don't make a noise," said the receptionist. "No noise after ten."

Faither looked at her without understanding a word she said. What does she mean? Don't make a noise? There was a black void thundering from the stairs that led upstairs to the rooms. The television behind his back was switched off, but even so it was informing the empty sofa in front of him in deafeningly loud tones about a festival that had just been held in the capital. Along its terrifying corridors and bandaged bathrooms, the hotel wailed about how painful it was for it to stand here, to grow old here, that it had a tooth that urgently needed extraction. Aren't you that tooth, Faither? Outside there was a buzzing and a feasting coming from that battle cruiser, the Emperor Paul. Like a healthy provincial town heart, it couldn't stop for a second.

What silence is she talking about?

The receptionist interpreted his silence in her own way.

"You're the only guest in the hotel," she made a start on the registration form. "But that does not mean that you can behave here as if you were at home. Do not forget that this is a hotel, and a hotel has its own set of rules ..."

He made a real effort to listen to her, but did not understand anything she said.

"Did you come here by car? Any children with you? Any animals? Write it down here."

Finally he was given a key: third floor. Last time he was on the second floor—a step up the ladder. The receptionist's eyes followed him with a suspicious gaze. If she could only see what he was holding in his hands. Although, of course, that was something no one could see. It was no more than a feeling, but it was so powerful, so vivid that Faither had been unable to rid himself of it for the whole day.

The feeling of a submissive child's hand in his coarse, adult hand. As if he had torn that hand off and was unable to throw it away.

He unlocked the door and walked into the room. If the receptionist could see him, she would be bound to reproach him with the words: "Just like he's entering his home." So what? A man from the forest will inevitably walk like that.

A pathetic, cramped room, as yellow as the flowers that Margarita held in her hand. A stain on the carefully folded sheet. A good sleep means wasting precious working time. Then the ashtray, spotlessly clean, like someone's insistent voice. An ashtray in which you could get the urge to drown yourself. The same black television set. Do you want me to tell your fortune? Switch me on. You're going to die. You're already dead. Except that if you switch me on, everyone will get to know of your death. And if you go on standing there with your mouth gaping open, it won't be Paradise you'll end up in, it'll be here, this hotel. A provincial hotel that instead of star ratings has a Board of Honour by the entrance, displaying the heads of the best people in the province.

Just like last time, Faither didn't even sit down; he stood frozen to the spot beneath the light bulb, inside which—again, just like last time—its immortal, exhausted slave, a tiny, puny, gilded homunculus, was dancing on hot coals. A hotel to die in. Hurriedly, trying to get ahead of the race. Squalor and damnation: There's nothing you can do about it. There's no way out. There never will be.

And then he remembered her song. The song of the woman who gave birth to Alicia. His wife used to sing it when she was pregnant. A song about the final room that's left to us. He could no longer remember, but it may well have been her final song. After that they decided to destroy her, to drive her out of the Leid.

It was a lengthy song. You could fall asleep to it if you didn't understand the words. And if you did understand them, you could fall asleep to it and not wake up again. How long ago it all was: Faither had even forgotten the words and rhymes; only scraps were fixed in his head. He tried to recall the melody, quietly humming to himself what he could remember of it; the result was pitiful and incomprehensible. The song was hers alone; no one else could sing it as she did.

She sang of the many rooms we enter and leave in our lifetime.

The first room: the maternity ward—all that remains of it in our memory is the sunlight.

Your parents' bedroom, where you have the right of place between them, these two people that you do not yet know. The time will come, and you will discover that they are not at all like the persons they pretend to be.

The child's bedroom, in which your own people live and you

are their hostage, because you are their God. Well, what did the rest of you think?

Offices, prison cells, railway compartments, washrooms, barracks, hospital wards, workshops. Hotel rooms.

And this one—the last room of all.

They took her away early in the morning, when the pigeons had only just woken up. He was the one who called the ambulance. Alicia was still very young, so he locked her in the bathroom and went to meet the medics. It did at times seem to him that Alicia had never forgiven him for this brief imprisonment; she never had the chance to say goodbye to her mother. But there was no other way he could have done it. She was sitting on the windowsill holding a knife when he awoke, sitting and peeling herself like an apple. Right down to the bone. She was cutting off even strips of skin, and the blood was dripping down into the yard below—as if someone had just watered the flowers for her. He awoke and rushed over to her, and she simply smiled at him guiltily, like a little girl. Who gave her the knife?

They took her off to the capital. He went to visit her just the once.

"Ah willna laisse her tae thaim," he whispered to her impulsively. "Ah'll dae iverything jist as we reckoned!"

But his wife didn't recognise him. She ran her clouded eyes across his face, yawned, guffawed, and then shut herself off again. There was only one thing she wanted—sleep. And Faither realised he was on his own.

What's more, the journeys would have cost him a lot of money. And he had Alicia to think about, as well as the message that she had to deliver.

He fell on the bed and covered his face with his hands.

Here ah'm, jyled awa as if ah'm feart o somethin. Patientfu. Oan a staundart cot, as if ah'm a widden dall. Oan ma richt airm,

---

jyled awa: shut away   *widden*: wooden

close up tae the shouder, a gey wheen o tottie wee patches o white skin, likes o a widwirm nibbelt m'airm. Thay're o various size, yon patches—awbesit's no really possible tae condescend oan size whan the muckle maist o thaim's no bigger than a drap or spreckle. Time, o coorse, maks a braw surgeon, but no the baist beautician. Yon patches growe mair snaw-like o'er time, an ah'm awreddy lang o'er thirty, but a body can yet spy them oot bi nakit ee, if ye shuve yer sleeves up faur eneuch.

Yon patches'd aye been explained tae us as merks left bi a big jag gien tae us whan we wur jist wee bairns bi a body wha wisnae a daub haund. Sae wee, in effect, the only merk we coud get afore it wis yon bullet dunt o conception. Big yins used tae say: big jag, vaccine, BCG. Yon last yin soonds nestie—it's goat stench o the seek clinic aboot it, shite kept i spunkboxes, caird gemms an unco cairving oan auld bowls … An we troued whit the big yins tellt us. We growe'd up disenchauntit, we thocht tae be cannier, but we aye kept oan believin. We believed, withoot pittin ony sarious thocht tae it—nae hummin an hawin here—we believed thare wis nae way t'adduce hou we'd wance been wee, wee bairns. The mynd's myndless frae sicca range, its seegnal vades, the film o whit's been fails tae load. Yet yon pale patches endure—visible oan skin fir tae keep somethin o import i mynd.

An anither thing folk say: fremmit folk ayeweys, ayeweys hae cognisance o whare we cam frae bi yon merks o vaccination. Only folk, thay say, born east o cultur an north o histoire get yon merks. Folk frae places whare streets e'en the noo get named fir murtherers; whare statues get lookit eftir likes o thay're flouers; whare they scrieve i the Cyrillic script an thair life's guidit no bi Law but bi law o' isms.

a gey wheen o: a great many   *tottie*: tiny   *the muckle maist o thaim*: the great majority of them   *bi nakit ee*: with the naked eye   *daub haund*: dab hand   *dunt*: wound   *seek*: sick   *spunkbox*: matchbox   *troued*: trusted   *the mynd's myndless*: the memory doesn't work

Ae-times ah believed aw this as weel: i BCG, i bairnhood, i fremmit folk. No that ah'd taen awthings oan faith, but ah semply dinna fash maesel wi sic things. Truelins, certaine suspeecions did arise oan rare occasions, but ah hae boust thaim likes o a jealous gadgie fechts wi yon firsten, ghaistly shaws o treichery. Ah believed i luve an meanin. Ah dinna think thare wis onything wharein ah didna believe; i hame-comin o a nation an soor plooms; i freendship an faimily; i the Leid an coffee; i revolution an lustration; i Zianon an Plato; i leeteratur an the Turau Gospels...[40] The truith's catchtin up wi me. It brocht me here, i this God-left hotel in a toun naebody kens aboot—forby the folk wha bide thare. Whan Alicia reads this, she'll be awmaist a growen-wumman. Ah wunner if she'll unnerstaund the langage it's scrievit wi. Or mebbes she'll hunt oot ancient beuks fir tae translate these mad scrievlins intae a langage o the Futur an ayont? He tried to picture Alicia as a grown woman, but could not. Children like her—they're a race of dwarf adults. They don't grow taller; they torment their parents when they look up on them from below with eternally reproachful eyes.

In a previous life, long ago, Faither and Alicia used to listen to music together, so that no one should hear them talk. He would switch on some pop music so that no one would ever suspect anything. However, they often listened to music that was more worthy. Sia, the Nile wagtail, had to remain a noble bird. Over breakfast they would listen to Schnittke. Occasionally they would even listen to his music before going to bed. Faither reached out for his telephone on the table. Most of all he liked a piece that some people call "Mindlessness" in the Lingo.[41] He found the piece on his telephone, and Schnittke began to play in this forlorn room. The telephone could scarcely cope with the sound and continually distorted the melody, but however much it slowed down the frenzied pace of the disturbing music, there was still enough of it for ghosts to begin to stir in the cor-

hae boust: drove away   *hame-comin*: rebirth   *God-left*: godforsaken
forby: except   *ayont*: beyond

ners of the room. And soon hotel room 42—where there was a man lying on the bed who called himself Faither—was filled with mysterious *beings*. They surrounded his bed, placed their hands on his fevered brow, talked to him in the Leid, helped him remember where the purpose of his journey lay.

"Ah wis semply eftir saufin ma bairn," he explained to them. They nodded; there were more and more of them in the room. An empty hotel, in which a light was burning only in one room.

Someone was knocking at the door. Timidly at first, but then more and more firmly.

Myndlessness . . . Ah'd a parfait mynd, but noo ah'm feart ah'm no thare. Ah'm withoot it. Langage is a wunnerfu thing, ye ken? Ye can dae whit ye like wi it, it'll mak ye hale, it's puir an michty, likes o a bairn's bonnie ee.

Bot first thow sal considdir commodities
Of our gardyng, lo, full of lusty trees.

Buzz, buzz, busy bee, buzzing all around . . .

Our lady is yonder, bissy as the beis,

"My inmost being hardly knows/If it's my demency that rambles/Or your own melody that grows."[42] Yon's a weird wird, yon demency. Latin myndlessness. Whit we say i the Leid soonds like "variety"; think oan variety shows, guid times, loadsae scran an bouze, hingowers an sair heids. Hou gaes ma demency? Is it aye haverin? For why havnae thair bardies scrievit onything likes o yon? Yon langage's nae guid fir yon . . . Is it yon weys?

Na mair I understude thir numbers fine,
Be God, than does a guko Cuculus canorus or a swine.

ah wis eftir saufin: I was trying to save   *loadsae scran*: lots to eat

287

Why no laisse a wee bit demency seep intae thair poesie? "An August night when summer-drunk/Threw open its black bags/ Fivescore thousand ripened stars/Poured down on warm, damp moss."[43]

Quhare precious staynes on treis doyth abound
—In sted of frute, chargyt with peirlis round.

Black bags, warm, dampit moss: are ye mine, demency? Tell me, Jew, whit am ah t'dae? The door began to shake again with the loud banging.

"Dinna schnittker! Haud aff wi yon iverlestin schnittkering!

Ye've goat a wean therr that's greetin!

Whit ur youse schnittkering it fur?

Haunds aff the wean!

Rag-folk likes o youse, ah'd slaughter them right oan the spot!

That does not mean that you can behave here as if you were at home. The deid dinna keech!"

Busy buzzing bee buzzing business.

Our lady is yonder, bissy as the beis,

large bees with red behinds, reid-airsies, *Bombus lapidaries*. Buzz aff, buzzybuzzybuzzyness.

"Whaaat d'ye waant me t'dae? Caw the fuckin cops? Switch that fuckin light aff an get tae fuckin bed. Get tae bed, ah fuckin said."

Tae Byzantium ma demency rambles, buzzing, nae messin', nae shirkin'.

Oh ye dour people descend frae Dardanus,
The ilk grund, frae wham the first stock came
O your lineage, wi blythe blossom the same

keech: defecate

Shall you receive thither returnin again.
Tae seek your auld mither mak you bane.

Tell me, Jew, whit shoud ah dae? Vive? Whit shoud ah dae, Sir Nowers? Praise you?

"Whit fir?" asked a voice from beneath a helmet that shone like the sun, a voice from out of a fair beard, as just as a field of wheat. "Aiblins ye shoud phone her, yon dame wi yon yellae hair. The wan ye think's belongin tae ye."

"Kenzy?"

"Aye. We wir aw that fond o her."

Kenzy. He heard her voice immediately after dialling her number, a voice so amazingly pure—as though she had been waiting only for this moment. As though she was standing there, behind the doors of this night, listening to his busy rambling. As though she knew that she held the key to the locked dimension of his demency in her hands.

"Kenzy."

Kenzy had placed the key in her mouth. She was sucking the cold key, and what he could hear was the ringing sound of the key striking against her marvellously young teeth. He listened to this melodic ringing, and she went on saying some strange things which Faither did not even try to understand:

"Give upal lowth emto hell pyou; doo knot foe near enny maw."

The sounds were clear and pure. A miraculous language, perfect in its incomprehensibility. Hell! Hell! Hell! Foe! Maw!

"Spit the key out."

"Eye ambi ing tree Ted."

"Spit the key out, Kenzy."

"By the very best doctor."

"The key, Kenzy."

"I don't understand a single word. The connection is terrible."

The key was still in her mouth, but the ringing stopped. By now, a fist was being drummed on the door. It was as if there was

289

a drummer trying to play along with Schnittke's music, but he couldn't get the rhythm right.

Faither opened the window and sat on the ledge. Before him lay the whole of the little town, a place where these people so much want to return to that they weep when they're singing about this "street with three apartment blocks/that we know so well."[44] Karaoke sounds were drifting over from the Emperor Paul, and in a strange way they fitted neatly into Schnittke's notes, but the drummer behind the door was ruining the whole effect. Beneath the window there were people eating and drinking, eating and drinking. They didn't notice him right away, but when they did it was too late. No doubt he was a strange sight, sitting in the window with the light behind him and his legs dangling down from the ledge.

"Awright, pal? Come oan doon here an huv a wee bevvy wi us wans." Tell me, Jew, whare maun ah gang?

"Ah'm tellin yese, get doon here, it's ma shout! Aw us wans is gonnae be heres aw night, so youse'll no be gettin any shuteye! Ah'm fu' o't the day. Ah've jist hud a wee lassie born!"

"En place o whom?" asked Faither from above.

"Whit y'talkin aboot, 'en place o'? 'Insteid of,' ur youse meanin? Ur youse a sicko or whit? Eh? Ah've jist hud a wee lassie born! C'moan, a wee deoch an doris!"

Faither stretched out to reach the glass that was being offered to him. He drank it down in one gulp. It took his breath away, and there was a painful sensation in his stomach. This was followed by something to eat that crunched under his teeth, like having a mouth full of sand or glass.

It's suppertime, an Faither's nae hame yet,
Daes he ken the road weel eneuch yet?
Aiblins he's loast, an Maggie his cuddie's stravaig'd;

his cuddie's stravaig'd: his horse has got lost

Aiblins he's somewhare aff the road an strayed?
Aye, yon's a kittlesome road, but weel Maggie kens her route,
An she'll no budge athoot she's felt her Jockie's boot.
But wha gangs here? His cuddie onweys spurrin'
An rantin an "Wag awa! Wag awa!" cawin?
Yon's the neebor, wow! an fancies bearin,
An buits an shaes Faither's laddie an lassie'll suin be wearin …
Aye an oan, an Faither's no yet came,
Forseuk be us bairns, an forseuk be his hame.[45]

---

kittlesome: difficult   *wag awa*: gee-up   *fancies bearin*: carrying presents   *forseuk*: forsaken

20

It was probably a Sunday. Or maybe a Friday

It was probably a Sunday. Or maybe a Friday. For all the time Alicia and Avi had been together, they had given up counting the days; there were much more important matters to attend to. Alicia was now going over this in her mind, and she again felt somewhat embarrassed. She was so grown-up and was even on her way to Bremen with her brother, and they had been through so much, and here she was not knowing what day of the week it was, just like a little kid, honest to God.

They would have laughed at her in the Camp. Especially those girls in the first troop. They were always laughing at her, but on the sly, behind her back. Goodness knows why—there was nothing noticeably different about her that made her stand out. Perhaps it was because they were a little bit afraid of Avi. Avi had some kind of special way of looking at people that wiped the smiles off their faces and instilled in them instead a sense of disquiet. That's the kind of brother she had. And once again it occurred to her that she couldn't say exactly what kind of person he really was. He's awmaist unknawist tae me, she thought, sneaking a glance at Avi, who was stepping along the forest path next to her. Maist likely acause ah've nae shawn muckle interest fir his vive. Whit sort o tittie am ah?

It was at that moment that she decided it would be better if today were a Sunday. First off, she intuitively felt that within her there was some kind of special clock that showed not only the time, but also the day, month and even year. If thare's a clock likes o yon tick-tockin awa insides o me, thought Alicia to herself, than it's rinning twinty fower oors en avaunce. It's aye the morn wi me. Yon's richt raison as tae why me and Avi ayeweys manage tae win thru. We're ayeweys timeous acause ony danger tae come aboot's en retard.

And secondly: Sunday was always visiting day in the Camp. Parents would turn up with tasty treats and presents, and it was only Alicia and Avi that no one ever came to see. That's perhaps why they were always making fun of her, those girls from the first troop. And anyway, Alicia and her brother were always dressed in the Camp uniform; they would exchange their T-shirts and shorts for exactly similar T-shirts and shorts whenever it was time for them to hand in their things for washing. The children in the Camp who had parents who came to visit them were able to introduce some variety into what they wore. They were always so colourful, those other Camp children, while Alicia and Avi were always dressed in just the one colour.

"Whit weys d'ye ween, Avi?" asked Alicia, when the forest track suddenly gave out and they had to make their way across a broad meadow where the grass reached right up to the chest, and she from time to time lost sight of Avi, who would suddenly jump out in the most unexpected places, as if he had emerged from water—"Avi! Thare y'are! Whit d'ye reck tae yon trees o'er thare i the forest, dae thay hae cognisance o bein pairt o a faimily?"

Avi raised his eyes skywards and thought for a moment.

"Aye mebbes some," he said in a sombre tone. "An some non. *Quercus robur*, aik trees, ah ween they knaw. *Thay* even tend thair ain. But birk trees, *Betula pendula*—naw, thay're sillies. An flichtie."

"Yon's the beuks y've read spoutin wirds fir ye," said Alicia. "Ye've read that much aboot the aik tree bein lang-heidit, man-heidit an faither-heidit, leavin the birks wi saft, hen-heidit thochts alane. Thochts oan luv an bein mairit tae men. Use yer loaf! Dinna

ween: guess   *reck*: reckon   *aik*: oak   *birk*: birch   *lang-heidit*: wise
hen-heidit: woman-headed

jist repeat whit ye've read i yer beuks. Whit aboot junipers, *Juniperus communis*, par exemple? D'thay no ken wha's thair bairns?"

"Communis shmonunis," grumbled Avi. "Stairt wi the cone-gatherin, an yon junipers'll haud thair wheesht frae th'aff. Aye, but if ye sae much as lay a haund oan yon aik tree's aik-nits, yon'll cast ye sic a leuk as gies ye hen's plouks aw o'er ..."

The meadow came to an end. They entered a bright wooded area full of squirrels and merry sunbeams, and then came out again on to a road which soon led them into a dense mass of tangled trees. They hesitated, stopped and again took each other by the hand. The road lost itself in the semi-darkness, somewhere beyond the trees' intertwined paws. They didn't wish to venture any further in that direction. They had managed to warm themselves in the sun, and the air that wafted towards them from the thick forest was damp and chilly.

They could also sense that someone was watching them closely from the forest—not a very good feeling to have. True, this was a feeling they had frequently had in the forest. Alicia knew that they were not alone.

"Let's awa an skirt yon forest," said Alicia, and Avi was for some reason very quick to agree.

They retraced their steps, and very soon realised that they must have taken a wrong turning at some point. Then Alicia (thinks to herself "*wha*aweese") and Avi (thinks to himself "*whau*raweese") decided to make for the place where they could see the sun breaking through the canopy of trees. This was exactly the right thing for them to do, for they found themselves once again on a road; on both sides of it there were so many wild strawberries and bilberries that they made up their mind: this is the right road. And no one would ever know where the road might have taken them if Avi—filling his mouth for the umpteenth time with a handful of berries—had not seen out of the corner of his eye something

aik-nits: acorns   *hen's plouks*: goose bumps

amidst the spruces, something that seemed to be growing out of the ground like a kind of plant, simply standing there, pointing ahead with a dry, branch-like finger ...

A signpost.

They had, of course, encountered signposts before. Lots of different kinds. Most of them had nothing interesting to say, and others said something in the language of numbers. However, this particular one was completely different. If Alicia and Avi had not known how to read, they would probably have simply continued on their way, stripping the berries from each little bush beneath their feet, but they were intelligent children, their father had been very concerned about developing their minds, and at one time they had even been going to school, although Alicia could not recall ever having seen her brother there. In a nutshell: they could both read very well, perhaps even a little better than their peers—the two of them could even read what was written in the old atlas, and that was something that not every child in their age group would be capable of. That's why they went right up close to the signpost and read it again, and then once more. On the signpost that was so self-assuredly pointing straight ahead, there were just two words, but very important these words were, crooked letters in white paint:

To Bremayne.

"Yon means we maun be oan the cairt bi nou," said Avi.

"Aye, seems yon wey," said Alicia, but there was a hint of doubt in her voice.

Naturally, they took each other by the hand as brother and sister should and went off in the direction that the signpost pointed out for them. The way they strode forward so resolutely, so purposefully, gave the impression that the signpost had hypnotised them. But Alicia was not smiling and was not thinking at all about how she would bang on the drum when they reached their final destination. Because something was not quite right.

Indeed, there was once again something not quite right.

Avi did have a smile on his face, but one that looked somewhat forced, however much he pretended to be happy. He was probably thinking the same thing.

Meanwhile they were making speedy progress along the forest road that stretched out before them like a carpet. All of a sudden, they again found themselves in some kind of meadow, where the grass was even higher, punctuated here and there by stunted apple trees. This must at one time have been a collective farm orchard. Here it was not at all difficult to walk, because someone had passed along there before them; the grass had been beaten right down to the ground. Without giving it a moment's thought, the children tried to stick to this path; it simply cut right through the grass like a corridor.

With their legs badly scratched, they reached the end of the path and stopped by a dilapidated brick house. It obviously hadn't been lived in for ages, but somebody was definitely in there now. Alicia and Avi could hear someone pacing about, breathing heavily and kicking stones and broken bricks around. In the grass there were crickets chirping away like tiny typewriters.

A man emerged from the house, wearing an army helmet that was pushed down right to his eyes.

"What's the purpose of your visit?" he asked in a hostile tone.

"We're gangin tae Bremen," said Alicia. "Ah'm Alicia, an this body here's ma brither Avi. We set aff yon wey indique'd wi yon signpost, an nou . . ."

She spread her hands out wide to show that she was a little confused and didn't know what to do next.

"This yer gear?" asked the man in the helmet brusquely. "Whit youz goat in therr? This is a border. Can youz no see that? Youz've baith goat eyes, aye?" And he pointed at something behind his back. Sure enough, there on the brick building that was staring at Alicia and Avi with its blank windows hung a board with writing on it: "Boarder Cuntrol." The letters looked exactly like those on the signpost—white and crooked.

"If we gang throu yon 'Boarder Cuntrol' we'll shuirly win Bremen?" asked Alicia.

"Aye," barked the man in the helmet. "Whit aboot the gear? Ah've awreddy askit youz wance!"

"Jist this," said Alicia. After a moment's thought, she handed over the road atlas and the manuscript of the unknown author. "That's aw."

The border guard seized the road atlas and the papers, and in a flash passed them over to someone standing behind the door. The door was hanging on just one hinge and swaying slightly.

"Dinnae move! They wans'll gie ye a shout ..." he said, and then he too disappeared behind the door.

Alicia and Avi stood there, shifting from one foot to the other. There was something wrong, but what exactly? A wind blew up, and the sun disappeared behind a border cloud. The fields around were wild and uninviting, all overgrown with weeds. The children had the feeling that someone was going to jump out of the greenery at any moment. They did not, however, have long to wait.

"Come!"—they heard a voice from inside the brick building. Holding each other by the hand, they stepped carefully over the broken glass and brick dust and entered. And inside—waiting for them, lying strewn all over the floor—were old placards, piles of human excrement, empty bottles of cheap booze, tattered newspapers, a deflated rubber ball, a broken umbrella, some bronze busts and several plaster statues of historical figures, generals and various other long-dead heroes, a number of them nearly full-size ... Lengths of wood, dog-ends, mattresses, mouldy blankets, pieces of tarpaulin ...

In the midst of all this mess there was a table, at which another border guard was sitting. He looked exactly like the one the children had met first—even his helmet was pushed down low over his eyes. There was a typewriter in front of him, and he was typing something with one finger. Once again Alicia had the feeling that something was wrong.

"He's ayeweys duntin jist same an same key," whispered Avi. "Ah knaw bi soond."

They stood for a bit, and then the border guard stopped hitting the key and slowly lifted his head.

"Ah'm Alicia, an this here's Avi ..." Alicia began to explain patiently; she knew only too well that grown-ups do not like to share information with each other, but prefer to obtain it direct from primary sources.

"I know." With one hand the border guard at the typewriter raised his helmet slightly, and gave an impatient, dismissive little wave with the other, and suddenly the light was blocked out of all the windows in the decrepit building, just as though they had been bricked up.

"Bannock the Bogill!" gasped Alicia.

"Bannock the Bogill!" said Avi in a voice that sounded like he was swearing.

And there before them were those selfsame eyes that looked like they had been drawn on his face, staring vacantly and indifferently at Alicia and Avi as though their fate had already been determined.

"What did the two of you call me?" demanded the great gob beneath those unseeing eyes, a deep gob full of needle-like teeth. "Who's this Bogill, eh? I'm Private Bannock, that's who I fuckin am. Private Bannock!"

Bannock the Bogill arose from the table and ran towards them. He was nearly as high as the hole-ridden ceiling, through which an ominous sky shed its light. He grabbed their road atlas and manuscript from the table and tore them to tiny shreds in a single movement; it was as if the paper itself had turned into white fluff at the mere touch of those terrifying hands.

"Sweet little girl," he hissed, trampling on the torn shreds. "A nice, tasty, filthy little girl with a dirty voice! No, that nasty Doctor won't be getting his hands on you with his cold metal toys, oh no! You'll be mine. It's you that's off to the Doctor ..."

He pointed his finger at Avi.

"The Doctor needs little boys, he loves them so very much! And you, little girl, well well well, we'll tell him the little girl died! It just happened! And we won't be lying to him either!"

And then he licked Alicia on the knee. Only a moment earlier he had been taller than they were, his head had reached right to the ceiling, and now here he was beneath their feet. But they had no time to do anything before Bannock the Bogill once again resumed his full height, up to where a lamp was now burning—it was dark in the house, and the windows had disappeared.

At this moment a telephone rang. Bannock the Bogill unwillingly reached into the pocket of his military trousers.

"Yup," he said, and thick, pink saliva dripped down on to his chest. "Yes! Yes, yes, yes!"

"No sweat, I'll still have time," said Bannock the Bogill, hiding the telephone in his pocket. "A little girl, a little tongue, not much trouble at all at the end of the day ... When I get back, you'll be sleeping like logs. Sleep well!"

He left the house, locking the door behind him. Alicia and Avi were left in total darkness.

And the brick house, which still had a board hanging from it that said "Boarder Cuntrol," started filling up with gas.

The gas smelled of sweet meadowland flowers. For a moment it seemed to Alicia and Avi that this wonderful aroma was being wafted into the house by the breeze. But then Alicia began to yawn, and her eyes started to beg her to allow them to embrace each other a little. Avi looked at her with concern, but how could she possibly see him? The gas was coming from somewhere to one side of them. Avi tried to find the precise spot where it was coming from, but it was so dark that all he found was a mouse. A dormouse that had been asleep for ages.

They could hear Bannock the Bogill impatiently stamping around outside on the broken bricks.

"Alicia," Avi called out to her, but she didn't answer straight-away.

"Whit? Avi, hyst ... hyst this dwaum frae me. Ah knaw hou ye're able tae."

"Ah'm no able," said Avi sadly. "Ah'm no able."

"Avi," now it was Alicia's turn to call to him in a feeble voice. "Wha ye be, Avi?"

"Ah dinna ken," said Avi. "Aforesyne ah'd cognisance o masel as an ordinary laddie, but nou ah hae ma doutes. But ah'm yir brither, ye can be sure o yon."

The room was now filled with a scent that made Alicia and Avi feel they were being stifled by a whole bouquet of flowers.

"Mebbes the Doctor'll turn up this moment fir tae sauf us yins," said Alicia. She was invisible in the darkness and sounded like she was barely alive.

"Naw, he'll be ahint the haund," said Avi. "An d'ye really hae sic a notion tae be back at Camp? Whit aboot Bremen? We waur verra near."

"Daft Avi," he heard Alicia's whisper, quieter even than the hissing of the gas. "Ye'd nae idea, did ye?"

"Whit d'ye mean?" Avi burst out laughing. "Nou, tak tent, Alicia—"

"Whit? Tak tent o whit?"

"Ah ween th'oor's come whan we maun say fareweel."

"Am ah tae dee?"

"Non," uttered Avi in an offended tone. "Whit's the maiter wi ye? Huv the wulves bitten ye? Y're na aboot tae dee. It's jist that nou we maun bid one anither *adieu*. For aye. Ye'll tak the high road, an ...

O braw Charlie Stewart, dear true, true heart,
Wha could refuse thee protection.
Like the weeping birk on the wild hillside,
How graceful he looked in dejection.

hyst: lift   *aforesyne*: previously   *he'll be ahint the haund*: he won't make it in time   *tak tent*: pay attention   *oor*: hour

O ye'll tak' the high road, and I'll tak' the low road,
And I'll be in Scotland a'fore ye,
But me and my true love will never meet again,
On the bonnie, bonnie banks o' Loch Lomond.

Aye. Jist list tae me the nou ..."

And then a lot of things happened. Alicia was never fond of recalling what took place. After all, who would ever want to recall spending a long time, a very long time, sitting inside their own brother?

Daith is wappin whan it comes—like birth;
I ken—I hae warstled throu, an focht wi baith.

Because, when Bannock the Bogill eventually returned to the dilapidated house, and the malevolent sun—it was in a bad mood on that particular day—was shining through the windows, he could not find either Alicia or Avi. Everything was as it was when he left, except that neither the delicious dirty little dish of a girl nor the little retard was anywhere to be seen.

She wis blue, ma bairn, blue as the breist o a bird
I seen oan the banks o the Tweed thon day; then grey,
Aw wrang ...

All he could do was pace stupidly from corner to corner around the room, aware solely of his resentment and hunger. It was all hopeless ...

The naelstring windit ticht aroon her neck;
I ettled tae lowse it, aince, twice, but it aye slippit ...

Broken bricks, lengths of wood, dog-ends, mattresses, mouldy blankets, pieces of tarpaulin. Tattered newspapers, a deflated rubber ball, a broken umbrella … Old placards, piles of human excrement, empty bottles of cheap booze, some bronze busts and plaster statues of historical figures, generals and various other long-dead heroes, a number of them nearly full-size and several with their noses broken off.

He had already gone off into the forest when the Doctor's men arrived. They waited for a bit, walked around the house, had a smoke while sitting on piles of bricks, cursed and then left bare-handed. By this time, Private Bannock was already a long way away. He was following a bloke out collecting mushrooms and listening to him muttering to himself under his breath. He's going to have to talk to the Doctor all the same. An idea occurred to Private Bannock of how to soften him up. For example, what about this bloke with the basket?

Meanwhile Alicia had waited for as long as necessary; she began to move her arms and legs, and the pedestal at last gave way. She had found it not at all suffocating to sit inside the beautiful statue into which her brother had metamorphosed. He had left her his breath, right until the very last moment. The only thing was that her arms and legs had gone numb …

Ma haunds couldnae grup, ma mind skalit frae the jizzen fecht, ma mooth steiket: no tae scratch, no tae scratch, lat nane hear …

Avi was smaller in stature than she was, and however much he had tried to puff out his chest and stretch out his arms, sitting in his insides was quite uncomfortable.

She hastily did some physical exercises, and her blood began to flow around her veins exactly as it should. She then placed the statue on its feet and covered it with a piece of tarpaulin. She reckoned that she would be back.

Surprisingly enough, she almost didn't cry. Well, maybe just a little. It was all—and here she was trying to convince herself—just a matter of a straightforward chemical reaction.

I stottert oot, doon tae the watter, thocht tae douk him in its cauld jaups, but ower late.

By now the damp clay had dried out and gone hard. And there was no way in which it could be turned back into Avi. He had explained it all to her just before they said their goodbyes. Moistening the clay would simply turn it into a lifeless lump. Clay like that, he had said, can be transformed only once. And then you need to know the special magic words, and it's only grown-ups who know them. And even then, not all of them know the words. That's how someone had deemed it should be. The question is: who?

Being alone in the forest wasn't exactly terrifying, but it certainly was extremely unusual. She hadn't been left so utterly alone for a long time … Adroitly skirting around the grey spruces—trees which, like the birches and pines, had long become her sisters—Alicia made her way through the forest. She sensed that Bannock the Bogill was somewhere close by and so covered her tracks as best she could. Her legs were, however, becoming weaker and weaker.

At night she recalled how Faither—back in the days when she still lived with him—had once left her all alone in the flat. He thought that she was asleep, but she had woken up in the middle of the night—there was someone walking around in the flat. Obviously, her first thought was that it was Faither, so she took hold of her bravest doll and looked out into the corridor. There she saw someone's back, a stranger's back. She noticed that the nape of the stranger's neck was clean shaven.

The stranger was walking around the flat, opening drawers and cupboards and rummaging around in them. He was obviously searching for something. He also went into her room, and she—holding her bravest, most super, courageousest doll (what did she call it?) in front of her—stood behind the curtain trying not to breathe.

He threw back the blanket on her bed and shone his torch on it. He shrugged his shoulders and began to examine the laundry basket. Then he got himself right into the corner where all her toys were kept in a cupboard. She was standing behind the curtain, thinking: if he finds her, will she have to speak to him? She wasn't allowed to speak the Lingo; Faither forbade it. She wanted to shout out loud, but she knew she mustn't. No one was supposed to hear the language that the girl in this particular flat spoke.

The stranger left and neatly turned the key in the lock of the front door. She had no idea if he had taken anything with him. She had no idea what he had been looking for. She wanted to tell Faither all about it on the next day, but she took pity on him. He was so tired. And he was drinking a lot from those little bottles. There were times when she would go to the kitchen whenever she woke up at night. He would be sitting with his legs stretched out, either moaning or mumbling something under his breath that sounded like a prayer. He used to think that she couldn't understand the Lingo, that Faither of hers. He used to think that not speaking was a sign of not understanding. How funny he was, and how much she loved him—until that morning when he went off with all the grown-ups, leaving her behind with a load of people she didn't know, people who kept on and on asking her about something or other. People in general are very fond of asking questions just for the sake of asking questions.

In the morning Alicia trudged through the fog-enshrouded forest, stretching her arms this way and that like a marionette to warm herself up a bit. Not many people know, she thought to herself, that the word "marionette" comes from the name of a little girl who lived a long time ago in a totally different country, one much closer to Bremen than to the Camp with an image of a sun above the gateway. Marionette—that's a little girl called Marie-Annette; her arms are attached to strings. The strings pull her in any direction, and she does what she's told to do. Alicia had never liked what her faither and mither had called her. No one in the whole world is called Sia. That's how she probably became Alicia. But perhaps being called Marie-Annette is even prettier.

At that moment Alicia came hard up against a barbed-wire fence.

Really hard, grazing her face nastily—adding to the scratch marks already left by badly brought-up forest plants.

She wiped the blood away and started walking along the fence. She was very hungry. Just like—it does happen sometimes—wanting to go to the loo badly. When you can't wait any more. She was even looking hungrily at herself. Well, there's this finger, for example ... So what if it's dirty?

The forest came to such an abrupt end that she let out a startled yelp.

Right in front of her was a gate, and above the gate—in the middle of a circle of rusty metal strips—was an image of the sun to greet her.

She turned her face towards the forest, ready to flee. However, the Camp exuded such a tantalising smell of breakfast that she hesitated, looked around while still clinging on to the branches of a spruce tree, and avidly inhaled the scents of human habitation.

"One of ours?" she heard a voice from behind her back.

"She certainly is," said someone in a satisfied tone, and took her by the hand. Firmly, just as Avi used to do. But not in such a debonair fashion.

It was the troop leaders. Right then, her other hand found itself in the tenacious grip of another set of fingers.

"Ah'm faimish'd," she said without raising her eyes.

"Right away," said one of the troop leaders. "Come on, off we go. We haven't seen you for ages."

"How dirty you are," said the other one. "What on earth do you look like? Just like you've crawled out of somebody's grave. You've even got fungus growing out of your hair."

Alicia burst out laughing. The two troop leaders chuckled—she knew that they couldn't laugh properly, after all they were the Authorities. She even snuggled up to one of them—with her cheek on the uniform shirt with the short sleeves. From the Camp kitchen there came such an intoxicating smell. Uncle Vasya the cook was preparing something that he could make better than anything, but Alicia had forgotten what it was called in the Lingo.

She would remember what it was called, she said to herself, she would remember everything. The troop leaders had already brought her to the gate, but then something completely unexpected happened. This was the road to the gate that was used on Sundays by parents bearing tasty treats and child-sized tracksuits, and on other days by the Camp minibus with its tinted windows. But on this occasion a dark red car came flying—no other word for it—up to the gate. From it, while the troop leaders were deep in conversation with the guardians of the gate, emerged a tall, good-looking woman all dressed in black. No, this was not the woman with the blonde hair, nor was it the old woman who looked young; it wasn't the woman from the bus or Miss Edwardson from the school. She was someone totally different, and yet at the same time very familiar to Alicia. And in this lay her most distinguishing feature.

"Let her go." They heard her voice, so quiet, yet so authoritative that the troop leaders at once loosened their grip.

"Come here, girl," said the woman, keeping a disdainful eye on the troop leaders. But Alicia stood where she was. Life had taught her that running was for when you needed to escape from something.

"I'm waiting," said the woman in black, smiling. Then Alicia took one step, then another, and so hesitantly approached the dark red car and stood beside it.

"Do you know who I am?" asked the woman in black with another smile.

"Aye," said Alicia.

"Who then?"

"Ma mither."

The troop leaders stood talking by the gate, and soon the Director himself came out, a little unsteady on his feet and hastily doing up the buttons on his ridiculous shirt. Alicia's mother handed him some papers. He put a great deal of effort into making sense of all the official stamps and signatures; then he compared several photographs and demanded still more evidence. She pulled everything necessary out of her little handbag, just like a magician.

"Are you going to come with me?"

"But ye war deforce'd frae ... Deforce'd frae the Leid. Ye war deid. Awmaist," said Alicia, looking wide-eyed at her mother.

"Luckily only from the Leid," and her mother smiled so sweetly that Alicia had no wish to stay silent next to her; she wanted to tell her all sorts of things, never mind what, even utter drivel, provided her mum would keep smiling.

"But ye ..."

"You know, I really don't like thinking about it," said Mother. "It was so long ago.

An mercy? Nane they gied me at ma trial—
The verdict? Hingin.

Which means that it never happened. So, are you coming?"

"Bi fegs! But whaur'll we gang tae?"

"You'll see."

It took another hour to draw up all the documents. Alicia sat gnawing yesterday's cheese rolls in her mum's car, continually honking the horn and categorically refusing to get out. The car's constant howling filled the forest, and a startled choir of birds replied. By the gate stood their kind Doctor; he stood staring intently at Alicia, as if he wanted to ensure that he could remember what she looked like. As if he knew that they would never see each other again.

bi fegs!: sure!

Mother shook the Doctor's hand, and he held hers in his—rather longer than was necessary.

The duimster slippit the towe ower ma heid ...

He whispered something to her: Alicia couldn't hear what, but she kept sounding the horn, and then ...

He drapt the flair—but I'd lowsed ma haunds,
I grupped thon raip, aince, twice, thrice at ma thrapple—
I'd dae it this time! The duimster duntit me wi his stick,
dunt, dunt, an the dirdum dinged in ma lugs,
"Clure the hure! Clure the hure!" Syne aw gaed daurk ...

Mum tore her hand away and came quickly over to the car.

"Mither, let's awa an pick up Avi," asked Alicia. "It's nae faur ... Ah'll pit him i ma chambie an clean him aw masel, sae dinna fash!"

"What do you mean? What Avi?" Mother asked, puzzled, as she started the car. "Please, Sia, don't make things up. We still have a lot to do."

They finally got underway. The journey was not all that long—just a few hours, and while the capital city baked in the stifling heat, Alicia was sitting naked in the bathroom of Mother's flat, and Mother was rubbing her back so hard that Alicia said she hated her.

"You speak Russian very badly," said Mother, shaking her head. "You're going to have to do some learning. When we've reached our final destination, you'll have a tutor called Herr Günsche. He knows something of the dead language that your father taught you—why he did that I have no idea. You will have to try very hard. I hope that by the New Year you will also start speaking German."

"Ah can speak yon a wee bit awreddy!" said Alicia. "Faither an ah used tae read Goethe i the oreeginal!"

"I just can't imagine how you could have lived here." Mother was horrified. "With that sort of pronunciation, not knowing any Russian ..."

"It's jist thare's a wee bane." Alicia opened her mouth and pointed to it with her finger. "Ah've been gettin traitment, but the Doctor's said ..."

"What's this about a little bone? Don't talk such nonsense, Sia!"

The look on Mother's face was so sad that Alicia meekly decided not to say any more.

Then there followed a night with a nice soft pillow and a new doll that Alicia called Avi, although it bore no resemblance to a boy. Aye but sometimes it did happen that a laddie leukit likka lassie, an th'ither wey roun, thought Alicia to herself. Just like that famous painting where St. Jerome teaches translators that language is in reality not a problem.

On the next day Alicia's journey continued. They drove for a long time in the car, then took a train.

"What a pretty little girl," said the border guard, a man very much like Bannock the Bogill, except that his eyes had been drawn on expressively, with obvious talent. As if they really were alive. "Do you have a younger brother?"

"Ah used tae," said Alicia, looking at the well-drawn eyes almost without fear. She liked it when things were done tastefully by the hand of an expert. "Aye, ah did hae a wee brither. He turnit intae a stookie, an ah went inside o him, an yon gas didna affect me."

"What on earth?" The frontier guard's eyes opened wide; that's exactly how they should be drawn, thought Alicia.

Aye so he remeen'd thare next tae the but 'n' ben, like he wis howked frae a block o puir ice,

said Alicia in all seriousness.

Ice-bund nae langer, stiff-frozen nae mair, nor droukit bi deidly

stookie: plaster statue

310

cauld watter; nou sculpit frae bronze, warmit frae sonne, for aye
he'll staund wi pride oan this airth.[46]

The border guard didn't bother them again, but from time to time cast sympathetic glances at Alicia's mother.

Later that day they found themselves in a completely unfamiliar town, where the people spoke a language that even Faither hadn't taught Alicia. After a good lunch a taxi took them to the airport. Alicia realised with horror that for several hours there wouldn't be any solid ground under her feet, but there would be endless forests, tiny and harmless when looked at from a great height, just like vast expanses of grass. Forests and roads. It turned out that everything up in the sky was very similar to what there was down there on the ground. Except that up here the forest was completely shrouded in white mist, just like it is in the morning. And the roads were the kind where Alicia was bound to get lost if she ever found herself alone again.

But now she really was at last on the map. She didn't need to consult any atlases to convince herself of this. The atlas was down there, beneath her feet.

A chink o licht. The smell o wid, warm—a cuddie's pech; ma
Een appen. I lift ma nieve, chap, chap oan ma mort-kist lid,
Chap, chap!

They were fed on the plane. As she was finishing off her yoghurt and muesli, Alicia finally decided that the time had come to ask Mother a question ... In fact, to ask her the most important question of all.

"Whaur are we fleein tae?"

"Guess," said Mother, concentrating on her notebook.

Alicia sat and thought for a bit, glanced out of the window, and only then did she react, in a voice that was half inquiry, half confirmation.

"T-tae B-bremen?"

"Well, of course," her mother waved the question away with a dismissive hand gesture.

I heeze masel, slaw,
Intil ma ain wake, at the Sheep Heid Inn. Folk heuch an flee:
"A ghaist, a bogle, risin fae the deid!" I sclim oot, caum.

"Tak the clasp oot ma hair. It's daft an it's nippin me."
"Naw, ah willna," said Mother irritated.

The braw brewster gies her a wink, haunds her a dram.
She sups lang the gowd maut, syne dauners back tae life, an hame

and gave Alicia such a look that the girl slid forward to the very edge of her seat, pouted her lips in a sulk and resolved to keep silent, even if Mother should ask her about something.

The clouds parted in front of them, Alicia's ears became blocked and she shut her eyes. When she opened them, she could see beneath the aircraft wing the scattered lights of a strange, big city glittering in the twilight. Swaying slightly, the aircraft began its slow descent. The stewardess straightened Alicia's seatbelt, although there was absolutely no need for it. Alicia watched her indignantly as she walked away, but then the stewardess turned round and smiled at her. She reminded Alicia a little of her mother—tall and fair-haired—but the stewardess had a smile that was clearly fake, and her fingers were cold. Jist laisse her keep up wi yon, thought Alicia, an

I'll sup lang the gowd maut, syne dauner back tae life.

And spitefully she stuck out her tongue at the pretty stewardess.

The Belarusian Dimension

Translator's note
In the notes below, on the specifically Belarusian aspects of the text, I have used the Latin-script spelling for Belarusian place names and personal names that has been adopted by the Minsk government:

c = ts
č = ch (English "church")
ch = Scots "loch"
j = y in "yet"
š = sh
ŭ = w
ž = s in "pleasure"

The letters ć, ĺ, ń, ś and ź represent sounds that differ slightly from their unaccented equivalents.

In the actual text of the novel, I have used the simplest possible transliteration of Belarusian words, without special letters.

The Scots Dimension
(poems and songs)

Chapter 1

"To a mouse on turning her up in her nest with the plough, November 1785" —Robert Burns (1759–1796)

Much has been made of this poem's connection to Adam Smith's *The Theory of Moral Sentiments* (1759), a key text in the moral philosophy of the Scottish Enlightenment, and precursor to *The Wealth of Nations* (1776). Burns admired Smith, and wrote of *The Wealth of Nations*, "I could not have given any mere man credit for half the intelligence Mr. Smith discovers in his book."

"The Lass of Cessnock Banks, A Song of Similes" —Robert Burns

Written when Burns was a teenager: the lass is identified as Ellison Begbie, a servant wench, daughter of a farmer.

"Mally's Meek, Mally's Sweet" —Robert Burns

Burns was actively involved in contributing to and editing *The Scots Musical Museum*, the most important of the many eighteenth- and nineteenth-century collections of Scottish song. He gathered songs from a variety of sources, and also included his own work.

Chapter 2

"Landlady, Count the Lawin" (tune: "Hey Tutti Taiti") —Robert Burns

"Hey Tutti Taiti" is a traditional Scots air, age unknown, although it is reputed to have been played by the army of Robert the Bruce before Bannockburn in 1314 and during the Siege of Orleans in 1429, when France and Scotland were in alliance. Also used as a basis for other songs, including "Scots Wha Hae" (see chapter 16).

"Ye Hae Lien Wrang, Lassie" —Robert Burns

Some of Burns's most admired works were sanitised versions of the bawdy originals. This piece comes from Burns's collection *The Merry Muses of Caledonia; A collection of favourite Scots songs, ancient and modern, selected for use of the Crochallan Fencibles.* Burns was admitted to this "convivial" Edinburgh club in 1787; as he both wrote and collected this material there is no knowing how much of it is actually his.

The Merry Muses was considered to be so explicit that its existence was denied for more than one hundred years after Burns's death. When it was finally acknowledged, it was banned in the UK until 1965.

Chapter 3
"For the Sake o' Somebody" —Robert Burns

The "Somebody" in this short song is Bonnie Prince Charlie (Charles Edward Stuart, the "Young Pretender"). It is derived from a piece by Allan Ramsay from his *Tea-table miscellany: or, a collection of choice sangs, Scots and English* (1733).

"Epistle to Mr. Tytler of Woodhouselee, Author of a Defence of Mary Queen of Scots" —Robert Burns

In May 1787 Burns composed this epistle for the historian Mr. William Tytler (1711–1793). The verses were inspired by Tytler's publication *An Historical and Critical Enquiry into the Evidence Produced by the Earls of Murray and Morton, against Mary Queen of Scots. With an Examination of the Rev. Dr. Robertson's Dissertation, and Mr. Hume's History* (1760).

"The Bonnie Moor-hen" —Robert Burns

The moor-hen hiding in the heather in this poem is Bonnie Prince Charlie, forced to go into hiding after defeat at Culloden.

"McPherson's Farewell" —Robert Burns

Jamie McPherson, a "Highland freebooter," was hanged at Banff on November 16, 1700. As the noose was placed around his neck he played on his fiddle the tune to which Burns's words are set. In the run-up to his execution McPherson composed his famous "Rant." A legend was born and Robert Burns was instrumental in developing the cult of McPherson with his rewrite of the Rant.

"Such a Parcel of Rogues in a Nation" —Robert Burns

This song is usually ascribed to Burns, but is in fact another where he has taken elements from elsewhere and made them his own. The phrase "Such a parcel of rogues in a nation" is found in James Hogg's *The Jacobite Relics of Scotland* in a poem called "The Awkward Squad," attacking the "thirty-one rogues," the Scottish commissioners who were alleged to have sold the nation out in the Union with England Act of 1707.

"O Can Ye Sew Cushions?" —Robert Burns

This old lullaby, sung by a mother whose husband is away at sea, was one of many which Robert Burns collected and published, sometimes with his own embellishments.

"Does Haughty Gaul Invasion Threat?" —Robert Burns

Written while Burns was simultaneously helping to organise the Dumfries companies of Volunteers against a proposed French invasion in the spring of 1795.

"John Anderson My Jo" —Robert Burns

A polite adaptation of the traditional bawdy song of the same name.

"A Bard's Epitaph" —Robert Burns

After the first stanza in the vernacular, the poem warns us in English of the dangers of reckless and impulsive living, ultimately revealing that if a reputation is to be saved and wisdom attained, life ought to be lived prudently.

"Rusticity's Ungainly Form" —Robert Burns

Theme for this poem—hypocrisy.

Chapter 4

"On the Late Captain Grose's Peregrinations Thro' Scotland" —Robert Burns

The etymology of *jocteleg* became clearer when an old knife was found with the cutler's name marked "Jacques de Liège."

"Contented Wi Little" —Robert Burns

Burns composed this song on November 18, 1794, two years before his death, and he considered it as something of a self-portrait. Indeed, when the painter Alexander Reid came to create his portrait miniature Burns wished to link the two together, so that "the portrait of my face and the picture of my mind may go down the stream of time together."

Chapter 5

"That a general inability to read, or speak, with propriety and grace in public ..."

These words open the first of the lectures on elocution given by Thomas Sheridan—father of the playwright Richard Brinsley Sheridan—in Edinburgh in June 1761. He also gave a lecture course on the English language.

"My Wife's a Wanton Wee Thing" —Robert Burns

While the first two stanzas are based on an old folk song, the remaining verses, the bawdiest of all, have been attributed to Burns.

"Epigram: To a Club in Dfrs. Who styled themselves the D Loyal Natives and exhibited violent party work and intemperate Loyalty... 10th June 1794" —Robert Burns

The Loyal Natives were formed in January 1793 and were among the more reactionary of the Dumfries citizenry. They unwisely produced verses lampooning Burns and other radicals, which provoked a stinging attack from the Bard.

"The Bonniest Lass" —Robert Burns

Written to the tune of "A Man's a Man for A' That," though its subject is somewhat different.

At the formal opening of the reconvened Scottish parliament in 1999—disbanded since the Act of Union in 1707—Sheena Wellington sang "A Man's a Man" and encouraged all the MSPs to rise and sing the last verse together. MSP Winnie Ewing said this was "a sensational moment of unity and plain Scottish speaking which typified the best things of our country."

"How Can I Keep My Maidenhead?" —Robert Burns

Contains explicit sexual scenes.

Chapter 6

"What Mum and Dad Say" —Anon.

Takes the form of a single stanza conversation between husband and wife to explore contemporary domestic arrangements.

"The Cotter's Saturday Night" —Robert Burns

"The Cotter's Saturday Night" is about tradition, but it also started a tradition in English poetry; it was frequently imitated. Later poets, in particular John Clare (1793–1864), took this poem as a model in writing poetry about the lives of ordinary people. Robert Burns made a huge contribution to the emerging idea of a national culture, the principles and significance of which are boldly stated in this poem.

"The Farmer's Ingle" —Robert Fergusson (1750–1774)

Fergusson wrote of Edinburgh scenes and Edinburgh people. Even more than his predecessor, Allan Ramsay, he had a considerable influence on his successor, Robert Burns.

Chapter 7

"Coulter's Candy," also known as "Ally Bally" or "Ally Bally Bee" —Robert Coltart (1832–1880)

Coltart was a weaver in Galashiels; this song was an advertising jingle for the aniseed-flavoured confectionery that he manufactured in Melrose, and sold around the markets of the Border towns. The recipe is no longer known, but the song lives on.

Chapter 8

Medley: "Scottish Soldier" & "Donald, Where's Your Troosers?"

"Scottish Soldier": Andy Stewart (1933–1993) wrote the lyrics and based the tune of his best loved song on "The Green Hills of Tyrol," which had been transcribed to the pipes in 1854 during the Crimean War by Pipe Major John MacLeod of the 93rd Sutherland Highlanders.

Chapter 9

"O Whistle and I'll Come tTo Ye, My Lad" —Robert Burns

Believed to be Burns's version of a traditional song, and eventually published in George Thomson's A Select Collection of Scottish Airs (1793).

"On Fergusson—Lines Written under the Portrait of Robert Fergusson, the Poet, in a Copy of that Author's Works Presented to a Young Lady in Edinburgh, March 19th, 1787." —Robert Burns

Rebeccah Carmichael, an aspiring poet, was the recipient of Fergusson's book and Burns's verses. Fergusson died at the age of 24 in the Edinburgh "mad house."

"Tam o' Shanter" —Robert Burns

Composed to accompany a drawing of Alloway Kirk in the second volume of Captain Francis Grose's *Antiquities of Scotland* (April 1791).

Chapter 10

Medley: "No Awa Tae Bide Awa" & "Wee Deoch an Dorris"

"No Awa Tae Bide Awa": Originally a drinking song with a number of regional variations of words—though most people only know the chorus.

"Wee Deoch An Dorris" (composed and sung by Sir Harry Lauder, 1870–1950): A convivial drinking song, but only a real Scot can properly get his tongue around "It's a braw bricht moonlicht nicht." "Deoch an doras" in Scots Gaelic and Irish means literally "drink of the door" or "one for the road."

Chapter 11

"A Drink Eclogue: Landlady, Brandy and Whisky" —Robert Fergusson

The poem takes the form of a singing (or rather flyting) contest between a bottle of brandy and a bottle of whisky.

"Nature's Law" —Robert Burns

Burns is writing here to his friend and landlord Gavin Hamilton, preferring the man, "wha multiplies his number," to the life-destroying warmonger.

Chapter 12

"Epitaph for Hugh Logan" —Robert Burns[?]

While there is no evidence to attribute the epitaph to Burns, the poet often revelled in crude verse. It is possible that Burns is the author. The verse may have been inspired by Laird Hugh Logan of Cummock (1739–1802).

"O an Ye Were Dead Gude Man" —Robert Burns

Burns's version of an earlier song. His addition of the cuckold's horns in the third stanza brings out the humour of the lyrical persona, who sings of her preference for another.

Chapter 13

"A Drunk Man Looks at the Thistle" —Hugh MacDiarmid, [pseudonym of Christopher Grieve] (1892–1978)

"MacDiarmid approached Scots from an entirely different angle: he rejected the 'kailyard' tradition with the sentimental picture of Burns surviving in the Vernacular circles. He seized on the Makars, on Scotland's Gaelic tradition (hence the pseudonym), on its independent, non-English individuality; on the language, finally, as the source of 'words and phrases which thrill me with a sense of having been produced as a result of mental processes entirely different from my own and much more powerful,' and 'which cannot be reproduced in English.' Besides his native southwest Border Scots, MacDiarmid used all accessible sources: the other dialects, older literature, and works of scholarly research including Jamieson's *Etymological Dictionary* … [It] might certainly be asked how MacDiarmid could set out to reach the masses and at the same time write in a language the only user of which was apparently he himself." (Renata Korpaková)

Chapter 15

Medley: "Bonnie Charlie/Will Ye No' Come Back Again?" & "Ane Godlie Dream"

"Bonnie Charlie" (Carolina Oliphant, Lady Nairne, 1766–1845), also known as "Will Ye No Come Back Again?" is set to a Scottish folk tune. As in several of the author's poems, its theme is the aftermath of the Jacobite Rising of 1745, which ended at the Battle of Culloden.

"Ane Godlie Dream" (Elizabeth Melville, Lady Culross, c. 1578–c. 1640): In 1603 Melville became the earliest known Scottish woman to be published when Robert Charteris issued the first edition of this Calvinist dream-vision poem. She was a friend of leading figures in the Presbyterian opposition.

Chapter 16
"Robert Bruce's March to Bannockburn / Scots Wha Hae"
—Robert Burns

Burns implies in a letter to George Thomson in August 1793 that he was inspired by the French revolution.

Chapter 18
"Lucky Spence's Last Advice" —Allan Ramsay (1684–1758)

Ramsay wrote this poem around 1718. It parodies the broadside publications of "last words" or "dying advice" which offered moral instruction. The narrator, Lucky Spence, is a brothelkeeper, and her advice consists mainly of teaching her "girls" how to exploit their clients.

Chapter 19
"The Palyce of Honour" —Gavin Douglas (c. 1474–1522)

Douglas was a Scottish bishop, makar and translator. His major achievement was *The Eneados*, published in 1513—a full translation of Virgil's *Aeneid* into Scots, the first translation in any Germanic language.

Chapter 20
"Bonnie Banks o Loch Lomond" —Andrew Lang (1844–1912)

Lang was a Scottish poet, novelist and literary critic. In about 1876 he wrote a poem based on a song, the original composer of which is unknown. It begins:

> There's an ending o' the dance, and fair Morag's safe in France,
> And the Clans they hae paid the lawing,

Morag—"great one" in Gaelic—refers to Bonnie Prince Charlie.

"Hauf-hingit Maggie" —Gerda Stevenson

From her collection *Quines: Poems in Tribute to Women of Scotland* (2018). This poem tells the story of Maggie Dickson (c. 1702–c.1765), charged and condemed for mudering her newborn child. After surviving execution by hanging, Maggie was considered legally dead and could not be rehanged.

Glossary

a brammer of: a really good
aebody: everybody
aforesyne: previously
a gey wheen o: a great many
a glittie faiple: a lower lip shining
  with grease
a growen-body: an adult
ahint: behind
ah'm eftir askin: I want to ask
ah've loast haud o masel: I've lost
  hold of myself
ah wis eftir saufin: I was trying
  to save
aiblins: perhaps
aik: oak
aik-nits: acorns
airt oot: find
a muckle hale: a whole load
atweesh: between
avaunt: go ahead
awbesit: albeit
aw bodies: everyone
a wee dicht: a little tidying up
aw thegither: all together
ayont: beyond

bampot: idiot
banes: bones
bawbees: money
bawhair: testicular hair
bawheids: fools, idiots

baws: balls
befaw: befell
befylit: befouled
beuks: books
bidin': living
bi fegs!: sure!
bi nakit ee: with the naked eye
birk: birch
birlin: running
birl roon: turn round
brammed up: dressed up
braw: good
breekums: shorts
brig: bridge
but 'n' ben: cottage
byganes: in the past

cairt: map
cantie: cheerful
carle: fellow
cawin: calling
chaft: jaw
chambie: room
chaunt: speak in a stylised
  manner
check: key
chib: knife used as weapon
chizors: scissors
chored: stole
clacht haud: caught hold
claes: clothes

clart: dirt
clype: inform
coof: fool, simpleton
coud ah hae len o: could I borrow
courie: snuggle
couthie: nice
cowp: mess
craiturs: creatures
cry: call
cry in by: drop in

daintees: delicacies
daub haund: dab hand
daunder: walk
daupit: stupid
daupit coo: stupid cow
deek: look
dicht: wipe
dominie: teacher
doon the wey: down the corridor
douce: kind, straight
drag: road
droukit: sopping wet
dry boak: dry retching
dugs: dogs
dunt: blow, push, drop, wound
durna: dare not
dwaum: stupor

ee (plural "een"): eye
echas: echoes
eik-name: nickname
elf-shot: shot by elves using
  invisible arrows (superstition)
endure: exist
eneuch: enough
ersten: first

fancies bearin: carrying presents
fantice: fantasy
fash: worry
fasht: bothered
faw: fall
firstlins: at first
foostie-baws: mushrooms
forby: except
forseuk: forsaken
fou: drunk
fr'ane: from an
fremmit: foreign
fud: arsehole
fundit: found

gadgie: bloke
gait: goat
gallus: bold, daring, unmanageable
gang: go
gars: makes, forces
gemm: game
gey: very
gin: if
girnin: pulling a face
glamourie: magic
glit: slobber
God-left: godforsaken
gorble: gobble
gorblin: unfledged bird
goury: (lit.) the refuse of the
  intestines of salmon
gree: favour
greetin: crying
growthiness: fertility
gub: gob
gullied: cut, knifed
gutties: plimsolls

haar: mist
hae a leukie: have a little look
hae boust: drove away
hae the hang o miracles: can work miracles
hale: whole
hame-comin: rebirth
Hame'll Dae Me: home will do me
hamelt: native
harnless: brainless, stupid
harnpans: brainpans, skulls
hashie: carelessly
haudit: held
haud yer wheesht: keep quiet
haund-festin: betrothal
haunds: hands
heave out: dispose of
heid bummerz: top dogs
he leuks gey fey: he looks so naive
he'll be ahint the haund: he won't make it in time
hen: girl
hen-heidit: woman-headed
hen's plouks: goose bumps
heuchter-teuchter: (contempt.) pertaining to the Scottish Highlands
hinnied: sweet, honeyed
his cuddie's stravaig'd: his horse has got lost
hoormeister: whoremonger
houghmagandie: fornication
houts touts: like hell
hout tout: good heavens
howk: dig

howked up: heaved up
hummer'd: murmured
hures: whores
hyst: lift

jaggie: stinging
jaloused: guessed
Jimmy: bloke
jocteleg: pocket knife
jyled awa: shut away

kailyard: kitchen garden
keech: defecate
keek: look
kegs: underpants
kent: knew
kittlesome: difficult

lang-heidit: wise
lee: lie
leet: list
loadsae scran: lots to eat
lues: loves
lum: chimney
lumbers: one-night stands

maks nae recks: it doesn't matter
maun: must
mercat: market
ming: stink
mingeour: something that produces a bad smell
Monro o clarty ashets: mountain of dirty dishes
moot: mention
mooth-airns: mouth gags
muckle: big

nameliheid: fame
neb birsies: nose hairs
nyaff: brat

oan the bevvy: on the booze
ochone: alas
oor: hour
ootlander: stranger
ova: egg cells

paip: stone of a fruit
panshite: panic
parritch: porridge
peel: pill
pertect: protect
pits: puts
playock: toy
pledgin: promising
pootch: pocket
prood: proud
purvey: food for a special
  occasion

quoth: speak

raebuck: roebuck berry
ramshin: chewing
raxed: reached
reck: reckon
redding oot: getting rid of
reid een: red eyes
rerr: great
roon: round

sair: sore; hard
sauf fur: save for
scalies: scabies

scaur: scar
schilpit: pathetic
screenged: scrubbed
scrieve: write
scrift: book
scuddy: naked
scunners: loathsome objects
seek: sick
shaidae: shadow
shoogled: shook
short syne: recently
shot the craw: scarpered
shuggle yer wallies: (lit.) "shake
  your false teeth"
siller: (lit.) silver, metal
skelf: splinter; small, thin person
skive: pare
sonne: sun
souk: someone who curries
  favour
spauldin: splitting open
spiel: put on, play, act
sprach: speech
spraff: talk
spunkbox: matchbox
starns: stars
stoatir: stunner
stookie: plaster statue
suiner or syne: sooner or later
sup: drink
swatch: look
swithly: indeed

tache: moustache
tae a baund playin: till the cows
  come home
tae be cried: to be called

tae yer howff: to your place
tak tent: pay attention
tak tent o: take notice of
t'ane: to a
tapsalteerie: topsy-turvy
teuch: tough
thaim: them
thay: those
the bygane: the past
the day: today
thees: thighs
the gither: together
the morn's morn: tomorrow morning
the muckle maist o thaim: the great majority of them
the mynd's myndless: the memory doesn't work
the nicht: tonight
thole: suffer
thrapple: throat; strangle
thrawart: perverse, contrary
thruive: thrived
timmer: tree, timber
tittie: sister (there is a phrase that denotes the close relationship between brother and sister: "tittie-billie")
tongue-tackit: tongue-tied
toot sweet: tout de suite
tottie: tiny
touk: beat
trews: trousers
troued: trusted
tummel tae l'amour: fall in love
tumshie heid: turnip head
twa heid: two heads

unchancy: dangerous
unco: strange
unspeal: wind back
unsteekin: opening

wabbit: exhausted
wag awa: gee-up
wean: little child
ween: guess
weygait sign: road sign
wey o' th'ongae: the way forward
wheeriorum: thingummyjig
widden: wooden
winching: wenching, trying to attract females

ye'd mynd o: you would remember
ye hae plichtit: you gave a solemn promise
ye moot yer cry: you mention your name
yestreen: yesterday evening
yett: gate
youse perr: the pair of you

Endnotes

1. A slight misquotation from the last line of the poem "Pahonia" by the Belarusian poet Maksim Bahdanovič (1891–1917), "None can conquer them, stay them or halt" (trans. Vera Rich). "Pahonia" means *pursuit*. It was the national emblem of the Grand Duchy of Lithuania, depicting a knight seated on a rearing horse with sword raised. The Grand Duchy was a medieval and early modern state that covered the whole of Belarus and the modern Republic of Lithuania. Predominantly a Slavonic state, it is viewed by many Belarusians today as an early form of Belarusian statehood.

2. Street named after the day in 1939 when, under the terms of the non-aggression pact between the USSR and Nazi Germany of August that year, the Soviet Union occupied what had been Eastern Poland. It is now Western Belarus.

3. The name of an international music festival held annually since 1992 in the Belarusian city of Viciebsk.

4. Vilnia is the Belarusian form of the name of the capital of the modern Republic of Lithuania.

5. A reference to the novel *The Master and Margarita* by Mikhail Bulgakov (1891–1940).

6. A line from the popular Belarusian folksong "Kupalinka," which in its present form may have been written by the poet Michaś Čarot who was shot by the Bolsheviks in 1937.

7. Neznaika ("Dunno"): the main character of three books written by the Soviet children's writer Nikolai Nosov (1908–1976).

8. Cheburashka: a character in Soviet cartoon films for children. "The blue railway carriage that rocks from side to side" is a line from a song that Cheburaska and his friends sing.

9. Doctor Aibolit ("Ouch, it hurts"): a character in poems and a novel by the Soviet children's writer Kornei Chukovskii (1882–1969), and modelled on Hugh Loftus's Dr. Dolittle.

10. This is a reference to the suggested name Staglava, literally "one hundred heads."

11. Ikhtiandr ("Fish-man"): a character in the 1928 novel *Amphibian Man* by the Soviet science fiction writer Alexander Belyayev (1884–1942).

Gyulchatay: a character in the popular 1970 Soviet film *White Sun of the Desert*.

12. The structure of Russian names is first name + patronymic (derived from the name of the father) + surname. Patronymics were unknown in Belarus until the expansion of the Russian Empire westwards from the late eighteenth century onwards.

13. A reference to the First World War poem "When Bazyl died, far on the march" by Maksim Bahdanovič (1891–1917).

14. The law in Belarus requires everyone to be registered with the police at their place of residence.

15. The form "Miensk" is the original Belarusian name of what is now the capital of Belarus. "Minsk" is in fact the Polish form of the name, which was taken over by the Russians.

16. Alfred Schnittke (1934–1998): Russian composer.

17. A bat-and-ball game similar to baseball.

18. The quoted line and the seven that follow are taken from the poem "Things will be bad" by the Belarusian poet Francišak Bahuševič (1840–1900). The speaker of these lines in the poem is Alindarka.

19. This, and the preceding quotations in this chapter—with the substitution of certain words—are taken from Hitler's *Mein Kampf* in the translation available at http://www.hitler.org/writings/Mein_Kampf/mkv1ch02.html.

20. Eliezer Perelman, later Eliezer Ben-Yehuda (1858–1922), born in Lužki in eastern Belarus. He was a major contributor to the revival of Hebrew as a modern language for everyday use. There is another way in which Perelman could be said to be a model for Faither: he brought up his son entirely in Hebrew, shielding him from his surroundings. The son (later Itamar Ben-Avi, 1882–1943) became "the first native speaker of Hebrew in modern times."

21. Ostarbeiter: worker from the east, name given to Soviet citizens in occupied areas, sent to Germany by the Nazi occupiers 1941–44.

22. Lines from the Bahuševič poem "Things will be bad" (note 18).

23. Zhyguli cars are called Lada when exported outside Russia.

24. The school year in the countries of the former Soviet Union always starts on or as near as possible to this date, the "Day of Knowledge."

25. Janka Kupala (1882–1942): pen name of Ivan Lucevič, without doubt the greatest poet-prophet of the Belarusian nation before the 1917 revolutions in the Russian Empire. In the 1930s, however, he seems to have become one of Stalin's court poets and was rewarded with a Chevrolet—the only one in Moscow at the time—and a driver. He died in Moscow when he fell down the stairwell of the Hotel Moskva. The unanswered question is: did he fall or was he pushed?

Stierlitz: the main character in a series of spy novels by the Soviet Russian writer Yulian Semyonov (1931–1993). Stierlitz was a Soviet spy who worked his way into a senior position in the Nazi security services during the war. He is best known for the novel and subsequent 1973 TV series *Seventeen Moments of Spring*.

26. Moisei Uritskii (1873–1918): chief of the first version of the Soviet secret police.

27. An echo of the Bahuševič poem "Things will be bad" (note 19).

28. A type of puppet theatre presentation popular in Belarus.

29. Aliaksiej Dudaraŭ (1950–): Belarusian playwright.

30. "Things will be bad"

31. "Nowers" is the translator's version of the knight's name in the Belarusian text, Niahorša, literally "no worse."

32. Jakub Kolas (1882–1956), one of the creators of the modern Belarusian literary language and founders of modern Belarusian literature. Kolas is a pseudonym; in Belarusian it means "ear of corn."

33. The name in Belarusian is Michaś Baradaŭkin. Baradaŭka means "wart."

34. The name in the Belarusian text is "I. Shakoŭski"; there is no writer of that name. "Ishak" is one of the Russian words for donkey.

35. A line from the song "Belorussia" by the 1970s cult group Pieśniary (The Singers).

36. In Russian the word has two meanings with the same spelling, depending on where the stress is. If it is on the second syllable it means "armour." The issue does not arise in Belarusian, where the word for armour is spelled "brania." What follows is the beginning of the novella *The Victims* by the Belarusian writer Ivan Šamiakin (1921–2004).

37. What Mike McFinnie now reads is not a continuation of the story begun in the previous chapter, but one that Bacharevič himself invents.

38. See note 21.

39. The Committee for State Security (KGB). This name is retained in independent Belarus.

40. Zianon Paźniak: the major advocate of independence for Belarus at the time when the USSR was collapsing at the end of the 1980s. He was an archaeologist who revealed the extent of mass shootings in the Kurapaty forest near Minsk by the Soviet secret police in the period leading up to the German invasion of 1941. He now lives in exile.

Turau Gospels: an eleventh-century manuscript discovered in the small town of Turaŭ in southern Belarus in 1865.

41. See note 16. The reference here is to the fifth movement of Schnittke's Concerto Grosso no. 1, to which some listeners have given the title "Bezumie," literally "without-mind-ness," insanity. The composer himself did not use this title.

42. Three lines from one of the poems in *The Gift*, a novel by Vladimir Nabokov (1899–1977) (trans. Michael Scammell).

43. A verse from a poem by the Belarusian poet Pimien Pančanka (1917–1995).

44. Line from the song "Gorodok" (the little town), sung by the Russian pop star Angelika Varum (1969–).

45. Lines from the epic poem *The New Land* by Jakub Kolas (see note 32). This must surely be one of the first translations of any Belarusian poetry into Scots.

46. Lines from the much-anthologised poem "The Komsomol Card" by the Belarusian poet Arkadź Kuliašoŭ (1914–1978).